To

Good Talking!

Best Regards

J. RYAN FENZEL

J Ryan Fenzel
1-Sept-12

ALLIED IN IRONS

A NOVEL

Ironcroft Publishing

This book is a work of fiction. Names, characters, places, and incidents are the product of the author's imagination or are used fictitiously. Any resemblance to actual events, locales, or persons, living or dead, is coincidental.

Allied In Irons

Cover Artist: Julie L. Hamilton

Interior Design: Thomas Gideon

Printed in the United States of America

First Printing: August 2012

Library of Congress Information:

Fenzel, J. Ryan.

LCCN: 2012909651
Allied In Irons / J. Ryan Fenzel
1st ed.
Hartland, MI : Ironcroft Pub., 2012.
p. cm.

ISBN-10: 0-9771688-2-4
ISBN-13: 978-0-9771688-2-8
1. Fiction – Action & Adventure
2. Fiction – Thrillers

In memory of my mother
Carol Ruth Bliss

"Now this is not the end. It is not even the beginning of the end. But it is, perhaps, the end of the beginning."

– Sir Winston Churchill

PROLOGUE

From the cabin of an MH-60 Seahawk, Rear Admiral Abner Wilson surveyed the distressed salvage vessel *Aeneas* floating in the Atlantic five hundred feet below. The ship looked dead to him. She wasn't making way or cutting through the waves on any sort of heading. She was drifting. And she was silent. The admiral cursed under his breath.

A marine dressed in fatigues with lieutenant's rank sat next to the admiral, listening to a report through his radio earpiece. "Admiral," he said. "The ship is secure."

Admiral Wilson raised an eyebrow. "Sheridan?"

The lieutenant shook his head. "We don't know yet."

"Get me down there," the admiral said. "Now."

The helicopter descended through a stiff crosswind and thumped down on the salvage vessel's cargo deck. The lieutenant and two PFCs hopped from the cabin with rifles in hand and spread out beyond the wind from the rotor spinning overhead. Admiral Wilson followed on their heels and scanned the deserted deck. Two bodies lie sprawled near the stern. They were dressed in black garb, light body armor, and combat boots. Not quite the standard uniform of the Neptune's Reach crew. They had obviously been part of the mercenary team that had seized the vessel two days before. Admiral Wilson called to the lieutenant over the winding down helicopter engines and nodded toward the bodies. "SEAL kills?"

"No, sir, the SEALs didn't fire a shot. Those two were already dead when we got here."

Admiral Wilson turned from the bodies. "Where is the crew?"

"Below deck."

"Take me there."

"Yes, sir." The lieutenant led Admiral Wilson into the vessel through a hatchway amidships. They entered a corridor that appeared to the admiral to be the crew quarter deck. Cabin doors hung half open on their hinges. Some looked to have been kicked in. Belongings and gear were strewn about, but nobody was there. The deck was empty. The desolate stillness got the admiral feeling like he was walking a ghost ship.

The lieutenant led them two decks deeper into the vessel and into another corridor, this one along the central axis of the ship above the keel. Admiral Wilson felt the atmosphere change. He was not aboard a ghost ship any longer. He was on a battlefield.

Bodies littered the deck, nearly a dozen from the admiral's count, all lying in the frozen grip of death. More men dressed in black combat garb, but bodies wearing shirts emblazoned with the Neptune's Reach logo were among them too. Spent shell casings scattered beneath the admiral's boot. Pock marks and chipped paint scarred the corridor walls, apparently imprints from errant bullets in the violent gun battle that had taken the lives of the dead men the admiral now walked among. He could smell gun smoke in the air.

At the end of the corridor, a crude barricade of overturned workshop tables and scrap metal plates barred entrance to a hatchway. A narrow path had been cleared through the barricade and Admiral Wilson saw activity in the compartment beyond. "I assume the survivors are in there."

"Yes, sir," the lieutenant said. "They barricaded themselves in the engine room." He glanced about the corridor. "Looks like it was a hell of a fight."

Admiral Wilson squeezed through the path into the engine room behind the lieutenant. The ragtag remnants of the *Aeneas* crew sat exhausted and beaten amid the stench of diesel fumes in the vessel's engine compartment. Marine medics worked among the fifteen survivors, tending to their bullet wounds and burns. Admiral Wilson searched their faces. He found the man he sought seated on a starboard stairwell, leaning forward on his knees with a Colt semiautomatic pistol locked in his hand and tired eyes focused on the crew.

Admiral Wilson approached him. "You can stop watching the flock, Jack, the marines are here."

Jack Sheridan looked up and offered a weary smile. "I'm a lousy shepherd."

The admiral shook his head. "I'm sure these crewmen feel otherwise."

Jack did not reply.

"Seriously," Admiral Wilson said, "it's good to see you alive. I thought we lost you."

"Me too."

"Is Connor okay?"

Jack nodded. "He and Markus are showing the SEAL team our makeshift brig in the forward hold. Got a couple of guys in there."

The admiral appraised the wounded crew. "How close did it come?"

Jack glanced at the barricade. "This was our last stand." He ejected the magazine from his pistol and showed the admiral it was empty. "My last round is in the chamber. If they had kept pressing we wouldn't be talking right now."

"The important thing is we are talking," Admiral Wilson said. "And you stopped Rafferty."

Jack shook his head. "He never should have gotten this far. I should have seen through him."

"Don't beat yourself up. He was a pro." Admiral Wilson offered his hand.

Jack took it and pulled himself up. "Was?"

"Yes. Two F-18s from the Theodore Roosevelt battle group caught up with Rafferty's ship a hundred miles east of here and put a pair of Harpoon missiles into her broadside. She went down in ten minutes, and she took the Doppelganger prototype with her."

Jack lifted his chin. "Do you have confirmation that Rafferty went down with the ship?"

"They're still sorting through the casualties. No sign of him yet."

"I really hope they got him," Jack said holstering the Colt. "Because this thing won't be over until they do."

"Why do you say that? The *Aeneas* is secure. Our prototype radar defense system is not up for bid on the black market. And you and I are still around to throw back a few beers together. It's over, Mr. Sheridan, and thanks to God for that."

"He won't let it be over," Jack said quietly. "For all the reasons you just listed, he won't let it end here. Not as long as he's alive."

Admiral Wilson scoffed. "He's fish food. And if he did somehow find a way to escape those F-18s, he's heading for the hills with his tail between his legs, never to tangle with Jack Sheridan again."

"That's not how it's going to go down," Jack said. "I got to know him pretty well these past few days. He put a lot of effort into this plot to steal Doppelganger, and I just pissed in his Cheerios. He's not going to forgive and forget."

"How can you be so sure?"

"Because he told me." Jack looked the admiral in the eye. "The last thing Rafferty said to me before he left was that he wasn't finished with me. If he isn't dead, he's going to come back…and I've got to be ready when he does."

BOOK I:
DOMINOES

- ONE –

Two Years Later

Jack Sheridan swept pieces of gravel off the cover plate of his new driveway barrier like an umpire cleans sand off home plate in a baseball diamond.

Connor Sheridan watched from the shade of a maple near the road. "Really, Dad?"

Jack stood and admired the device. "What?"

"That thing is going to be covered by gravel every day. What's with the hand broom?"

"Ever hear of taking pride in your work?" Jack gestured to a box sitting in the grass next to his son. "Toss me the remote."

Connor threw him a small remote control unit from the box of parts. Jack hit a button on the remote, and the narrow cover plate that spanned the driveway rose up on four hydraulically driven steel bollards and stopped at the height of headlights on a standard SUV. Jack approved.

"So tell me," Connor said. "How much of the money from the Coates coins are you going to spend on security measures?"

"As much as it takes for me to relax."

Connor laughed. "You don't have that much money."

Jack lifted his boot and kicked his heel against the steel barrier. It didn't budge.

"You know," Connor said, "most people just install a gate to secure their driveway, not a barrier capable of stopping a tank."

"Most people don't have a professional mercenary stalking them." Jack slapped his hands against his dusty jeans and surveyed his property line. "Those old maples form a nice picket line along the road. A vehicle can't get through them." He creased his eyes in a squint against the sun. "The new iron fence supplements the trees. Anyone less than seven feet is going to have a hard time getting over the spires, and if they try they'll get a surprise." He faced Connor. "Speaking of money, I don't see you driving a new car or living in a big house with your cut. What toys are you buying?"

Connor frowned and lifted the box of parts. "Not going there."

"Going where?"

Connor started up the sloping drive toward the house.

Jack gave his new toy one more admiring look and started after him. "Why are you still doing contract work for CCG?"

"I like it. It keeps me busy."

"Yeah? How did you like working on smiling Lloyd's retrofit over the winter?"

Connor did not reply.

Jack caught up with him. "Connor, come on, you're young and wealthy. Why don't you relax and enjoy it for a little while? Not everyone gets an opportunity like this."

"Money doesn't relieve stress." Connor glanced at the new barrier. "You're proof of that."

Jack frowned. "Touché."

Connor walked a little farther in silence. "In case you didn't notice, I did not end up with the girl after the big treasure hunt."

"That's a good thing," Jack chuckled. "Alyson *is* your sister."

"The point is I'm single, and now that I have some cash I'm afraid of jumping into a relationship only to find out later that my woman is really dating my bank account. I guess I'm a little paranoid. I'm sure you know the feeling."

"Funny. Keep jabbing at me, boy."

They reached the porch that wrapped around the brick ranch house and picked up glasses of ice water they had left there on the steps. "You need work on your self-esteem," Jack said. "I thought we farmed that territory pretty well when you were growing up."

Connor took a swig of water. "That's what you get for thinking."

The sound of tires crunching over gravel arose from beyond the maple trees along the dirt road. Jack listened a moment, judged the car to be slowing down. Yes, he expected company, but he reached for the shoulder holster lying behind the toolbox near the porch steps just the same. He threaded his arms through the holster and positioned the Kimber semi-automatic comfortably against his side as a navy blue Ford Explorer turned into the driveway. Jack's German shepherd Ike bounded around the corner of the house on a barking tirade. The dog made for the vehicle at the bottom of the drive, but Jack shouted a command. "Ike, stand down. It's a friend."

Ike stopped barking immediately.

The Explorer rolled to a stop in front of the steel barrier and the driver's window scrolled down. A man in his mid-fifties with a white crew cut and a bulldog nose looked up the driveway at Jack Sheridan through dark sunglasses. He considered the barrier blocking his SUV and the pistol in Jack's shoulder holster. "You did invite me here, didn't you?"

Jack smiled and approached the Explorer. "Abner, it's good to see you."

"Hey," Abner said. "You shaved your moustache. Are you trying to look younger or something?"

Jack smiled. "I was shooting for a decade. How'd I do?"

"Missed it by a couple of years."

Ike hopped the barrier and trotted around the SUV. He got up on his hind quarters and put his front paws on the driver's door. Abner scratched behind the dog's ears. "Bet your master's working you overtime. Don't hold it against him."

Jack hit the button on the remote again. The barrier lowered to the driveway. "Head up to the house," he said to Abner. "I'll meet you on the porch."

Abner pulled the Explorer forward. Jack rejoined Connor near the porch steps. "You didn't tell me Admiral Wilson was coming over," Connor said.

"I wanted it to be a surprise."

"Why?"

Jack didn't reply. Abner parked the Explorer near the house and stepped out of the vehicle. He stretched his large frame and studied the wrought iron fence on the property line. "Judas priest, Jack, has Rafferty got you spooked?"

Jack shrugged. "Good fences make good neighbors."

"You don't have any neighbors."

"Back in November I thought up some home improvement projects." Jack surveyed the new fence line. "Had to wait for the ground to thaw to sink the posts." He climbed the porch steps. "I haven't heard from Rafferty since Labor Day."

"And while waiting for another call you're beefing up security with these *improvements*."

"More or less. I'm having bullet-resistant glass installed in the Jeep next week too."

Abner regarded his friend a long while. "Sometimes you worry me, Jack. But I've got something for you to ponder besides paranoid thoughts. Interested?"

"That's why you're here."

Connor gave his dad an inquisitive look. They all gathered on the cedar porch around a circular patio table. The screen door behind them creaked opened, and Lauren Sheridan stepped from the house.

She smiled at Abner and a warm breeze blew her auburn hair into her eyes. She brushed it back and hugged him. "How long has it been, Abner, a year?"

"I think you're right," Abner said. "Has Jack been keeping you on the edge of your seat?"

"As always."

Jack frowned. "You want a beer, Abner?"

"Affirmative. It's a beautiful spring weekend, and I'm officially off duty." He sat in a chair. "We'll have to talk shop unofficially."

"I'll get the beer," Lauren offered. Jack caught her before she went into the house and gave her hand a squeeze. She kissed him and disappeared inside.

Connor took a chair next to Abner's. "What kind of shop are we talking about?"

"My kind of shop," Jack said. "Abner's got a new job and thinks I might be useful to him."

"In a nutshell that's right," Abner said. "A year ago the government decided it needed an office to deal with special interest projects on U.S. waters, projects involving historical, commercial, or national security concerns. They dubbed it the Maritime Affairs Office and tapped me to be the director. I'm here to talk your dad into helping me out on our first project."

"This sounds interesting," Connor said. "I might want in too."

"Two Sheridans with one pitch? This could be my lucky day." Abner leaned forward as if crowding around a campfire to tell a ghost story. "This project involves history, unexplained events, and the potential to save thousands of lives. It starts with a tragedy seven decades old."

Jack rolled his eyes. "He's already hooked, Abner. Just get on with it."

Admiral Wilson cast an annoyed glance at him and settled back. "On the eve of June 23rd, 1950, Northwest Orient Flight 2501 took off from LaGuardia Airport bound for Seattle. She was a DC-4 carrying fifty-five passengers and a crew of three. The flight plan had her touching down at her first stopover in Minneapolis at 10:00 p.m. but she never made it."

"What happened?" Connor asked.

"She crashed into Lake Michigan."

"Any survivors?"

Abner shook his head. "No, and because the wreckage was never found, the cause of the crash remains a mystery."

"The leading theory points to weather conditions on the night of the crash." Jack gave Abner a knowing smile. "I did a little research on my own."

"Right," Abner said. "Weather is the prime suspect. Thunderstorms were moving through the Midwest that night, and the captain of Flight 2501 requested permission to descend to twenty-five hundred feet to avoid severe lightning and gusting winds. The Civil Aeronautic Authority denied his request due to dense air traffic at the lower altitude. Soon after the denial Flight 2501 flew into a squall line over Lake Michigan and disappeared from radar."

"What kind of search took place?" Connor asked.

"The best search that the coast guard and the naval reserve could muster at the time. They made an educated guess as to the point of impact, which they theorized was off the West Michigan coast between South Haven and St. Joseph, and hit the area with their old sonar equipment. They even dredged the bottom of the lake with trawlers. Nothing turned up. All they ever found was light debris floating on the surface of the lake."

Lauren returned from the house and set down a bottle of beer in front of each of them. "Keep talking, Abner," she said. "I can tell Jack is almost sold."

Jack's eyebrow twitched. "You used to get upset when I'd take off on a salvage project."

"That was different. Those projects were half a world away. They kept you from home for months at a time while Connor was growing up. This one is practically in our own backyard, and it seems like Connor might go with you. Anyway, I don't see it taking six months to find a plane wreck in Lake Michigan."

"You'd be surprised how long these things can take," Jack informed her.

"Well, you need something to keep you focused. Without it..." Lauren glanced at the new fence and driveway barrier.

Jack made eye contact with her and smiled, and then turned his gaze on Abner. "So why is the government interested in finding this plane after so many years?"

"Cholera," Abner said. "One of the passengers on the flight was a microbiologist who had brought with him a bio case containing vials of a unique cholera vaccine that was to be studied and developed at Washington University's bioresearch department. Some smart guys who wear lab coats believe that if we retrieve the material remaining in those vials, they can reproduce the vaccine today."

Connor took a swig of beer. "Hold on a minute. We have effective cholera vaccines already. Why go through all the trouble to retrieve this one?"

"Like I said, the vaccine on this plane is unique. They used it to treat a strange mutated form of cholera that was spreading through the Philippines at the time. Unfortunately this same form of cholera has shown up in Haiti in recent months, and modern day vaccines are not terribly effective against it."

"Doesn't the government have documentation on this special vaccine?" Connor said. "Doesn't anyone have a sample of it on hand to develop a new batch?"

"It's been over sixty years since we've seen this form of cholera," Abner said. "Lab equipment and practices weren't too high tech back then, and any samples we had were lost or destroyed decades ago. The microbiologist on the plane had with him critical documentation that did not exist anywhere else. Remember, in 1950 computer memory and flash drives were still pipe dreams."

Jack ran a finger over some condensation on his beer bottle. "Abner, you want me to do what the coast guard and naval reserve couldn't accomplish with all their resources."

"Yes," Abner said flatly. "Sonar and search technology has advanced a lot over the last seventy years, and your knowledge and experience in finding things that are lost is unsurpassed." He gave Jack a puckish smirk. "Don't get a big head."

"I learned a few other things in my research," Jack said. "A lot of people have tried to find Flight 2501 over the years. They all failed. A Michigan shipwreck organization mounts an annual search. No joy for them either, and they're funded by Clive Cussler for crying out loud."

"Clive who?" Abner said.

"Come on, Dad," Connor said. "This sounds like a very cool opportunity."

"Yes, cool and challenging. Just what you need," Lauren added.

Jack rocked his chair back. He and Lauren stared at one another for a long while. Her smile is all he needed. He felt a little rush and brought the chair down on all four legs. "Okay, Abner, you got me. What's the timetable?"

"The sooner the better."

"I'll need to secure a vessel rigged for salvage from Neptune's Reach. Lloyd might be a problem."

Abner smiled and lifted his beer from the table. "If Lloyd Faulkner kicks up a fuss, you let me know. In the meantime, welcome into the service of the Maritime Affairs Office."

They tapped their beer bottles together and drank to success. The clink of the glass seemed to snap Jack into search and salvage mode. It surprised him how quickly it came back. He began listing and prioritizing tasks in his head. Details of the crash had to be researched; logistics for the salvage effort needed to be calculated. He had to assemble his team. Jack took another swig of beer. His mind jumped into the search for Flight 2501, but like a shadow the thought of Rafferty fell over him, and his eyes drifted to the security fence encircling his home.

- TWO -

The long-range directional microphone planted sixty yards east of the perimeter fence picked up Jack Sheridan's voice and transmitted it through the air. A digital processing console amplified the signal, filtered background noise, equalized the tones, and fed the clean signal to a set of output speakers in the rear of a Buick Enclave parked a mile away. The vehicle's darkened windows blocked the afternoon sun and enhanced the effect of the LEDs on the audio surveillance equipment inside the car, as well as the flame from the stainless steel cigarette lighter in Donovan Rafferty's hand.

Rafferty lit the cigarette between his lips and listened to the end of Sheridan's conversation with Admiral Wilson. Their voices sounded as clear as if they were seated five feet away from him at an outdoor café. It intrigued him, not just the content of their discussion but the visceral emotion he felt hearing Sheridan's voice so clearly again. Two years had passed since their conflict aboard the *Aeneas,* a Neptune's Reach salvage ship he had taken control of in his attempt to steal a prototype radar defense system named Doppelganger. Jack Sheridan had gone from a benign salvage project manager to the leader of a crew rebellion that eventually bested Rafferty's hand-picked team of mercenaries and prevented them from attaining Doppelganger. Rafferty had spent eighteen months planning that operation and exhausted millions of dollars in resources to execute it, but in the end it was all thwarted by Sheridan. Rafferty had not been able to reconcile the fact that his divine charter to humble the U.S. government was brought down by a maritime garbage man.

He had wanted Jack Sheridan dead, and indeed at one point literally had the man in the crosshairs of a high-powered rifle. Why he had not squeezed the trigger is something Rafferty did not understand at the time. He rationalized that the simplicity of a single bullet would not have satisfied the vengeance due him. But in some deep recess of Rafferty's mind Sheridan deserved more. After all, the man proved himself under fire and claimed victory that day on the Atlantic. In the end it was Donovan Rafferty and not the U.S. government that learned a lesson in humility. That made Jack Sheridan special. It afforded him a measure of respect. And it persuaded Rafferty to stay his hand until a more fitting opportunity arose to balance the scale.

It took a year, but the opportunity that presented itself was well worth the wait. A series of encounters set Rafferty on an unexpected path. One event tumbled into the next like a string of dominoes winding their way back to Sheridan. Rafferty understood now why he had not taken that rifle shot. As the song goes, to everything there is a season: a time for war, a time for peace, and a time for tormenting Jack Sheridan in a manner befitting his worst nightmare. True, Rafferty would have chosen a different path to get there, but he saw the divine design in it and seized the opportunity with vigor. He now understood. A single bullet a year ago would have tasted bitter in comparison to the delicious irony about to unfold.

Rafferty blew a stream of smoke from his lungs and allowed himself a brief smile. "Mr. Ferguson," he said to the man seated next to him in the back of the Enclave, "did I hear Admiral Wilson mention cholera in Haiti?"

Ferguson checked sound levels on a digital recorder. "I believe that's what he said."

Rafferty thought about that a while. "Jack needs some new friends, wouldn't you say?"

"I don't care who his friends are," Ferguson said with dark inflection. "My knee aches every time it rains because of him. If I had my way, I'd be over that fence in five minutes and I'd put a slug—"

"That's not an option," Rafferty warned. "We execute the plan as I've laid it out. You will not stray to the left or to the right. Do you understand?"

Ferguson remained silent one second too long.

Rafferty glared through cold, grey eyes. "Do you understand?"

"Yes, sir," Ferguson said, acquiescing his stance. "It's just that Sheridan deserves some payback."

"I know what he deserves," Rafferty said sharply. "Vengeance is mine, sayeth the Lord." He leaned forward just a touch. "And I'm the Lord's sub-contractor. You'll do well not to forget that."

Ferguson nodded.

Rafferty put his attention back on Jack and Abner's closing conversation coming through the speakers. "They're moving quickly on the crash site. We have to move quickly too." He checked the time on his watch with the night glow button. "Naughton should have Simon secured by now." He grabbed his satellite phone and speed dialed a number.

A man's voice answered, crisp and assertive. "Yes, Colonel."

"Mr. Naughton, events are accelerating. I need Simon up here in one day. We move in two."

"That won't be a problem."

"Wexler will transport the lab equipment. You escort Simon. No delays. No complications."

"Understood."

"Contact me when you cross the state line."

"Yes, sir."

Rafferty disconnected. He puffed on his cigarette and took a moment to consider the habit. Sheridan had once warned him about the dangers of smoking. He had found the comment amusing at the time given the volatile environment surrounding them, but months later he had actually thought about quitting. Sitting there in the darkened SUV, contemplating the falling dominoes, the idea seemed a pointless effort. Rafferty stifled a laugh. To everything there is a season.

"Mr. Ferguson, shut down your hardware. We're leaving."

"Yes, sir."

Rafferty made his way toward the driver's seat. He paused midway and glanced back. "By the way, that impulse you had to breach Sheridan's fence would not have worked out for you. Sensors would have detected you climbing over, and the iron would have been immediately electrified. You would have woken up stunned on the ground in time for his guard dog to tear your throat out, or perhaps to face the business end of a .45 caliber semi-automatic."

Ferguson did not reply.

"Jack Sheridan is creative. He has a tactical mind and abundant financial resources. You continue to underestimate him. That's a mistake I refuse to repeat." Rafferty continued forward and settled behind the steering wheel. "On the contrary, I'm counting on his abilities to make my whole plan succeed."

- THREE -

Alec Cohn stood at the bow of the *Liberty* just clear of the jib, breathing in the air of a southwesterly wind sweeping over Lake Erie. The ship was an eighteenth-century sloop replica, fully rigged and stretching 106 feet from bowsprit to stern, with a twenty-foot beam and an eight-foot draft. Cohn had her sailing on a port tack with a broad reach, keeping a general northerly heading and making way at twenty knots. He watched his crew trim the sail in answer to a slight shift in wind direction. He had trained them well. After spending so much time on the water over the years, he had come to feel more comfortable on the pitching deck of a ship than on static ground ashore. With years of experience came a wealth of knowledge, and he imparted all he could to his men. They were a sharp crew. They knew traditionally rigged craft inside and out and responded well to orders. Cohn mused, however, that crew structure and chain of command cut sharply against the grain of his overall objective on this voyage.

He aimed his eyes to the peak of the top mast and checked the canvas telltale affixed there. The narrow strip stood perpendicular to the mast, vibrating in the air showing the southwesterly wind direction had changed slightly to favor the western component, which explained the crew's trim adjustment. He walked to the main cabin and zipped up his nylon windbreaker halfway. Although the sun warmed the air on shore just fine, the wind on the lake packed a rather chilly punch.

Cohn was lean and strode across the wooden deck as surefooted as a cat. He hadn't touched a razor since they left port, and a three-day beard shaded his cheeks and chin crimson, except where jagged scar tissue ran along his jaw line. He stood tall at six feet and some change, and the man he stopped next to had to tilt his head slightly to look him in the eye. "Did you figure out the problem below deck?" Cohn asked the man named Speers.

"Yes," Speers replied. "A circuit breaker on the freezer unit had tripped." The short, black hair on Speers' head blew wild in the wind, and the fair skin over his narrow cheekbones seemed to redden in the gust. "Byrne must have shorted something out when he wired the controller. The refrigeration system is functional now, and we're charging it with the liquid nitro."

Cohn scanned the lake ahead of the ship, considered the narrowing channel of water between Michigan and Canada. "We've got about five hours until we reach Sarnia. Just make sure the damn thing is on line when we get there."

"It will be," Speers said.

Cohn noted the holstered pistols on some of the crew working on deck. "Tell the men to stow their side arms before we make port. We don't need to draw the Canadians' attention. The whole point is to hide in plain sight."

Speers nodded.

"We can't afford mistakes," Cohn added.

"The men understand. They know the potential rewards if we manage to pull this off."

"If?" Cohn regarded the crew working on deck. "I don't remember instructing them in doubt."

Speers waved off the comment. "Don't misunderstand. There's no shortage of confidence with this crew. If our task can be done it will be done. I merely allow for the random element of chance."

"We make our own chance," Cohn reminded him. "We determine our own future. Failure can only come at our hands as well." He walked to the port gunwale and silently studied the waves for a long while. "*When* we pull this off," he finally said, "the shock waves will ignite half the world."

Speers smiled in agreement. "And what will happen to the other half of the world?"

"The other half?" Cohn faced him. "The other half will be arming up. Clear your calendar for the next ten years. There'll be lots of overtime."

"Already planning for it."

Cohn returned his gaze to the vista surrounding the ship, watching industrial buildings along the Canadian shoreline shoot smoke and steam into the air. "I heard from Nix this morning," he said abruptly. "The colonel has popped his head up."

Speers raised an eyebrow. "Where?"

"Very close. Just around the corner in Southeast Michigan as a matter of fact."

"What is he doing?"

"I think he's working on his bucket list." Cohn thought about the colonel a moment. "Whatever his intentions, his actions could benefit us."

Speers didn't follow. "How so?"

"The colonel is a person of interest to intelligence agencies."

"So are you after the Dubai incident."

"That's my point," Cohn explained. "If the colonel becomes active, if he starts throwing red flags in the FBI's face and bends the antenna of Homeland Security, then he's drawing their resources away from what we're doing. In essence he'll open a second intelligence gathering front. That might give us more breathing room to operate."

"More breathing room or more exposure?"

"Don't be concerned," Cohn said. "Information is the currency of our trade, and I'm a very stingy man. The details of our plan are safely in my pocket."

Speers inspected the mainmast shrouds in conspicuous silence.

"Brooding doesn't suit you," Cohn told him. He added, "I instructed Nix to stay on task and report any developments."

"Not leaving anything to chance?" Speers said with just the hint of a smile.

Cohn fixed him with a glare but did not reply.

Raised voices from astern turned both their heads. Two crewmen near the quarter deck shoved one another and hurled crude insults. One man struck the other with a quick right jab, and they broke into a full-on fistfight. Speers shook his head. "It's Anders and Duvall. Those two mix like oil and water." He moved to intervene but Cohn took his arm and held him back.

"Let this play out," Cohn said. "Wait until one of them is clearly winning and then break it up. Confine both to quarters below deck until we reach Sarnia."

"Done."

Cohn added, "Promote the winner of the fight to squad leader."

Speers cocked his head as if he had heard the order wrong, and then seemed to make a connection. "A man is limited only by his power to obtain what he desires."

"Without regard for God, state, or morality," Cohn said to finish the creed. "That's what it's all about, isn't it?"

"It is," Speers said. "But what if one of them decides your position of leadership is what he desires?"

"Then he will discover the limit of his power, and we will perform a burial at sea."

"Let's hope they're all content at their current station. We've got a dozen men sailing a ship that carried twice the crew compliment back in the day."

Cohn faced the shoreline again. "We're not out on extended duty. We'll be off the lake within a week. I'm certain they can hold it together that long." He shifted to scan the water in their wake. Three other tall ships of similar vintage to the *Liberty* trailed behind in a staggered formation. Cohn noticed them begin to fall in line for entry into the Detroit River ahead. The commotion astern began to die down. "Somebody is winning," he said to Speers. "Head back and take care of the situation."

"On my way." Speers moved to secure the unruly crewmen.

Cohn looked forward. He was hours away from having the catalyst of his greatest ambition in his hands, and mere days away from achieving the first stage of his ultimate goal. The thought exhilarated him, but a dark memory reached up from the depths. For an instant his mind filled with images of a cold concrete cell, a dark, rancid hole in the floor, and the butt of a pistol splitting the skin along his jaw line. He detested the weakness in him that allowed his mind to wander in such a way, but lingering on it a bit longer made sense to some degree.

The memory was the beginning.

This voyage will be the conclusion.

Cohn had his greatest desire in sight, and he had no doubt in his ability to seize it.

- FOUR -

Monday
Port Huron, MI

Jack parked his Jeep Cherokee in the west lot of the Neptune's Reach North American operations facility. The blue and gray two-story complex sprawled out on a piece of property bordering Lake Huron. A brand-spanking-new sign sat in front of the Jeep with three-foot tall, illuminated letters spelling out the company name and a large silver trident spanning the entire length. Jack and his passenger Joshua Rezner studied the sign a short while.

"I see how Lloyd spent some of the money from the coin recovery," Jack said.

"Looking good is our first priority," Rezner added. "Same old Lloyd."

Jack had parked next to Lloyd Faulkner's Cadillac CTS, so close that Rezner could not open his door enough to exit the Jeep. Rezner frowned. "Jack, I can't get out."

"That's okay," Jack said. "Lloyd can't get in. Come through this way."

Rezner nodded. "Good point." He climbed over the center console and followed Jack out of the Jeep. He noticed the stock of a weapon tucked into a makeshift compartment in the driver's door panel on his way over. "Hey, where did you get that Remington short barrel?"

"Huh?" Jack glanced back. "Oh, I got it on eBay."

"EBay! I could have gotten you a better model at cost through my store."

"I wasn't thinking, Rez. Come on." Jack headed for the lobby entrance.

"Speaking of such things," Rezner said. "How's that Kimber working out for you?"

Jack patted the pistol under his dark blue jacket. "It feels like the Colt with a little more speed. Good recommendation. By the way, I noticed you're not carrying today. That's odd."

"Ankle," Rezner confessed. "Snub .38."

"Kind of small caliber for you."

"I knew you'd be covering the power today with that .45." They walked a few steps in silence. "So why did you ask me to join in this Abner Wilson project?"

"We had so much fun last time in the Atlantic with Rafferty that I thought we should try to recapture some of the old magic."

"No thanks to the old magic, but I am interested in this airplane wreck."

They pushed through double glass doors into a classic Roman-themed lobby with faux coliseum pillars and white marble tile. The attractive blonde receptionist across the room recognized them both and greeted them with hugs. "Great to see you guys again."

"Great to see you too, Meg," Jack said. "Can you buzz us in for our meeting with Lloyd?"

"Sure thing," she said. "Let me make sure he's ready for you. He has a busy schedule this morning."

While she rang up Lloyd, Jack and Rezner looked at artistically framed photographs of the company's past salvage and exploration activities hanging on the wall. One photo in particular caught Jack's eye. "You've got to be kidding me."

"What?" Rezner asked.

"Get this." Jack read a placard below the picture. "*Neptune's Reach: Recovering our Past.* This is a picture of the Coates coins. That weasel Lloyd is taking credit for finding them."

"This surprises you how?" Rezner said.

"Lloyd's ready for you in the main conference room on two." Meg pressed a button on her desk and the door behind her clicked.

Jack pulled it open. "Thanks, Meg. We'll catch you on the way out." He led the way into the building and up a flight of carpeted steps. He didn't have the patience to wait for the elevator.

Rezner hurried to keep up. "I'll hold him, you hit him."

Jack kept marching forward. "Sounds like a plan."

"I hate being the voice of reason," Rezner said, "but you need Lloyd to secure a salvage ship for the project. If you want his nose broken at least let me do it."

Jack stopped in the hallway just short of the conference room. "You're right."

Rezner smiled. "Now, hand me that .45 before you go in there."

Jack huffed and walked into the conference room. It hadn't changed much. A long, elliptical table of lacquered mahogany consumed a lion's share of floor space. Dim lights glowed in recessed ceiling canisters and kept the extents of the room hidden in shadow.

More photographs of Neptune's Reach's storied past hung on the walls beneath track lighting. Lloyd Faulkner stood at the far end of the table wearing his trademark dark suit and a smarmy smile on his round, clean-shaven face. His hair was slicked back as always, and he greeted his former employee with a cheery voice. "Hey, Jack, it's really great to—"

"Does truth in advertising mean anything to you?" Jack said cutting him off.

"It means a lot of things to me. Depends on the context."

Rezner entered the room and stood beside Jack. It took Lloyd a moment to recognize his other former employee. "Joshua Rezner, what a pleasant surprise." Lloyd studied his flannel shirt, jeans, and untrimmed beard. "Looking rustic, I see."

"I'm not following Neptune's corporate appearance guidelines these days," Rezner said.

Lloyd nodded. "Good for you. Now can you tell me what Jack is talking about?"

"I'm talking about the Coates coins," Jack said. "The coins that I found and you're taking credit for in that lobby display."

Lloyd's smile fell. "Now wait just a minute. Neptune's Reach did recover those coins from the bottom of Lake Michigan. You can't deny that."

"I found them. I provided the locator tag frequency to pinpoint the spot where I had stashed them. I led the effort to pull them up. How does Neptune figure into any of it?"

"That placard says recovering our past, not discovering our past. It's accurate in my book."

"And what happened to the confidentiality agreement we had to keep the incident quiet."

"That was before you had taken the coins to auction, and before everyone was settled up with their shares of the sale. The dust has settled, the courts have cleared everything, and I decided it was okay to add the find to Neptune's portfolio."

"How can we do business when you pull crap like this every time I turn my back?"

"That's callous, Jack. I'd think after working together eighteen years you'd know me better than to level a ridiculous charge like that."

"That's exactly why I'm saying it."

Lloyd feigned disappointment. "This isn't getting us anywhere. Let's start over." He gestured to the chairs around the table. "Gentlemen, please take a seat and let's discuss Abner's project."

Jack realized he had let that photograph bother him more than he should have. Lloyd had done it to him again. Damn. He exchanged a glance with Rezner, and they reluctantly lowered themselves into chairs.

"Joshua," Lloyd said. "I heard you had opened a hunting supply store somewhere in the wilderness. How did Jack get you out of the backwoods to join his little expedition?"

"He asked me." Rezner shrugged. "I wouldn't be here if anyone else had."

"That's amazing." Lloyd regarded Jack across the table. "After all the trouble you put him through, he still admires you."

Jack's face flushed red. "You really want to go there, Lloyd? You want to talk about trouble and bad decisions on the Rafferty project?"

"No, I'm just making a comment. I want to leave the past in the past."

"Then leave it there and move on."

Lloyd smiled. "I'd prefer to talk business with you and make good decisions today."

"Right. Let's make this quick." Jack checked his watch. "I know you have a busy schedule this morning." He settled back and calmed himself. "I need a ship rigged for surgical salvage. I don't need muscle for mass, I need tech for precision."

"You're familiar with the fleet. Do you have a vessel in mind?"

Jack had thought about this all night after Abner had left his house. He knew what he wanted. "The *Aeneas* would be perfect."

"No can do," Lloyd said without hesitation. "The *Aeneas* is allocated to a project in the South Pacific. I can give you the *Achilles*. She's been retrofitted since you used her to recover the coins last year. As a matter of fact Connor did some work on her in January installing new stabilizing thrusters, and his friend Sweetwood had a hand in updating her ROV deployment rig."

"Markus Sweetwood?" Rezner said. "If that jackass had something to do with it, I'll be spending half my time undoing his work."

Jack crinkled his brow. "Markus is good. It'll be fine."

"She's had other tech goodies installed too," Lloyd continued. "Looking Glass system in the operation center, state-of-the-art sonar array. She's a first-class vessel."

"Sold," Jack said, "I want Garcia to captain her."

Lloyd sucked in a breath through clenched teeth. "Garcia's on the Eastern Seaboard working a freighter recovery." He chuckled. "That last hurricane has been good to Neptune's Reach." He rocked his chair back and forth in thought. "I can give you Malcolm Braddock."

"Negative," Jack said. "We don't like each other."

"Do you two still have issues over the Columbian thing?"

"Four crew members were killed by privateers during the Columbian thing, as you call it, and Braddock blames me."

"That was a long time ago. Surely you two can come to terms over that incident."

"Lloyd, you and I can't come to terms over the Rafferty thing. Why do you think the Columbian thing would be any different?"

Lloyd made a flustered gesture with his hands. "You two are adults, and you're professionals. You can find a way to work together. Compartmentalize for crying out loud. You and I, on the other hand, do not technically have to work together. We meet, we discuss, and in a way you work *for* me. It's a different dynamic, and so we relate on a different level."

Jack stared at him. "Do you know how hard you make this when you talk bullshit like that?"

Lloyd sat back a bit stunned. "What?"

"Never mind."

"Is the *Achilles* available for this project now?" Rezner asked.

"Not now but very soon," Lloyd said. "She returned from her shakedown voyage a few weeks ago and is having all the bugs in the retrofitted systems ironed out here in Port Huron."

"I plan on shipping out within two weeks. Is that possible?" Jack asked.

"Anything is possible."

Jack frowned at the non-answer. "Muskegon is our home port for this project. It's close to the crash site, and they have excellent marine facilities. How soon can you get the *Achilles* on-site?"

"With Braddock on the bridge?" Lloyd asked.

Jack held his breath. "Fine, with Braddock, when can she ship out?"

Lloyd scanned the ceiling in thought. "I'll have to get back to you on that. It could be as early as this week, but I need the maintenance crew report to gauge their progress."

"That might be helpful." Jack sat quiet a moment and considered Lloyd across the table. "This is a government-funded project," he said at last.

"I know. Legal is already beginning to fill out the paperwork."

"Really." Jack stirred in his chair. "Have you talked to Abner direct on this?"

"About an hour ago," Lloyd admitted. "The margin on this project is a little higher than I'm used to for an Abner Wilson opportunity. That's a nice surprise."

"Why did you go around me to Abner?"

Lloyd raised his hands in defense. "I didn't go around you. Abner called me. He wanted to get the red tape rolling. I wasn't going to tell him to hold on until I talked to you."

Jack sat up straight. "Why not? I'm the primary contact. Everything should go through me."

Lloyd stood. "Look, you, Abner, and I have a history. We've worked projects together before and I'm not going to do a little dance just to make you happy." He checked the time on his Blackberry. "I've got to be in Grand Rapids by noon. Meg's got the standard contract pulled together for you downstairs. Remember to take it with you when you leave. I'll need it signed by week's end. I'll get back to you on the *Achilles* ship-out date. Okay?"

Jack smoldered. "Don't go around me again. I don't care what history we have or how many times Abner might call you. Got it?"

Lloyd headed for the door in a rush. "Same old Jack."

Jack grabbed his arm. "No joke. Everything goes through me."

Lloyd stopped and flashed his best disarming smile. "Of course. Ground rules are set. Gotta run." Jack released him and Lloyd bolted. He turned back at the door. "Hey, you might get a kick out of this. A group of tall ships arrived in Port Huron last night. Why don't you and Joshua take a walk to the marina and check them out while you're in town. They'll be heading out tomorrow afternoon for their next stop." A wink and a nod and he was gone.

Jack corner-eyed Rezner. "I'm not interested in seeing tall ships today."

"Nor I," Rezner said.

"I'd rather get a sneak peek at the *Achilles* retrofit. Let's go say hello to our old co-workers."

"I'm right behind you."

Jack led Rezner out of the conference room. He made a mental note to chastise Abner Wilson for intervening in the project. If the admiral wanted him to run the show, then he was going to run it all. As he started down the carpeted stairs a thought made him smile, and for a moment he considered running down to the parking lot to watch Lloyd Faulkner crawl into his Cadillac thorough the passenger door.

- FIVE -

Bangor, MI

Donovan Rafferty parked the Enclave in a weed-infested gravel driveway in front of a neglected two-story house. He switched off the engine and studied the vacant home. White paint peeled from the walls and patches of shingles were missing from the roof. Aged oak branches encroached over the east peak and the gutters had saplings growing out of them. At one time the place had been a thriving farmhouse, but it had been years since the surrounding fields had yielded anything more than straw grass, or perhaps the occasional marijuana plant. Rafferty scrolled the driver's window down and listened. Birds chirped in the nearby trees. Quiet.

A black Acura was parked next to the house ahead of the Enclave, and Rafferty identified it as a rental by the license plate. It matched the make and model Naughton had told him he'd be driving. Rafferty unsnapped the flap on his belt holster and freed the Sig Sauer for quick access, and then flipped open his cell phone and speed dialed Naughton.

"Yes, Colonel," the voice answered.

"Is everything okay?" Rafferty asked him.

"Yes, we arrived a half hour ago and are settling in."

"I'm in the driveway now."

"I know. I see you...I've got a perfect shot."

"You best not take it. I'm coming in." Rafferty glanced at his passenger. "Mr. Ferguson, sweep the perimeter. Make sure Mr. Naughton's arrival has not attracted unwanted attention."

Ferguson acknowledged the order and they exited the Enclave. Rafferty moved toward the front door while Ferguson started into a wide circle around the house and through the field up to the tree line. Rafferty felt a tickle in his nose and sneezed. He reminded himself that tree pollen levels spiked this time of year and it usually took him a number of days to adjust to the season.

The porch steps creaked and the wood siding gave off a musty smell. He reached for the door knob but the door opened on its own. A tall, muscular man with bleach blond hair and a handsome face stood behind the threshold. The MP5 submachine gun in his hands belied the California surfer appearance. "Mr. Naughton," Rafferty said. "I trust your trip up here went without incident."

Naughton scanned the yard behind Rafferty and lowered the weapon. "Yes, Colonel."

"Wexler is en route. I expect him to arrive within the hour." Rafferty walked into the house. A folding table and chairs had been set up in the front living room, and a dark-haired man in his mid-twenties sat there chugging a Monster power drink. His unkempt hair was longer than corporate standard length, and the dangling left earring and barbed wire forearm tattoo painted a picture of a punk who could not possibly do what Rafferty needed done. The punk, however, had checked out in every way and even performed advance research proving his collegiate credentials. "You are a microbiologist," Rafferty said. "How can you drink those things knowing what the chemicals can do to you?"

Simon the punk set down the power drink. "Donovan Rafferty, dude, you are boring me to death." He gestured to the sparse room. "I've got nothing. No equipment. No lab set up. How am I supposed to get my work done with nothing but a card table, a condemned house, and a Long Beach lifeguard for a babysitter?"

Naughton shot him an annoyed glance and shouldered the MP5.

"Your lab will be here shortly," Rafferty said. "Then you'll have plenty to keep you busy." He addressed Naughton. "Has the power to the house been switched on?"

Naughton flicked on a light switch and a bare bulb in a ceiling fixture illuminated. "The whole ground floor is hot, but only the front bedroom upstairs has power. Something's wrong with the wiring feeding the other rooms."

"That isn't a problem," Rafferty said. "I didn't pick this house to be a vacation resort."

"That's another thing," Simon said. "Not only did you put me in a crap-hole house and confiscate my cell phone, you parked me in the middle of a nowhere town. I mean, Bangor? Really? The place consists of a hardware store, a feed supply store, a greasy diner, and a set of railroad tracks that carry the rest of the world right by without stopping."

"This house is located perfectly," Rafferty countered. "It's secluded, functional, and only twenty minutes from South Haven, which is essentially ground zero for our purposes."

Simon tilted his chair onto its back legs. "At least spring for a big high-def TV. I need my downtime."

Rafferty eyed him with disapproval. "You'll get downtime when your work here is done. I'm paying you a year's salary for a month of effort. Try to wrap your sharp but immature mind around the fact that this is a good deal for you."

Simon cocked his head. "My dad used to talk to me like that. Not cool, Donovan."

"I'm not your father. I'm your employer. We have a contract, and you will honor it."

"I'm thinking renegotiation. I didn't plan on these working conditions."

Rafferty tensed and felt anger take root. The punk obviously did not fully understand what he was into or with whom he was dealing. "Our contract stands as is. There will be no changes."

Simon laughed. "Agreements are made to be broken, or at least reconsidered. What are you now, Donovan, fifty years old? You may not be keeping up with the world, but things move pretty fast these days. I can't afford to let them roll right over me."

"I expect a man to keep his word." Rafferty said with an icy gray glare. "Did I expect too much from a boy?"

"Call me what you want, my price just went up 30 percent."

"Do you really want to reconsider our agreement? I guarantee you won't like my new terms."

Simon laughed again. "You need me, Donovan. You know it's true. You can't start over. There's not enough time." He grinned with self-assurance and stared hard at Rafferty. "Thirty percent."

Rafferty waited three seconds for Simon to reconsider his demand and then moved without warning. He crossed the room in two steps and swept the rear legs of the chair out from under the punk with a side kick. Simon fell hard on his back onto the wood floor and lost his breath. Rafferty dropped a knee onto his chest and drew the Sig Sauer. He set the barrel firmly into the punk's forehead. "Negotiations open."

Naughton watched close from the other side of the room with the MP5 in his hands.

Simon struggled for breath and his panicked eyes darted around the room as he tried to adjust to his new situation. He managed to force a few words from his gapped mouth. "But…you can't…start over."

Rafferty's expression remained stone cold. "Did you really think that I failed to consider this course of action on your part? I have the names of two other microbiologists in hand, and they are waiting to hear from me at a moment's notice. You are not indispensible. Your bargaining position is substantially weaker than you have assumed."

Simon didn't seem to understand. "You can't kill me...You can't afford it."

"I expect a man to keep his word. I take that very seriously." Rafferty applied a little more pressure to Simon's forehead with the gun barrel. "You're intelligent but you made a serious miscalculation. You see, I'm willing to put a bullet in your brain and pull in my number two man if you insist on changing our original agreement. On the other hand, if you decide to honor that agreement, we can move forward from this point as if this unpleasant incident never happened." Rafferty gave him a moment of silence to think. "What is your decision?"

Simon closed his eyes, swallowed hard, and slowed his breathing. "Okay, okay, you win."

Rafferty considered the sincerity of the answer and then removed the pistol from Simon's head. "It's not about winning."

He motioned for Naughton to help the punk off the floor. Naughton shouldered the submachine gun and pulled Simon to his feet. Rafferty holstered the Sig Sauer. "Despite the silver in my hair, I'm not quite fifty yet."

The front door opened and Ferguson walked in. He scanned the room with a little question in his eyes as to what had just happened. "Uh, Wexler is here."

Rafferty and Simon stared at one another. "Are we good to carry forward?" Rafferty said.

Simon gave him an unsteady nod. "Yeah."

"You have about a week of preparatory work to do before I return with the samples, correct?"

Simon nodded and his earring dangled back and forth.

"Then I suggest you help Wexler and Ferguson unload the equipment from that van and set up your lab right away."

"Yeah, sure, I'm on it." Simon headed for the door and exited the house with Ferguson.

Naughton walked over. "You're giving him a second chance. How can you trust him after he tried to weasel on the deal?"

"I'm a good judge of character. Simon won't be a problem." Rafferty faced him. "You shouldn't be so critical. I gave you a second chance two years ago. Be thankful for it."

Naughton didn't reply for a long while. "You said we were making our move on Sheridan tomorrow. Is that still the plan?"

Rafferty fished the cigarette lighter from his pocket and sprung open the lid. Its metallic ring sounded musical to him. "Tomorrow we head back across state; me, you, and Ferguson." He set a cigarette into his mouth and let it dangle. "We'll make final preparations for our long overdue date with Jack." He conjured a flame into his palm with the lighter and smiled. "I have to admit I'm looking forward to it."

"That's no lie," Naughton said.

Rafferty heard a little more intensity in Naughton's voice than he thought appropriate. "You will do as instructed, Mr. Naughton; nothing more, nothing less. Just because Sheridan bested you on the *Aeneas* doesn't give you free reign to even the score." He lit the cigarette.

Wexler, a short and stocky man, burst through the door with a cardboard box in his arms. He dropped it onto the floor. Simon and Ferguson followed with their arms full as well. Simon noted the markings on Wexler's box. "Dude, be careful. That's a centrifuge. You can't get those at the Bangor hardware store."

Wexler chuckled. "If it breaks, you'll figure something out."

Simon checked the package in Ferguson's arms. "That's an autoclave. Also delicate. Set it down carefully over there." He recognized the box in his hands as an electronic scale and gently set it beside the centrifuge. "There's still an incubator and a vortex machine out there, along with plenty of tubes, Petri plates, and filters. Everybody take it easy."

The three disappeared for their second trip to the van.

Rafferty took a draw off his cigarette and blew smoke. "Wexler will babysit Simon while we're gone. If all goes as planned, we should be back in about a week with the material he needs to finish the job."

"How certain are you that Sheridan can, or for that matter, will do his part in your grand scheme?" Naughton asked.

"He'll do it," Rafferty said slowly. "He'll put every fiber of his being into the effort. I know him. I know what motivates him, and trust me," Rafferty smiled. "Jack Sheridan will be motivated."

- SIX -

Tuesday
South Haven, MI

Jack followed Route 43 into South Haven and steered the Jeep around the welcome sign in the circular median on Phoenix Street. It being so early in the tourist season traffic was light, and Jack appreciated not having to dodge cars pulling in and out of the spaces lining the storefronts in town. He had turned the Jeep's ignition key before sunrise and had picked up Connor from his Brighton apartment by 7:00 a.m. They had made the two and a half-hour trip west to recruit the last member of the salvage team under clear skies. Rolling through town now, Jack glanced over at Connor and the laptop computer he had open and running.

"What are you doing?" Jack asked.

"Making sure Markus is here."

Jack didn't get it.

"Markus has a GPS transponder in his boat," Connor explained. "I can pinpoint his location using an online GPS tracking site and the ID number of the transponder."

"How are you doing that on your computer in my Jeep?"

"Oh." Connor tilted the computer to show a card plugged into the side USB port. "This is a 4G card. It's sort of like a cell connection for your computer."

"Technology is on the move." Jack stopped at the Phoenix and Kalamazoo Streets traffic light and gazed at the South Haven Marina straight ahead and down a shallow hill to the right. "Why wouldn't Markus be here? You confirmed the time and place, didn't you?"

"Yeah, it's just that Markus has been AWOL a lot this past year. Before yesterday I hadn't talked to him in three months. I think he's going through his mid-life crisis twenty years early."

Jack sat silent for a moment. "Is Alyson still with him?"

Connor shrugged. "We didn't get to that topic on the phone. It was a short conversation."

Jack pointed through the windshield. "There's the marina. Do you see him on your screen?"

"Uh, I think so, but…" Connor shook his head. "He's not in the marina. Make a left."

The traffic light turned green and Jack turned left. They rolled slowly past the Black Water Bookstore on Kalamazoo Street. "Now what?"

"Make a right up here on Erie. Head into South Beach."

Jack drove the Jeep down a hill into the parking lot for South Haven's South Beach. There weren't too many cars, and he easily found a spot. He switched off the engine. "Well?"

Connor closed the computer. "He's just off shore next to the pier."

Jack put on a pair of sunglasses and got out of the Jeep. Across the sandy beach and seventy yards offshore floated a forty-foot Boston Whaler. She was anchored just south of the concrete breakwater. Across her stern in black letters it read, *Grande Pomposo*. "It's Markus all right."

Connor exited the Jeep and joined his father near the front grill. "He either couldn't find an empty slip last night or didn't want to pay for one."

"Speaking of payment…" Jack held out an open hand to his son. "Five dollars to park."

"Why do I have to pay?"

"Because Markus is your friend. We wouldn't be here if he'd pulled in at the marina."

Connor grumbled and slid a five-dollar bill from his wallet. "Let's go."

They walked onto the beach, Connor inserting the folded Abe Lincoln into the yellow collection box as they passed. It was shaping up to be another warm day. A strong breeze blew in off of Lake Michigan, capping swells and rocking *Grande Pomposo* back and forth. Only a handful of people had come to the beach this weekday morning, and none of them had ventured into the lake yet. Instead they lounged on beach towels drinking in the warmth of the sun. Jack and Connor trudged through the sand up to the waterline. Connor dialed Markus Sweetwood's number on his cell. It rang six times and went to voicemail. "He's not answering."

"What do you suggest?" Jack said.

"The water is shallow for quite a way out, and it's a nice day."

"Call him again."

Connor started unlacing his tennis shoes. "Let's wade out to the boat."

"Let's call him again."

Connor slid off his shoes. "Are you trying to tell me the great undersea salvage expert Jack Sheridan doesn't want to get his feet wet?"

"It's May in Michigan. I know how cold that lake water is still."

Connor tucked his socks into his shoes and carried them as he stepped into the water. "Whoa! Hey, you're right, but we've got to walk the walk."

Jack cursed and pulled his shoes and socks off. He splashed in and caught up with Connor. "Son-of-a—this is why I like Caribbean salvage operations. Hypothermia is not an issue."

They were up to their waists in water when they reached *Grande Pomposo*. Connor pulled himself onto the spacious swim step at the stern and boarded through the transom door. Jack followed him up. Cold lake water dripped from their clothes as they surveyed the towels and snorkel equipment strewn across the fiberglass deck. A wetsuit was draped over the back of the captain's chair in the cabin. Slips of paper with scribbled navigation notes and worn sections of lake charts covered the nav console. No Markus. "Okay, so he's not up and waiting for us." Connor said. He entered the cabin and found a hatch to below deck. "Come on."

Connor crawled through the hatch to a close quartered lower deck in shambles. A collection of worn Bermuda shorts, T-shirts, hoodies, and sweat pants littered the floor, and an eclectic variety of empty beer bottles stood on a little table beneath the starboard porthole. More bottles sloshed in a cooler filled with melted ice. A barley malt aroma mixed with the smell of leftover Chinese food that was caked inside cardboard cartons on the table. A mountain of blankets covered the port side bunk, and a form roughly resembling a human being stirred beneath them. Connor took hold of the top layer of blankets and yanked them off the bed.

Dressed only in red cotton briefs, Markus Sweetwood's tall, athletic frame winced at the sudden inrush of cool air. His short, brown hair was matted against his head on one side but stood up in impossible directions on the other. He pressed his eyelids closed to block the morning sun streaming in through the porthole. Connor reached into the cooler and flicked water droplets into his face.

Markus recoiled. "Sheridan, I'm going to kick your ass."

Jack stepped down through the hatchway. "Which Sheridan are you talking about?"

Markus lifted his head and opened one eye. "The young Sheridan. I respect my elders."

"Why did you anchor over here?" Connor asked.

"Forgot to call and reserve a slip at the marina. They were full up when I got in." Markus dropped his head back down. "I like it better at South Beach anyway."

Connor sat on the edge of the bunk. "So what have you been up to these past three months?"

"Spending money." Markus rolled onto his back and stretched. "Going places. Hey, your pants are wet and you're soaking the mattress."

"Sorry, had to wade out to the boat." Connor sniffed the air. "You reek of alcohol."

"That must be why my head is throbbing."

"Where have you been spending your sabbatical from reality?" Connor asked.

"Virgin Islands, Jamaica, Florida Keys…and some other places I can't think of right now."

Jack crossed his arms. "Have you seen my daughter lately?"

Markus didn't reply. He struggled to sit upright and then settled with his head in his hands. "Yeah, about that." He scanned the cabin floor through his fingers. "When Alyson and I got back from the Keys we had what she called an adult conversation."

"Uh-oh," Connor said. "That doesn't sound good."

Jack cleared dirty laundry from the bench seat behind the table and sat. "I'll bet she wanted you to get some direction in your life and stop floundering."

Markus regarded him a second or two. "She's definitely your daughter, Mr. Sheridan." He swiped a not-so-dirty T-shirt from the floor and pulled it over his head. "She said she was getting tired of living bohemian all the time. I mean, really? Who gets tired of that?"

"Sounds like Alyson did," Connor offered.

"Well, she gave me thirty days to clean up my act."

"And then what?" Jack said.

"And then she's done with me. That's a bit harsh, don't you think?"

"Not really. It would have been harsh if she had not given you the thirty days."

"When did the clock start running on this ultimatum?" Connor asked.

Markus thought a hazy moment. "About a week ago."

"You're not making much progress in your rehabilitation," Connor noted.

"I'm working on it."

Jack reached down into the scattered clothing and lifted a black bikini top. "Who owns this?"

Markus stared at the scant garment through bloodshot eyes. "Uh…"

"Before you speak," Jack said. "Know that from my point of view there is no good answer to this question."

"Then I have no idea where that came from." The boat rocked over the wake of a passing fishing charter and Markus steadied himself. "A hangover really messes with your sea legs."

"Maybe you need something in your stomach," Connor said. "How about some of that leftover Chinese?"

"How about I gak down the front of your shirt?" Markus focused on a picture tacked to a cabinet door across the cabin from him. In it, he and Alyson stood together on a Key West beach. "We went to some pretty nice places and I got her some pretty nice gifts, but none of it impressed her." He let loose a sarcastic chuckle. "Why did I think it would? She had more cash from her share of the coins than I did. Money is definitely not the problem." Markus stood. "Apparently I'm the problem." He staggered toward the head in the bow of the boat. "Gotta take a leak. Don't go anywhere, gentlemen." He stepped in and closed the paneled door.

Jack and Connor stared at one another a long while in silence.

"Do you think he's up for the salvage project?" Connor said, trying to be quiet.

"It doesn't matter if he's up for it." Jack replied. "He needs a schedule and a goal. Having the money from the coins derailed him."

"I'm not sure how much money he has left. He's been spending it like crazy. He might actually need this job to earn living expenses."

"This door is kind of thin," Markus called from the head. "And the hangover is not impairing my hearing." He opened the door and came out wearing a pair of khaki shorts. "Yeah, I've pissed away some cash, but I wasn't going to be a freak like Connor and not spend anything."

Jack considered them both. "I'm sure there's a happy medium between you. Connor, you can loosen up a bit. Markus, I'll ask you straight up. Are you broke?"

Markus plopped down on the bunk. "Not yet. But the joyride is almost over. Believe it or not, I've been thinking about coming back to earth even before you two came to visit. I actually considered calling Stan Crittenden to get my old job back. I came to my senses after four beers."

"Don't go off the deep end," Connor said. "We've got something better in mind."

Markus leaned forward and clasped his hands together. "Lay it on me."

"We're getting the team back together for an Abner Wilson salvage operation," Jack said.

Markus seemed to perk up. "Where this time? Pacific? Atlantic?"

"Somewhere closer to home." Jack pointed through the porthole. "The salvage site is about twenty miles that way in Lake Michigan. That's why we had you meet us in South Haven."

"Okay, I'm interested. What are we going after?"

"Wreckage from a 1950 airplane crash," Jack said. "There was a case in the cargo hold containing a unique cholera vaccine that may or may not have survived the crash intact. We need to find this case and get whatever vaccine material is inside it to the government so they can reproduce the vaccine."

Markus smiled. "So we get to save humanity. I like it."

"Saving humanity is a bit of an exaggeration, but the government believes it's important to find this vaccine in order to combat an outbreak of cholera in Haiti."

"When do we get started?" Markus asked.

"I'm already on it. Rezner and I met with Lloyd yesterday and secured a ship for the search."

"And that ship is the *Achilles*," Connor said. "While I was being a freak this past winter I worked on her retrofit. Didn't you have something to do with her too, Markus?"

Markus sat up straight. "I upgraded her ROV system. It was my last job for Crittendon."

"That's why we're here." Jack slapped his back. "You'll be more help than usual."

Markus looked cross at him. "You're lucky I like you, Mr. Sheridan."

Jack chuckled. "Markus, let's take your inflatable to shore to get coffee in town and discuss details. You've got five minutes to get yourself together. I'll be on deck."

Jack climbed through the hatchway to the Boston Whaler's main deck. He stood with his back to the sun to dry his wet jeans. A hundred yards beyond the red South Haven lighthouse at the end of the pier, a speedboat skipped across the waves at full throttle. Farther out near the horizon of lake and sky, a pair of sailboats glided along on a southwesterly wind. Beyond the horizon, roughly two points off dead west, the crash site of Flight 2501 waited to be found. Jack felt a wave of exhilaration. He loved to hunt for something lost, and what made this hunt all the better was that Lauren had put her full support behind him. That made all the difference to Jack. He could not wait to climb aboard the *Achilles*. Things could not get much better.

For the first time in two years he had managed to forget all about Donovan Rafferty.

- SEVEN -

Sarnia, Ontario

Alec Cohn carefully fitted a suppressor onto the barrel of his 9 mm Glock. He screwed the attachment until it seated snug, and then opened a cabinet near the hatchway door inside the *Liberty's* main cabin and placed the weapon on an easily accessible shelf. He mused that his earlier order for the crew to stow their side arms while docked in Canada did not apply to him. He closed the cabinet, ducked through the hatchway, and stepped out onto the deck.

Their voyage up the Detroit River and past the city had gone without incident, and their passage through the navigational channel of Lake St. Clare went much the same. After navigating up the St. Clare River, the small flotilla of tall ship replicas reached their next stop in the shadow of the Blue Water Bridge.

The suspension bridge spans a mile and a quarter of water separating Michigan from Canada, and as the ships approached the structure, two had veered west to dock at the Seaway Terminal in Port Huron and two had veered east to dock at the Sarnia Bay Marina. Cohn commanded the *Liberty* and led the way around the marina breakwater late Sunday evening. They glided into their slip, which barely accommodated the sloop's length, moored the vessel, and bedded down for the night.

Cohn commended himself again on utilizing the tall ship flotilla as nautical camouflage. Authorities are less likely to find you if you parade around right under their noses. The overt nature of Cohn's cover, however, carried with it increased risk by allowing tourists to roam about the deck during tour hours. He calculated the trade-off was worth it, and by restricting access to the lower deck he mitigated some of that risk. He simply did not allow anyone the opportunity to see what the *Liberty* was carrying. The cryogenic freezers and other suspect equipment below just weren't standard fare on eighteenth-century sloops. And although cannon, shot, and powder were common aboard a war ship, the type of armament Cohn had below deck possessed a decidedly twenty-first-century flare.

Cohn considered this stage of the plan again as he had done a dozen times since making port and again concluded that designating Sarnia as his way station was the correct choice. Generally lax security measures throughout the Canadian provinces made the job of importing and transporting illicit material relatively easy. The United States posed a more formidable challenge. Despite reports to the contrary, security at U.S. entry points had tightened up considerably post- 9/11. An array of traveler identification systems, cargo screening equipment, and sophisticated profiling methods had been implemented. But there were blind spots. Crossing a Great Lake from Canada to Michigan was an Achilles heel authorities had yet to sufficiently address. Trafficking of narcotics and people on the great inland waterways was a thriving enterprise, and Cohn had decided to fully exploit it.

It was early afternoon and Cohn watched the last pair of tourists descend the gangplank to the dock. One of his crew pulled a chain across the entry to bar anyone else from coming aboard. They were due to ship out in two hours. Cohn checked his watch. The couriers were scheduled to arrive any minute.

Across the deck crewmen prepared to get underway. Speers descended the starboard steps from the deck amidships and met Cohn beneath the yard arms of the mainmast. "Can we restart the generator yet?"

Cohn nodded. "The last tourists just left. Fire it up and get those freezers to temperature."

Speers snapped his fingers at a passing crewman. "Anders."

The crewman stopped and turned. A bruise darkened his left eye, and the crusted scab of a cut bisected the right side of his nose.

"Captain, meet your new squad leader," Speers said.

Crewman Anders acknowledged his superior with a quick nod.

"Congratulations on your recent promotion," Cohn said.

"Thank you, sir," Anders replied.

Cohn felt a little uneasy being addressed as "sir" because it reeked of traditional military hierarchy, but for lack of a more suitable title he let it pass. "Don't do anything to make me regret that promotion."

Anders shook his head. "That will not happen."

"We're clear to restart the generator," Speers said to Anders. "Take Byrne below to bring the freezers online."

Anders acknowledged and moved to collect Byrne from his topside duty.

Cohn observed the movement of a cluster of white clouds overhead and determined wind direction. He made a mental note of the tack he would need to set when the *Liberty* got underway. "I received another report from Nix," he said.

Speers turned from watching crewmen take down rope barriers that restricted tourist access to sensitive areas of the ship. "What's the colonel up to?"

"I was right," Cohn said. "He's watching a man named Jack Sheridan."

"I know that name."

"You should. Two years ago Jack Sheridan derailed the colonel's attempt to steal an air force jet fitted with a new radar defense system. Sheridan wiped out half his team."

"Is this guy Special Forces or something?"

"No, he's a civilian." Cohn laughed. "That's what really pissed off the colonel. How could an ordinary man defeat a skilled mercenary force?"

"Apparently he's not ordinary."

"News stories profiled Sheridan after the incident. He had served a stint in the navy, and half the crew of his salvage ship was ex-navy, but it goes beyond that. He should not have been able to do what he did."

"I understand the colonel's frustration," Speers said. "You think he's planning to kill Sheridan?"

"If you were in the colonel's shoes, wouldn't you?" Cohn scanned the dock. On the walkway astern of the *Liberty,* a pair of men dressed in generic brown pant and short-sleeve uniforms pushed a cart loaded with four crates through the thinning crowd. Cohn checked his watch. "Anyway, it makes sense, except for the house."

"The house?"

"Nix shadowed the colonel to a house in West Michigan. He couldn't get close enough to determine what they were doing, but some of the colonel's men met him there. It's likely a staging point for whatever they have planned for Sheridan."

"You'll obviously keep Nix on task."

Cohn smiled. "Obviously. I can't wait to see how it turns out. Now, our delivery is here. Get Duvall and Erikson to help carry our packages aboard."

Speers acknowledged and headed toward the bow where the requested crewmen were inspecting the staysail prior to leaving port. At the foot of the gangplank the uniformed couriers stopped the cart and locked its wheels. Four wooden crates about a meter square were stacked side by side and two high. They were held fast to the cart by nylon straps. Black stenciled letters spelled the words *Northeast Marine*

Supply across the front of each one. The couriers loosened the straps and lifted one crate off the top, and then maneuvered toward the gangplank. Duvall and Erikson strode down to them, removed the chain across the entry, and grabbed a second crate off the cart.

Cohn absently ran a finger over the scar tissue on his jaw line and watched the couriers carefully make their way up the gangplank. He moved to meet them. "Right on time," he said to the first courier. "Just as advertised."

"We weren't going to be late with this delivery," the tall courier replied. "The sooner we drop, the better. Where do you want it?"

Cohn turned. "Speers." He motioned to the main cargo hatch forward of the cabin amidships.

Speers ordered two crewmen to man the block and tackle rig above the cargo hatch. They spread a mass of netted rope on deck, and the couriers set the crate in the middle of it. At Speers' urging the crewmen heaved a line of rope through the pulleys. The rope sling lifted the crate off the deck. Speers helped guide it over the hatch, and the crewmen lowered it into the hold. The couriers headed back to the cart as Duvall and Erikson stepped onto the deck with the second crate.

Cohn felt his heartbeat quicken. He went into the main cabin and climbed down the steps to the lower deck. He made his way through a narrow corridor and entered the main cargo hold. On the starboard side of the hold, the diesel generator rumbled through a silenced exhaust pipe. Cohn walked around the waist-high stainless steel freezer units and stepped over the power cables from the generator to observe his men receive and stow their cargo. Speers joined him near the freezers. Anders and Byrne lifted the first crate from the rope sling as it settled in the hold and carried it toward a freezer unit, but Byrne stumbled on one of the power cables and it crashed onto the deck. "Shit!"

Anders and Byrne scattered. Speers stepped back. Even Cohn flinched, but he knew better.

He knew the design of the packaging and the containers within, and that such an impact should not have caused any damage. He also knew that if a rupture had occurred on an inner container, there would be no corner aboard this ship they could run to that would be safe. "Anders, stand fast! Pop the lid off that crate and let's have a look."

Anders hesitated but then swiped a short crowbar from a toolbox beside the generator. He wedged the claw up under the wooden lid and pried the corner nails loose. He worked his way around the edges. Byrne came over to help and they lifted the lid off. The last few nails screeched in protest and the lid broke free, spilling Styrofoam packing peanuts onto the deck. Anders and Byrne stood still. They were not eager to go further. Cohn stepped forward and dug into the crate, clearing away packing peanuts until he reached a solid inner case. He felt around the top and sides and cleared away more peanuts. Fingers of vapor rose from the surface of the case.

"Everybody relax. There are no cracks." Cohn unlatched a series of clasps around an upper seam in the case. "Speers, hand me that extractor on the table behind you." Speers handed him the tool, and Cohn opened the lid of the case. A cloud of icy vapor billowed from inside. It dispersed and thinned and revealed the top plates of six stainless steel canisters seated in a honeycomb-like nesting rack. Cohn felt a rush of frigid air on his face. He took the extractor tool by the handle and actuated its trigger. Three articulating steel fingers opened and closed like a set of jaws at its base. He positioned the tool above one of the canisters, carefully lowering it into position so the fingers enclosed the end of the canister like a mechanical hand. He actuated the trigger and locked the mechanism, and then gently pulled the canister from its sub-zero nest.

Warm ambient air swirled around the canister's stainless steel surface and it steamed like it was on fire. Cohn turned the extractor tool, inspecting the canister. No dents, no cracks, no damage. Engraved Asian characters ran vertically along the length of the twenty-inch canister. Cohn knew it was Korean writing but he could not read it. He did understand one section, however. The number 731 stood out amongst a string of engraved symbols.

Cohn stood. "Byrne, open that freezer."

Byrne threw back a latching lever and pulled open the top door of a freezer unit. Another cloud of arctic vapor spilled into the cargo hold, this time from the empty belly of the cryogenic freezer. A honeycomb-like nesting rack exactly like the one in the crate occupied the freezer compartment. Cohn aligned the canister with one of the cylindrical compartments and lowered it into place. He unlocked the jaws of the extractor tool, stood back, and handed the tool to Byrne. "Inspect the rest. Transfer them. Be careful but be quick."

Byrne reluctantly took the tool. "Right…no problem."

Cohn and Speers watched the remaining canisters from the crate get transferred to the freezer. The rest of the crates were quickly lowered into the hold, and their contents were placed inside the cryo freezers as well. Cohn leaned toward Speers. "Come with me to close the deal with the couriers." He walked around the freezers and climbed the steps into the main cabin. Through the hatchway door he spotted the two couriers standing near the main cargo hatch on the deck. Cohn stood near the door and called to them. "Gentlemen, if you would step inside for a moment."

The two men who had delivered the crates ducked into the cabin and stood beneath the low overhead. Cohn greeted them with a business smile. "I'd like to thank you for your prompt service." He opened the lower cabinet near the hatchway and lifted a blue plastic container that looked like a fishing tackle box. He set the box on a table in the center of the ten-foot wide cabin. Speers climbed up from the lower deck and stood on the other side of the cabin. The tall courier stepped over to the table and opened the box. Stacked and banded hundred-dollar bills took up every bit of space inside. The tall man smiled, as did his partner. "Count it," Cohn said. "Make sure it's all there."

The tall courier lifted a stack of hundreds and fanned the bills with his thumb. His smile slowly receded. He put the stack back in the box and closed the lid. "I trust you."

Cohn smiled and shook his head. "Don't trust me."

The tall courier lifted the box from the table. "It looks like it's all here. We need to leave. Whatever we just delivered can't be legal, not for this kind of money."

"Well, I want to give you a bonus for getting it to me on time." Cohn turned and opened the top cabinet. "Are you heading back to Toronto right away?"

"Yeah, as soon as we get back to the—" He never finished his sentence.

Cohn spun around with the silenced Glock in hand and put a bullet right in his forehead, spraying blood and matter on the other courier's face. The second courier jumped in panic and spat a curse as his partner collapsed. He frantically reached under his shirt for something but Speers advanced and seized his arm. A small caliber pistol was holstered on the courier's waist. Speers grabbed the gun and shoved the man against the wood bulkhead. Cohn fired two silenced rounds into the courier's chest. The man gasped and gurgled and was dead before he dropped onto the deck.

Cohn considered the blood spatters and bodies, and then searched the tall courier's pockets and found a set of car keys. He picked up the blue box of money and set it back on the table. "Speers, get Anders up here and clean this mess. Pack and stow the bodies in the hold. We'll get rid of them in the middle of Huron." He turned and stepped out onto the deck under the afternoon sun. "Duvall, Erikson, get over here."

The crewmen hustled over from the cargo hatch. "Yes, sir," Duvall said.

Sir again. Cohn figured he had to get used to it. "Take these keys." He slapped the ring into Duvall's hand. "Wheel that cart at the bottom of the gangplank back to the marina parking lot. Find the courier's van or truck or whatever they drove. Use the key fob. Load the cart and drive the vehicle off marina grounds. Find a nearby parking lot and stash it there. Get back quickly because we leave port in under an hour. Understand?"

Duvall and Erikson acknowledged and headed down the gangplank.

Cohn climbed up to the foredeck and surveyed the marina for any signs that someone saw or heard any of what had just transpired. The thin crowd milling about the docks was just as calm and uninterested as before the couriers had arrived. Cohn took a moment to slow his heart rate and breathing. It wasn't shooting those men that had keyed him up. No, it was the fact that he had just taken the biggest step of the operation and he finally had the means in his hands to set the tripwire. The thought brought a smile to his face and made the scar tissue on his jaw tingle.

- EIGHT -

Linden, MI

Jack Sheridan took a moment to watch Lauren through the frosted glass of the shower door in their master bath. She still mesmerized him. Through twenty-four years of marriage the feeling never waned. Although there were times when Jack thought their marriage might not survive it was not because he didn't love her. His previous job with Neptune's Reach had wreaked havoc with their relationship. It kept them apart too often, drove a wedge between them. Three years ago the strain had led to separation. Ironically, Jack's near-death experience with Donovan Rafferty on that ship in the Atlantic proved to be the turning point for them. He realized what mattered in life and what deserved to take a back seat. When he made it home alive he changed some things. First and foremost he quit Neptune's Reach.

Jack stepped in front of the mirror above the sink and checked the small cut on his chin. He had been in the shower after returning from his trip to South Haven and was shaving when Lauren had walked in and surprised him. He flinched enough to draw blood, but the surprise ended up being worth the sting. Now he assessed the damage. Not too bad. Wearing only a towel around his waist, Jack made a cursory appraisal of his overall condition at forty-seven years of age. He had managed to stay fairly fit, and although he didn't have a full six pack you could tell he had abdominal muscles. The scar under his left rib cage served as a memento of the gunshot wound he suffered during the Columbian incident. His left hand still ached every morning around the bones that broke while escaping from the hand cuffs on Garity's yacht during the treasure hunt ten months ago. A fair amount of silver had worked its way between the brown on his head to give him what Lauren called the appearance of wisdom. He still hadn't come to appreciate the comment. And yes, he'd recently shaved his moustache, perhaps to feel a bit younger, but he hadn't fully admitted that to himself yet.

Lauren came up behind him wrapped in a white towel. She kissed the back of his neck and dripped water from her hair onto his shoulders. He looked at her reflection in the mirror and smiled. "How does Stillwater Grill sound for dinner to celebrate the new project?"

"Sounds good." She went into the walk-in closet to get dressed.

Jack pulled on a pair of jeans and searched through a dresser drawer for a shirt. Ike trotted into the room and circled around his legs. "Looking for trouble?" he said to the shepherd. Ike growled and panted, and Jack became uneasy.

A memory from early morning surfaced as he wound down from the South Haven trip. Before sunrise Ike had stirred Jack awake with a low growl. It wasn't uncommon for the shepherd to spot a raccoon out a window and get vocal during the night, but this time the dog was sitting in the center of the bedroom floor alert with ears perked. Jack had walked the house and had checked the security fence monitor but saw nothing out of the ordinary. He figured Ike had just heard some nocturnal animals scrapping in the woods beyond the tree line. Looking back, Jack realized that he had neglected to fret over Rafferty all day, and he supposed his subconscious was simply trying to give his paranoia equal time.

Then again maybe his sixth sense had pinged his conscience for a reason.

Jack found an olive green polo shirt and pulled it over his head. In the kitchen he read an article about a Hartland bank robbery in yesterday's newspaper while waiting for Lauren to finish getting dressed. When she stepped out of the bedroom she looked amazing, as she always did to Jack. She'd climbed into a comfortable pair of faded jeans and a sleeveless brown shirt, which showed that she too had kept herself in good shape. A gold necklace and small hoop earrings set off the shirt perfectly, and she'd pulled back her hair with a clip to reveal the graceful lines of her face and neck.

"Whoa, you really know how to throw yourself together," Jack said. "What do you say we delay dinner for half an hour or so."

"I'd say first, I'm hungry." She walked over and kissed him. "And second, you're not up for it after the shower."

"Now that's just cold."

"Let's go before we have to wait for a table."

Jack slipped on his shoulder holster and chose a dark blue spring jacket to conceal it. They left the house and jumped into the Jeep Cherokee. Jack felt another ping in his head before he turned the ignition key. He glanced around the yard, listened to the wind blowing through the trees. A thin cloud of dust from a car that had just passed dissipated over the dry dirt road at the end of the driveway.

"What are you doing?" Lauren said.

"Appreciating Mother Nature." He started the engine and turned the Jeep around. He had Lauren press the button on the new remote and the barrier at the end of the drive lowered to ground level. Jack drove off his property and wound his way over the back roads to get to the expressway. He accelerated down the Silver Lake Road entry onto US 23 and headed south.

Jack settled behind the wheel. "When Rezner and I toured the *Achilles,* the maintenance crew said they'd be finished in a couple of days."

"Then she could be ready tomorrow," Lauren said. "When do you think you'll ship out?"

"Not sure. I've got to research meteorological records for the night of the plane crash, see if I can pick out something everyone else missed that will help find the crash site. Plus Lloyd has to get the *Achilles* to our staging port in Muskegon and load her with logistical supplies. If things go smooth we could ship out within a week."

"Connor is looking forward to working with you again."

"So am I," Jack said. "I mean me working with him, not me working with myself."

"It's sad about Markus."

Jack glanced at her. "What's to be sad about? He's had quite a year of travel and toys."

Lauren shook her head. "He's realizing that money doesn't make you happy."

"He just needs to get grounded." Jack switched lanes. "This project will do him good."

"It'll help that he's spending more time with Connor too," Lauren added.

"That will help both of them. As far as Markus has spun out, Connor has pulled back. I think their opposite personalities balance each other."

Lauren sat quiet a moment. "And what about Alyson?"

"She's doing the right thing. Markus has to decide what he wants. Her staying out of the picture until he figures that out is a smart move." He added, "That's how I'd play it."

"Like father, like daughter?"

"Something like that." Jack's cell phone rang with the "Apocalypse Now" ring tone. "It's Rezner." He answered. "What's up, Joshua?"

"Hey, Jack, I was thinking," Rezner said. "When we're criss-crossing the lake we'll be out on a limb. Know what I mean?"

Jack frowned. "Strangely enough I do know what you mean."

"Right. If our old friend picks this boat ride as his opportune moment to pay a visit, we're cut off from outside help. Ten miles out on Lake Michigan is beyond the reach of a 911 call. You following me?"

"Yeah," Jack said. "What do you want to bring with you from the JR Supply and Ammo stock room?"

"Oh, just something with a little more power behind it than a snub-nose .38. Keep in mind we're fending for ourselves out there."

"As long as it fits inside a standard sized suitcase you can bring it. Okay?"

Silence on the line. "Balls. Okay, let me think about this. I'll get back to you."

"All right, let me know." Jack closed the conversation and returned the phone to its clip.

Lauren sat and waited for an explanation.

"It's Rezner. Don't ask." They drove in silence a while. Jack merged onto 96 and then took the Grand River exit into Brighton. He pulled into the Stillwater Grill parking lot a minute past six o'clock. They got a table without a wait and placed their orders. After the waitress brought a beer and an iced tea to their table Lauren said, "Do you mind if we run an errand in town after this? I need to pick up a few things."

Jack checked the time on his cell. "Sure, but let's not make this a shopping marathon. I want to get going on that weather research tonight."

Lauren squeezed a lemon wedge over her glass of tea. "Yes, that does sound exciting."

Their orders arrived, salmon for Jack and a Caesar salad for Lauren. They ate with casual conversation. Midway through the meal Jack glanced around at the restaurant crowd. Clinking plates and the drone of fifty conversations filled his ears. "It feels like we're being watched. Do you feel that?"

"Honey, do you know how many times you've asked me that in the last two years?"

"More than I can count," Jack admitted.

"Does it feel different this time?"

Jack frowned. "Not much." He regarded Lauren across the table. "Maybe I'm just picking up all the guys staring at my beautiful wife."

She gave him a sarcastic smirk. "Nice try." She shuffled a piece of Romaine lettuce with her fork. "You know, you're close to becoming the little boy who cried wolf."

"Boy?"

"You know what I mean."

"I hope I do, or our marriage could be in trouble."

"Okay, you're the big man with the big problem."

"Hey, let's not get carried away." Jack lowered his voice. "Let's just keep the man big and the problem small."

She couldn't help but smile and continued eating her salad. A short time later Jack finished the last of his beer and threw a tip on the table. In the parking lot he verified the locked Jeep Cherokee was still locked. He peered inside at some papers he'd left on the seats to confirm they had not been moved or crinkled. Lauren waited by the passenger door and tapped her open-toed shoe. "Any time now."

Jack unlocked the doors with the fob and they climbed inside. He started the engine and pulled out of the restaurant parking lot onto Grand River. He found a parking spot in the middle of the lot of a merchandise store that had a bull's-eye for a logo. He remembered seeing a T-shirt on display with that logo across the chest. Although that's how he felt a lot of the time, Jack figured there was no need to make Rafferty's quest any easier by wearing one of them.

Jack and Lauren walked inside the store. Lauren headed to the ladies footwear section. Jack followed. "Are you serious? You came here for shoes? You've got thirty pair at home."

Lauren walked down an aisle and inspected the selection of sandals. "Exaggerator."

Jack's eyes glazed over. He stood at the end cap and waited. And waited. He glanced down the main aisle at the shoppers drifting through the store. Lauren switched aisles and he switched end caps. After a few minutes she said, "I'm going to housewares for some towels."

"Right." He checked the overhead signs and found the housewares section a few rows away. He headed that way via the main aisle but got distracted by an electronics display. He studied smart phones through a glass case a minute or so before getting back on course.

His mind suddenly tore him from the store and dropped him on the deck of the *Aeneas* two years ago, because four aisles down and straight ahead stood a man who was a dead ringer for one of Rafferty's men. Jack reached for the Kimber but did not draw it. The man in his sights perused cell phone accessories on an end cap display and appeared not to notice him. Jack took a tentative step forward. The man tilted his head, and then Jack wasn't so sure of his identity. The man stepped around the corner.

Jack walked straight for the aisle the man had disappeared into, slowly at first but with increasing speed. He withdrew the pistol halfway from the holster but thought better of it and set it back in place. He peered around the corner. No one there but two teenagers checking out phone chargers. He stepped over to the next aisle. Nobody. He began to doubt what he had seen.

And then he thought about Lauren.

"Damn!" Jack rushed toward housewares with his hand still locked on the Kimber, checking aisles to his left for the elusive phantom from the *Aeneas* and aisles to the right for his wife. He grabbed his cell from its belt clip and tried to speed dial her number. No service this deep inside the store.

He reached the housewares section and searched the entire area. She wasn't there. He spun around and double-checked the aisles. People passing by gave him uncertain looks. He pushed past a couple holding hands and rushed to the front of the store, scanning the staggered checkout lanes with a nervous stride. There in the last lane he spotted Lauren setting a group of towels on the conveyor belt. "Hey," she said to him. "I tried to call you but I didn't have any bars." She saw that he was short of breath and had beads of sweat on his face. "Are you okay? You look like you're having a heart attack or something."

Jack walked to her and tried to calm himself. "Big man, big problem. Remember?"

"What happened?"

"I saw someone, or rather, I think I saw someone." He checked behind them in line.

She handed her credit card to the cashier. "This isn't the first time you thought you saw…" She made quotation marks with her fingers. "*Someone.*"

"This time was different." He leaned in close to Lauren's ear. "It's a guy I shot in the leg."

She faced him. "Which one?"

He gave her an odd look. "What does it matter which leg?"

"Not which leg, which guy?"

"The one you haven't met. Let's go."

Lauren signed for the purchase, stuck the credit card in her purse, and grabbed her bag of towels. "How sure are you about this?"

Jack didn't reply right away. "Just humor me this time." They hustled through the automatic doors to the parking lot. They got halfway to the car when the cashier called after them from the sidewalk. "Miss, you forgot a bag."

Lauren stopped. "My shoes."

Jack took her arm. “Leave them.”

Lauren exhaled. “You’re not even sure you saw this guy. Go back with me.”

Jack looked skyward and mumbled something. “Fine, let’s go.” They headed back to the store. To their left a black Enclave with tinted windows had its brake lights lit up. They stopped in case the vehicle was going to pull out of its parking space. Instead of pulling out, the Enclave seemed to shift back into park and the brake lights went dark. Jack and Lauren dashed into the store. She collected her bag from the checkout lane and they returned to the parking lot. The Enclave was still there. Jack rushed past it and unlocked the Jeep. The ping in his head came at regular intervals now.

They climbed into the Jeep. Jack started the engine and pulled forward out of the space. The tires squealed as he exited the lot. He connected with Grand River and hopped onto I-96E. Nobody seemed to be following in the rearview mirror. Jack shook his head. “I thought for sure…” He picked up his cell phone and speed dialed Connor’s number.

“Yeah, dad,” Connor answered.

“Where are you?”

“Working at home.”

“Is everything okay?”

“Yeah. What’s up?”

Jack thought a long moment. “Probably nothing, but stay alert.”

“Got it. I’ll check in this afternoon.” They disconnected.

Jack grabbed the steering wheel with both hands. “I know what you’re thinking,” he said to Lauren. “This was different.”

“How so?” she asked.

“It just felt different.” He took the US 23 North exit. “I know that’s not helpful to you.”

She sat quiet in the passenger seat a few minutes. “We need a better way to deal with this.”

Jack had calmed a bit with the uneventful drive and the silence in the Jeep. He took one hand off the wheel. “I know.”

A mile or so ahead on the expressway cars began to cluster with brake lights illuminated. It seemed traffic was stopping dead. “Must be an accident.” He nodded to the M59 exit sign they had just come up on. “Let’s get off here and bypass the tie-up.” Jack drove down the off ramp. At the light he merged onto M59 East and switched lanes to turn onto Hartland Road.

“Wonder what happened on 23,” Lauren said.

Jack turned on a local radio station while waiting at the light. He drove through on the green, passed the shopping plaza to the right, and entered a roundabout. A top-of-the-hour newsbreak came on the radio. The news director reported a rollover accident involving multiple cars that had shut down the northbound lanes of US 23. The Livingston County Sheriff's Office and emergency vehicles were responding, and travelers were being advised to seek alternate routes around the incident. The news director closed with an unsubstantiated report that gunshots from off road may have played a part in the accident.

Jack put both hands back on the wheel and drove past the middle school. To the west he could see the traffic backup on US 23. He stopped at the intersection of Hartland and Crouse. The rearview mirror showed clear behind the Jeep. He checked the three incoming routes to the intersection. An old, white pickup truck rolled up from eastbound Crouse and turned right onto Hartland, passing them in a cloud of blue exhaust smoke.

"What are you thinking?" Lauren said.

"You don't want to know." He continued forward and drove through Hartland's tiny downtown, looking past the café, music hall, and residential side streets. Hartland Road dropped down a low-grade hill, with Cromaine District Library on the right and the Hartland Village Cemetery on the left. Farther ahead, the road banked right. Jack pictured the terrain beyond the curve. It was a desolate section of pavement that turned to dirt and wound through a wooded field with large trees peppering either side of the soft shoulder. An S-turn limited forward visibility to short sections of the road. In Jack's mind it seemed the perfect spot for an ambush. "This is my alternate route when 23 is backed up. He's been watching. He knows that."

He slowed the Jeep at the crest of the hill. A car parked alongside the upcoming curve came into view. It was a clean, black Acura with rental plates and hazard lights flashing. "That car isn't local," Jack muttered.

Lauren seemed to be growing nervous. "Okay, Jack, now this feels different."

In the rearview mirror a black Enclave with tinted windows appeared from a side street behind the Jeep. "Damn right it's different." Jack gunned the accelerator and pulled hard on the steering wheel. The Jeep swerved off the pavement and bounded up an embankment, smashing through the black iron fence that surrounded the cemetery.

Lauren thrashed with the lurching vehicle and clung to the door handle. "What are you doing?"

Jack veered around a large marble headstone and headed down a long grassy path between plots. "That accident on 23 is no accident. Rafferty caused it. He drove us into an ambush."

"Where are you going?"

"Trying to loop back to the side streets."

Lauren checked through the rear window. "They're coming after us."

Jack glanced at the driver's side mirror. The Enclave paralleled their course on Henry Street. It closed the distance faster than Jack thought it would and cut hard into the side entry of the cemetery. "So much for that idea."

The Jeep's front tires suddenly skidded across the gravel of a little road that wound through the tombstone landscape. Jack regained control in time to miss a group of Civil War headstones and passed over a pair of ground markers before getting the Jeep squarely onto the dirt road. The Enclave surged forward, coming within inches of his bumper. "Hang on!" Jack shouted. He hammered the brake pedal. Deceleration threw them forward until the inertia belts locked across their shoulders and jerked them to a stop. A split second later the front grill of the Enclave slammed the rear of the Jeep. The crash of steel smashing steel resounded in the cab, and the force of impact threw their heads back against the rests. Jack let off the brakes and kicked the accelerator. The Jeep lurched forward. In the rearview mirror the Enclave swerved off road with both front airbags deployed and crashed over a low headstone.

"Watch out!" Lauren shouted.

Jack spun his head and focused through the windshield. A string of tall headstones bounded a hard right turn in the road ahead. Jack slowed the Jeep and crowned the curve, sliding up onto the grass and nicking one of the headstones in passing. The exit to Hartland Road lay just ahead and he zeroed in on it. The black Acura suddenly appeared. It slid to a stop across the gateway with its passenger side blocking the exit. The driver got out of the car. It was Naughton. His bleach blond hair and submachine gun sparked another flashback. "Shit, it's a mercenary reunion."

Jack swerved right to avoid Naughton's aim. The Jeep slid across loose dirt from a fresh grave. He let off the gas and turned left to compensate, but the front quarter panel struck a large tree trunk and the Jeep bounced like a billiard ball. Jack fought the wheel for control, sideswiping a great marble memorial. A massive oak tree with a spread of headstones beneath its branches loomed ahead. Jack hit the brakes and slid to a stop inches from the stones. He reached for the Remington's pistol grip in the side door compartment. "Stay put," he said to Lauren, and then threw open the driver's door.

Naughton was weaving through the headstones with the submachine gun leading the way. Jack chambered a round in the Remington and fired at him. Naughton flinched right and fired a burst of rounds across the tops of the tombstones that echoed off the stone and leafy overhead. Not very close to the mark, Jack thought. He pumped another shell into the chamber and blasted again. This time the spread of stinger rounds pelted Naughton in the neck and shoulder, staggering him back but not taking him down.

Jack had loaded the shotgun with non-lethal loads thinking altruistically that he did not want to kill if it wasn't absolutely necessary. Now in the thick of things it didn't seem like such a good idea. Jack pumped the Remington again and hit Naughton point blank with a full spread of rubber shot. It threw the blond mercenary off his feet and landed him writhing on the ground.

The sound of gunfire from behind turned Jack around. The Jeep's side mirror blew apart and the windshield cobwebbed under a hail of bullets from an automatic pistol in the hands of the man Jack had seen in the store: Ferguson.

Ferguson had taken up a position behind a four-foot tall headstone thirty yards in front of where the Jeep had come to rest. He kept shooting into the Jeep, and Lauren screamed as she scrambled beneath the dashboard to escape the lead and pieces of tempered windshield. The bullet resistant glass Jack had ordered would come a week too late. He raced back to the Jeep, dropping the Remington and drawing the Kimber, which was fully loaded with lethal rounds. Any fear he felt transformed into anger.

Ferguson had stopped shooting, probably to reload, and Jack pulled open the Jeep's passenger door. Lauren was crouched below the dash. "Are you okay?" he said.

She looked into his eyes, half panicked and half relieved. "Yes."

"Do you have your pistol in your purse?"

She gave him a look that told him she didn't.

He grabbed her hand. "Let's go." He pulled her out of the Jeep and they dashed through the cemetery, crouching low near headstones for cover. Ferguson must have loaded a fresh magazine because gunfire sounded again. Bullets ricocheted off marble and split the bark on a three-inch red maple to their left. Jack pulled Lauren down behind the massive trunk of an oak tree. He pivoted around the tree, set his stance, and fired two thundering rounds from the Kimber. The first missed clean but the second struck Ferguson's headstone cover, dislodging a fist-sized sliver of marble and sending shards into his cheek.

Lauren shrieked and recoiled like she'd been hit. Jack crouched beside her. She cradled her arm. "I'm okay," she assured him. He considered the wound. If she had caught a slug in her arm it couldn't have come from Ferguson. He didn't have the angle. It had to have come from…

Jack swung the Kimber around to target their rear. Down on one knee and sighting down the barrel, he found himself face to face with the boogeyman.

Donovan Rafferty stood ten yards away with arms half raised and hands open and empty like he intended to surrender. Jack froze at the sight. Rafferty had haunted his dreams and lurked in every daytime shadow for two years, and the day had finally come to end it. But something wasn't right.

If Rafferty had been aiming a weapon or rushing forward, Jack would have already plugged him with seven bullets, but it seemed he had something else in mind. Jack wasn't in the mood to find out what it could be.

Rafferty smiled. "Good to see you again, old friend."

Jack fired a .45 caliber slug just shy of Rafferty's temple.

Rafferty flinched and his smile disappeared, but it spread slowly across his face again. "I missed you too. It's good to know your moral core is intact. You still can't shoot an unarmed man."

Jack felt that core melt down. "After all you've done, the deaths, the threats, the betrayals, killing you will be a service to humanity." He steadied his aim and curled his finger around the trigger.

"Before you dispense your self-serving brand of justice, know this," Rafferty said with the confidence of a man who held all the cards. "If you kill me, Lauren dies too."

BOOK II:
SILVER BULLET

- NINE -

Jack kept Rafferty's chest dead center of his aim. This wasn't playing out as he'd imagined. He'd always figured their meeting would be brief and violent, with one of them ending up dead in the first few seconds. For the moment Jack held the upper hand, but a shred of doubt prevented him from sealing the deal. Rafferty's threat to Lauren seemed a desperate gambit to stay alive. Jack was certain of it. She'd just caught a graze or a ricochet in her arm, nothing life threatening. Even if the wound was more critical, how would keeping Rafferty alive help her? No, it had to be a ploy, one that Jack would not entertain. The steel trigger felt cold against his finger. He stared hard into the boogeyman's eyes, searching for evidence that the gambit was a lie…or one small hint that it might be the truth.

"You know me," Rafferty said calmly. "Do you really believe I'd hand you this advantage if I didn't have a hammer hanging over your head?"

Jack didn't reply. He eased his finger off the trigger. In his peripheral vision, Ferguson cautiously worked his way closer. Several yards back over Rafferty's right shoulder Naughton picked himself off the ground, obviously tender from the stinger rounds. Jack stepped back toward Lauren. "Tell them to stop where they are," he said to Rafferty. "If they keep coming, if they get within ten feet of us, I'll blast a hole through your heart."

Rafferty smirked and signaled to Ferguson. "Stop where you are. Turn around and get our vehicle drivable. We'll need it soon." He checked over his shoulder. "Mr. Naughton. Stand your ground."

Jack noticed the red mark on Rafferty's face for the first time. "Looks like that airbag tagged you pretty good."

Rafferty slowly lowered his arms. "I have to admit you are a challenge."

"Keep those hands clear." Jack checked for Rafferty's belt holster but did not see it.

"I didn't shoot her with the Sig," Rafferty said. "I hit her with that."

Jack followed Rafferty's leading glance to a pistol laying in the grass a couple of yards away. He hadn't noticed it there before. It wasn't Rafferty's favored Sig Sauer semi-automatic. Jack walked backwards to Lauren and crouched beside her. "Are you okay?"

"I think so," she said. "It just stings now…It wasn't a bullet."

Jack took his eyes off Rafferty. "What do you mean?"

She held a small, black object that looked like a dart from a tranquilizer gun in her hand. A flood of deadly thoughts rushed through Jack's mind. "What did you do?" he said to Rafferty.

Rafferty dropped his arms. "Do I have your full attention?"

Jack stood. "What the hell did you do?"

Rafferty relished Jack's moment of anguish. "A bacterial plague has been introduced into your wife's bloodstream. It is antibiotic resistant and there is no ready cure. It will incubate and replicate until she is ravaged by full-blown plague symptoms."

Jack narrowed his eyes on Rafferty.

"It starts with nausea," Rafferty said with cool detachment, "perhaps a fever, nothing too dramatic at first. Stage One is just mild enough to be confused with a minor case of the flu. In Stage Two the fever intensifies and is accompanied by delirium. The immune system collapses in Terminal Stage, and open sores burst through the skin from head to toe. Systemic organ failure and internal bleeding precede death. It's not a pleasant way to go."

Jack clenched the Kimber and his hand turned white. "You're lying."

"Look at me, Jack. You know I'm telling the truth."

"Why are you doing this?"

Rafferty found that amusing. "You have to ask?"

Jack set his jaw. "You want to play hardball?" He laid his finger across the trigger. "If you've condemned her to death, then I'm sending you to hell right now."

"I'm the only one who can save her," Rafferty warned, "and unless you do exactly as I say, and I mean exactly, she will die in the manner I've just explained."

"I'm not buying."

"You had better. She's infected and I'm her only hope."

"I won't be your puppet."

"I know what matters to you. If you love your wife half as much as I presume you do, you'll tie the marionette strings to your arms and legs yourself."

Jack stood rigid with the pistol locked in his hand and his thoughts racing. "There is no plague."

"Think about it. Would I go through this much trouble to bluff you?"

Jack didn't reply.

"I don't envy your position," Rafferty said, taking a step to the side. "You have two choices: Kill me now and end this drama between us, or believe what I've told you and follow my instructions."

"I like option number one."

"Then Lauren dies and you have no one to blame but yourself."

"How stupid do you think I am? You're playing me."

"Of course I am. That doesn't change the truth of the matter."

"Your version of the truth is always open for debate."

Rafferty chuckled. "What is truth?"

"Pontius Pilate," Lauren said.

Rafferty looked at her with a bit of surprise.

"That's what Pilate said to Jesus before he had him crucified," Lauren explained.

"Bravo," Rafferty said clapping his hands. "I appreciate someone well-read in scripture."

"That's right," Jack said. "You think you do God's dirty work. Is that what you're doing now? Is this another divine mission?"

"Let's just say the Lord's agenda and mine line up nicely at the moment."

"How convenient for you."

Rafferty frowned. "Let's not waste any more time. Although the local authorities are busy on the expressway, our conflict here will soon draw their attention. I'll need your decision now." Rafferty walked forward.

Jack stood awash in doubt.

Rafferty stopped three inches from the barrel of the gun. "Lauren's life depends on what you do next. Kill me or agree to my demand."

Jack wanted to empty the magazine into Rafferty so bad he could taste the gunpowder on his tongue, but indecision chipped away at his resolve with each passing second. If he pulled the trigger and the plague story happened to be true, then Lauren would die and there was no reset button to get her back. The stakes were simply too high to make a rash judgment. An avalanche of frustration overcame him and he swung the butt of the pistol hard into Rafferty's temple. Rafferty didn't expect the move and recoiled. Naughton snapped to attention and rushed forward with the submachine gun raised.

Rafferty spun and warded him back. "Stand down!"

Naughton stopped dead but stayed on his toes ready to spring with eyes shifting back and forth.

Rafferty felt a small cut over his temple and studied a smear of blood on his fingertip. He looked at Jack. "As a show of good faith, I'll let that pass without punishment. I will not be as charitable next time. Now, we were discussing your decision."

Jack settled back on his heels and struggled for calm. He bit his tongue and prayed for direction, and in a moment that felt like defeat he knew what he had to do. His heart pounded and he drew in a long breath. "What do you want?"

"That didn't hurt as much as you imagined, did it?"

"Don't push it, Donovan. What do you want?"

"I want you to continue doing what you've already started."

Jack didn't get it. "Explain."

"Abner Wilson has asked you to find the wreckage of an airplane for him."

Jack's jaw fell open despite effort to keep it closed.

"Yes, our meeting today is not a coincidence. I know what you're up to, and I know Abner has told you that you're searching for a cholera vaccine. That is not the truth."

"There's that word again," Jack retorted. "Why would Abner lie to me about the vaccine?"

"Ask him. It's his lie."

Jack scowled. "If it's not a cholera vaccine, then what is it?"

"You're actually going after a bacteriophage."

"What the hell is a bacteriophage?"

"It's a virus designed to attack and destroy bacteria. The phage that went down on that airplane was designed to target the bacteria found in something called the 731 Plague. When you find the case with the bacteriophage, you will give it to me."

"Why do you want it?"

"The reason I want it is unimportant. You need to concern yourself with why you want it."

Jack caught the gist of Rafferty's comment and his face went pale.

"That's right," Rafferty said. "The 731 Plague is coursing through your wife's veins at this very moment. With the remnants of the phage in that case, I can reproduce a living strain and treat her."

Jack mulled it all over a long while in silence.

"I see the wheels turning in your head, Jack. You're thinking perhaps microbiologists who work for Abner might be able to reproduce the phage as well. Don't consider it. A government lab will take three months to conjure up an effective bacteriophage. I have a man with a head start on the project that can do it in three days." He added, "Lauren doesn't have three months to wait."

Jack exhaled. "How do you even know about this?"

"You forget that in my past life I served twelve years in Military Intelligence. I still have contacts that provide me information to this day. You'd be frightened of the classified things that I know."

"Finding that plane might take weeks." Jack relaxed his grip on the pistol. "How much time do I have?"

Rafferty caught sight of the Enclave rolling around the corner of the cemetery road. He returned his attention to Jack. "This is where Lauren has a fighting chance. The 731 Plague was engineered to be a weapon. Its key tactical quality is its slow, passive progression to Terminal Stage to ensure a widespread outbreak. People infected with 731 can expect to enter Terminal Stage four to five weeks after exposure." Rafferty extracted a plain white plastic bottle from his jacket pocket. He shook the bottle and it rattled, and then he tossed it to Jack. "Of course that's if they take the pills in the bottle at the onset of symptoms."

Jack considered the bottle. "You said the phage was the only way to stop the plague."

"It is. Those pills contain an enzyme inhibitor that retards bacterial growth. It will help to slow the progression of 731, but will not stop it."

"It might take longer than four weeks to find this plane."

"For her sake it had better not."

"No," Jack said. "For your sake it had better not."

Rafferty considered the threat but did not find it as amusing as Jack thought he would.

Lauren lifted herself from the ground. "How soon until I'm contagious?"

The calm manner she asked the question surprised Jack.

Rafferty regarded her. "In the second week, your body fluids will be capable of transferring the infection. Saliva, perspiration, even tears become an effective contagion. In the third week, the plague becomes airborne in the infected person's breath or cough."

Jack holstered the Kimber and put his arms around Lauren. He held her a long while in silence.

"I can save her," Rafferty said. "You give me that case and everything in it, and I can save her. Do you understand?"

Jack released Lauren and faced him. "How do you expect me to trust you on this?"

Rafferty smiled. "I don't expect you to trust me. I expect you to obey."

"Whatever I do for you, don't mistake my actions for obedience. But if you want my cooperation, I want something from you." Jack paused to consider the value of the demand he had in mind. "I want your word," he said at last. "I want your word that you will treat Lauren with the phage within three days of receiving it, just like you said."

Rafferty chuckled. "What good will my word be if you don't trust me to begin with?"

"Humor me."

Rafferty's expression took on a rather serious cast. "You have my word."

Jack knew it was folly but he actually found a measure of hope in Rafferty's oath. "I'll get you the damned case."

Rafferty motioned for Ferguson to stop the Enclave and pulled open the passenger side door. He turned around. "You made the right call, Jack" He stepped into the vehicle. "I'll be in touch."

Jack thought he saw Ferguson picking stone slivers from his cheek before Rafferty closed the door. Naughton glared at Jack a second before jogging off to the Acura. Both vehicles drove off cemetery property and headed north on Hartland Road.

Jack watched them go. "And when this is over, Donovan Rafferty, I'm going to plant you right here at my feet to make sure you never threaten my family again."

Lauren took his hand. "What do we do now?"

A police siren wailed off in the distance. "Let's get out of here."

"Shouldn't we report this to the police?"

"No," Jack said sharply. "If this whole thing is for real, then I need to get out there and find that plane right away. Filing a police report on Donovan Rafferty will open a can of worms that will attract the attention of the FBI and half a dozen other agencies. Abner will catch wind of it and will lock down this salvage operation so tight with security that I will never be able to get the case to Rafferty. I've got to think it all through."

"No," Lauren said. "We have to think it all through. We don't even know why Rafferty wants this bacteriophage. What if he is lying about infecting me and just wants the phage to actually reverse engineer the plague to use it himself?"

Jack considered that a bit. "Or maybe he wants the phage so he can alter the 731 Plague to be resistant to it. Then there would be no stopping it. This is getting more frightening by the second."

"That siren is getting closer. What do we do?"

"Let's go. If we decide Rafferty is lying, we can file a report at the police station. Better yet, with Abner."

"If Rafferty's story is true, then Abner did lie about the cholera vaccine."

"That's something I'm going to address right after I get you to a doctor. Come on."

They climbed into the Jeep and drove off cemetery grounds. A smattering of people had begun filtering out of the library and surrounding homes to check on the commotion outside. Jack leaned out his window and spoke to a man on the sidewalk. "Did you see those kids tear out of here? I think they were driving an Acura and an Enclave. Damn vandals. Look at my car. I'm going to file a police report." He scrolled up his window and drove as casually as he could to deter attention. He considered the bullet holes in his windshield and turned down a side street. He didn't need the police seeing that. It would only complicate matters. The Jeep blended into the residential background as a squad car from the Livingston County Sheriff Office sped down Hartland Road toward the cemetery.

"Rafferty doesn't have much of a head start," Lauren said. "You think they'll get him?"

Jack shook his head. "Rafferty has been eluding the FBI, the CIA, Homeland Security, and Interpol for years. Livingston County might have some difficulty catching up." Jack grabbed his cell phone and scanned through his contacts.

"Who are you calling?"

Jack pressed the send button. "Dr. Clarke."

- TEN -

Lake Huron
44° 16' N / 82° 6' W

A full moon lit the lake and cast a pale glow on the sloops sailing ahead of the *Liberty,* illuminating their sheets like a trio of Flying Dutchmen. The ships made their way north in a single file formation. A light wind from the northeast had them close hauled with a port tack, and crawling along at six knots. Cohn stood on the quarter deck near the helm, studying ghostly wisps of cloud passing through the moonlight. "We won't make the Straits of Mackinac before Thursday at this rate," he said to Speers.

Speers pulled his jacket collar tight around his neck to ward off the open water chill. "We figured a slow passage through the lakes in our timeline, didn't we?"

"I'd rather be ahead of expectations," Cohn said. "We started off so strong too. The last two hours have just killed our progress. Seventy miles out is less than I'd hoped for at this hour."

"We can fire up the diesel and move ahead of the pack," Speers said.

Cohn thought on it a while. "No need to yet." He took account of their distance from the Michigan shore, listened to the hull creak and cut through the calm lake with a continuous wash against the planks. "Give me a course adjustment," he said at last. "Bearing zero-six-zero. Ease out some sail."

Speers acknowledged and relayed the order to the helmsman, who at this hour was Duvall.

"Tell Anders and Erikson to bring the couriers up from the hold," Cohn said. "As soon as we're out of sight of the other ships, get the bodies over the side."

Liberty veered to the east and the distance to the other ships increased. Before long Anders and Erikson emerged from the main cabin carrying a body mummified in plastic wrap. They'd wound a length of heavy chain around the legs, and when they threw the body over the side it splashed into the lake and sank straight down. They returned to the cabin for the second body.

"Foley is manning the short wave," Speers said to Cohn. "He says Nix has a report for you."

Cohn took one more look at the horizon and then pulled open the aft hatch to the lower deck. He climbed down through the hatchway and found his footing on the planks below. He stepped into the tiny port side compartment where they'd placed the communication gear. Foley, a skinny, sandy-haired man, sat at the controls and handed him the microphone.

Cohn took it and keyed the switch. "Go ahead, Nix, what do you have?"

"Something very strange," Nix said through the radio receiver.

"Didn't the colonel meet up with Sheridan?"

"He did but it didn't go down like you thought it would. They both walked away alive."

Cohn palmed the mic and stared at LEDs on the radio console.

"Did you hear me, Alec?"

"Yes. Tell me exactly what happened."

"The colonel executed what looked to me to be a first-rate take-down. He staged an elaborate diversion to drive the mark to a chosen location where he'd positioned assets to strike. A lot of surveillance and target profiling went into the effort. It impressed the hell out of me."

Cohn keyed the mic with a little more force than was necessary. "It's just what I'd expect from the anal son-of-a-bitch. How did it go sideways?"

"Sheridan is smart," Nix said. "He read the situation, tried to break out right before the jaws of the trap closed. The colonel had to scramble. Sheridan almost made it but they corralled him in a cemetery."

"I'm waiting for the part where Sheridan escapes."

"You said to tell you everything."

"Damn it, Nix, what happened?"

"I'm not exactly sure. There was gunfire followed by a long period of silence, and then they both left the scene going their separate ways."

"You're leaving a big hole in this report," Cohn said with a bit of agitation.

"Hey, I can only get so close to the action, and I sure as hell wasn't going to walk into their crossfire."

Cohn processed Nix's report. "The colonel should have killed him," he said absently.

"You didn't key," Foley said.

Cohn rebuked him with a glare and then keyed the mic. "I want to know why the colonel didn't kill him."

A burst of squelch preceded Nix's voice. "Maybe they settled their differences and exchanged addresses for their Christmas card lists."

"Doubtful," Cohn said. "The colonel's primary obsession was to exact revenge on Sheridan. He had that revenge within reach and didn't take it. He must be working another angle."

"Maybe he has a new obsession."

Cohn pondered that and scowled. "Not a new obsession, just another one."

"Orders for me?" Nix asked.

"I want to know why Sheridan is still alive. He just escaped death, and I'm sure he's going to talk about it to someone. Get a bug in his car and record 24/7. Find out where he lives and plant one in his house too."

"What about the colonel?"

"Keep eyes on him. I want to know what Sheridan says, but I need to see what the colonel is doing. He's the one driving whatever is happening between them." Cohn thought about logistics. "Can you handle this alone, or do I need to send in someone from the bench?"

A long pause on the radio. "I can handle it. The colonel went back to the house in West Michigan. I'm calling from Bangor now. This is his base for the moment, and I'm certain he'll stay through the night. I'll start collecting personal information on Sheridan and get ears on him tomorrow. I got a feeling if I stick close to Sheridan, the colonel won't be far away."

"I agree," Cohn said. "Report back tomorrow at noon."

"Got it."

Cohn handed the mic back to Foley and stepped out of the radio room into the narrow corridor. A voice called to him from the starboard compartment across the way. "Captain, I have an unidentified surface contact."

It was Byrne. He was sitting in front of a monitor watching reflections captured by the radar array mounted on the *Liberty*'s main mast. "Report," Cohn said.

Byrne read data off the display screen. "Mid-sized vessel one-point-five miles to starboard bearing zero-seven-five, inbound at fifteen knots."

"They're coming from the Canadian side," Cohn said. "Odds are it's a patrol boat."

"That would be my guess too," Byrne replied.

Cohn faced the radio compartment. "Foley, what channel is reserved for Canadian Coast Guard operations?"

Foley searched his memory. "Nineteen A."

"Dial it in now and monitor."

Foley switched the radio to channel 19A – the 156.95 kHz frequency setting. Less than a minute elapsed before a voice emerged from the radio. "Patrol vessel *Simmons* maneuvering to investigate contact of interest. Expected intercept time four minutes."

Cohn cursed. One thing he didn't need was to host a Canadian Coast Guard boarding party. Their search of the *Liberty* would be extremely problematic. He thought over his options and found them very limited. "Failure can only come at our hands," he said to himself. He surveyed the radio room and against the bulkhead found a black trolley-type case with a cluster of coaxial cable jacks and quick-connect receptacles on its surface. "Foley, break out that tactical jammer. Program it to disrupt all Canadian and U.S. Coast Guard operational channels. Activate on my command."

Foley acknowledged and pulled the black case from the bulkhead. He went to work connecting antenna cables and entering frequencies into the high-power RF jammer. Cohn rushed up through the hatchway in the overhead. He found Speers standing aft, conversing with Anders and Erikson.

"Speers," Cohn said. "A Canadian patrol boat is inbound. Intercept time three minutes."

"Just passing by or are they coming after us?" Speers asked.

"We've drawn their interest. Maybe our move away from the flotilla caught their attention. It doesn't matter now. When they get here they may want to board. That's a hell of a bad idea, given the fact we're transporting canisters of a bacterial plague engineered in North Korea."

"Can't argue that. How do we play it?"

"Get both squads topside armed with muzzle-suppressed HKs. Disperse the men around the gunwale and out of sight. We fire only on my command." Cohn addressed Anders. "If I give the word, our action will be lethal and overwhelming. Do you understand?

Anders nodded.

"I think we should bring the LAWs topside as well," Speers said.

Cohn considered the recommendation. The M72 LAW, or Light Anti-Tank Weapon, is a shoulder-fired missile packed with enough explosive charge to penetrate the steel hull of any coast guard or commercial vessel on the Great Lakes. Cohn had figured that if the authorities found out what he was up to, they would come after him with serious force. He needed the capability to respond in kind. Unleashing an M72 now would end the coming confrontation quickly, but the resulting nighttime explosion would be visible to the three sloops far off their port quarter and any other vessel within miles of their position.

"Deploy two LAWs topside," Cohn said. "Stage one behind the center gun port starboard and the other likewise on the port side." He added, "We fire them as a last resort."

Speers acknowledged and headed below with Anders and Erikson to rally the men.

Cohn turned to Duvall at the helm. "Keep our course steady. Don't do anything to spook the Canadians." He crouched beside the hatchway to the lower deck. "Byrne, report on the inbound."

"Still closing. Range, three-quarter mile."

"Foley, are you set?"

"Thirty more seconds."

Cohn studied the dark horizon to starboard, hoping the full moon would reveal the approach of the patrol vessel, but he couldn't make out anything yet. Men began popping up through the deck hatches and fanned out around the perimeter of the ship as ordered. Dressed in black clothing with light body armor, they moved silently into position with only the dull clunk of their footsteps on the wood deck to accompany the maneuver. Within seconds four men had settled into concealed positions behind the starboard gunwale and four more had done the same on the port side. Erikson knelt over a narrow, black case at the base of the center gun port on the starboard side. He popped a set of clasps on the case and opened the lid to reveal an M72 LAW lying inside. "Should we clear for action?" he asked.

Cohn almost smiled at the eighteenth-century terminology. A war ship of the era would clear for action by opening the gun ports and sliding the cannons forward to fire. "Keep the port closed," he said. "The guardsmen just might understand the intention."

"Here they come," Duvall announced.

Half a mile off the *Liberty*'s starboard bow a search light flashed on. The Canadian vessel closed the distance and the shape of a sixty-foot fast patrol catamaran became visible. The pitch of her engines dropped as she slowed her approach. Speers took up a position next to Cohn. "Mid-shore patrol vessel," he said, "crew compliment of five, maybe eight if they've got some RCMPs aboard."

Cohn felt the pulse pound in his temple. "Stand ready. If it looks like they're going to board, we jam their communications and rake their ship with gunfire." He called through the hatchway, "Foley, get your finger on the switch."

A voice through a bullhorn came from the patrol boat. "Unidentified vessel, heave to."

Cohn glanced at Speers. "Heave to and take in the sail. Keep the men calm." Speers nodded and instructed the four men on deck without weapons to begin trimming sail. They went to work on the rigging while the concealed crewmen hunkered down with their automatic weapons.

The guardsman called again through the bullhorn. "State your designation and status."

The search light swept over the sloop's deck. Cohn did not turn from the glare. He shouted across the water. "We are United States registered sailing ship *Liberty*, outbound from Sarnia and travelling with the three sloops off our port bow on a prearranged circuit of the Great Lakes. We are currently in route to Grand Traverse Bay."

"Are you disabled or having difficulty with navigation?" the guardsman inquired.

Cohn considered the question. They seemed to be fishing for information. That could mean they did not have particular knowledge about *Liberty,* just curiosity. A good sign. "No, all our navigational aides are functioning. We know where we are."

"Do you need our assistance?"

"Yes, a good twenty knot westerly wind would be nice."

A short pause. "How did you become separated from the other vessels?"

"We have a midshipman at the helm," Cohn said. "I decided to give him some time with the wheel, let him get a feel for the rudder."

The bullhorn remained silent, and the patrol vessel began a long circle around the sloop.

"They're coming about, crossing our beam," Cohn said just loud enough for his men to hear.

Anders crouched behind the port gunwale with one hand on a LAW and the other working the line to open the gun port. Cohn crossed the deck and gave him a sharp kick in the ribs. Anders winced and released the line.

"Keep the damn thing closed unless I say otherwise," Cohn warned.

The patrol ship came astern of the *Liberty*. Without the glare of the searchlight in his eyes Cohn saw the .50 caliber machine gun mounted on the vessel's bow and a guardsman with a rifle standing aft.

Speers spoke in a low voice. "Maybe the OPP discovered the couriers' van back in Sarnia and traced their last delivery to us."

Cohn considered the theory and agreed with its plausibility, but if it were the case he was certain the Canadian Coast Guard would not be so cordial now. Cohn's gut told him the missing couriers weren't part of the equation. "They just suspect we're smuggling cigarettes across the border."

"They still may want to board," Speers said.

"Anders," Cohn said, "there's a .50 cal on the bow. If we move you target the gunner." He spoke to the next man in line. "Gates, you target the rifleman on their stern." Cohn placed a hand on the Glock beneath his jacket. "I'll take out the search light." He moved closer to the deck hatchway to communicate with the men below.

The patrol ship's engines dropped to idle and she glided twenty yards abeam of *Liberty*'s port side. The bow gunner leveled the machine gun amidships. A guardsman came out of the cabin and he walked the length of the catamaran. The searchlight stayed focused on Cohn. A minute ticked by. And then another.

"I don't like Canadians," Speers said.

"They're checking out our registration and cover story." Cohn kept his eyes from staring into the glare of the searchlight. *What the hell is taking them so long to make their next move?* And then it came to him, and a subtle smile crossed his face like a passing shadow.

Another guardsman emerged from the cabin and spoke with the rifleman at the stern. The bullhorn speaker clicked on and a voice boomed. "Sailing vessel *Liberty*…"

Cohn drew a breath. "Foley—"

Anders and Gates prepared to spring over the gunwale.

An amplified crackle came from the bullhorn as if the switch had been double keyed. "Sailing vessel *Liberty*, you are free to continue your voyage to Grand Traverse Bay."

The searchlight went dark and patrol vessel *Simmons* revved her engines and moved off.

"Stand down," Cohn said. "Everybody stand down. Foley, keep off the switch. Byrne, watch their departure, make sure they're leaving. Speers, ease out the sail and get us underway. Correct bearing to previous course and get us back in line with the other ships." Cohn exhaled and released the Glock. "Anders, Erikson, keep your men in position until I'm satisfied we're in the clear."

Cohn walked to the bow and watched the patrol boat disappear into the night. Her engines droned off in the distance. Speers came up beside him. "We dodged a bullet," he said. "If they had tried to board us the rest of our voyage would have been very difficult."

"They weren't going to board," Cohn said. "They couldn't."

Speers cocked his head. "Why do you say that?"

"If you check our position on the GPS system, I think you'll find we're just inside United States territorial waters. The Canadians didn't have jurisdiction to board us."

"That may be so," Speers said, "but why didn't they just call up the U.S. Coast Guard and have them join the party?"

"They probably did. Foley is monitoring the Canadian Coast Guard channel, not the U.S. channel. I'll bet the U.S. Coast Guard didn't have enough interest in us to dispatch a cutter. A group of tall ships circumnavigating the Great Lakes is a highly visible and very common event. Giving an anal exam to a straggler from such a flotilla doesn't rate high on their priority list. If we were a cigar speedboat launching from a pitch black port of call it would be another story."

Speers chuckled. "You talk good logic, but I still believe we just got lucky."

"We make our own luck. Hiding in plain sight wasn't an arbitrary decision." Cohn felt a gust of wind on his face and heard it flutter the sails. "Wind is picking up. It's shifting too. We may not have to pinch to stay on our heading. Let's make the most of it."

Speers nodded and moved to help the men adjust the running rigging.

Cohn stared off to where the patrol boat had disappeared. He'd already managed to put the incident behind him and had gone on to consider the rest of the voyage. The *Liberty* would continue on with the flotilla into the Straits of Mackinac and tie up for a day at the Mackinaw City Marina. They would then hoist sail and head into Lake Michigan for their scheduled two-day portage in Grand Traverse Bay. Finally, the flotilla would set course for Chicago, where the final leg of the journey would begin on land. Events seemed to be accelerating, and the big day was quickly approaching. Cohn would have been bursting with anticipation if it weren't for one thought that kept rolling thorough his head.

What the hell are you up to, Donovan Rafferty?

- ELEVEN -

Wednesday
Fenton, MI

Jack Sheridan watched Dr. Clarke flip through pages on a clipboard. The doctor had dark-rimmed glasses up on his head of black, curly hair, and he pursed his lips as he read. Jack held his tongue and reached for Lauren's hand as she sat on the padded exam table in the small examination room. *How long does it take to read the results of a blood test?*

Dr. Clarke set the clipboard on the table and straightened his white lab coat. "Hmmm."

Jack lifted his chin. "What does that mean?"

"It means I don't see anything terribly interesting." Dr. Clarke gave Lauren a smile and lifted her arm to examine the puncture wound from the dart in her bicep.

"What does 'terribly interesting' mean?" Lauren said.

Clarke pressed his thumb around the wound. "The cultures from the blood draws we did last night show no bacterial growth as of yet. Your white cell count is slightly elevated but not enough to be of any concern."

"So she doesn't have anything?" Jack said.

"So far so good, but it takes three days to get complete culture results." Dr. Clarke released Lauren's arm. "Tell me again how this injury occurred."

Jack and Lauren exchanged a glance. "We were walking along an old wire fence around some farm land," she said. "I lost my footing, and a rusty wire got me."

Dr. Clarke listened with arms crossed as if waiting for more information.

"The end," Jack said.

Clarke looked unconvinced. "Jack, I've been your primary physician for fifteen years. I've treated you for far more serious injuries, and you've been far less concerned. You came in once with a gunshot wound and joked about it for crying out loud."

"That was different. I'm not concerned about myself."

"By the way, how's that hand healing up?"

Jack opened and closed his left hand. "It aches in the morning. What can you do for it?"

Clarke inspected the metacarpals. "Keep up with the exercises I gave you and take an NSAID as needed."

Jack sat up straight. "What's an N-said?"

"A nonsteroidal, anti-inflammatory drug."

"Ibuprofen, dear," Lauren said.

"Right, I've heard of that." Jack nodded to the clipboard. "Is it possible she has something in her blood that will take longer than three days to show up?"

"Anything is possible but it's very unlikely. We're pretty good at identifying bacterial growth and infection at an early stage."

"I hope so," Jack said.

Dr. Clarke regarded him. "What are you expecting me to find?"

"Nothing, I just want to be on the safe side."

"Lauren, how do you feel? Do you have symptoms you're not telling me about?"

Lauren shrugged. "No. I feel fine. My arm is sore."

"Well, those perimeter fences are vicious. You're the fourth barbed wire attack I've seen this week." Clarke glanced at Jack.

Jack stared back nonplussed.

"Are you up to date with your tetanus shots?" the doctor asked Lauren.

"Yes, I had a booster last year."

Jack fidgeted, unsure if he should ask the question on his mind. "Doc, uh, do you know anything about bacteriophages?"

Dr. Clarke sat on a stool beside the exam table. "That's a pretty big word for a guy who didn't know what NSAID meant a minute ago."

"I'm trying to broaden my knowledge base."

"I see." Clarke crossed his legs. "A bacteriophage is basically a phage, or a virus, that infects and destroys cellular structures in bacteria. Before antibiotics were developed in the 1940s, it was the principal focus of modern medicine to combat infection. The Russians and Japanese spearheaded the research in this area. As a matter of fact Russia is still developing bacteriophages as a firewall against drug resistant tuberculosis they're dealing with. Why do you ask?"

"Don't you watch the news?" Jack said. "It seems a new superbug is popping up every day. Staph infections and MRSA, and that new antibiotic-resistant bacterium in India; we're running out of ways to treat this stuff. I'm just trying to see over the next medical horizon."

"It's not all doom and gloom, Jack. Modern medicine isn't stopping at antibiotics to fight infection. Now we're into genetics, DNA, nanomaterials, and even bacteria versus bacteria. Of course, a lot of this research is years away from producing effective treatments."

Jack pondered the doctor's assessment. Lauren didn't have years. She didn't even have months. According to Rafferty she had weeks, but that assumed the bastard had actually told the truth. "Have you ever heard of the 731 Plague?"

Lauren squeezed Jack's hand.

Dr. Clarke searched his memory. "No, I haven't. What is it?"

"Uh, some new plague threat I read about in a *Newsweek* article. I forget where it turned up, but it's just something else to worry about. Right?"

Dr. Clarke shook his head. "You worry too much. You have a better chance of getting in a car accident than catching a superbug."

Jack thought back on the cemetery chase. "Tell me about it."

"Lauren, you feel fine and have no symptoms of illness. I say go home, get some rest, and we'll call with the final blood culture results. I don't suspect we'll see anything. You seem healthy. You just had a run in with a killer barbed wire fence, and luckily you survived."

Lauren smiled and stood up from the exam table. "Don't think I'll be resting. I've got some flower beds behind the house that need attention."

Dr. Clarke shook Jack's hand. "Good to see you and not treat you for once."

"It's early in the day. There's still a chance I'll be back."

Lauren slugged his arm. "Stop it." She exited the examination room.

Jack followed but stopped at the door. "Doc, is there such a thing as an enzyme inhibitor that can slow bacterial growth?"

"What is with you today?"

"Humor me."

"Yes, I imagine an enzyme inhibitor can exist somewhere. There are variations of antibiotics that target enzyme function. An enzyme inhibitor would work along the same lines."

Jack slapped the doorframe. "Thanks." He met Lauren in the hallway and they walked to the lobby. He peeled thirty dollars from his wallet for the office visit co-pay and handed it to the secretary. He and Lauren walked to the Jeep in the parking lot. Before getting in they looked at each other across the hood. "I feel fine," Lauren said. "Rafferty lied."

"Clarke just confirmed the validity of everything Rafferty told us."

"Everything except the existence of the 731 Plague. Let's go." She climbed into the Jeep.

Jack opened the driver's door and plopped behind the wheel, not noticing the sheet of paper he'd left on the seat was crinkled and twisted. "Rafferty said the plague bacteria replicated very slowly. It might not show up in a three-day culture."

She glared at him. "Are you trying to scare me?"

Jack paused. "No. I'm sorry. Rafferty is a liar. I'm just expounding on possibilities. It's what I do best." He absently inspected the new windshield he had installed that morning and recalled the bullet holes that had been blasted through the old one. Rafferty played his games with live ammo. This airplane salvage would not be a fun ride. He started the Jeep and backed out of the parking space. As he drove out of the parking lot he thought about his new partner.

Jack knew Donovan Rafferty better than most. He knew the man had no compunction to tell a lie, but Rafferty also dished bits of truth when it suited him. In this particular case Jack felt strongly that the bacteriophage story was true. What bothered him most about that was the correlation that if Rafferty had told him the truth about Flight 2501 then Abner Wilson had lied about the cholera vaccine.

Jack grabbed his cell phone and speed dialed Abner's number.

The admiral answered with a cheerful voice. "Jack, how goes the salvage preparation?"

"Moving right along. It could be better."

"Anything I can help with?" Abner offered.

"For one thing you can stop dealing directly with Lloyd Faulkner. I need to be his single contact."

"I was just getting the red tape going. Government contracts have a lot of it, and you don't need to be bogged down with useless paperwork."

"Right."

"You sound like you've got a burr under your ass about this. I didn't mean to step on your toes, Jack, I'm sorry."

Jack didn't reply.

"Are you really that steamed over me calling Lloyd?"

"There's more." Jack changed lanes to catch the on-ramp to 23. "We've known each other twenty years, and to my knowledge you've never lied to me. Correct?"

Abner paused. "This is starting to sound ominous. What's going on?"

Traffic cleared and Jack accelerated onto the ramp. "Have you told me everything about Flight 2501?"

"I told you everything I know. What are you getting at?"

"Okay, Abner, it's like this. You told me the U.S. government is interested in a cholera vaccine in the wreckage of that plane, but I have reason to believe it's something else."

"Something else? Like what, a garment bag full of Zoot suits from 1950?"

"No, I think you've got me searching for a bacteriophage effective against the 731 Plague."

Lauren anxiously watched Jack from the passenger seat.

A long pause played out on the phone. "I didn't understand a single word you just said."

Jack changed lanes and picked up speed. "You know nothing about a bacteriophage?"

"I don't even know what language you're talking. Enlighten me."

Abner's confusion seemed genuine. Jack pressed. "If you've been holding back it's time to come clean. Is there an engineered virus in that airplane wreckage that was designed to destroy something called the 731 Plague?"

"No, there's a cholera vaccine in that wreckage. Why the hell are you asking this?"

"Because." Jack swallowed hard. "Donovan Rafferty told me it isn't a vaccine you have me looking for, but a bacteriophage."

"Rafferty! You're joking. Rafferty contacted you and started talking about my airplane salvage? How the hell—"

"He served twelve years in Military Intelligence and still has a pipeline for information, or so he says."

"He did serve," Abner admitted. "That's one of the things that make him so dangerous."

"If he's got an inside source of information, then his story might be true."

"No, I'm telling you it's not. I was commissioned by the Homeland Security director to locate Flight 2501 and recover a cholera vaccine. That's how it was laid out, and that's what I'm doing. Since when does Rafferty's word carry an ounce of weight with you? Did he convince you the CIA killed Kennedy too?"

"Kennedy didn't come up, but this bacteriophage did. He told me you lied about the vaccine."

"I'm telling you he lied about the bacteriophage. Now who are you going to believe, the deceitful bastard who once tried to kill you and your son, or your close friend of twenty years? Don't answer right away. I'll give you a minute to think about it."

Jack noticed Lauren literally sitting on the edge of her seat. She hung on his every word, and why not? Her life depended on what was decided in this conversation. Jack switched the phone from one ear to the other. "Why would Rafferty suddenly appear and tell me this lie? How does it benefit him?"

"You tell me," Abner countered. "What does he expect you to do with this knowledge?"

Jack didn't reply. He thought about the 731 Plague replicating in Lauren's blood stream. He thought about weeks not months. "I don't know," he said at last. "I don't know what he expects me to do."

"I think he's jerking your chain. It's a game of some kind. He wants you to bite, to do a little dance for him. Why give him the pleasure?"

Jack held the steering wheel tight. "Is it possible you weren't told the truth by the Homeland Security director?"

"You're getting my blood up, Jack. Why would the director lie to me? I'm on his team. Maritime Affairs falls under the Homeland Security umbrella."

"It's in the nature of intelligence agencies to lie. They arbitrarily decide who does and doesn't need to know certain information on a daily basis. I'm simply asking if it's possible for Rafferty's story to be true."

"Negative," Abner said firmly. "But because I'm sensitive to the concerns of my close friend of twenty years, I'll investigate the matter. I'm in the perfect place to do it. I've got a temporary desk at the MIOC in Lansing during this project. I'm surrounded by intelligence and law enforcement officers. If there's any truth to Rafferty's tale, I'll find out."

"I appreciate it, Abner."

"And if Rafferty contacts you again, you let me know immediately. I won't have him disrupting my salvage project. I'll send a detachment of marines with you on the salvage ship if I have to, just to keep you and my vaccine safe."

Jack bit his lip. He couldn't have marines crawling all over the *Achilles*. That would make it very difficult to transfer the bacteriophage to Rafferty, if need be. "We're not there yet. Let's just see if Rafferty is on the mark with his story. We'll figure out why and how later."

"Give me a couple of hours," Abner said. "I'll let you know what I find out."

They ended the call.

"You didn't tell him about me," Lauren said.

Jack shook his head. "I couldn't. He's already thinking about putting marines on the salvage ship. If the phage exists and Abner thinks Rafferty is actively engaged in trying to steal it, he'll lock down the whole operation. I know he'll put a team of government microbiologists to work on developing a living phage ASAP if it turns out you're infected, but we don't have the time it would take for them to succeed."

"So you not only believe Rafferty but you trust him to keep his word."

Jack frowned. "I don't like hearing you put it that way."

"There's no other way to put it."

Jack concentrated on the road ahead. "I know."

- TWELVE –

Lansing, MI

Admiral Wilson had set up his temporary desk at the heart of the Michigan Intelligence Operations Center (MIOC) on the third floor of the State Police Headquarters building in Lansing. He'd picked a cubicle right next to the operations area, where eight large, flat-screen monitors displayed a constant flow of news feeds from around the globe, and a compliment of State Police lieutenants monitored 911 dispatches and dozens of Internet media sites 24/7. Abner enjoyed being close to the flow of all that information. It felt a bit like the old days in the navy when he had worked with Military and Central Intelligence on covert operations.

He had met Jack Sheridan on one of those operations over twenty years ago. The government had contracted Neptune's Reach to recover a sunken Russian spy vessel in international waters off the northeastern seaboard. Jack had been assigned to head up the project on Neptune's end. His youthful self-confidence read as cockiness to Abner, and their relationship got off to a rocky start. But they managed to get around the breadth of each other's egos and forged a strong friendship that lasted nearly a quarter century. Today, however, that friendship suffered the first instance of mistrust.

Having Jack question Abner's honesty was bad enough, but the fact that Rafferty had put the idea into his head was salt in the wound. There could not be any truth to Rafferty's story of course, but the mere fact that Jack had taken it to the point of confronting Abner raised a major red flag. The admiral decided to put a quick end to the issue so they could move forward unobstructed by this nonsense.

Fueled by a measure of righteous indignation, Abner rose from his desk on the analysts' side of the floor and headed toward the offices of reps with higher pay grades. One of the screens in the operations area caught his attention with a news report on North Korea's latest round of saber rattling. That tiny half-country had been such a thorn in the side of the United States, Abner wondered if perhaps the solution in 1952 should have been to incinerate Pyongyang.

Abner paused at the desk of one of his maritime brethren, Lieutenant Gabriel Walker of the U.S. Coast Guard. "How goes it in the Ninth District today, Lieutenant?" Abner said.

"Fairly quiet, nothing to tweet home about," Lt. Walker said.

Abner chuckled. Lt. Walker was one of a dozen representatives on staff at MIOC from various law enforcement and security agencies in the region. The concept of an intelligence fusion center matured after the dust from September 11th had settled. The inability of the nation's security network to connect the dots and prevent the devastating terrorist attack was due largely to bureaucratic walls dividing the flow of information between agencies. Fusion centers addressed this problem by providing an intelligence clearinghouse where the thousands of bits of information received daily could be coalesced and parsed by all relevant organizations, including Homeland Security, the FBI, the DOD, the INS, local law enforcement, and Lt. Walker's organization, the U.S. Coast Guard.

As Maritime Affairs director Abner worked under the authority of Homeland Security, and as such his on-site DHS liaison was the State Intelligence Officer (SIO) stationed at the fusion center. In this case that person was Paul Dutello. Abner had worked with Dutello in the past. In different roles and in a different setting Abner found Dutello to be a bright, intelligent analyst, and it was not a surprise to find him at MIOC.

The SIO had an office with real walls, not just a cubicle, and Abner strode up and knocked once on the door before entering. Seated behind his desk, Dutello looked up from a manila folder. As usual he was dressed casual in a dark green polo shirt and khaki pants. Abner could never get over that Dutello looked fresh out of college even though the man was thirty-five years old.

"Morning, Paul," Abner said before realizing the SIO was not alone. Special Agent Benjamin Chatfield of the FBI was also present, sitting on the corner of the desk with arms crossed, crinkling the sleeves of a dark blue suit that looked to have gotten a lot of mileage. Abner grumbled to himself. Chatfield was not among the admiral's top five favorite reps at MIOC. "Am I interrupting?" Abner said.

Dutello gave him an affable smile. "No, Abner, what's up? Have you started fishing around the lake for that airplane yet?"

Abner closed the door behind him. "I've assembled the team but haven't put them on the field yet. We're just about good to go, however, and that's why I'm here."

Special Agent Chatfield uncrossed his arms and seemed to become more attentive.

Dutello sat back in his chair. "Do you need DHS to shake loose more resources?"

"Not quite." Abner set a stance in front of Dutello's desk like he was forming up at the line of scrimmage. "All I need is an answer to a question. You may know it off the top of your head or you may have to dig a little to find it, but one way or another I need this answer." Abner glanced at Chatfield. "Listen up, Ben. You might be of some use here."

Chatfield chuckled in what Abner perceived to be a sarcastic manner. "The Bureau is happy to help however we can," he said.

Dutello regarded Abner. "What's the question?"

Abner shifted his weight from one leg to the other. "Director Hoekstra instructed me to locate the wreck of Flight 2501 in order to recover a bio case containing a unique cholera vaccine."

Dutello nodded. "Yes..."

"That's wasn't a question," Chatfield said.

"Be patient, Ben, I'm taking it slow so you don't fall behind." Abner paused and caressed his chin. The closer he got to asking about Jack's bacteriophage the more hesitant he became. It galled him that he was actually reacting to one of Rafferty's tricks, but he had to follow through to clear his conscience. He needed to reassure Jack without a doubt that the vaccine was the true objective of their salvage mission.

"Is that Alzheimer's acting up again, Abner?" Chatfield said.

Abner gave Chatfield's thinning black hair and crow's feet around the eyes a once over. "Careful, Ben, you don't exactly represent the Bureau's bright and shining future yourself."

"Hey," Dutello said, "can you two act like my colleagues and not my kids? Abner, what do you need to know?"

Abner looked him in the eye. "Is it really a vaccine in that wreck?"

"Of course it's a vaccine."

Dutello almost pulled if off, but Abner caught the slightest twitch in his eye when he answered. Chatfield directed his stare into the carpet. Abner could hardly believe it. He'd hit on something, and both of these men knew it. "Paul, I've been dealing in secrets since you were in junior high school. I know when someone is fudging the truth."

"Maybe you've been dealing with them too long," Dutello said. "Sometimes a cigar is just a cigar."

"Or a vaccine is just a vaccine," Chatfield added.

Abner rolled his eyes to the special agent. "I got the analogy."

Dutello glanced over papers on his desk. "There's an outbreak of a special strain of cholera in Haiti. Director Hoekstra learned about the existence of this vaccine and its fate on Flight 2501 and decided it a worthy cause to try and recover it. Why is that so hard to believe?"

Abner got the feeling in his gut that he was smack in the middle of a calculated deception. "I'm sure Director Hoekstra learned about the existence of something on Flight 2501, but it wasn't a vaccine."

"What else could it be?" Chatfield said.

"A bacteriophage," Abner said, "some kind of virus that can kill the 731 Plague."

Dutello pushed away from his desk and cursed. Chatfield let out a breath.

Abner suddenly felt the dynamics in the room shift. "Judas Priest, it's true?"

Dutello stood. "Conference in the back room. Now."

They marched out of the office single file following Dutello's lead. Abner stayed on his heels. No one spoke. Some heads in cubicles turned as they passed. One lieutenant in the operations area tapped the shoulder of another and they watched the procession enter the analysts section. They knew something was up. Abner knew too. If the discussion was headed to the back room, his question must have opened a classified can of worms.

Abner joined Dutello and Chatfield in throwing their cell phones onto a filing cabinet in front of a door to the secured section of MIOC. Dutello passed his RF badge in front of a reader on the wall and the door lock clicked. They all entered a room about the size of a closet and let the Kevlar-backed door close behind them. An identical door and badge reader lay ahead. Dutello swiped his badge again and the second lock clicked open. Abner followed them into a short corridor lined with doors fitted with drop locks. Dutello pushed into the first room on the right.

The small conference room seemed like any other you might find in corporate America, with a six-foot long, rectangular table in the center and uncomfortable looking chairs all around. A dry-erase board hung on the far wall and an overhead projector was suspended from the ceiling. It was all generic except for the fact that the room had been secured for conversation up to Secret classification. Soundproofing material filled the walls, Ethernet cables from a isolated server fed into the room through hard pipe conduit, and a secure LAN line connected into the telephone.

Dutello faced Abner. "Where did you hear about the 731 Plague?"

"I sure as hell didn't hear it from you, did I? I've got a problem with that."

"Need to know," Chatfield said.

"Don't throw that bullshit at me," Abner retorted. "I've got Top Secret clearance. And since I'm the one who's going to pull that bio case out of the lake, I've got a damned righteous need to know."

"You're working with civilians at a private organization to recover this plane wreck," Dutello said. "Those people don't have TS clearance and they don't need to know about the bacteriophage or what it has to do with the 731 Plague."

"And no one thought I could keep my mouth shut?"

"I haven't seen it yet," Chatfield said.

"Back off, Special Agent Numbnuts, or you'll find yourself hogtied in that cheap suit."

Dutello gestured for silence. "Everybody calm down. We're on the same team."

"Then start acting like it," Abner said. "What's this 731 Plague all about?"

"You need to tell us where you heard about it first."

Abner shook his head. "Time to stop jerking my chain, Paul. Tell me what's going on or I'll derail this entire salvage operation right now."

"No deal," Chatfield said. "This is a matter of national security—"

"We're in a secured conference room talking about a goddamned plague! I think I figured out the part about national security."

Dutello stared at Chatfield. "Abner deserves to know."

Chatfield threw up his hands.

"The name says it all," Dutello said. "731 is an engineered plague bacterium with a progressive contagion component and a 90 percent mortality rate. It's completely antibiotic resistant, and there is no known modern medicine alternative to treat it…And there is a very high probability it will be introduced on American soil in an upcoming terror attack."

"That's why the viral material in that plane wreckage is so damned important," Chatfield added.

It didn't add up for Abner. "That plane went down in 1950. How can the viral goop that went down with it be effective against a modern engineered plague?"

"Because the 731 bacterium wasn't engineered today." Dutello slid back a chair and sat at the table. "It was engineered in 1943 by the Japanese."

Abner smiled. "I know my history. We won that war. Sure, the Japs did a lot of experiments with biological weapons, but we captured their bio-warfare facilities and all their bugs should have been secured."

"They were secured," Chatfield said, "in all the facilities that we knew about."

"We missed one? Where the hell was it, Iraq?"

"North Korea," Dutello said. "It's in an underground complex near the Chinese border. The Japanese built it during their occupation of the Korean Peninsula."

Abner stared at him a second. "Of all the places to miss a bio-warfare facility." He punched his fist into his palm. "Why did all this come to light now? That war ended a long time ago."

"We're not the only ones who missed the facility." Chatfield loosened his tie. "Even the Korean's didn't know it was there. The place went undiscovered until a year ago when some People's Republic geologists, if you can imagine, found the place during a survey of the area. Intelligence intercepts went crazy with talk of the find."

"The Japanese apparently believe in redundancy too," Dutello added. "Based on what we've gleaned from our intercepts, this Korean facility is a duplicate of their infamous Manchurian complex, including Building #731."

Abner straightened his back. "I presume that's where the 731 Plague was engineered."

"Gold star for the admiral," Chatfield said. "It's also where we got the bacteriophage that went down on Flight 2501. Thank God the Japanese were afraid of their monster too. If they hadn't engineered a phage to kill the plague bacteria, we'd have no hope at all."

Abner thought over the scope of the story a long while. Something didn't make sense. "Paul, you said this plague was engineered in 1943. That's before antibiotics were developed, isn't it? How do we know the plague is resistant to them?"

"The North Koreans made some improvements," Dutello said. "Now the only way to stop it is the bacteriophage that we don't have."

Abner felt his temperature rise. "You can't tell me we haven't been able to replicate this phage in the last seventy years."

"There hasn't been a need," Chatfield said. "It's true that at the time of the crash everyone was scared to death of what might happen if the plague escaped our bio-warfare lab because the microbiologists of the day had not figured out how to replicate the bacteriophage yet. That's why they were bringing that sample to Washington University on Flight 2501 in the first place. But by 1960, some of the antibiotics that had been developed proved effective against the plague samples we had on hand in our Plum Island facility. Fear of a pandemic faded away."

Dutello shook his head. "This North Korean plot caught us off guard. It was bad enough when the plane went down in 1950. At least then we had the plague contained. This time the threat is worse. This time an enemy state has the plague, and if it comes to America it will be no accident."

Abner connected dots in his head. "That news report I just saw in the op area, the North Korean threat, it's about this plague isn't it?"

Dutello nodded. "CIA analysts believe Memorial Day is the most probable date of an attack, but we don't know where yet."

"That's less than two weeks away," Abner said.

Chatfield stared into the blank white board. "If they do execute a terror attack with the plague, it will be different than any other. There will be no massive explosions or dramatic assaults. It might even go unnoticed at first. The 731 bacteria can be introduced into the air or in a major city's water system. By the time we find out it will be too late. We have no way to fight it."

"Our only chance is to find the phage material lost with that plane and pray we can replicate a living strain," Dutello said. "Or pray the North Koreans don't use the plague on us."

Chatfield grabbed a dry-erase marker from the board. "Even if we recover the phage material, our microbiologists estimate it will take three months to develop a living strain."

"If the plague is dispersed on Memorial Day, there could be a hundred thousand dead Americans by then." Dutello added, "I'm really hoping they decide not to use it."

Abner huffed. "I'm sure as hell not going to bank on the North Koreans' moral ethics."

Chatfield drew a big red question mark on the white board with the marker. "Your turn, Admiral. How did you learn about 731?"

Abner took a minute to digest all he'd just been told. A dark cloud hung over the salvage project that had not been there a half hour ago. And it didn't feel like a project anymore, it felt like a mission. Abner stared at Chatfield's red question mark. It seemed appropriate. "Donovan Rafferty was the source."

Dutello sank in his chair. "You can't be serious."

"I am. He contacted my salvage leader Jack Sheridan and told him it's the bacteriophage and not a vaccine that is in the wreckage. That SOB is still connected."

Dutello slapped the tabletop. "Shit!"

"Who the hell is Donovan Rafferty?" Chatfield said.

"He's a colonel-turned-mercenary," Dutello answered, "and the man who nearly stole the Doppelganger system two years ago."

"And thanks to Jack Sheridan he didn't get it," Abner retorted.

"How so?"

"Sheridan and his crew overpowered Rafferty's mercenaries and stopped the theft. It was sort of a big deal when it happened, but I guess I'm not surprised you missed it."

"Oh yeah, I remember now. Doppelganger was another Admiral Wilson, debacle wasn't it?" Chatfield thought it over a minute. "So Sheridan defeats this guy on Doppelganger, yet years later he contacts Sheridan to tell him his latest salvage is a cover up?" Chatfield shook his head. "It doesn't make sense."

"There's some deep, personal animosity between those two," Abner said. "Rafferty wouldn't have told Sheridan about this unless he thought it would hurt him somehow, and because of you two, Jack is going to think I've been lying to him right along."

"There's got to be more to it than that," Dutello said. "What else did he say to Sheridan?"

"According to Jack that's it. No threats, no predictions, no dire warnings. It's possible that Rafferty discovered what Jack is working on and pulled this information just to screw with him. He may not have anything to do with the terror plot, the North Koreans, or any of it."

Dutello gave Abner an uneasy smile. "That's wishful thinking."

"You bet. I intend to meet with Jack this afternoon and sort this whole thing out. He received Top Secret clearance after the Doppelganger affair and is still certified. I owe him the truth."

Chatfield erased the question mark. "Officially I'm opposed to telling Sheridan."

Abner huffed. "I officially don't care what you think."

Dutello cleared away invisible clutter from the tabletop. "Ben, if we're letting Jack Sheridan inside on this Flight 2501 business, we might as well let him in all the way."

Chatfield cursed and shook his head. "Your call."

"What do you mean let him in all the way?" Abner asked with a measure of suspicion.

Chatfield turned from the white board. "There's one more thing..."

- THIRTEEN –

Lake Huron
45° 30' N / 83° 21' W

Alec Cohn stood with arms crossed in the tiny radio room below deck on the *Liberty*, listening to the tail end of a digital recording Nix had sent him through their satellite uplink. Foley watched the progress bar on the playback monitor reach the end. "That's about as clean as I can make it with my filtering software," he said. "You want to hear it again?"

Cohn nodded. "Yes, but start one minute into the recording."

Foley indexed the file to the requested timeframe and initiated the playback. Jack Sheridan's voice came into the radio room through the audio speakers. He and his wife were discussing a blood test and an illness. Ambient road noise indicated they were in a vehicle. Sheridan calls someone named Abner and they begin to discuss an airplane wreck, a vaccine, and a bacteriophage. Cohn leaned toward the speaker at Sheridan's mention of the 731 Plague. At the end of the recorded conversation, Cohn concluded that he'd heard it right the first time. The U.S. government was searching for a bacteriophage effective against the very plague bacteria he carried in his cargo hold, and the colonel was somehow angling into the process.

Cohn understood what the colonel had in mind and found a reason to smile. "Very desperate, Donovan."

Speers had listened to the playback from the corridor. "Do the North Koreans know about this bacteriophage?"

Cohn turned. "I'm certain they do. They probably have it in their lab back home, but I'd say they're unaware of the sample that went down on the airplane. That's an unexpected twist in this odyssey of ours."

"What are the chances Sheridan will find the wreckage?"

"Slim. It's been over sixty years and no one has found it yet. Even if he manages to locate the wreck it will take him weeks to do so. And if he actually recovers remnants of a bacteriophage, it will take another several weeks if not months to develop a living strain of the virus. By then the damage will be done."

"If the government is searching for this bacteriophage, they must know an event involving 731 is coming." Speers let that thought hang out there a few moments. "They might have information that will lead them to us."

"Not yet they don't," Cohn said. "If they did the Canadians would have detained us and the U.S. Coast Guard would have had enough interest to dispatch a cutter to board us. If anything, they have fragments of intelligence that doesn't make enough sense to be useful."

"Then we ignore the issue?" Speers asked.

"No. We've come a long way, and I will not allow anything to endanger our success, not even a long-shot gamble by the U.S. government."

"Then what do we do?"

"For the time being we stick with the plan and tie up with the flotilla at the Mackinaw City Marina. To do anything different at this point would raise suspicion." Cohn checked his watch. "We should be five hours from the docks. Is that correct?"

"Dead on," Speers said.

"Good, that almost gets us back on schedule." Cohn addressed the radio operator. "Foley, hail Nix on the shortwave. Tell him to stick with Sheridan right into Lake Michigan and to report all activity to me."

Foley acknowledged.

"Odds are Sheridan won't begin his sonar sweeps before we crack open the plague canisters in D.C."

Speers thought a bit. "What if something extraordinary happens and he gets the bacteriophage in his hands before we hit D.C.?"

"I'll deal with the extraordinary when it happens."

"Why don't we take him down before he has a chance to find it?"

"That would be a tactical error," Cohn said sharply. "Sheridan will be too late. Moving against him now will only show the government where we are and what we're up to."

Speers hesitated a moment. "The colonel is a wild card. He's already proven himself unpredictable by sparing Sheridan's life and putting him on to this bacteriophage. I think we need to be concerned about his end game."

"We know his end game," Cohn retorted. "And there is no road for him to get there."

"But the colonel is well connected. Somehow he pulled the story of this airplane crash right out of his ass. What other critical information does he have?"

"Having information is one thing, what you're able to do with it is another." Cohn stepped from the radio room. "The colonel is painted into a corner, and even though he believes himself an unstoppable force of nature there is very little he can do."

"How are you so certain?"

"I'm the one who put him in that corner."

"And what about the North Koreans?" Speers said. "Do we tell them about the government's attempt to find the phage?"

Cohn stroked the scar tissue on his jaw. He'd been kicking around the same question since hearing the recording. "If we want to maintain our status as good business partners, we should tell them. I'm sure they do not want the U.S. to possess a silver bullet against the monster I'm unleashing for them. If I frame the facts properly, they'll want me to keep that bullet out of the game."

"That will cost a little more I presume," Speers said.

"Damn right it will. And we better grab all we can from them before it's too late." Cohn stood in the warmth of a beam of sunlight streaming through the overhead hatchway. "The North Korean government launched this operation intent on gaining stature and power for their country. They don't see it will only lead to their annihilation." He laughed. "The pride of nations is the most destructive plague the planet has ever known, far more deadly than the bacteria we carry aboard this ship."

"Then it's fair to say we intend to kill a plague with a plague," Speers said.

"Well put." Cohn peered inside the radio room. "Foley, establish the satellite uplink. I need to send an urgent message to our North Korean contact. Their terror plot is in danger of imploding, and I'm willing to offer my assistance in any way I can."

- FOURTEEN -

Harrison Township, MI

Jack Sheridan stared through the passenger window of Admiral Wilson's Explorer, fist clenched on the armrest and struggling to keep himself collected. Abner had just laid it all out for him, the bacteriophage, the plague, the imminent terror attack. It sent Jack's head spinning. Rafferty had told the truth and Abner, unknowingly, had lied. The world was upside down. But what really seized him like a pair of hands around the throat was the realization that Lauren had in all likelihood been infected with the 731 bacteria. Regardless of what Dr. Clarke's blood culture tests showed, Jack had to assume the worst. And now with the added complication of a Memorial Day terror plot factored in, his agreement to give Rafferty the bacteriophage had exploded into quite a moral dilemma. The inner turmoil had him so distracted he didn't bother to ask why Abner had driven him to the front gate of Selfridge Air National Guard Base.

"If it will make you feel any better," Abner said, "reach over and knock a tooth out of my mouth. I should have sensed the cover story Hoekstra told me. I must be getting complacent in my old age."

Jack turned from the window. "Why didn't they tell you the truth from the beginning?"

Abner frowned. "These post-9/11 intelligence punks grew up watching *The X-Files*. 'Trust no one' is their motto. They hold their cards a little too close to their chest for my liking."

"How confident are these punks of the Memorial Day terror plot?"

Abner slowed the Explorer to a stop behind a car at the main gate. "Confident enough to throw a Hail Mary pass at Flight 2501. If the plague hits we need something in our arsenal to fight it. Dutello and Chatfield said this thing has the potential to cause a hundred thousand deaths."

A shiver passed through Jack's body. That many lost lives would be a devastating tragedy, but he couldn't help but focus on just one of them. "I imagine this will accelerate our timetable."

"The *Achilles* shipped out of Port Huron at her best speed three hours ago," Abner said. "She'll be on station in Muskegon by nine bells tomorrow." He glanced over the top of his sunglasses at Jack. "Sorry, but I called Lloyd direct this morning and told him to cast off the mooring lines."

"Guess I'll overlook that breach in protocol." Jack considered the guard station at the main gate and the air base beyond. "Why did you bring me to Selfridge?"

Abner looked through the windshield. "Showing is better than telling."

A security guard waved the car ahead of them through the raised gate and gestured Abner to come forward. Abner let off the brake and rolled the Explorer to the check point. He lifted the ID badge hanging from a lanyard around his neck.

The guard scrutinized the photo, the name, and the Homeland Security - Maritime Affairs seal. "Good afternoon, Admiral Wilson. Who on base are you here to see?"

"Major Campbell," Abner said. "We're meeting in Maintenance Hangar Three."

"Just a moment, please." The security guard went to the guard station and spoke with another sentry through the doorway. He returned after a minute of conversation. "Major Campbell is expecting you, sir. May I see your guest's identification?"

Jack knew this was coming and handed over his ID card. The guard studied it a moment and handed it back. "Thank you, Mr. Sheridan." He stepped back from the window. "Admiral Wilson, do you know the way to your destination?"

"I believe I do. The Major mapped it out for me in some detail."

The guard waved him through and Abner pulled forward, turning onto a perimeter drive beyond the gate.

Jack could not get his mind off the bacteriophage. It seemed foolhardy to give it to Rafferty after the revelations this afternoon. If Rafferty really was behind the terror plot, his promise to treat Lauren was surely a lie. To deliver the phage on a silver platter to him could make Jack complicit in thousands of American deaths, including Lauren's.

But to renege on his deal with Rafferty held very little upside either. Lauren would just as likely die. She simply did not have the time it would take government microbiologists to reverse engineer the phage. But then Jack considered that all his calculating was based on information Rafferty himself had provided. Yes, some of it happened to be true, but could it all be true? And did Rafferty leave something out? Historically speaking Rafferty never presented the whole picture, and that clarity was something Jack desperately needed to set his course of action. It all began to feel overwhelming.

He realized his thinking was just running him around in circles. Jack decided that he had to rely on his instincts to move forward like he had done in Columbia, and on the *Aeneas*, and with Garity. But the thing his instincts told him to do surprised him.

He would give Rafferty a chance to honor their agreement. Jack could not explain his rationale. There really was none. All he had was a sense of something genuine in Rafferty's word, an intangible feeling that told him the promise to develop the living phage was just as important to Rafferty as it was to him. But Jack's conscience would not let the decision come without cost, and he vowed to get the phage into Abner's hand as well. How he would do that was still a mystery, but his appeased conscience let him kick that can down the road to worry about later.

Abner glanced across the cab. "You're awfully quiet. What are you thinking about?"

"You don't want to know." Jack took in the surroundings and finally processed where they were. Ahead and to the left a great open field crisscrossed with runways, landing lights, and taxiways sprawled out to the horizon. The roar of a fighter jet climbing into the sky penetrated through the windows. A large building that housed the Selfridge Air Museum passed slowly on the driver's side. "Abner, I enjoy history just as much as the next guy, but shouldn't I be home packing to ship out tomorrow? I don't have time to visit an air museum."

"We're not going to the museum, but history is the point of our visit."

Jack regarded him a moment. "How so?"

Abner read a passing street sign. "Flight 2501 crashed in the eye of a geopolitical hurricane, six months after the first Soviet Union A-bomb test and one *day* before the start of the Korean War. President Truman had a lot on his plate and he didn't want to explain to an already anxious nation how we just lost the only defense against a deadly weaponized plague."

"So he did what any president would have done," Jack said. "He classified the whole thing secret and kept it under wraps."

Abner nodded. "And then he ordered the search for Flight 2501 to begin."

"Where are you going with this history lesson?"

"Straight down this little road here."

A side street named Platsburg came up on the left, and Abner turned into it. Up ahead a pair of sentries dressed in full camouflage with AR-18 rifles slung over their shoulders guarded a tiny intersection. They stood vigil in front of a gate in a tall chain-link fence. Behind the gate a corridor of hangars and maintenance buildings ran down the length of a wide concrete road. One of the sentries approached the Explorer.

"Good afternoon, gentlemen. May I see your identification?"

Abner and Jack presented him their ID as they had done at the main gate.

"Admiral Wilson, sir, Major Campbell is expecting you in Maintenance Hangar Three." The sentry pointed through the gate. "It's the fourth building on the west side of the road." He completed his set of instructions with a crisp salute.

Abner responded in kind and drove the Explorer forward through the gate that the second sentry had pulled open. Jack considered the intersection a moment. "The security guards at the main gate were ANG personnel. These guys are regular army. What's up with that?"

Abner didn't reply. He pulled up to the fourth building on the west side and switched off the engine. The structure was about two stories in height with flat gray corrugated walls, no windows, and one entry door near the south corner. "I give up." Jack said. "What do Truman and the search for Flight 2501 have to do with an unimpressive hangar at Selfridge?"

Abner unlatched his door and stepped down to the concrete. He gave the building a once over with hands on hips. "You have to believe me, Jack. I heard about this just this morning."

Jack got out of the Explorer. "Heard about what?"

The door near the south corner swung open with a metallic screech. A man in uniform with a major's insignia stepped out of the building. He was Abner's height with a little more girth, and he sized up the visitors quickly. "Admiral Wilson, welcome to Selfridge."

Abner flashed his official business smile. "I've got my salvage expert with me, Major Campbell, so let's make this visit worth our while."

"That's my intention," the major said, gesturing his guests to step inside the building. "It will help to actually see it, don't you think, Mr. Sheridan?"

"See what?" Jack said.

Major Campbell seemed surprised. "You don't know what you're here to see?"

Jack tilted his head toward Abner. "The admiral and I were trying to get to the point of the matter, but a pesky history discussion got in the way. We haven't gotten to the good part yet."

"This is the good part," Abner said stepping through the threshold of the doorway.

Jack followed him in. Incandescent lights hung from overhead trusses and threw down barely enough light to see the cracked and grease-stained concrete floor of the barren hangar. The aroma of machine oil and metal filings hung in the air. "This isn't impressive, Abner."

"I'm not impressed myself," Abner said. "Major, I hope there's more."

Major Campbell pointed across the empty space to an ancient cage elevator in the shadows against the back wall. "We're set up in the bay below ground. Follow me." He led them toward the elevator. Their footsteps echoed off the cool, steel walls. Major Campbell chuckled. "When Command decided to pull it out of mothballs they almost couldn't find where they'd stored it."

Jack didn't bother to ask what "it" was again. He crowded into the metal-framed elevator with the major and the admiral. Campbell pulled the gate closed and threw the lever to start them down. The hum of an electric motor clicked on and the gondola cage slowly dropped through a shaft in the floor. "This better be good," Jack said.

Light from below shined up through the space between the elevator and the shaft. There seemed to be much better illumination down there than on the ground level of the hangar. The elevator passed through the concrete foundation. And then they were in the underground bay.

Jack took in the scene with eyes wide. "What the…?"

Large sections of aircraft fuselage and a giant dismembered wing lie like disjointed puzzle pieces on a clean, concrete bay floor under brilliant halogen lighting. The nose of the craft was totally disconnected from the cabin and tilted to one side just thirty feet from the base of the elevator. The wing had been positioned on the port side of the aircraft and looked to be fairly intact, complete with engines still mounted, although dents and deformation showed evidence of a significant impact. Two long and tore-up sections of fuselage approximated the main cabin. White lettering in a painted blue band above the porthole-type windows on one of the sections was legible and spelled out *Northwest.* Two-thirds of the tail section stood on end at the rear of the pieced-together craft. Twisted and jagged metal around the edges of the wreckage gave the impression that the airplane had been ripped apart in the hands of some mythical giant.

Jack read a number off the red tail fin. "N95425…Is this some kind of joke?"

"No joke," Abner said. "You're looking at Flight 2501."

"Or rather sixty percent of it," Major Campbell added.

"This is why the wreckage was never found," Abner said. "The naval reserve had already recovered it."

The elevator came to rest on the bay floor, and the motor kicked off. Major Campbell pulled open the gate. "We've had the pieces laid out a little over a week now, ever since Homeland Security gave the green light to launch the new search."

Jack stepped from the elevator and surveyed the wreckage. "You already have the plane. Did they dredge up the bio case too? Is this whole damned thing a wild goose chase?"

"No, you need to find the rest of it," Abner said. "They only recovered these big sections. They did not locate the other parts or any of the luggage or cargo. They were short on time and the technology to get the job done."

Jack walked up to the nose of the plane and placed a hand on the skin. "The government kept the families of the passengers in the dark about this even after they thought the plague threat was contained. What was the point?"

Abner stood beside him. "Once you tell a lie it's easier to just keep telling it."

"Not everyone would agree with the reason this incident was classified in the first place," Major Campbell said. "People lose perspective when years distance them from an event."

Jack studied the beaten engines on the wing. "So what's the upside of this revelation, Abner? You just shrank my target and made it harder to hit."

Abner lifted a folded piece of paper from his pocket and handed it to Jack. "Your birthday is coming up soon, isn't it? Here's an early present. Don't say I never gave you anything."

Jack unfolded the paper and found a handwritten set of longitude and latitude coordinates inside. "Is this what I think it is?"

"If you think it's the actual coordinates that the naval reserve recovered this wreckage from you are correct. Official reports place the crash site eighteen miles off shore. These coordinates say it's more like ten miles out. Assuming the point of impact and the debris field from the crash are in relative proximity, those numbers should put you real close to the mark."

Jack's hand shook with excitement. The coordinates on that paper could eliminate weeks of useless searching. Lauren's chances to survive this mess had just improved significantly. Jack folded the paper and held it tight in his fist. "I've got work to do tonight."

"Atmospherics on the night of the crash, right?" Abner said.

"You know it. We've got to be quick about finding that debris field."

Abner smiled. "I see that fire in your eyes, Jack. You're going to get me that bio case well in advance of Memorial Day, I feel it."

A shot of guilt tightened Jack's stomach. "Don't get too confident, Admiral. Finding the case is still a long shot. It's been underwater for almost seventy years. It may not have survived."

"If it's salvageable, you'll get it. I know that for a fact."

I may get it, Jack thought, *but you may not see it. At least not until Lauren is cured.* He surveyed the wreckage again and lifted his cell phone.

"You won't get a signal down here," Major Campbell said.

"I'm not making a call. I want pictures. This wreckage will give me clues as to how the plane came apart and hit the water." Jack began snapping photos with his cell phone.

Major Campbell suddenly looked nervous. "I don't think I can let you do that. This is still classified material. Those pictures can't get out to the general public."

Abner's face turned red. "Major, the U.S. government wants Jack Sheridan to find this bio case for them, and he's going to get any pictures, files, or scraps of evidence he needs to do so without restriction. If you have a problem with that, I suggest you contact Homeland Security Director Hoekstra immediately."

Major Campbell clenched his jaw and exhaled his displeasure. "My orders are to keep this thing under wraps. The threat of an unstoppable plague outbreak is greater today than it was in 1950. What kind of panic do you think will follow if this information gets out?"

"It won't get out," Jack said. "Trust me. I want this whole affair kept secret just as much as you do. It'll work best for everyone involved."

"It will be secret and secure," Abner said.

Jack lowered the phone. "What do you mean?"

"The *Achilles* will have a coast guard escort. Two cutters will flank you out of port tomorrow. And instead of marines you'll have a Special Forces team on board just in case."

"I understand the cutters, but I won't buy off on Special Forces. They'll just complicate matters with the crew and raise a lot more questions than you want asked."

Abner shook his head. "This voyage must be secured, especially with Rafferty sniffing around the perimeter. The Spec Ops guys will guarantee we don't have a replay of the Doppelganger business."

"The cutters will guarantee that. Look, we're in the Great Lakes, not the Atlantic. It's our own backyard and you're right around the corner if I need your help. Hold back the soldiers. I'll work faster and the crew will be more effective without them getting in the way. It's the least you can do after the whole vaccine misfire."

Abner stewed on that note. "Okay. No strike team on board. But a team will be ready to go at the first sign of trouble. You give the word, and they will be in the air thirty seconds later."

"Agreed." Jack took a few more pictures, much to Campbell's chagrin, and then closed the cell phone. "Let's move. I have to inform my team we're heading out tomorrow."

- FIFTEEN -

Thursday
Muskegon, MI
Mart Dock Marine Terminal

Jack leaned against the starboard handrail on the *Achilles* cargo deck and watched for the arrival of Connor and Markus dockside. A lake breeze washed over him and the morning sun warmed his face. The brilliance of a new day helped to melt away some of his exhaustion. He hadn't slept more than two hours all night. After returning home from Selfridge, he had briefed Lauren on his meeting with Abner and revealed to her that the 731 Plague was real. She took the news well, much better than Jack imagined he would if the tables were turned. Again he had to marvel at her courage in the face of a very scary situation. And then he got to tell her the good news about the crash coordinates. She liked that information better, as did he. The rest of the night Jack plunged into researching weather reports and lake conditions on the night of the crash to help determine how the debris from Flight 2501 may have dispersed and settled on the lake bottom. He dozed off on the small leather couch in his study with a bathymetric map of Lake Michigan on his chest.

Lauren woke him at dawn. They showered, packed, and hit the road to Muskegon in under an hour, and made it to the marine terminal by 10:00 a.m. Just as Abner had told him, the *Achilles* was laid up along the heavy piled frontage of Mart Dock waiting for their arrival.

She truly was a beautiful vessel with her sculpted bow and lean structural lines. Following her retrofit the *Achilles* represented the highest level of maritime tech afloat on the lakes. She stretched nearly three hundred feet from bow to stern with a sleek three-tiered forecastle housing operations and crew quarters, and a clear aft working deck large enough to land a pair of Apache helicopters if the need arose. That should make Abner happy.

A gantry bridged the water between the dock and the *Achilles* starboard side, and crew members trudged up and down the walkway bringing aboard supplies that had not gotten loaded in Port Huron before the hasty departure. Jack recognized some faces from previous voyages and greeted them as they stepped on deck. An attractive young woman with brown eyes accented by Asian features caught his attention. She hefted an overstuffed duffle bag onto the ship, and her pure black ponytail whipped behind her. "Mai," Jack said.

She looked up and smiled. "Hey, Jackson."

He gave her a hug. "Are you my sonar operator? I heard you left the company."

Mai set the duffle bag down with a grunt. "I did for a little while. I needed some time away."

"We all did," Jack said. "A lot of us are coming back to the water, though. We must love what we do."

"It definitely beats data entry at a production plant."

"Is that what you did after you left Neptune?"

Mai nodded. "Yeah, eight months is all I could take of it."

"I would have hired you," Joshua Rezner said as he walked up from a hatchway in the forecastle. "I need a front counter girl at JR Supply and Ammo."

"Rez!" Mai hugged him and lightly scratched her nails through his beard. "What's up with the whiskers?"

"My customers are mostly mid-state hunters, so I went native. I'd be there now if it wasn't for Jack. He asked me to come along on this project, just in case."

Mai's smile faded a bit and her dark eyes narrowed in question. "In case of what?"

"In case Braddock gets preoccupied badgering me," Jack said. "Where is our captain anyway?"

"Oh, he's stomping around on the bridge complaining about you," Rezner said.

"I haven't seen the guy in three years, and he's still pissed at me for something I didn't do."

Mai hoisted the duffle bag to her shoulder. "I need to get my gear to my cabin and pre-flight my station. This is going to be fun." She playfully slugged Jack in the arm and headed off.

"Connor is going to be glad to see you," Jack called after her.

Mai turned and her eyes brightened. "Connor's with the crew too? Great. Tell him he still owes me a phone call." She continued on to the forecastle.

When she'd gotten a good distance away, Jack turned to Rezner. "Don't bring up Rafferty aboard this ship, especially to crew who were on the *Aeneas.*"

"I didn't mention Rafferty. I merely implied his name."

"Don't even imply it. No need to dredge up those memories and sidetrack this crew's thinking." Jack returned to the handrail and faced the dock.

"Speaking of Rafferty," Rezner said, "any new developments?"

Jack bit his lower lip. "No."

"We're shipping out kind of sudden. I figured it might have something to do with him."

Jack kept watching the crewmen carrying boxes up the gantry. "Abner made the call. Our schedule has tightened but it doesn't have anything to do with Rafferty." He regarded Rezner with a side glance. "I presume you're carrying. That jacket is too warm for a morning like this."

Rezner patted a bump at his waist. "Smith & Wesson .40 cal semi-auto."

"Keep it discrete. Guns on a salvage recovery will spook these people too."

A revving car engine swelled from the port facility service drive off Fifth Street north of the dock. Jack and Rezner watched as a midnight blue Heritage Ford Mustang gathered speed on the cracked cement. It rumbled over a set of railroad tracks and barreled into the twenty-acre lay down space in front of the *Achilles*. The car veered clear of a pallet of non-perishable food boxes and began spinning in three hundred sixty-degree circles with its rear tires smoking and screeching on the concrete. The driver pulled out of the doughnuts and set a beeline course for a group of cars parked in the far corner of the lay down area. The Mustang reached about sixty miles per hour before the driver slammed the brakes and slid to a sideways stop just three feet from the side of Jack's Cherokee.

"Who's that jackass?" Rezner said.

Jack frowned. "Markus Sweetwood."

The Mustang's doors swung open and Markus and Connor sprang out, ranting and waving their arms at one another as if arguing. They pulled out duffle bags that were jammed tight in the rear seat of the car and headed for the gantry. Jack watched them approach. "Here they come, Ying and Yang."

"I like your son," Rezner said, "but hanging around with Sweetwood is going to corrupt his common sense."

"Come on, are you telling me you don't remember what it's like to be twenty-four?"

"I remember not being a reckless, disrespectful punk."

"Markus respects me. Maybe you haven't earned it from him yet."

Rezner scoffed "It's a good thing I know you're just jerking my chain."

Connor and Markus climbed the gantry, greeting crewmen they knew with handshakes and embraces as they went. At the top Markus tossed his duffle bag onto the deck, leapt from the walkway, and offered Jack a lazy salute. "Private Sweetwood reporting for duty."

"You'd be a private if you were in the army," Connor said stepping off the gantry. "Since you're boarding a ship you should have used a naval analogy."

Markus thought about it. "What would I be in the navy?"

"You'd be Seaman Sweetwood," Rezner said through a laugh. "Sounds fitting to me."

"Hey, nobody told me my friend Joshua was coming with us." Markus offered his hand and Rezner reluctantly shook it. "I hope you're ready for another humbling experience at the poker table," Markus said.

"Name the time, wise guy. All that money from the coins must be heavy in your pockets. I'll do you a favor and take some of that burden off your hands."

"He's emptied his pockets enough already, Rez, go easy on him," Connor said.

"I appreciate you guys getting here *before* we left the dock," Jack said, "but that driving demonstration wasn't necessary."

Markus smiled. "It wasn't necessary but it was fun."

"So why are we shipping out today?" Connor asked. "Is that cholera outbreak in Haiti worse than they thought?"

Jack almost corrected the false story but remembered that the particulars of their voyage were classified Top Secret. Furthermore, he'd not yet told his son about Lauren's exposure to the 731 Plague, or what he had planned to do with the bacteriophage once they found it. He realized he had a great number of things on his mind but precious little he could actually say. "Abner is calling the shots," he finally said. "We can assume any number of things, but the fact is we are shipping out today and we need to locate that plane wreck as quickly as possible."

Connor nodded to a catwalk outside the forecastle where Lauren stood surveying port activity. "Is mom taking a tour, or is she coming along for the ride?"

Jack considered how to answer the question. "She's coming along. I guess after all those years of waiting for me to come home from a project she's decided not to wait anymore."

"Good for her."

Something drew Jack's attention down the gantry. He glanced there briefly but felt a slap on his shoulder.

"Mr. Sheridan," Markus said. "Do they have my ROV prepped in the bay?"

"ROV?" Jack refocused his thoughts on the ship. "Uh, yeah, it's set up on a test stand for you to do a dry run of its systems."

Rezner slapped Markus' shoulder. "Respect your project leader. Don't slap him like that."

The image of the gantry flickered in Jack's mind. A few crewmen were ascending, two with boxes and one without. He couldn't make out their faces.

"Dad," Connor said. "Who do we have manning the op center?"

"Not sure yet." Jack shifted gears in his head again. "Wait, Mai is our sonar operator."

"Mai's back with the company?" Connor smiled.

"Yes, and she says you owe her a phone call."

"Way to fumble the ball, Sheridan," Markus said.

Something didn't feel right to Jack. The day seemed to darken as if a cloud had drifted in front of the sun, or an unexpected shadow had passed overhead, but neither event had actually happened. He looked up to the catwalk where Lauren had been standing, but she had gone into the ship through an outer hatchway. Connor and Markus bickered in the background. Jack turned to silence them but froze when his eyes settled on the person standing behind them: Donovan Rafferty.

Panic slammed in Jack's chest like a hammer on an anvil. Why is he here? Jack's hand flinched to draw the Kimber but he resisted. Rafferty held the key to Lauren's survival. As much as it betrayed Jack's instincts, he had to let that man live. And on realizing this fact an immediate problem suddenly became apparent. Nobody else aboard the ship knew about Lauren's dilemma or Rafferty's role in it. No one else knew...

Jack sensed a flash of movement to his right.

"It's him!" Rezner shouted and drew the Smith & Wesson from its holster.

Connor and Markus scattered from the barrel of the gun.

Rezner leveled the pistol at Rafferty.

Jack anticipated the bullet. At point blank it would be lethal. *Rafferty had to stay alive.*

"Joshua, no!" Jack seized Rezner's arm and forced the gun barrel toward the deck.

Rezner struggled for control with wild eyes. "It's Rafferty. He's here!"

"You can't shoot him."

Markus realized Rafferty was standing behind him and wheeled about with a powerful right hook, fully intending to remove the man's head from his body. Rafferty saw the fist coming and ducked under it. He rose with the Sig Sauer in his hand. Markus staggered after his thrown punch missed the mark, and he found himself staring straight down the barrel of Rafferty's pistol.

Connor had begun an advance on Rafferty too but stopped in mid-step.

Jack caught the skirmish in the corner of his eye. He released Rezner's arm and spun around with hands raised. "Donovan, wait."

Rezner sidestepped and reestablished his aim at Rafferty's chest.

Rafferty stood firm, holding the Sig an inch from Markus' forehead.

Nobody moved.

"I need Jack," Rafferty said cooly. "I don't need you, Mr. Sweetwood."

A sheen of sweat glistened on Markus' face.

Jack took a cautious step forward. "You need me but I need them. If this goes down any other way we fail, and I know you don't want that."

Rafferty shifted his gaze to Jack. "It doesn't seem your team is on the same page we are. Why didn't you bring them up to speed?"

"I didn't think you'd be joining us."

"I wasn't about to let you orchestrate this search on your own. You need to be managed."

Rezner stared at both of them. "What the hell is going on?"

Jack glanced at him. "Rez, lower your gun. We'll be okay."

"What are you talking about?"

"You have to trust me on this."

"Sorry, no can do. This bastard's gotta die."

Jack raised his voice. "Joshua, I've got a damn good reason. Now put the gun down."

Rezner shook his head.

Jack turned back to Rafferty. "Donovan, you've got to give me something. You can't blame them for wanting you dead, can you? Just holster that pistol and we'll set the ground rules."

Rafferty assessed the tactical standoff. "Mr. Rezner doesn't look much in the mood for discussing rules."

"He won't shoot if you put that Sig away. Isn't that right, Joshua?"

Rezner's hand shook. "Don't do this, Jack. We've been waiting for him to come back for two years. Now he's here and you want us to surrender?"

"It's not a surrender, it's a truce. I'll explain everything but you have to put away the iron."

Rafferty looked Jack in the eye. He seemed to find something agreeable there and his lips curved into a faint smile. "Mr. Sweetwood, consider this the luckiest day of your life." He lowered the Sig, stepped back, and holstered the weapon.

Markus straightened up. "I was about to tell you the same thing."

Jack faced Rezner. "Your turn, Joshua."

Rezner didn't budge. "I don't understand what you're doing."

Jack reached out and took hold of the Smith & Wesson. "I'll explain, but you need to give me that chance."

Rezner seemed lost in anger and confusion, but he let Jack guide the pistol back to its holster. "No matter what you tell me, I won't trust him," Rezner said.

"This isn't about trust."

Jack looked about and found himself at the center of everyone's attention. Rezner and the guys stared in total disbelief while a handful of crewmen on the periphery gawked as if watching the aftermath of a fatal traffic accident. Jack had to contain the situation, get events back on track. He put a hand on Connor's shoulder. "Give me five minutes and I'll explain everything. Take Markus and Joshua forward and wait for me there."

Connor gave him a hesitant nod.

Jack approached Rafferty. "We need to talk."

"I agree."

"Let's take it aft." Jack started toward the empty deck space near the stern. The small gallery of crewmen cleared the way for him to pass. Jack studied their faces. None of them had been aboard the *Aeneas* so they would not know Rafferty's identity. That was a plus. And the whole event had unfolded in under two minutes, so exposure to witnesses was limited.

"Hey, Jack," one of the crewmen said. "What's going on? That guy was just standing there, and your posse went after him."

"It's just a misunderstanding."

"Yeah, a big one. Who is he anyway?"

Rafferty flicked open his stainless steel lighter and lit a cigarette. "I'm with the FAA and I'm here to monitor the Flight 2501 recovery effort." He took a drag off the cigarette. "You know us government types; overworked, under stress, and always carrying guns."

The crewman offered a wary smile.

Another said to Rafferty, "I'd file an assault charge if I were you, dude."

Jack bristled. Rafferty pressing assault charges would mean the world really was upside down. "How about it, Donovan?" Jack said deadpan. "You want to file a police report?"

Rafferty consumed the irony with a wide smile. "I'm not certain. I'll have to think it over. I'm very flustered right now."

Jack dispersed the crewmen to their duties and walked aft with Rafferty following just half a step behind. He stopped at the stern and crossed his arms so he could feel the butt of his pistol beneath his windbreaker. Rafferty leaned on the aft gunwale and casually observed an inbound freighter making way through Lake Muskegon.

"What are you doing here?" Jack said.

"I told you. You need managing. You're far too creative to have free rein of this search."

"What's that supposed to mean?"

"It means you're as skilled at deception and duplicity as any mercenary I've dealt with."

"I'm not sure how to take that."

"Take it as a compliment."

Jack uncrossed his arms. "You can't stay on this ship."

"What's the matter? Are you afraid of me?"

"Any sane man would be."

Rafferty puffed on the cigarette and inspected the glowing embers. "You didn't answer the question." Smoke escaped his mouth with each word. "If I were you I'd be scared shitless."

"It's a good thing you're not me." Jack studied Rafferty a short while. "Why are you alone? Are your men waiting out on the lake to intercept and take over the ship?"

"Where's your tactical mind, Jack? Seizing this vessel would be counterproductive to my goal. You need to work unfettered to find our bio case quickly."

"Your very presence here is fettering me."

Rafferty smiled. "I will not seize this ship. Does that make you feel any better?"

"You leaving would make me feel better."

"That isn't an option. I will be here when you open the case." Rafferty wiped a bead of sweat from his temple.

"If you can't stand the heat get off my ship," Jack said.

"I'll leave when the bacteriophage is in my hands."

Jack moved closer and looked him in the eye. "Why do you want it?"

"That's not your concern. I thought we covered this in the cemetery."

"Are you planning something with the 731 Plague on Memorial Day?"

Rafferty took another drag off his cigarette. "Did Abner tell you that?"

Jack shrugged. "Let's just say he implied some things."

"Did he also explain why he lied to you?"

"Someone lied to him."

Rafferty chuckled "It's hard to know who to believe anymore, isn't it?"

"It's not so hard with some people."

"If I told you I have nothing planned for Memorial Day, would you believe me?"

Jack did not reply.

Rafferty flicked ash onto the deck with a hint of aggravation. "Why ask the question if you've made up your mind?"

"I have a problem handing over the only defense against a deadly plague to a guy who just might turn that plague loose in a city. Maybe my subconscious wants to hear you say you have no such intention so I can justify our agreement."

Rafferty squared up with him. "What if that is my intention? What difference does it make to you? Would you really sacrifice Lauren's life in exchange for the mere possibility of saving thousands of faceless people you don't know, you don't love, and many of whom don't deserve saving?"

"Twist it around however you want, but you can't make me responsible for your actions. One life or a thousand, any blood shed will be on your hands alone."

"What if I drop the plague into a penitentiary of convicted murders? Would your conscience accept that any easier?"

Jack stood nose-to-nose with him. "It's not your place to judge the value of one life over another. If you're God's tool of retribution like you say, I'm sure he would tell you that."

"What if releasing the plague isn't my plan at all?" Rafferty retorted. "What if keeping the phage from me actually causes the death of that faceless multitude as well as your wife? Could you live with yourself then?"

"Are you actually suggesting Saint Donovan is bent on saving the world? That's a stretch."

"I'm suggesting no such thing," Rafferty said blithely. "I'd never save the whole thing."

Jack turned away. "I'm tired of your damned head games."

"Whatever you believe about me and this situation, you need to understand that this is no game."

Jack faced the forecastle where he'd last seen Lauren. Things were getting murky. Instinct and emotion were at odds, and he couldn't tell which held the advantage. He faced Rafferty again. "You can stay aboard the ship, but you have to keep away from the operations center and the bridge. You will remain alone, no Neanderthal back up team, and you will give me that Sig."

Rafferty smiled and flicked the cigarette butt over the gunwale. "I will access any area of the ship I see fit, Mr. Ferguson will be joining me, and I will under no circumstances surrender the Sig."

Jack shook his head. "My salvage, my rules."

"You forget who's pulling the strings," Rafferty said.

"You need me."

They stared hard at each other a long while in silence.

"Admit that we need each other, Jack, and this voyage will go much smoother."

"That's the first candid thing you've said." Jack looked out over Lake Muskegon. "Ferguson will be unarmed, and you will not interfere with search operations in any way."

"I think we're finally getting somewhere." Rafferty fished for another cigarette but reconsidered and put the pack back into his pocket. "Now it's time to get the rest of your team on board. You can start with him."

Jack turned. A towering man with a barrel chest and a five-day beard approached with a very purposeful stride. The sleeves of his charcoal gray Neptune's Reach shirt were rolled back to his bulky forearms, and his captain's rank insignia pin glistened in the sun. The name *Braddock* was embroidered over his left chest. "Sheridan," his voice boomed. "What the hell kind of trouble have you brought aboard my ship?"

BOOK III:
BAD COMPANY

- SIXTEEN-

"Bad company corrupts good character."
– *Thais*, Menander

Jack held back a sigh as Captain Braddock approached. "Malcolm," he said with as much artificial cheer as he could muster, "can you at least say hello before you start in on me?"

Braddock strode up as if approaching an opposing general on a field of battle. "I got three reports of a scuffle on deck. What the hell is going on down here?"

"Nothing to be concerned about," Jack said low key. "Your crew is exaggerating the incident."

Braddock wasn't buying. "Did Rezner pull a gun on someone?"

"That was a misunderstanding. You know how Rezner overreacts."

Braddock gave Rafferty a once over. "Who's this?"

Jack scrambled for a cover story but Rafferty stepped in. "Raymond Shaw," he said. "I'm with the FAA. This is a government project and the plane wreck holds historical significance. I need to document the salvage of Flight 2501 to close this case once and for all."

Braddock scrutinized him. "Are you friends with Sheridan?"

Rafferty laughed. "Hardly."

"Then you and I might get along." Braddock scowled at Jack. "Keep your team in line. One more report of trouble and I'll bounce you into the lake."

Jack straightened his stance. "You may steer the ship but I'm running the operation. If anyone gets bounced it'll be you."

"Don't push me, Jack. I'm warning you." Braddock spat over the side. "No more trouble." He marched off in a huff.

Rafferty watched him go. "Jack, I'm shocked. He doesn't adore you like everyone else does."

"Don't be so surprised. You're half the reason he hates me."

Rafferty grinned. "I think I'm going to enjoy this voyage."

Forward on deck Connor, Markus, and Rezner huddled in conversation at the base of the forecastle. They seemed to be taking turns glancing aft. Jack needed to bring them into the fold.

"Where's Ferguson?" Jack said to Rafferty.

Rafferty checked his watch. "He'll be along shortly with our gear."

"I'm searching your gear," Jack said. "I won't allow you to bring any weapons aboard."

"Sig Sauer excluded."

Jack grimaced. "I'd consider it a gesture of good faith if you were unarmed."

"That may be true but it's not going to happen. Now why don't you show me to my quarters?"

"Give me a few minutes to think of a nice dark corner of the ship to stick you in. Until then wait right here. I need to talk to my team." Jack left Rafferty and headed toward the forecastle. He began thinking of ways to break the news of his deal with the devil to Connor, Markus, and Rezner when his cell rang. Caller ID displayed Lloyd Faulkner's name. Jack exhaled and answered. "What do you need, Lloyd?"

"Braddock just called," Lloyd said clearly agitated. "Did you have to kick the hornet's nest as soon as you set foot on deck?"

Jack cursed under his breath. Braddock certainly didn't waste any time complaining. "I didn't want him as captain to begin with," Jack said. "You forced him on me. Now you have to deal with his whining."

"Whining?" Lloyd squeaked. "He's telling me about fights on deck. Guns. And who the hell is this government guy you brought aboard?"

"I didn't bring anyone aboard."

"Braddock said it's some FAA guy, Shaw."

"Right, Shaw. I didn't bring him. The feds sent him to observe the recovery. Something about closing an FAA case file. He requested to come aboard, I granted, and then there was this misunderstanding with Rezner. It's no big deal."

"Braddock made it sound like a hell of a big deal."

"Consider the source. I'm sure he exaggerated every detail. Believe me when I say I've got it all under control."

"It better be under control. I don't want to hear another report like that."

"Try to remember that I don't work for you anymore, Lloyd. I'm the project manager and site representative for the Maritime Affairs Office, which is the contracting entity on this salvage operation. Technically you work for me."

"Don't pull that crap with me," Lloyd said flustered.

"Look, everything is green to go. We're shipping out this afternoon. We'll be on site by dusk. I'll report back when I have something to report. It's under control. Gotta run." Jack disconnected, and then got to thinking just how he would make that rosy report true. The first step would be to convince the three people staring at him that everything was okay. He stepped into the little circle that Connor, Markus, and Rezner had formed, and they waited for the explanation that he had promised.

"Why is Rafferty on this ship?" Jack said. "And why am I protecting him? I suppose those questions are front and center in your minds."

"I had him dead in my sights," Rezner said. "Why didn't you let me end it?"

"He's got leverage over me."

Markus crinkled his brow. "Does he have a bomb on board or a sniper team targeting you?"

"Worse," Jack said.

"What could be worse?" Connor asked.

"You'd better not be doing this to protect me," Rezner said, "or that jackass Markus."

Markus frowned. "I agree with Joshua in principal. Don't stand in the gap because of us."

"It's not us," Connor said.

Jack looked at his son and their eyes connected.

"Mom's never gone out on a salvage before," Connor said. "Why now?"

Jack tried to speak but the words didn't flow. His eyes reddened. "She's infected with some kind of bacteria," he finally said. "Rafferty exposed her. He says it's lethal and only he can save her, and he will save her only if I do what he tells me to." Jack added, "He's punishing me for what I did to him on the *Aeneas*."

Rezner scoffed. "The son of a bitch is lying, Jack."

"He's not lying. Abner confirmed the things he told me."

"Admiral Wilson knows about this?" Connor said.

"No, he doesn't know about Lauren. I can't tell him that part. And I definitely can't tell him that Rafferty showed up here."

"Why?" Markus said. "What does Rafferty want you to do?"

"He wants me to find Flight 2501."

"What a coincidence. That's what Abner wants. I see the conflict," Rezner said.

"Rafferty wants the cholera vaccine?" Connor asked.

"No, he wants something called a bacteriophage. That's what's really in the wreckage. There's a whole muddy story there, but I won't go into it now."

Markus ground some gears in his head. "Here's what we do. We get hold of Rafferty and restrain him, and then I start slicing around his carotid artery with a knife until he surrenders whatever medicine he has to cure Mrs. Sheridan."

"I like the spirit of your plan, Markus, but it won't work. Rafferty says the bacteriophage is the thing that will ultimately save her. He has a microbiologist ready to patch together a living strain of the phage from the remains in the bio case. We have to recover that case for Lauren to survive."

"Why does Rafferty want this bacterio-whatever in the first place?" Rezner said.

Jack glanced around to make sure no one was listening in on them. "He hasn't shared that with me yet, and right now I don't care. We have to find that case before the infection advances too far in Lauren to save her. Rafferty will treat her as soon as we get him the phage."

"You can't trust him to follow through," Rezner warned.

"I agree," Connor said solemnly.

"Don't you think I've considered that?" Jack said. "I've gone over it in my head a hundred times. Right now this is all I can do. Until I figure a way to turn the tables on Rafferty, I have to play along. We need to find that case, and I need you three to swear to me you'll keep this information secret and you'll not make a move against Rafferty." Jack looked at each of them. "I need to hear it."

One by one they took Jack's oath.

"We might be able to keep this under our hats, but there is a problem," Connor said. "There are *Achilles* crew members who were also aboard the *Aeneas,* and they know who Rafferty is and what he did. Mai is one of them. If Rafferty bumps into any of them, this whole ship is going to revolt."

Jack pondered the problem. "Then we take them out of the equation," he said. "You and Markus get a hold of the ship's roster and find the names of *Aeneas* crewmembers. I'll come up with a reason we don't need them aboard and I'll send them home."

Rezner scratched his beard. "The *Achilles* crew compliment is less than twenty. What if half of them were aboard the *Aeneas*? We can't get underway with half the crew missing."

"Let's hope it's not that many," Jack said. "It shouldn't be. I've been watching them load supplies this morning, and Mai was the first *Aeneas* alumnus I saw."

"Mai is a real good sonar jockey," Connor said. "She'd be a great help in finding the case in the plane crash debris."

Markus cleared his throat. "I never thought I'd be the one to say this, but stop thinking with your shorts, Sheridan. If she sees Rafferty, she'll freak and it'll be game over."

"I'm thinking of the best chance to save my mom's life, shit-for-brains. Maybe Mai can handle knowing Rafferty is aboard."

Jack shook his head. "No exceptions. Anyone who has seen Rafferty prior to this day is off the ship. Got it?"

Connor looked away. "Sure, whatever you say."

A man stepping off the gantry with two travel bags slung over his shoulders caught Rezner's attention. "There's a face I recognize, but I can't tag him with a name."

Jack glanced over his shoulder. "It's Ferguson. Come on, Rez, we need to get him and Rafferty out of sight. Connor and Markus, find that crew roster. I want it within the hour."

The group broke up. Jack and Rezner headed toward the new arrival near the gantry. Rafferty approached him too. Rezner's hand dropped to the butt of his pistol. Jack eyed the movement. "Cool it. I've got a tenuous working agreement with them, and I want to keep it that way."

Rezner grumbled. "I don't like this."

"You don't have to like it. We've just got to see this through. Lauren's life depends on it."

"Damn it, Jack. How do you get yourself into these situations?"

"If I knew I'd quit doing it. Now ease off that Smith & Wesson."

Rafferty and Ferguson watched them approach. Up close Jack saw the flesh-colored bandages on Ferguson's cheek and smiled. Ferguson's expression turned cold. "Hey, Sheridan, long time, no see." He laughed. "How's the wife and kid?"

Jack clenched his fist. "Still carrying Donovan's baggage I see." He gestured to the bandages. "Cut yourself shaving?" Jack snapped his fingers. "Oh, wait. The cemetery. That's right."

They glared at one another.

Rafferty found their posturing amusing. "Are you gentlemen finished getting reacquainted?"

Jack pulled back. "You two have a reputation with some of the crew that could prove problematic."

Rafferty set an unlit cigarette between his lips. "Nothing you can't handle, Jack."

"I am handling it. The first step is getting you out of sight."

"Show me the way," Rafferty said.

Jack led them to the forecastle while Rezner followed as rear guard. They all stepped through a hatchway that had a twelve-foot Zodiac mounted to the bulkhead beside it. They climbed a set of stairs from the main deck to the second tier deck that housed the crew quarters. Jack made sure the whitewashed corridor was clear before proceeding. The smell of fresh paint and new fiberglass from the recent retrofit tinged the air. Jack walked mid-way into the corridor, checking the doors on the left and right in passing. He entered a cabin on the port side of the vessel.

Rafferty and Ferguson followed him in and scrutinized the tiny compartment. With a disapproving sneer, Ferguson tossed the bags he'd been carrying onto the only bunk in the room. Jack snatched up one of them and opened it. Ferguson got angry. "Hey, back off!"

Rezner put a hand on his pistol.

Ferguson reached for the bag but Rafferty grabbed his arm.

"I made an agreement with our new partner," Rafferty said through the unlit cigarette. "This is part of it." Ferguson resisted his grasp a bit too much, and Rafferty jerked him close. "You will honor my terms." He seized the 9 mm Ferguson had holstered under his loose-fitting sweatshirt and handed the weapon to Jack.

Jack hesitated before taking it. He never thought he'd see the day when Rafferty would disarm one of his own men and hand him the weapon. He tucked the pistol under his belt and began searching through the contents of the travel bag.

Rezner eased off the Smith & Wesson.

Jack found nothing but clothing and toiletries packed in the first bag. He moved to the next and found much the same.

Rafferty finally lit the cigarette. "Satisfied?"

Jack regarded him. "You're just making me wonder if I'm missing something."

Rafferty smiled. "I like keeping you on your toes." He blew a stream of smoke.

"This is a non-smoking environment per the state of Michigan."

"Cigarettes are non-negotiable."

"Then keep it in the cabin. And stay in here until we ship out. I need to make crew adjustments." Jack moved to the door and tapped Rezner on the shoulder. "Let's go."

They left the compact quarters and closed the door behind them.

"I thought for sure you'd stick him in a cargo hold," Rezner said.

"Keep your friends close and your enemies closer."

"What idiot said that?"

"I think it was Machiavelli. Anyway, my cabin is at the end of this corridor. I want to know what Rafferty does and when he does it."

They walked a while in silence.

"I'm not buying any of it," Rezner said.

Jack looked at him but said nothing.

"That bit back there with Rafferty acting compliant, like he has every intention of honoring his deal with you. That's a load of crap. He's plotting something."

Jack started down a steep stairwell through the deck at the end of the corridor. "If he is we'll put a stop to it. In the meantime, we have to execute this search and salvage as if nothing is out of the ordinary, which means you need to get with Markus and make sure the ROV and deployment rig is ready for action."

"Don't know if I can focus with that mercenary aboard," Rezner said. "Just let me put a bullet in Rafferty's head, and I'll perform my duties much better."

Jack abruptly faced him. "This is Lauren's life we're talking about. Her survival hinges on Rafferty making good on his promise, no matter how unlikely that may seem. He can't do that if he's dead. Once she's treated and cured, you can do whatever you want, but until then you will not endanger Rafferty in any way. As a matter of fact, you'll protect him from harm if it becomes necessary."

Rezner stared back incredulous. "It'll be a cold day in hell when I protect him."

"This is serious, Joshua. He's the only chance she's got. I need to know right now if you're buying in or begging off."

Rezner rolled his head back and grumbled. "I'm in! Okay? I hate it but I'm in."

"That's good because I need your help." Jack pushed through a hatchway door that opened up to the bow of the ship. He and Rezner walked to the point and looked out over the water of Lake Muskegon. A pair of U.S. Coast Guard cutters steamed in through the inlet from Lake Michigan and set a course for the marine terminal where the *Achilles* was moored. Jack identified them right away as Abner's escorts. "Here comes our flank guard."

"What do you mean?" Rezner asked.

"Those cutters are Abner's idea. He wants them to escort us during the search just in case Rafferty shows up to derail our effort."

Rezner watched the vessels approach. "Are you going to tell him they're wasting their time?"

"No."

"Withholding from Abner again, eh? You really are going off the reservation on this one."

"I've got no choice. Are you still in?"

Rezner gave him a somber look. "You saved my ass on the *Aeneas*. You saved the whole crew. I'm all in."

"I didn't save anybody. We worked together to survive, and we're going to do it again." Jack regarded the cutters. "That lead boat is the eighty-seven-foot Marine Protector class. Nice vessel. High tech."

Rezner chuckled. "The other is an old Point class boat. Guess we didn't rate two state-of-the-art escorts."

Jack's cell phone rang. It was Connor. He answered. "Do you have the roster?"

"Yeah, I have it. The first officer printed it out for me," Connor said.

"What's the damage?"

"Out of fifteen regular crewmen, there are three who were crew-members aboard the *Aeneas* during the Rafferty project; Whalen, Hogan, and Mai."

"That's not so bad. You and Markus help me round them up. I'll meet with them in the galley."

"What are you going to tell them?"

Jack toyed with the phone a moment. "I'm going to say that after consulting with a corporate psychologist, I've determined that it is not a good idea to have a group of Rafferty project survivors serving together on another salvage operation. Having us all together in a setting very similar to the one in which a major traumatic incident occurred could trigger an episode of Post-Traumatic Stress Disorder, and I don't want that to happen."

Connor remained silent for a second or two. "That actually sounds pretty good, but what if they aren't concerned about the potential for PTSD?"

"They won't have a choice. This is my project, and I made it clear to Lloyd that I will be the one to make all operational decisions, including crew personnel." Jack added, "I'll also sweeten the pot and give each of them a check to cover two weeks' pay."

"You'll never get Lloyd to sign off on that."

"Son, I'm not Markus. I haven't burned through my share of the coin money yet. I'll cover the cost myself."

"Right. What was I thinking? Markus and I will find these three and meet you in the galley in thirty minutes."

"Sounds good." Jack ended the call and turned to Rezner. "I'm going to make this work."

At thirty minutes on the mark, Jack stepped into the galley and addressed the crew members who knew Rafferty's face. They took the news that they were leaving the ship with a good deal of skepticism, but the promise of a two-week paid vacation smoothed any ruffled feathers. Only Mai remained resistant to the idea. Jack apologized and assured her that disbanding the group was best for everyone. When she asked if Connor and Markus were being booted too, Jack gave her an evasive answer. She reluctantly agreed to leave and the meeting ended, at which point Jack wrote them checks from his personal account and wished them well.

He then went to his cabin and informed Lauren of Rafferty's unexpected arrival.

The *Achilles* was fully supplied by twelve o'clock. Her search and recovery systems were run through pre-flight diagnostics and secured by mid-afternoon. A tug guided her out of Mart Dock at 3:17 p.m. Her engines rumbled to life at half past the hour and Braddock ordered the helm to navigate through the channel to Lake Michigan at quarter speed. The coast guard cutters formed up to port and starboard and the small convoy headed out.

Jack chose the starboard wing outside the bridge to stand as they got underway. Not long ago he thought he'd never head out on a Neptune's Reach vessel again, but there he was with the wind in his face and open water dead ahead, undertaking the most important salvage operation of his life. He definitely did not see this voyage coming, not by a long shot.

His cell phone rang and he checked the display screen. Abner Wilson's name appeared. Jack hovered his thumb over the receive button but decided instead to close the phone. He slowly returned it to his belt clip and let the call go to voicemail.

- SEVENTEEN –

The *Achilles* cleared the Port of Muskegon and steered southwest, increasing speed to eighteen knots. The crash site coordinates Abner had provided were roughly seventy miles away, officially the shortest distance Jack had ever had to travel to reach a salvage site. Given the favorable marine conditions and the *Achilles'* present speed she would reach the coordinates just before sunset. Jack took one more look at the water and then left his post on the starboard wing, stepping through the hatchway door into the bridge.

The retrofit had not changed the basic layout of the ship's command center. Sitting at the top of the forecastle, the *Achilles'* bridge still contained ample deck space and an open design. Dozens of large windowpanes encircled the elliptical room to provide a full three hundred sixty-degree view of the water surrounding the ship. The changes became apparent to Jack in the command console that stretched across a lengthy section of the forward bulkhead. New panels and interface screens now populated the angled face of the console instead of the old switches, dials, and gauges that used to monitor the ship's systems.

A crewman Jack did not know served as conning officer and was seated in a new, comfortable-looking chair in front of a series of flat-screen monitors displaying navigation and radar information. Another crewman, Jack thought his name to be Cooney, sat in a similar chair before the helm controls. Braddock stood between them and seemed to be studying the new equipment, watching the ship's systems report in their status through the various monitors. The captain did a remarkable job of ignoring Jack's entrance onto the bridge.

Jack figured he'd try to smooth things between them. "How is the new and improved *Achilles* performing, Captain Braddock?"

Braddock kept his attention on the console and didn't reply.

"These system upgrades are as big a leap in technology as an airplane switching from cable-controlled flaps to electronic fly by wire."

Braddock straightened up and turned around. "Do you have a reason to be on my bridge, Sheridan?"

Jack's feeling of good will began to evaporate. "I just thought we could act like a couple of professional colleagues. Guess one of us couldn't handle it."

"Look, I've got a ship to captain and you've got a project to screw up, so let's just get back to doing what we're good at."

"If we're getting back to what we're good at, you better toss that captain's pin over the side."

Cooney concealed a grin.

"We'll be on station in four hours," Braddock said. "You and I will confer on ship's status at that point. Until then stay out of my way."

Jack nodded. "Okay, Malcolm. Be a hard ass, but I'm holding a mission briefing in the operations center in five minutes, and it might be a good idea for the captain to attend to have a clue as to what's going on."

"I don't need a briefing to learn you're going to drive us around in circles for six weeks before we head home empty handed. Of course, that's if you don't lead us into a nest of mercenaries who'll gun down half the crew."

"This is a simple search and recovery," Jack said. "Don't be so dramatic."

"Dramatic?" Braddock pointed through one of the port windows. "Why do we have a coast guard escort?"

Jack didn't reply.

"That's the problem, Sheridan. Your projects are never simple. They're complicated, and dangerous, and captains have a very short life expectancy around you."

Jack fumed. "Suit yourself. Screw the briefing." He marched aft of the bridge to where a cage ladder led down through a circular opening in the deck. He nearly racked his knee on the high-tech chart table in the center of the room. If he hadn't been so riled he might have asked Cooney for a demo on the thing, but Braddock's reference to Captain Beckett had set him off.

Beckett had been in command of the *Aeneas* when Rafferty and his men seized that ship. In Jack's first act of resistance, he and Beckett tried to retake the bridge. Beckett was gunned down by one of Rafferty's men. Jack had never forgiven himself for that. The revolt was an ill-conceived, spur of the moment plan that had little chance to succeed. If he had to do it over again, he would do it much differently. Stepping into the cage ladder, he hoped the *Achilles* would not be the stage for a second chance to do it right.

Jack descended two decks and stepped out of the cage into the operations center. The climb down helped to settle his temper, and he looked around at the updated nerve center of the ship's search and recovery systems with a cooler head. Dead center in the room about waist high, sat what seemed to be an oval table crafted from stainless steel with a tabletop of smooth, dark glass. It was the Looking Glass system Lloyd had mentioned; a graphical interface and informational display device operated by touch screen control. Jack planned on using it in his briefing. Although he and Rezner had gotten a quick training session during their walk-through in Port Huron, he knew he would need assistance from Connor to get it up and running.

Along the far bulkhead a control console with screens and keyboards stretched beneath a long ribbon of glass that looked down into the recovery bay. From that console Connor would operate the stabilizing thrusters to hold the ship in place while recovering pieces of wreckage and, God willing, the bio case. The console also contained the sonar station where Mai would have been stationed if Jack had not arranged for her departure. Markus would man the end section of the console to pilot the remote operated vehicle.

A smart board hung on the starboard bulkhead. Mounted beside it was a flat-screen monitor for video conferencing, which Jack was certain Lloyd would try to utilize as often as possible. A series of overhead fluorescent panels lit the space quite well, but as he saw in Port Huron the room darkened to half lighting during active salvage operations to clarify the information displays and speed identification of color-coded keypads. In a way the op center reminded Jack of a CNC compartment aboard a warship at general quarters.

The operations center had really gotten a facelift, and all the new tech gave Jack an added level of confidence that he would find the wreck and recover the case in time to save Lauren. Before he could linger too long on her plight, however, voices spilled in from the corridor through the port side hatchway door. The team was gathering for the briefing.

Rezner stepped in first with a handful of maintenance techs and operators from the recovery bay, chatting about the retrofit that took place over the winter. McElroy, the XO, walked in behind them looking just a bit intimidated by the team and the technology surrounding him. Jack knew the XO from his days with the company. McElroy had been standing in Braddock's shadow for a number of years. From Jack's observation that's just how the captain liked it; a second who preferred to stay second.

A pair of engine room mechanics Jack did not know rounded out the crewmen who would hear the briefing.

Markus entered behind the *Achilles* entourage and gave Jack an awkward glance. Connor followed wearing an expression that Jack had come to know as the "it's not my fault" face back home. Their behavior didn't make much sense to Jack…until he saw Mai walk in.

She was supposed to have disembarked the ship. Jack shot a peeved look at his son. Connor gestured his innocence. *It's not my fault.*

Jack locked his gaze onto Mai and opened his mouth to speak but she held up a hand to stop him. "Don't bother, Jackson. I'm not afraid of Post Traumatic Stress Disorder and I'm here for the duration of the project." She showed him the check he had given her for the two weeks' pay, ripped it in half, and handed him back the uneven pieces. "You said you needed a good sonar operator, and I'm it."

"I said you needed to leave this ship, whether you're afraid of Post-Traumatic Stress Disorder or not." Jack looked at Connor. "You were supposed to escort her to the dock."

"I did," Connor said. "At least I thought I did."

Markus stepped up. "Technically she's a stowaway. You can lock her in the brig."

Mai set her knuckle like a spike and punched him in the arm.

"We don't have a brig," Jack said.

"Well, now I'm here and you have to deal me," Mai said.

Jack fixed her with a stern eye. Mai had just made things a lot more complicated, and he couldn't do a thing about it. Her expertise at reading and calibrating the sonar equipment was the only upside to her staying. "Connor," Jack said. "Keep an eye on her. Make sure she doesn't experience anything that would trigger PTSD. Understand?"

Connor nodded.

Mai rolled her eyes. "I don't need anyone to keep an eye on me."

"Hey," Rezner said, "What's Mai doing here?"

Jack exhaled. "She's our sonar operator, where else would she be?"

"But…"

Jack turned and tapped the surface of the Looking Glass tabletop to curtail the conversation. The entire five-foot oval screen flashed on, turned blue during a start-up routine, and then displayed a large Neptune's Reach logo. Everyone in the op center gravitated to the display. "You all know why we're aboard this ship," Jack began. "We'll be at the search coordinates by sundown and will begin our sonar sweeps at sunrise, and I want everyone to know what to expect—and what is expected."

He swiped his hand across the tabletop and the Neptune's Reach logo slid off the side of the display. An array of icons swept in from the other side. Jack scanned through the application options and tapped an icon that looked like a scroll. A full-color graphic of Michigan and the Great Lakes filled the screen. The high-definition rendering provided texture to the land masses and ripples to the water. Longitude and latitude numbers ran along the perimeter of the oval display. Jack tapped another section of the tabletop and tried to open a second application, but the interface frame kept opening and closing and sliding left and right. "I can't get picture-in-a-picture to work on my TV back home, so I haven't got a prayer here."

Laughter rippled through the room.

"Connor," Jack said. "Get that modeling software running and open the file I e-mailed to myself on the ship's server."

Connor came forward and manipulated the touch screen with a bit more dexterity than Jack. He fired up a 3D model viewing application, accessed Jack's shipboard e-mail account, and downloaded the attached file. In less than two minutes he had a 3D rendering of a Douglas DC-4 slowly rotating in circles above South Haven.

Jack studied the image a few seconds. "Flight 2501 crashed when she flew into a squall line of heavy thunderstorms moving over the lakes. The most prominent theory out there says massive turbulence hit the plane with a gust load that broke her back and tore her apart. Based on pieces of light debris found floating on the surface she fell into the lake here." Jack touched the virtual model of the airplane and dragged it over to Abner's coordinates ten miles offshore in Lake Michigan.

McElroy wagged a finger at the screen. "No one has ever found the wreckage. How can they say a gust load tore her apart?"

"I said it was the leading theory. I think it's a very plausible one."

"How close do you think those coordinates are to the actual crash site?" Mia asked.

Dead on, Jack thought, but instead said, "No way to know for sure. There are a lot of theories as to why Flight 2501 crashed and where she went down. If we consider them all we get a search area that looks like this." He nodded to Connor.

Connor tapped a soft control button on the display and a scaled red rectangle materialized around the crash site coordinates.

"That rectangle encloses two hundred square miles of water," Jack said. "Worst case, we blanket the entire area with high frequency sonar scans. The high freq will restrict our speed to five knots. I estimate it will take us eleven days of around-the-clock sweeps to complete our first pass, and that's assuming minimal recalibrations along the way."

"Sounds like I'll have a lot of time to practice my golf swing." Markus said.

"Use it to get that ROV operating at peak performance. It won't do us much good to find the wreckage if we can't snatch up that bio case."

"What depth do you think the wreck is at?" McElroy asked.

"That's a good question." Jack opened a small application window and enabled a program. The rippling water of Lake Michigan transformed into a bathymetric map of the lakebed. The virtual DC-4 now hovered over the rim of an apparent abyss. White division lines dropped down into the underwater canyon like rungs of a ladder, each one numbered to denote increasing depth. "The crash site sits on the edge of the South Chippewa Basin. At its deepest point the basin reaches down one hundred seventy-five meters."

Markus tapped Rezner's shoulder. "That's about five hundred twenty-five feet for you old timers."

"Metric," Rezner scoffed. "Old timers like me and dad did pretty well using Imperial caliber bullets to win a bunch of wars against countries armed with metric ammunition."

Jack continued. "Flight 2501 was flying west at an altitude of three thousand five hundred feet. The storm front she flew into was moving east with recorded wind gusts topping eighty miles per hour. Given the assumption that she broke apart under a gust load, I did some calculations based on the plane's speed, weight, and trajectory, and the most likely manner of structural failure she suffered to define a hot zone for our search."

Jack double-tapped the airplane model and it separated into random pieces. "Once she came apart the individual sections scattered. Heavier pieces like engines and the cargo hold would drop quicker than wings and hollow sections of fuselage that could be tossed around more easily in the storm. Eventually it all came to rest at the bottom of the lake. In my theory of things, the most likely dispersion pattern of the wreckage looks like this..." Jack nodded to Connor.

Connor touched some controls and the pieces of the DC-4 dropped into the basin, coming to rest mid-way down the decline. A light blue circle blinked on and isolated the area.

Jack caressed his chin. "The center of that circle is one hundred twenty-five meters down, and its diameter is eight miles across. I apologize for mixing my units of measure, but that's a little over fifty square miles of area and it's where we will concentrate our search effort. We'll be able to sweep the entire area in two and a half days. Best case scenario is we find the wreckage by Sunday night."

A baritone voice boomed from the cage ladder across the room. "And when we don't find anything there, we'll expand our sweeps in concentric circles from here to eternity."

Jack cursed under his breath and turned to face the owner of that voice. "Do you have an alternative approach you'd like to share, Captain Braddock?"

Braddock put on a sarcastic smile. "You run the search, I steer the ship. Remember? I am, however, entitled to my opinion of the operation."

"Well, you know how I value your opinions," Jack said.

Braddock gestured to the Looking Glass table. "You're too far to the east with your crash site. The consensus is that plane went down about twenty miles from shore, not ten. That's where that Cussler guy conducts his annual searches."

"They haven't found it yet, have they? If I do what everyone else has done, I'll get the same results that they did. Nothing. We can't afford that. We need to find the—vaccine. Too many people are depending on it."

"You're the expert," Braddock said derisively.

"Mai," Jack said. "You're key here. Finding the wreckage will be easy in comparison to pinpointing the bio case within the debris field. We're looking for something the size of a suitcase that will likely be surrounded by other suitcases. We don't have weeks to sift through a hundred pieces of junk."

Mai nodded.

"I'll get you a picture and specific dimensions of the bio case. You need to train your eye to pick up anything that resembles it in the sonar image."

Mai studied the search area on the display screen. "The new sonar system has a sensitive shape recognition tool," she said. "It can determine the size of an object within a couple of centimeters. It will filter out a lot of debris we don't want to waste time on."

Jack began to feel less irritated that she had decided to stay aboard. But he still had to figure out how to keep her from seeing Rafferty for the duration of the salvage. To that point, it seemed time to close the briefing. He didn't need Rafferty catching wind of it and wandering down to poke his head in.

Jack stood back and addressed the crew. "Okay, we all know what we're after, why we're after it, and where we'll find it. I've no doubt you'll execute your duties with the professionalism I've come to expect from Neptune crews, but I want to impress upon you the importance of this operation. A lot of lives are depending on what we find, so let's make sure we come back with that bio case."

Approving comments and some hand claps rose from the crewmen.

"Get some rest tonight, because we hit the ground running tomorrow at oh-five-hundred." Jack led the way out through the hatchway into the corridor, not giving Braddock a second look. He peered left and right just to make sure Rafferty wasn't snooping around. Connor and Markus caught up with him.

"I'm going to check on your mother," Jack said to Connor. "You stick with Mai. She likes you, so it shouldn't be a problem."

"How do you know she likes me?" Connor said.

Markus laughed. "No wonder you're single, Sheridan. Can't you sense these things?"

McElroy, Rezner, and the rest of the crew filed out of the op center behind them. Mai talked with one of the recovery bay techs as they exited. Jack poked Connor. "Go."

"Right." Connor headed off.

"What about me?" Markus said.

"Go with him. He might get all swoony around her. If that happens Rafferty could pop up right in front of him and he won't notice."

Markus nodded and joined his friend.

Jack climbed the stairs to the crew quarters at the end of the corridor. He walked to Rafferty's cabin door. Before checking inside he felt for the pistol under his jacket. All set. He opened the door and found Rafferty and Ferguson sitting in conversation. "What are you up to?" Jack asked.

"We're plotting the overthrow of this vessel," Rafferty said.

"Not funny."

"Who said I was joking?"

Jack frowned. The man just loved to push his buttons. "We'll be on station by sundown, and the search begins at dawn. I recommend you stay put in here until then."

"Recommendation noted," Rafferty said in a very non-committal tone.

Jack closed the cabin door and walked down the corridor to his quarters. He entered and found Lauren sleeping on the bunk. Not wanting to disturb her, he crept out again. He walked the ship from stem to stern, touching his boots on every deck to get fully acquainted with the layout of the vessel. He ended his tour on the bow at the base of the forecastle.

The sun had fallen near the horizon and the sky glowed deep amber. Jack felt the engines rumbling inside the ship. It was nearly eight o'clock, and he figured they had to be close to the crash site coordinates. Far off the starboard quarter a tall ship sailed. Jack estimated her to be about sixty feet long, sparred length around a hundred. She seemed to be adjusting her heading to angle toward the *Achilles.* Jack watched her as she approached. He recognized the shape of her wooden hull and the arrangement of her sails and rigging. She was the *Friends Good Will* out of South Haven, a replica nineteenth-century sloop built and operated by the maritime museum in town. In the summer season, the museum scheduled regular day and evening sails for tourists. Apparently she was out on one of her sunset cruises.

The sight of her reminded Jack of Wallace Garity's transom yacht, and his desire to own such a vessel. Money wasn't his problem any longer. The problem had become his pre-occupation with the inevitable return of Donovan Rafferty. Now that the man had indeed resurfaced, Jack was rather busy trying to save his wife's life, deter a Memorial Day terror threat, and end his conflict with the boogeyman for good. Peaceful days sailing the Great Lakes would have to wait just a bit longer.

Friends Good Will came a little too close for the coast guard's comfort. The cutters escorting the *Achilles* revved their engines and set a course to intercept the approaching sloop. Passengers on the sailing ship waved at the patrol boats. The voice of the lead cutter's commander called through a PA speaker. Jack couldn't make out his words but was certain the sloop was being warned to stay back beyond a certain perimeter around the salvage vessel. *Friends Good Will* responded to the order and adjusted course accordingly. Jack watched the scene play out and wondered how he had gotten entangled in another complicated, dangerous, salvage project.

It occurred to him that Captain Braddock just might have a point.

Jack returned to his cabin, this time finding Lauren awake although still lying in the bunk. She gave him a little smile. He walked over and sat next to her on the bunk. "Feeling okay?"

"A little better now," she said. "We got underway and I got queasy. Nauseated, actually."

Jack recalled the plague symptoms Rafferty had mentioned. "Nauseated?"

They looked at each other. She spoke first. "I get seasick. Remember?"

"Yeah, I know. It's just that…"

She sat up and settled back on her pillow. "I'm feeling better. It was just the movement of the ship."

"I don't mean to overreact, but how can we be sure of that?"

"*We* can be sure because *I'm* sure. Okay?"

"Okay." Jack noticed the little white pill bottle that Rafferty had given them sitting on the table near the bunk. If she had dug that out of the luggage, it meant that she wasn't as sure as she led on. "Did you take one of those?"

"No."

"Are you going to?"

She hesitated. "No. It's too soon to buy into this whole…situation."

He put a hand on her forehead to feel for a temperature.

"Jack, please. It's only been two days."

"People react differently to infection and illness."

"Well, if I have this plague I won't be contagious for about two weeks."

Jack smiled at her. "According to my plan we'll find the wreckage inside of three days. This whole thing will be over before it begins."

She bit her lip. "How can you be certain of that?"

"Trust me. I know what I'm doing. Why do you think Rafferty roped me into this?"

"Do you really think he'll deliver on his end of the bargain?"

"We're beyond that question. We've already bet the farm that he will."

Lauren beat her fists against her knees. "I can't believe that we're believing him." She looked at Jack and took his hand. "Pray with me."

"What?"

"I know it's an odd concept for you, but man up and humble yourself before God."

"I pray. How do you think I made it through—?"

"Shhhhh." Lauren closed her eyes and recited Psalm 23, and then asked Jesus to guide them through the tribulation with Rafferty, and the plague. Jack added his own prayer in silence that his nightmare with Rafferty would come to an end once and for all. Just so there would be no misunderstanding with the Almighty, Jack clarified that he wanted to be the one still standing after the dust settled.

When finished, he and Lauren sat with their hands clasped together, staring at the little white pill bottle and hoping their prayers had been heard.

- EIGHTEEN –

Mackinaw City, MI

The North Koreans said yes. Alec Cohn knew they would. After he had revealed to them the existence of the bacteriophage and the U.S. government's effort to recover it, he did not have to wait long for the official reply. The North Koreans quickly realized the blunting effect the phage would have on their plan to unleash the 731 Plague in America. They agreed to have Cohn neutralize the threat for them at a reasonable 40 percent above the original contract amount.

As a result Cohn had been extremely busy changing up his plans to include this new task on his schedule ever since sailing into port at the Mackinaw City Marina twenty-four hours ago. He wasn't sure how much manpower and resources would be necessary to keep the phage lost, but he wanted to be certain not to shortchange himself. Of course, drawing men and equipment from the primary operation meant delaying his march to Washington, and that in turn meant sailing with the flotilla into Chicago was off the table.

Everything had been thrown into the air but Cohn welcomed the chaos. Outside of the box is where he thrived. Kinetic freedom. That's what it was all about. He actually considered this mid-course adjustment a good thing. Cohn had been feeling uneasy about the plan ever since the close brush with the coast guard, and more so after learning about the colonel's recent activity. Staying the course had begun to feel wrong. Today was the first step in setting things right.

The sun had gone down and the lights of downtown Mackinaw City were lit. Cohn stood on the corner of Huron and Central in front of the Dixie Saloon. The sign on the front of the building boasted that the saloon had been there since the 1890s when the only route up the East Coast from Florida was the Dixie Highway. That pioneering expressway led right to the tip of Lower Michigan in Mackinaw City. Saloon lore tells that travelers would stop at the Dixie to celebrate reaching the end of the road. Cohn thought it an appropriate anecdote for his meeting here tonight.

He had left Speers to watch the ship back at the marina, and Anders stood next to him on the sidewalk. Earlier in the day Cohn had worked his contacts and found a man in the area named Peterson who seemed the right fit for the task he needed done. After speaking with Peterson briefly on the phone, Cohn set up this meeting at the Dixie Saloon. "Do you have any concerns over your role in this plan?" he said to Anders.

Anders shook his head. "No issues."

Cohn scanned a small crowd gathering for a light show on Shepler Street south of the saloon. "I've identified one set of eyes watching us, east on Central in front of the gift shop."

Anders nodded. "I see him."

Cohn lifted his cell phone and hit the direct connect button. "Byrne, anything to report?"

Byrne responded from his post at the Sheplers Ferry dock east of the saloon. "Yeah, Peterson is walking up Huron toward your position."

Cohn pocketed his phone and looked across the street. A man wearing a Wisconsin Badgers sweatshirt and a Red Sox baseball cap approached. The clothing combination was a pre-arranged signal to identify Peterson. "At least he's punctual," Cohn said.

"The guy in front of the gift shop is getting more interested in us. You sure he's with Peterson?" Anders said.

"He's definitely not law enforcement. Too sloppy." Cohn made sure his 9 mm was concealed beneath his jacket and observed Peterson's approach. The man appeared to be about forty years old and wore a scruffy red beard that seemed to have grown from neglect instead of intention. He was shorter than Cohn and Anders, and the Badgers sweatshirt didn't quite conceal his thick midsection.

Peterson met Cohn's gaze with a skeptical tilt. "Alec?"

Cohn gave a slight nod but didn't offer his hand. "Mr. Peterson, it's good to meet you."

Peterson glanced at Anders and snorted as if unimpressed. "I'm not alone either," he said to Cohn. "Let's go inside. There's a beer in there with my name on it."

Cohn and Anders followed him into the saloon. The place didn't look quite like it had during those turn-of-the-century days. Cohn guessed it had recently been renovated. A forest worth of cedar trimmed out an expansive open-air interior. Large cedar columns rose from the floor to the ceiling and intersected with cross members that spanned the width of the building to tie the whole structure together. The Dixie was fairly crowded for a pre-season weeknight. The loud drone of a hundred conversations buzzed in the air, and a man with an acoustic guitar sang a Gordon Lightfoot song on a raised stage near a small dance floor. Peterson apparently knew the place well and climbed a flight of steps to the left of the main entrance.

The second level offered a top-down view of the ground floor from a cedar handrail that circled the inner perimeter. Peterson took a seat in a booth next to a window overlooking the dock for Shepler's Ferry. Cohn and Anders sat across from him. A waitress greeted them right away and Peterson ordered a beer.

Cohn declined. As soon as the waitress left he said, "We only have five hours before I need your services, so let's get down to business."

"No bullshit," Peterson said. "I like that."

"You own an eighty-foot tug boat with ample deck space for hauling cargo. Correct?"

Peterson nodded. "There's good money to be made ferrying things across the lakes."

"And you'll make some tonight if we strike a deal."

Peterson grimaced. "It's a little too early to be talkin' about deals. You haven't told me what your cargo is or where I'll be taking it."

Cohn leaned on the table. "I'll tell you only what's required for you to get the job done. Do you have any concerns with that arrangement?"

Peterson read Cohn's face and grinned. "Yeah, I know what you're up to. It's plants or people, right? I'll bet you just came over from Canada too." He chuckled. "Guys like you are my biggest customers."

Cohn gave him an artificial smile. "You're very good at this. For the sake of discussion, let's say my cargo consists of exotic South American crickets shipped north to sell as food for pet reptiles. Call it bugs. I need to get these boxes of bugs off my ship and onto shore without going through the hassle of processing them through U.S. Customs. Understand?"

Peterson's beer arrived and he took a swig. "Perfectly."

"I have commercial incubators too, which are a couple hundred pounds each. Do you have a jib crane aboard?"

"Of course I do, except I'm used to talking in terms of kilos." Peterson laughed. "You sure those incubators don't weigh a couple hundred kilos?"

Cohn ignored Peterson's trade humor. "About eighteen miles west and twenty miles south of Mackinaw City is the town of Good Hart. Are you familiar with it?"

"Very," Peterson said. "That's why you called me, isn't it?"

"Tonight at 2:00 a.m. my vessel will be in the general vicinity of Good Hart. Can you get your tug into position in that span of time?"

"I need a little more positional information before I'll answer that."

"I won't give you specific coordinates yet."

Peterson grumbled. "What type of vessel are you sailing?"

"That's unimportant. All I'll tell you now is that Good Hart is within five miles of where I'll be. I propose to send Mr. Anders with you aboard your tug. Once you get underway from the marina, he will feed you the numbers."

Peterson drank his beer halfway down the mug and scrutinized Anders. "Do you talk?"

Anders sniffed and straightened up. "Three languages. Which one do you want me to use?"

"Keep it English. I've heard enough babbling from beaners, euro trash, and sand niggers to last a lifetime."

"It's not good business to bash your customers, is it?" Anders said.

Peterson looked to Cohn. "He has an attitude. I don't like him. Send someone else."

"There is no one else," Cohn said.

"Then find yourself another tug." Peterson finished his beer and slapped the mug on the tabletop.

Cohn faced Anders. "Apologize for offending Mr. Peterson."

Anders didn't hesitate. "Mr. Peterson, I'm sorry if my comment offended you in any way."

Peterson looked at them both. "You really need my boat, don't you?" He smiled.

"I estimate you'll need to make two runs from ship to shore to offload my cargo," Cohn said.

"I assume you want the transfer done before sunrise."

"I do."

Peterson thought a moment. "Is the coast guard, the FBI, or any other group that carries a badge on to your import business?"

"No, and I want to keep it that way."

"We have common ground there." Peterson rotated the empty mug with his thumb. "Ten thousand with half up front, like we discussed on the phone."

Cohn pulled a small package wrapped like a present from an inner jacket pocket and slid it across the table. "Happy Birthday, Uncle Bob."

Peterson took the package. "You shouldn't have." He ripped opened the end and confirmed it was filled with enough hundred dollar-bills to approximate five thousand dollars. "This is just what I wanted. You guys are too good to me."

Cohn climbed out of the booth. "After the party, you'll get the rest of your presents."

Peterson gestured to the mug. "How about a parting gift?"

Cohn fished a ten-dollar bill from his pocket and threw it on the table. They all descended the steps and walked out to the street. Peterson nodded to Anders. "Are you coming with me?"

"He'll meet you at the marina in twenty minutes," Cohn said.

"SlipFifteen. If he's not there in twenty, I'll assume you've changed your mind." Peterson signaled his man standing in front of the gift shop on Central Street to move out, and he walked into the street.

When Peterson had gotten well clear of them, Cohn spoke to Anders. "Byrne will shadow you to the marina and deliver the other half of the down payment. Call him in if you have any doubt about the situation onboard the tug."

Anders gave him a look like he'd just been insulted.

"Get familiar with Peterson's boat and its equipment," Cohn continued. "I want you driving that vessel by the time you reach the rendezvous coordinates. No passengers."

Anders smiled. "No problem."

"The other sloops left two hours ago," Cohn said. "We have to get the *Liberty* underway before too many people start asking why we're still here. I don't want Peterson to know we're the ones taking her out, so keep him busy."

Anders acknowledged and said, "Is the Chicago crew on the road?"

Cohn paused to decide how much information he should divulge. "Yes," he said, deciding Anders was safe to inform. "It took several hours to gather up the secondary crew this afternoon but they're finally on the way. They weren't expecting to take over for three more days, and that was going to be at Navy Pier. They'll be in Traverse City by morning. Speers will coordinate the crew exchange."

"That'll raise some questions from the crews on the other sloops."

Cohn brushed off the comment. "It won't matter. We'll have disappeared into the woods north of Good Hart by the time Speers hands over the helm."

"What's the word from Nix?"

Cohn started walking along Huron toward the marina. "He reports that the recovery vessel has stopped ten miles off the coast between St. Joseph and South Haven. He thinks they've reached their search site."

"Now what?" Anders asked.

"I go down there tomorrow and assess the situation with Nix. Based on what I see I'll decide what action to take next. Until then you and the rest of the men will hunker down in Good Hart under Speers' supervision."

"This is one twisted road we're on," Anders said.

Cohn chuckled. "Where is the fun in driving a straight path?" He checked the time on his cell. "You better meet with Peterson before he gets spooked."

"Right." Anders took off ahead of Cohn.

"One more thing," Cohn said.

Anders turned and listened.

"Get my money back from Peterson before you dump him over the side."

- NINETEEN –

Friday
Aboard the *Achilles*
42° 21' N / 86° 29' W

Jack stepped into the op center at half past five in the morning with a cup of bitter coffee from the galley in his hand. He'd given the crew a kick-off time of six o'clock, so no one else had arrived yet. He scanned the empty technology-packed room and felt the weight of the task ahead of him. He'd been here dozens of times before, standing at the ready minutes before the start of a new search operation, but never before had the outcome been so important to him. If he failed Lauren would die.

That cold, simple fact cut through all the complexity of the situation. In the grand view of things nothing else mattered, not the conspiracy or the deception, not the extortion or the threats, not even the road that got him here mattered anymore. The only thing that mattered was finding that bio case as quickly as possible.

The hand that he broke on Garity's ship ached, and Jack set the coffee down in a holder beside the Looking Glass table. He reached down and touched the tabletop. The big oval display flickered to life and the map of Michigan and the lake materialized. He swept his hand over the glass and zoomed in on the search coordinates. The translucent blue circle defining the prime search area grew to fill a quarter of the screen. The bathymetric image of the South Chippewa Basin appeared beneath it. At the edge of the blue circle an icon representing the *Achilles* materialized. The display software gave the image of the ship an illusion of depth to suggest it was floating on the lake above the basin. A block of text displaying the name of the vessel, her coordinate position, her speed, and her heading was tethered to the icon with a leader line.

Two other vessel icons blinked into existence on either side of the *Achilles*. The icon to starboard was identified as United States Coast Guard cutter *Thunder Bay*, the new Marine Protector class boat. The icon to port was the older Point class cutter *Commodore Perry*. Three other unidentified vessels drifted east of the search area closer to shore. Most likely they were sailboats or fishing boats that the *Achilles'* surface radar had picked up. Jack stood back and marveled at the virtual rendering of the lake environment.

"It's pretty cool stuff, isn't it?" Connor said.

Jack looked up and found his son standing in the hatchway. "Very cool. We never dreamt of this kind of tech when I started in the maritime industry twenty years ago."

Connor walked into the op center and absently cast his gaze around the room. He settled his eyes back on his father and stood silent. Jack could almost see the three hundred-pound gorilla in there with them. Connor cleared his throat. "Is Mom going to be okay?"

Jack hesitated. "I don't know."

"You're supposed to know," Connor said. "You always had the answer when I was growing up. How about one more time for old time sake you tell me you've got it all figured out and you're going to make it work?"

"I wish I could," Jack said quietly. "The truth is even if we're successful out here we can lose. There are no guarantees."

"That's not what I wanted to hear."

"It's the truth, Connor, I won't lie to you. You're not a kid I can impress with bravado and simple promises anymore. You're an adult. You don't need me to prop you up like that."

Connor stood mute a long while. "Yeah, I do," he finally said.

Jack walked over and put a hand on Connor's shoulder and looked him in the eye. "One thing I will tell you is we can't give up. We have to do whatever it takes to retrieve that bio case. Understand that if we fail on our end it really will be over. We have to succeed and have faith it will all work out. Your mother does. She's got more faith than both of us combined. We need to follow her example."

"You're right about that." Connor walked to the end of the Looking Glass. "So how do we attack that search area?"

Jack eyed the lake graphic. "We charge right down the middle." He walked around the table and glided his hand toward the crash site as if it was an approaching aircraft. "Flight 2501 broke up in mid-air, so her pieces would have hit the water with some forward momentum and would have dispersed from east to west; therefore, our first sonar pass will bisect the circle on that same vector." Jack touched the edge of the blue circle nearest the coast and traced a line along its diameter. An actual dashed line followed his finger. "We'll position the *Achilles* on the eastern tangent and plow westward. Once we reach the other side of the search area, we'll come about and parallel our path back. We'll keep it up until we've swept the entire area."

Connor nodded his agreement. "Okay, so what are we waiting for?"

Mai stepped through the hatchway door. "You're not waiting for your sonar operator. She's right here."

Jack checked the time on a panel readout. "You're fifteen minutes early."

"Just giving the company their money's worth." Mai plopped into the chair behind the sonar station and swiveled around. "PTSD notwithstanding." She went to work running the sonar equipment through a series of diagnostic tests.

Jack had to admire her spirited belligerence. He turned to the starboard bulkhead and keyed a switch on the communication panel next to the white board. "Bridge-Ops. Are we good to maneuver?"

Braddock's grumpy voice replied through the intercom panel. "Just waiting on you."

"Standby for set-up coordinates." Jack walked to the Looking Glass and tapped the point on the circle's radius where he intended to penetrate the search area. A dialog box popped up with longitude and latitude numbers inside. Jack returned to the comm panel. "Coordinates should be on the ECDIS now."

After a few seconds Braddock replied, "Cooney confirms receipt of coordinates."

"Position us at those numbers," Jack said. "And then we're off and running."

"Into the abyss," Braddock said.

"Ops out." Jack shook his head and turned from the panel.

Rezner and two crewmen walked in at that moment. The *Achilles* shifted under their feet. Rezner gave Jack a look. "You couldn't wait for us?"

"We're just maneuvering into position. Don't worry, there's plenty left to do." Jack motioned to the crewmen. "Hart, work with Connor on firing up the stabilizers. Parson, monitor atmospherics and surface traffic."

Connor settled behind his control station and threw a series of switches. "Powering up servos. Setting track mode." He glanced over at Mai. "Just like back in the day."

She smiled but kept her eyes on her monitor. "Diagnostic-A complete."

Hart walked over. "I zeroed the servos yesterday. Those pods should be telling you exactly where they are."

Connor glanced at a set of yellow indicators on a display screen. "Pods are green, but the over-current safety circuits for the thruster engines are tripped."

Hart cursed. "I forgot to reset them. I'll get down there right now and do it." He pushed through a hatchway at the end of the control console and made his way down a steep set of steel stairs that led to the floor of the recovery bay. He cautiously made his way across the floor in half-lighting. Standing at the observation window, Rezner searched a bank of switches on the bulkhead until he found a set for the overhead fixtures and flicked them on. The cavernous recovery bay beneath the op center lit up like day. Hart signaled his thanks and kept going.

The *Achilles* icon on the Looking Glass came about and approached the entry tangent of the search area. The coast guard cutters gave the search vessel a wide berth. Jack watched the activity rather pensively, silently praying to defy the odds and find the wreck on their first pass. Someone touched his hand.

"How are we doing so far?" Lauren said.

Jack looked at her and smiled. She must have slipped in while he was occupied with the display. "We're just getting started," he said. "Why aren't you sleeping?"

"I didn't want to miss the first day of the rest of my life."

"Diagnostic-B complete," Mai said. "Calibrating - Narrow beam, high frequency."

Connor leaned toward her. "Pick it up. It's almost game time."

"Just worry about your station," she said. "I'll be ready."

Connor glanced across his monitors. Hart had not reset the engine safeties yet. And then he saw a blank field where there should have been numbers. "Hey, I'm not getting atmospheric input from Looking Glass."

Parson searched through a series of display screens at his station on the Looking Glass table. "That's one we missed in Port Huron," he said. "I'll pop in some code to transfer the feed to you, Connor."

Lauren tugged on Jack's sleeve. "What's atmospheric input and why does Connor need it?"

"Atmospherics is the environment surrounding the ship," Jack said. "Wind speed, wind direction, wave height, water currents, everything that could affect the ship's course. Connor needs that information to instruct the thrusters to compensate for those outside forces. This ship must run straight and true to the extreme."

"Why is that so important?"

"We're using high-def sonar imaging. Subtle shifts in course can blur the image of the lakebed." He squeezed her hand. "We don't want to miss anything down there."

One by one the yellow indicators on Connor's monitor turned green. "Mr. Hart, you are the man." He switched display modes and a 3D rendering of the underside of the ship appeared on his screen. Eight thruster pods arrayed around the hull showed their status to be green. "All set," Connor said, "except for those atmospheric inputs."

"A few more seconds," Parson said.

Braddock's voice crackled into the op center. "We'll be on the numbers in one minute."

Jack turned and toggled the transmit switch. "Once we hit the mark, lay in course two-seven-zero and reduce speed to five knots."

"Acknowledged."

"Calibrating," Mai said. "Wide beam, high frequency."

Connor chuckled. "You're going to miss the first thirty seconds of our first pass."

Mai frowned. "Look who's talking. Got your atmospherics yet?"

Connor glanced at the empty data field just as the feed appeared. "Sure do."

Mai linked her sonar station into the bathymetric chart on the Looking Glass. "A coffee from the galley says I'm online and scanning by the time we cross the line."

"That's a small wager," Connor said. "You must not be too confident."

"If I make it in time, you'll have to bring me a coffee every morning we're out here."

"With only fifteen seconds left? You're on."

Mai hit a key on the console and settled back in her chair. "Scanning."

Connor looked at her display screen and a crystal clear grayscale image of the lake bottom passing beneath the *Achilles* appeared.

"Adjusting course and speed," Braddock's voice said. "We're in the zone."

"Shouldn't you be stabilizing me?" Mai said to Connor.

"Crap." Connor reached for his controls and fired up the thruster engines. "Thrusters coming online, quarter speed in tracking mode."

Mai observed the resolution of her sonar image. "One cream, two sugars, please."

Lauren glanced over Mai's shoulder and studied the picture of the lakebed produced by sound wave reflections. She turned to ask Jack a question but caught sight of someone standing in the hatchway to the corridor. "Visitor," she said.

Jack lifted his head from the Looking Glass display. Donovan Rafferty met his gaze. Jack quickly checked to make sure Mai had her back to him, and then stepped around the display table to position himself in front of the uninvited guest. "I told you to stay away from the op center," he said quietly to Rafferty.

"I told you I would access any part of the ship I chose," Rafferty retorted.

"There's someone in here who knows your face from the *Aeneas*, and if that person sees you our effort is going to grind to a halt."

"That sounds like your problem," Rafferty said. "Not mine."

Jack took a step closer but Rafferty didn't budge from the hatchway. "It's our problem, so if you want to throw a monkey wrench into the works before we get off the starting blocks just step inside."

Rafferty peered into the op center and seemed to be contemplating the merits of ignoring Jack's warning. "It's the Asian girl at the sonar station, isn't it? I recognize her."

Jack didn't reply.

"If memory serves she knows her job well." Rafferty considered the situation a moment longer. "You should have planned this better."

"Maybe you should have told me you were coming along."

"I can't tell you everything." Rafferty stepped back into the corridor. "I won't play this game the whole voyage. Figure out a solution."

"How about you climb into a lifeboat and paddle away? That would work."

Rafferty ignored him. "I expect frequent progress reports." He left the op center hatchway and headed for a stairwell that led topside.

Jack turned back into the room and found Lauren staring into the space where Rafferty had been standing.

- TWENTY –

Topside Cargo Deck: *Achilles*

Rafferty walked across the cargo deck and met Ferguson near the starboard gunwale. Ferguson had his hands jammed into his pockets and tucked his head like a turtle as a wind gust buffeted his thick sweatshirt. Rafferty didn't feel the chill quite as severe and decided not to expend much thought as to why. He set a cigarette between his lips and scanned the deck. At this early hour topside activity was non-existent, with the exception of Markus Sweetwood driving golf balls into the lake off the stern. Rafferty grabbed his cigarette lighter but held off igniting it in another wind gust. "They've started their search," he said.

Ferguson nodded toward Markus. "Why isn't that ass-wipe in the op center with the rest of them?"

"They don't need him yet. They've only just begun scanning the lakebed."

"How long?" Ferguson asked.

"Unknown." Rafferty opened and closed the lid of the steel lighter. "Sheridan thinks he can find the wreckage within three days."

"Do you think he can?"

"I wouldn't be here if I didn't."

"We're going to miss Chicago."

"I figured that would probably happen."

Ferguson gave Rafferty a look like he didn't get it. "So then what?"

"We shift our attention to Washington."

"It gets more difficult the farther east we go, doesn't it?"

Rafferty slapped the lid closed. "We are where we need to be. In case you've forgotten, this part of the plan is critical. Chicago is secondary to what happens on this ship."

"I haven't forgotten," Ferguson said. "I just want to hurry it along." He cast a glance at Markus. "Me and Marko have some unfinished business we started on the *Aeneas*. Bastard cracked me in the head with a golf club, probably the one he's using right now. Can I at least settle up and throw him and his bag of Pinnacles into the lake?"

"You seem to have an abundance of unfinished business." The wind subsided and Rafferty took the opportunity to light his cigarette. "I remind you again, this crew is untouchable until we get the bio case."

"And after we get the case?"

"I'll decide that when the time comes."

Ferguson frowned.

"Don't sulk," Rafferty said. "Make yourself useful. Recon the ship, watch the crew, keep appraised of all activity. We need to be on top of this effort."

Ferguson nodded and started off with a hint of rebellious hesitation his step. He looked over at Markus.

"Keep on task," Rafferty warned.

Ferguson averted his gaze and kept moving toward the forecastle hatchway beside the Zodiac. Rafferty took a drag off the cigarette. Far in the distance a boat trolled slowly through the water. She looked to be a thirty-footer with fishing lines in the water. Rafferty wondered what people saw in a sport that consumed so much time yet offered so little activity. Fishing just didn't fit his temperament. He closed his eyes and contemplated his end game. *Vengeance is mine, sayeth the Lord.*

He sensed someone standing nearby and dropped his hand to his pistol. He glanced left. Lauren Sheridan stood just ten feet away. Wrapped in a burgundy fleece sweatshirt with arms crossed and hair held up with a clip, she stared intently at the man who had planted the biological time bomb in her blood.

"You won't need that gun," she said rather dry. "You've already given me a mortal wound."

Rafferty moved his hand away from the Sig. "I thought you were in the op center observing the search effort. What brings you topside?"

"A question," she said.

"For me, I presume."

She nodded.

"Let me guess." He puffed on the cigarette. "You want to know--"

"Why?"

"Why I infected you with the plague? I thought I made that very clear."

"No." Lauren cocked her head with a weighty question creasing her brow. "Why do you do the things you do?"

Rafferty looked at her with an almost whimsical curiosity. "I'm afraid the question is a bit vague. Can you be more specific?"

"Why are you a mercenary?" she said directly. "What happened that turned you into a murderer, a thief, and a terrorist?"

"I disagree with that characterization."

"Do you deny you've killed people?"

"No, I deny I've murdered people. There is a difference."

"A difference, a nuance, a shade of gray; is that how you sleep at night?"

"It's simply the truth of the matter. Murder is a crime. Killing can be justified depending on the circumstances, and in each instance I've killed my action has been justifiable."

"Maybe to you," Lauren said with distain.

Rafferty studied the glowing embers of his cigarette. "The Bible says Joshua marched into Canaan under orders from God. He attacked and defeated several nations, and in many cities he put every living thing to the sword. To the Canaanites, Joshua's actions made him a murderer, a thief, and a terrorist. Is that how you see him?"

"Are you saying the things you do are comparable to the things Joshua did?"

"I'm saying perspective is everything."

"And when God is on your side, anything goes. That's convenient, isn't it?"

"God isn't on anyone's side," Rafferty said flatly. "He simply chooses certain people to do certain things. If you think about it with any theological honesty, you have to conclude that that is how he gets things done. The righteous and the sinner, the cop and the criminal, the good, the bad, and the ugly; they all have their role to play." Rafferty flicked a plug of ash off his cigarette. "All things serve God, Mrs. Sheridan. Even me."

"So that's it? God made you this way?" Lauren scoffed. "I used to teach a class of sixth graders. Some of them would try to defend their bad behavior using that same argument."

Rafferty scrutinized her. "You're familiar with scripture and seem to take your faith seriously, so how can you stand there and deny what I've just said?"

"Plenty of men have claimed their criminal actions were God's will. In the end it always turns out that it wasn't God that drove them to their crimes but their own selfish desires."

Rafferty felt his argumentative side stir. "You likened me to Pontius Pilate back in the cemetery. I rather like the comparison. He was a man destined to do the will of God too, although history is not kind to him."

"Pilate was a heavy fisted governor bent on keeping peace in his corner of the Roman Empire. The crucifixion was a means to an end for him."

Rafferty raised an eyebrow. "Do you deny God arranged for him to do it?"

Lauren did not reply.

"For who resists God's will," Rafferty said with a smile. "Does not the potter have the right to make out of the same lump of clay some pottery for noble purposes and some for common use?"

"Romans 9:21," Lauren said. "You twist scripture to suit your needs. A lot of evil men do that. They camouflage their actions with chapter and verse."

"Mrs. Sheridan, you do not see the face of evil when you look at me. Evil men build gas chambers to exterminate a race of people. Evil men fly airplanes full of businessmen and families into skyscrapers. Evil men murder millions of their own countrymen because they hold an opposing political view."

Lauren seared him with a glare. "Evil men release a deadly plague in a city full of innocent women and children."

Rafferty matched her. "Yes, they do."

"What are you going to do with the phage?"

"I'm going to treat your affliction."

"And after that?"

Rafferty turned from her and faced the watery horizon. "I'm going to do what I've always done. I will convince the leaders of this country they are not doing their best, and I will force them to improve their effort."

Lauren's eyes narrowed. "With a biological terror attack?"

"Spare the rod, spoil the child." He grinned. "But then again, not every measure of discipline involves harsh punishment. I'm afraid you're going to have to use your imagination."

"I am and I don't like what I'm coming up with." She stared at the cargo deck a long while. "If you didn't have me as a bargaining chip, you wouldn't get away with this."

Rafferty did not reply.

"What would you do if your leverage over Jack disappeared?"

"What are you suggesting, Mrs. Sheridan?"

She lifted her chin. "Use your imagination."

Rafferty threw his cigarette down and crushed it underfoot. "Don't be foolish. I told your husband and I'll tell you too. If you manage to sabotage my plan in some way, the ramifications could be more devastating than anything you've imagined."

"Devastating for whom?" she said with a sarcastic lilt. "For you?"

His cold, gray eyes fell heavy on her. "For everybody."

Neither of them spoke, and a wind gust blew around them.

Markus' voice broke the silence. "Are you okay, Mrs. Sheridan?"

Lauren and Rafferty turned. Markus stood a short distance away with a Pinnacle driver resting over his shoulder and a concerned expression on his face.

"I'm fine." She walked over to him. "Donovan and I were just having a conversation."

Markus gave Rafferty a suspicious look. "I was about to head down to the op center," he said to Lauren. "See how it's going. You want to come along?"

"Sure," she said. "I'm finished here."

- TWENTY ONE –

Lake Michigan

Alec Cohn steadied his footing on the deck of the thirty-foot Bayliner and lifted the binoculars to his eyes. He'd lost count of how many times he'd fixed that search vessel under the lenses in the past twelve hours, and each time it netted the same results. Nothing of interest. Cohn had determined that the Neptune's Reach ship was executing a search pattern of a circular area roughly seven or eight miles across. He didn't know how wide of a swath the ship's sonar scanned with each pass, but he estimated the vessel could not have covered more than 20 percent of the area yet. Once Cohn had figured out the search vessel's pattern he instructed Nix to set the Bayliner on a pattern of its own, one that kept them on the far fringe of visibility when the *Achilles* made her eastern-most turns.

"We're almost out of fuel," Nix said. "We need to head in soon. I don't think we're going to miss anything if we spend a few hours on shore tonight getting a beer, a burger, and a little sleep."

Cohn lowered the binoculars. "You're right about that. Even if they hit on something tonight, it will take some time to bring it to the surface. They'll still be out here in the morning."

"Back to the marina then," Nix said, easing the throttle lever forward.

Cohn lowered himself into a port side bench seat and watched the *Achilles* head west on another sonar pass. He focused on the two coast guard cutters shadowing her through the water. Depending how things played out, those cutters could pose a problem. Their very presence incensed Cohn, not just because of the tactical complication they introduced but because of what they represented; another tentacle of federal government reaching out to entangle everything and everyone it could reach. It's the very thing he sought to destroy, and not just the U.S. government but all central governments; they all had to be dismantled. After rotting away for three years in an Iranian prison cell for no crime other than possessing an American passport, he understood the evil of global politics. It amazed him how he had managed to learn in thirty-six months what the world had failed to learn in three millennia. The greatest atrocities inflicted on the people were caused by the very governments pledged to protect them.

Caesar, Napoleon, Hitler, Stalin, Mao, and Roosevelt all brought unprecedented death and suffering to their populations because of something as simple minded as political philosophy. The sins of the few imposed on the lives of the many. It had to stop. A man should not have to fight and die for someone else's ideas, but for his own desires and ambitions. That's what Cohn believed, it's what he wanted, and it's what he pondered as he watched the cutters fade into the distance.

"Did it go off without a hitch?" Nix said, stirring Cohn from his thoughts.

"Yes," Cohn said. "According to Speers they made port in Traverse City mid-morning and the Chicago crew showed up a bit after noon. He handed the *Liberty* over to them, and was with the rest of the men in Good Hart by three o'clock."

Nix checked the GPS unit and adjusted the Bayliner's heading. "So Chicago is off the itinerary. Which road leads to Washington now?"

"I'll tell you when you need to know." Cohn spotted a set of sails on the water north of their position. The sailor in him admired the vessel.

Nix saw the focus of his attention. "That's a sloop out of South Haven. She heads out a couple of times each day. I've watched her too. Nice reproduction."

Cohn pondered the information a moment and then turned back into the boat. Daydream time was over. "We'll be back on the water at dawn, so get right on refueling as soon as we put in at the marina."

Nix frowned. "Guess that beer is going to have to wait a little longer."

"Be sure to get your rest tonight," Cohn warned. "Tomorrow will be just as long, if not longer."

Aboard the *Achilles*

Markus stared intently through the binoculars, keeping the deck of the sloop in view while adjusting the focus. He steadied himself against the handrail that wrapped around the starboard wing off the bridge. "Come on, girls, where are you hiding?"

Connor stood next to him sipping a bottle of water. "There's a chill in the air this evening. I doubt you're going to see any skin on that boat."

Markus kept searching undeterred. "I swear I saw some bikinis a second ago. They adjusted their heading and now the damn rigging is in the way. I mean, with a name like *Friends Good Will* I expect a little charitable voyeurism."

"Wow, those were big words for you."

"Yeah? I have a couple of four letter words for you too."

Connor watched the coast guard cutter *Thunder Bay* break off from its parallel course with the *Achilles* and head toward the sloop under Markus' surveillance. "The show's about to end," Connor said. "The guard is on the way to ward them off again."

"Figures." Markus pulled back from the binoculars. "Where's your girlfriend? I thought you two might spend your off-duty hours together, work off that sexual tension you built up during the shift."

"If you're talking about Mai she's in her cabin winding down."

"Maybe you should be in there with her," Markus said.

"I haven't seen her in a year and a half. Our relationship hasn't progressed to that level."

Markus laughed. "I meant go there to distract her from doing something that might put her face to face with Rafferty. Play checkers. Fieldstrip a personal computer. Discuss the latest software patches. Do whatever you IT people like to do when you're not finger poking on a keyboard." Markus pondered a bit. "I actually like your idea better. I'd go with that."

Connor frowned. "It wasn't my idea."

"That's pathetic, Sheridan. Do I have to do all your thinking?"

"God help me if you do. You've got a point, though." Connor added, "About the Rafferty thing."

"I've got a lot of points. Just not everyone agrees with them." Markus peered through the binoculars once more and then faced Connor again. "How's your mom doing?"

"Good considering the circumstances."

"I saw her talking with Rafferty this morning," Markus said. "Don't know what they were talking about but both of them seemed a little intense."

"After what he did to her, they're not going to be all smiles."

"No, but he seemed irritated. Normally your dad is the only one who can rattle Rafferty. Your mom was doing a pretty good job herself."

Connor frowned. "I hope she didn't say anything to change his mind about treating her with the phage."

Markus did not reply. He snapped a pair of lens caps on the binoculars. "Have you stopped to think about why he wants the phage in the first place?"

Connor stayed silent a long while. "I try not to. It would only complicate things."

"I have a theory," Markus said.

The dull metal ring of someone climbing the stairs to the starboard wing halted their conversation. They turned as Mai stepped onto the walkway. She had her long, black hair down, and she wore a white cotton sweatshirt with an open v-neck zipper. Despite the chill she sported a pair of khaki shorts, which showed off a good portion of leg. Connor was distracted.

"Hey, there's our sonar jockey," Markus said.

Mai joined the guys at the handrail. "What's your theory about, Markus?"

"Poker," Markus said, "which reminds me, I've got a lesson in humility to teach Joshua at the card table." He gave Connor a slight wink. "Now don't get too geeky, you two."

"We'll do our best," Connor said.

Markus maneuvered around Mai and started down the stairs that she had just climbed.

Connor leaned on the handrail. "Who's covering the sonar station on second shift?"

"Nathan is covering," she said. "I've got the gear set to alarm if it detects bottom formations with characteristics of a debris field. He'll call me down if that happens."

Connor thought on that. "How can the system distinguish between rocks and airplane wreckage?"

Mai became animated. "The new software has a filtering algorithm that identifies regular geometric shapes. Most rocks and outcroppings have irregular shapes, so they will not trigger the alarm. We're high-def so we have the sensitivity to pick out machined parts from smooth rocks."

"Very cool." Connor realized they were actually discussing software. He'd never admit it to Markus. He looked to the horizon ahead of the ship. The sun was setting behind a thin layer of cloud. "Nice sunset. Pinkish-colored sky."

"Shrimp," Mai said.

"Shrimp? Are you serious? They have a color named shrimp?"

Mai laughed. "They've got one named salmon too."

"I've seen salmon. It looks pink. I think I'm color challenged."

They watched the sunset a while in silence.

"Why didn't you ever call?" she said out of the blue.

Connor felt a marble in his throat. "Good question." He faced her. "When I heard you were aboard I asked myself the same thing."

"What answer did you come up with?" she said. "I'd like to know."

"I never really came up with a good one."

"It's got to be better than what I'm thinking."

"What are you thinking?"

"That you just might be a typical guy who seems interested at first but when I tell him I'm interested too, a switch flips in his head and he disappears. After the *Aeneas* incident I thought something had started between us. Was I wrong?"

"No, you weren't wrong. It's just…" He avoided her gaze and rallied his thoughts. "After the *Aeneas* thing, that's a good place to start. That was a pretty intense event. We almost didn't make it off that ship alive. And, you know, they say traumatic experiences like that—"

"Don't you dare say Post-Traumatic Stress Disorder," she warned.

"No, no. They say intense trauma like that sometimes draws people together who may not have normally been drawn together, and when the experience is over that attraction fades away."

Mai's eyes narrowed. "Are you saying what you felt for me back then disappeared?"

"No!" He reconnected with her gaze. "I thought it might disappear for you."

She stared at him a long time as if parsing his every syllable and then punched him in the arm. "That's the stupidest thing I've heard you say."

He flinched and rubbed his bicep. "Well, sure, right now it sounds dumb."

She nodded but said nothing.

Connor stepped away, caressed his chin, and then returned. "I'm an engineer, right? I always need to know how things work, how the gears fit together, how the code calculates the answer. It must be the only way my brain works because I think that way about everything, even relationships. I look for external things that make or break them. The *Aeneas* incident is a good example. It's a good cog to explain the implausible."

"What's implausible?" Mai said.

Connor cleared his throat. "It's implausible that an attractive, intelligent girl like you would be interested in me."

"You should have let me decide that."

"I know, but believe me that all this garbage bouncing around my head is why I didn't call. It's nothing you did or said."

She stared at him. "Did you really just say, 'It's not you, Mai, it's me?'"

Connor considered her summation. "That's a pretty loose translation, but —yeah."

She slugged him again. "Figure out that cog."

"I think I understand that one."

She stormed to the ladder leading down to the deck. "One more thing." She returned and kissed him square on the lips with enough intensity to cloud his head. She pulled away. "It's two years later. Do you think the trauma of the *Aeneas* incident is still influencing my feelings?"

Connor stood there unable to think about anything but her kiss. "Uh, doesn't seem that way."

Mai raised an eyebrow. "Hmmm." She started her descent down the stairs and said, "See you in the morning. Don't forget my coffee."

- TWENTY TWO –

Saturday
Lake Michigan
42° 22' N / 86° 33' W

Jack walked into the op center with damp hair from an early morning shower. At half past five the second shift crew was still manning the consoles. He didn't know their faces as well as he did the first shift crew, but felt confident enough in their abilities to get a little sleep overnight while they ran the show. The reason he did not get a lot of sleep was the overall predicament he found himself in. Lauren was infected with a deadly plague bacteria and her only chance at survival required him to give up the phage to Donovan Rafferty, a man who had tried to kill him during their last encounter. And then of course there were the unknown implications for thousands of other people if he did surrender the phage to Rafferty. The deadly possibilities weighed heavy on Jack's shoulders. He had to find a way to navigate between a rock and a hard place. He had to find a way to save Lauren and deliver the phage to Abner.

Jack studied the graphic display on the Looking Glass table. The *Achilles* had covered roughly a third of the primary search area. Each pass they made improved the odds of locating the debris field. Time was getting short. Jack needed to figure out his plan of action in a hurry.

Conversation was sparse in the op center. McElroy served as the ranking deck officer and paced slowly from the Looking Glass table to the sonar console, his mouth stretching open in a wide yawn. He acknowledged Jack's presence with a casual nod that communicated nothing of significance had occurred on his watch. Jack walked over to the sonar station and observed the crystal clear image of the lakebed passing under the ship's keel on the flat-screen monitor. Sporadic rock formations beneath layers of sand and silt made the floor of the basin look like a desolate landscape in some post-apocalyptic movie.

The absence of airplane wreckage on that screen irritated Jack. "Are you sure Mai's alarms are turned on?"

Nathan, the sonar operator, looked back as if Jack had just jabbed him in the ribs. "Yes, sir." He opened a dialog window on the display screen and showed Jack that all the shape recognition alarms had been enabled.

"Just checking." Jack moved back to the Looking Glass and studied the virtual rendering of the lake environment. The *Achilles* icon neared the western perimeter of the search radius. The cutter icons dutifully matched her speed and heading. Closer to the Michigan shore a handful of unidentified vessels meandered back and forth. Jack figured some of them might be fishing boats and for a moment dreamed of being on one of them trolling for walleye instead of being aboard the *Achilles* trolling for a bacteriophage.

Captain Braddock's voice crackled through the intercom system. "Coming up on a southern turn. Executing in one minute."

Jack noticed McElroy yawning again near the stabilizer console. "I've got this," he said to McElroy. "Go get some rest."

The XO thanked him for the gesture and left the op center.

Mai walked in a few seconds later. "Morning, Jackson." She went to the sonar station and set a small backpack down behind the chair that Nathan was sitting in. Through the intercom Braddock informed the crew that the *Achilles* was beginning her turn. Mai watched Nathan as the ship executed the maneuver. Jack noticed she seemed displeased.

"Nathan," she said, "run my compensation program on the turns. Remember our speed and the beam's angle of incident to the lakebed change with the heading."

Nathan frowned. "It doesn't make that much difference."

Mai tapped the back of the chair. "Yes, it does. Get up, my shift is starting."

Nathan glanced back at Jack for support. He didn't find it.

"Let her in there to run that program," Jack said. "It's her baby."

"Right." Nathan rose from the chair.

"You did good covering second shift," Jack offered as consolation.

Nathan grumbled and walked past him.

The windows above the control console flickered with light. Jack looked through them into the recovery bay and found Rezner and Markus setting up the ROV for a systems check. The remote vehicle they were working on contained an intricate grappling mechanism that could gingerly lift delicate items off the lakebed, like a decaying bio case. Jack hoped they would have reason to drop it into the water soon.

The *Achilles* completed her turn and settled into another eastern pass through the search area. Jack paced to the Looking Glass with hands clasped behind him like a general awaiting the start of a decisive battle. He decided it was far too early in the day to be this tense and loosened his posture. Minutes eroded like hours. At six o'clock the rest of the day shift crew filtered into the op center. Parson took his position at the Looking Glass interface. Hart manned his station to monitor the ship's propulsion systems. Connor arrived carrying a coffee from the galley. He made his way to the control console and tapped Mai on the shoulder. She turned, smiled, and took the cup from him. Jack noticed a bit more substance to their interaction than the previous day.

The crew settled in and the search carried forward. Three hours and two turns later, the large screen on the starboard bulkhead flashed a message: *Incoming transmission.* It could only be one person and Jack did not want to talk to him, but he didn't have much of a choice. He thought about yanking the cable from the monitor, but the screen blinked on with a video feed of Lloyd Faulkner's face.

"Jack," Lloyd said gazing into the screen at his end, which gave him a wide angle view of the op center. "How are we doing with the search?"

Jack faced the screen. "We're doing just fine. What got you up so early on a Saturday?"

Lloyd sat back with a bemused grimace on his face. "You did. You failed to file a status report yesterday."

"There was nothing to report." Jack shrugged. "So I didn't."

"I don't care if nothing happens. I want to know about it."

"I forgot. You know all there is to know about nothing and you're always looking for more."

Muted laughter rippled through the op center.

Lloyd ignored it and continued. "You didn't even call Abner yesterday. That's not like you."

Jack crossed his arms. "You shouldn't be talking with Abner. I'm the single point of contact. Remember?"

"Abner called me. You're keeping us both in the dark. Why?"

Rafferty immediately came to mind, but instead Jack said, "Why would I be keeping you in the dark?" Jack turned and presented the op center like a magician presents his upcoming illusion. "Behold the crew of the *Achilles*, diligently manning their stations in search of Flight 2501. You are now up to date."

Lloyd set his jaw and leaned forward. "Why do you have to be so damned flip with me?"

"If you don't know after all these years, I'm not going to waste my breath explaining now."

"You're trolling around in a ship I've just invested four million dollars in. I'm entitled to know what you're doing with her."

"You know what I'm doing, and when we find the wreck you will be informed."

Lloyd stared through the video feed a long while in silence. "I don't like this contract arrangement between us. You're playing it too loose. You were easier to manage under the Neptune umbrella."

"That's exactly why I left. Is there anything else you wish to discuss?"

Lloyd fidgeted in his chair. Jack could tell his teeth were clenched behind his lips. "I want reports every four hours," Lloyd finally said, "regardless if you find the wreckage or not."

"I'll do my best," Jack said very non-committal.

"See to it that you do." Lloyd reached forward and hit a key on his desk computer to end the video conference. The screen went dark. Jack exhaled.

"That's no way to talk to the boss."

Braddock's voice came at Jack from the cage ladder across the room. Jack faced the captain who had just climbed down from the bridge. "He's not my boss," Jack said. "I'm his client, his customer. By logical extension I'm your customer too. Why don't you try something different for a change and keep the customer happy?"

"I know the pecking order," Braddock said, "and I know you. You and that admiral buddy of yours have got us deep into something. You snowed Lloyd somehow, probably waved a big check in his face. I don't distract so easy."

Connor, Mai, and the other crewmen began taking note of their conversation. Jack reprimanded them with a stern eye. "Mind your stations."

They turned back to their consoles.

Jack walked up to Braddock and spoke in a quieter tone. "We're just about halfway through the search area and I've got a feeling we're going to hit on that wreckage today, so let's just keep it together a little longer, okay?"

"I intend to. Just know that if I see a situation unfolding that threatens the ship or crew, I won't hesitate to shit-can the pecking order." Braddock nodded to Jack's side. "Looks like the FAA guy wants a word with you."

FAA? It took Jack a second to make the connection. He turned and found Rafferty studying the Looking Glass display. Unbelievable.

They were coming at him from all sides this morning. Jack headed over, keeping his eye on Mai. She and Connor were chatting back and forth at their stations. Fortunately, their attention wasn't focused toward the center of the room. Jack took a position on deck right in front of Rafferty. "Mr. Shaw," he said in a low voice. "You are in a restricted area once again."

Rafferty kept watching the unidentified boat icons drift east of the search area. "Does this device store the marine traffic information in an archive file?"

"You can't be in the op center," Jack pressed. "It's a ground rule."

Rafferty looked him in the eye. "You seem to be telling me you have not addressed your concern over my presence with the crew. As I've said before, this is not my problem."

"I saw no point in tormenting my sonar operator with the knowledge that one of her nightmares is roaming this ship. If you'd stay away from operational areas, we wouldn't have a problem. You can't seem to follow that simple instruction."

Rafferty smiled but resisted responding right away. "I have a purpose for being here," he said after a pause, "one that should be of interest to you."

"Then tell me and get off this deck."

"Your wife and I had an interesting conversation yesterday. She thinks she's come up with a solution to your dilemma."

Jack didn't follow. Lauren hadn't mentioned anything to him.

Rafferty read his expression. "No, I wouldn't imagine she'd discuss it with you. What a strange odyssey you're on; so many people keeping secrets from you."

"Are you finished?" Jack said. "I have things to do."

Rafferty's playful demeanor receded. "She's considering removing herself from the equation. Is that clear?"

Jack didn't speak. Lauren "removing herself" could only mean one thing, and the thought of her taking her own life sent an icy flash of fear through him. He forced a steady composure. "She'd never do it. It's against her beliefs."

Rafferty smirked. "Reality has a way of shattering beliefs on impact."

"You don't know her."

"I think I do," Rafferty said. "She believes her demise will free you to defy me. That's actually a sound bit of logic, but I'm certain you'd agree it's something neither of us wants."

"I hate when we agree. It means there's something very wrong with the situation."

"If your wife upsets the balance of our agreement, it would be a very bad thing for a number of people in Washington, D.C. I recommend you speak with her on the matter."

Washington? It's the first time a city had slipped from Rafferty's mouth. The Memorial Day plot began to feel more real. Jack checked over his shoulder. Connor had positioned himself behind Mai's chair to shield her view, but she was preparing to leave her station. Jack met Rafferty's gaze again. "I'll speak with Lauren. Our agreement stands. Now get out of here."

Rafferty judged Jack's resolve before turning to leave the op center.

Jack heard Mai's voice behind him. She mentioned a trip to the restroom. Bad timing. She couldn't leave her station until Rafferty had exited the room. Connor was already trying to delay her by asking a question about the sonar station he was to watch in her absence. She patted his shoulder, assuring him he knew what to do, and then stepped around him. Jack pivoted about to intervene but he was too late.

Mai hurried toward the exit hatchway. She looked up an instant before running into Rafferty. She began to apologize but froze when her eyes locked onto his face. Fearful recognition seized her. Survival instinct seemed to kick in and her hand flashed upward to strike him in the face. Rafferty blocked the blow and smiled. She retreated. Connor came up and put an arm around her.

"It's him," she said in a shaky voice. "He's here."

"It's not what you think," Connor said. "It's okay."

Mai looked at him with disbelief.

"It's good to see you again, Mai," Rafferty said in a pleasant tone. "I believe Jack owes you an explanation."

All eyes in the op center focused on the encounter.

Mai shifted her gaze from Rafferty to Jack. "What's going on, Jackson?"

Jack fumed. "Mai, believe me. Everything is all right. This is why I wanted you off the ship. I didn't want this misunderstanding."

"Misunderstanding?" She was clearly livid.

Braddock stepped forward. "What's the problem with our guest, Sheridan?"

"Not now, Malcolm," Jack snapped. He refocused on Mai. "Listen to me. This isn't the *Aeneas*. This isn't two years ago. And this is not the man you think it is."

Mai shook her head. "I know what I'm seeing."

The crewmen in the op center were tensing up. Jack felt it. He had to get the genie back into the bottle. "Mai, this man is here to observe the recovery effort. Nothing more."

Rafferty seemed to sense the atmosphere tilt toward hostility too, and he shifted his stance to a defensive posture. "We are all together for the same purpose," he said to Mai. "Whatever misgivings you may have, I suggest you put them aside."

"Go to hell," Mai spat. "I know you. I know what you do. I saw what you did on the *Aeneas*."

Wary eyes from every corner of the room fell on Rafferty.

Braddock came closer.

"That's not happening here," Connor said.

Jack scanned the op center. "Everybody stand down! Shaw is an observer. It's that simple. We are going to find the plane wreckage, recover the case, and we're going home. End of story."

"Mai thinks differently," Hart said from the propulsion station. "And she's pretty convincing."

Jack stayed close to Rafferty just in case someone got it in their head to take him down. If that happened, Jack would be forced to defend him. The thought of protecting his nemesis left a bitter taste in his mouth. He turned to Braddock. "Captain Braddock, are you in control of this ship?"

"Damned straight I am," Braddock dutifully replied.

"Are you afraid of losing that control to this man?" Jack said nodding to Rafferty.

"Hardly. I'm more concerned about your influence on my ship."

Jack frowned. "Fair enough. Since armed insurrection is not on my agenda, let's get back to searching for that damned plane."

"But Mai's got a problem with this guy," Braddock said. "And because of that, and the incident when he first came aboard, I think I need to detain him and do a little background check." He strode up and set his large hand on Rafferty's shoulder.

Rafferty immediately reached for the Sig holstered under his jacket.

Jack trapped his hand, stopping him from drawing the weapon. "Don't," Jack warned. "This whole thing will fall apart right now."

Braddock eyed him suspiciously. "What's your game, Shaw?"

Rafferty stared hard at the captain. Jack knew that expression. Rafferty was about to brandish the pistol and jump to the next level; the point of no return.

Jack inched closer. "Every fool is quick to quarrel."

Rafferty shifted his gaze to Jack. "A proverb? Your wife has great influence over you."

"She does and I want to keep it that way. Don't you want the same?"

Rafferty did not reply. He was still toying with the tripwire.

Braddock loomed over his shoulder, not budging from his menacing stance.

Deathly quiet settled over the op center.

Jack felt the tinder box about to explode.

And then a sharp alarm pulse split the silence like a wedge. Jack spun toward the source: The sonar station. "Mai!"

The rapid beeping drew her out of her shell of fear. She slipped from Connor's arm and turned to the sonar station. "It's a shape recognition alarm," she said.

Jack locked eyes with Rafferty. "This could be it." He broke away and went to the sonar screen. The distinctive shape of a DC-4 engine appeared in relief under a thick layer of silt. Mai's algorithm highlighted the contours of the grayscale image with a yellow outline. A large section of wing appeared close by. "We found it."

Jack returned to Rafferty and the captain. The discovery had transfixed them both. Rafferty had not drawn the Sig. Braddock had taken a step back.

"Very good," Rafferty said with beads of sweat on his forehead. "Now close the deal."

"I'll be damned," Braddock said to Jack. "Your theory was right." He glanced at Rafferty. "But he's still a problem."

Jack walked up to the captain. "Macolm, give me one hour before you do anything about Shaw. I'll explain the whole story. This is bigger than our feud. What we're doing here is important to a lot of people. It's important to me."

Braddock considered Jack's plea. He seemed to feel the weight of the situation and gave him a slight nod. "If there's a story behind those cutters shadowing us, I want to hear it. Lloyd just gave me the runaround on them. You're trouble, Jack, but you shoot straight when it gets down to crunch time. I'll give you that hour."

Jack faced Rafferty. "If you want me to get this rolling, you need to go."

"Talk to your wife," Rafferty said, "before she upsets the balance." He moved toward the hatchway and into the corridor.

Once he had disappeared from the op center, Jack projected his voice to reach everyone on station. "Okay, people, we found the crash site but there's still a lot to do. We need a clear picture of that debris field. All stations gear up for mapping."

The crew hesitated. Apparently the showdown had given them pause in following Jack's instructions.

Braddock noted their inaction. "Sheridan gave you an order," he bellowed. "Do it!"

The crewmen immediately turned to their stations. Satisifed, Braddock moved to the cage ladder in the back of the room. "I'll be on the bridge."

Jack acknowledged. When the captain had climbed out of sight, Jack went to Mai's side. "Are you all right to stay on duty?"

She glared at him. "You have a lot of explaining to do."

"I will, I promise. But right now you have to trust me about him."

"I do trust you," she said. "But I can't begin to understand what's happening on this ship."

Jack gave her a half smile. "Believe me. I have a hard time understanding this mess myself."

- TWENTY THREE –

Jack watched the sonar monitor over Mai's shoulder. The image of the engine moved slowly across the screen. The wing it had once been attached to lie at an angle unnatural to the original assembly, like the two pieces had drifted to the bottom independent from each other. Mai had enabled a filter in her shape recognition software, and the program now searched for objects approximating the size of the bio case. Each time the sonar beam reflected back from a candidate object, the station beeped and the program flashed a yellow outline around the perimeter of the target item.

"Connor," Jack said. "Give me a five-degree course correction with the starboard thrusters. Get us on the center line of that debris field. Coordinate the shift with helm control on the bridge." He watched the sonar screen a moment longer. "Are we marking these hits with GPS tags?" Jack asked Mai.

"Should be," she said. "All my data is routing to Looking Glass."

Jack turned. "Parson, verify we're logging these GPS numbers."

Parson switched modes on Looking Glass, and the virtual rendering of the search area blinked off. An electronic grid composed of light blue lines replaced it. A coordinate number in the upper left corner of each square identified the grid space. The image from Mai's sonar monitor faded in from black and filled the oval display beneath the grid. A white triangle icon tethered to a set of coordinates popped up over a handful of objects on the lakebed.

"There're your GPS tags," Parson said.

Jack nodded. He watched the display a bit longer, noting the slight course adjustment brought about by the thrusters along the keel. Another white triangle and a set of coordinates popped up over a half-buried piece of debris. He moved to the console between Connor and Mai and read status information off the equipment monitors. Rafferty's warning about Lauren distracted him. Remove herself from the equation? She would never do it, but then what did she mean?

"Dad," Connor said in a low voice. "Shouldn't you inform Lloyd we found the debris field?"

"I've got three and a half hours before I have to report to Lloyd."

"What about Abner?"

Jack didn't respond. He looked at Connor. "I'm still working on a plan for once we get the case aboard. A lot of lives depend on what we do here, your mother being on top of the list. I'll contact Abner when I get a better handle on a course of action." Jack peered through the windows above the console into the recovery bay. Rezner and Markus were down there working on the ROV. "I need to tell those two we found the plane."

Jack pulled open the hatchway at the end of the control console and started down the stairs into the recovery bay. His footsteps echoed off the steel bulkheads of the open workspace. The cube-shaped framework of the remote operated vehicle sat next to a retractable bay door in the center of the deck. Rezner had his hands inside the vehicle, reaching around a thruster pod to adjust a grappler arm. A bulky umbilical cord comprised of power, control, and communication cables was wired into the ROV and extended back across the deck to where it entangled Markus like a robotic boa constrictor.

"You two don't look ready," Jack said.

Rezner pulled his hands from the ROV and pointed to Markus. "Numbnuts over there crossed some wires and blew out three servos."

"Hey," Markus protested as he struggled against the boa. "It wasn't my wiring that was wrong. The source connections on the umbilical were screwed up."

"And who wired the source connections?" Rezner countered.

"Ask your buddies on the crew. I didn't do it."

"Enough," Jack said. "We just found the debris field. As soon as we're done mapping the site this ROV needs to drop."

Rezner and Markus fell silent and exchanged a pensive glance.

"How long do you think we have?" Rezner asked.

Jack shook his head. "Could be an hour, could be five. I don't know the density or the dispersion of the field yet." He eyed the ROV. "Do we have the parts on hand to fix that thing?"

Rezner deferred the question to Markus.

Markus dropped the bundled umbilical cable and stepped over it. "We've got two servos on the shelf in the crib. I'll have to pull the third off the observation ROV that we're not using."

"Get it done," Jack said. "This recovery is time critical." He added, "You know the stakes."

Markus and Rezner acknowledged the point.

Jack started back toward the stairs to the op center. Halfway there he stopped and turned.

"One more thing," he said. "Mai just saw Rafferty."

"Where?" Markus asked.

"The op center. Rafferty decided to pay a visit this morning."

"What happened?" Rezner said.

"It almost blew up in my face. When we hit on the plane wreckage it diffused the situation, but this operation just got a lot trickier. Mai's scared, the crew is suspicious, and I owe Braddock a complete explanation about this salvage in under an hour."

"You knew you were walking a tightrope with Rafferty aboard," Rezner said.

"I didn't have a choice in the matter." Jack gestured to the ROV. "Get that ready. You two are on deck." He climbed the stairs to the op center. The crew was still immersed in mapping and tagging the debris field. Mai gave him a look like she wanted to come after him about Rafferty again, but Connor distracted her with a question. The Looking Glass display showed that another object had been identified and plotted. Jack remained on station until the first pass was complete, and then ordered a starboard turn to begin the second pass over the wreckage. He left the op center and climbed to the crew quarters.

The news that Rafferty had brought him that morning preoccupied his thoughts. Before that conversation Jack was certain Lauren would never even contemplate suicide. She was the most selfless person he knew, and the thought of her life being saved at the expense of thousands of other lives would definitely trouble her. No, she wouldn't commit suicide, but she would run, jump ship, and hide away. Then how would he get the phage to her? He had to stop her.

A nervous twinge turned his stomach as he pushed open their cabin door. He expected to see Lauren sitting near the port hole reading, or lying in bed, but she was in neither place. The door to the tiny restroom was closed. "Lauren?" He listened for a response but did not hear one. He moved to the closed door. What if she had already made her break? He heard water running in the stainless steel basin inside the restroom. "Lauren, are you all right?" No reply. He reached for the door and worked the latch.

Click.

He threw open the door, but it jerked to a stop halfway through its swing.

"Ouch!"

Jack poked his head around the corner. Lauren hobbled on one foot and held the big toe of the other. A toothbrush dangled from her mouth and she frothed white foamy paste like a rabid animal. Her eyes narrowed at him. She spit into the basin and wiped her mouth. "Are you crazy, Jack?"

He stood agape a second or two. "Uh, I thought something might be wrong in here."

"There is now," she said. "My toe is bleeding."

Jack suddenly felt stupid. "Sorry, honey."

She scurried around him, exiting the restroom and sitting on the bunk in the cabin. Jack grabbed a bandage and an antiseptic spray from a little first aid kit on the bulkhead and followed her out. He knelt at her side and inspected the injured toe.

"What could have been wrong in the bathroom that you had to rush in?" she said.

Jack sprayed her cut with the antiseptic solution and she winced.

"You're not answering," she said through grit teeth.

He peeled the paper off the bandage. "Did you talk to Rafferty yesterday?"

She hesitated. "Yes."

"What did you talk about?"

She exhaled and lifted her foot to the bunk to look at the cut on her toe. "If you're asking the question, then you know the answer."

"He said you threatened to kill yourself to free me from my agreement with him. Is there any truth in that?"

She hedged. "I never said that. If he thought I implied it that's his problem."

Jack shook his head. "I didn't think you would do something like that, but you had me concerned you were going to make a break, try to get away somehow."

She looked at him with deadpan eyes. "And go where?"

"I don't know, out on a life raft, but that would be just as bad as if you slit your wrists. I wouldn't be able to get the phage to you."

She huffed. "Just put that bandage on."

He wrapped the elastic strip around her toe. "Why did you let Rafferty believe you were making an exit?"

She shrugged. "I wanted to get into his head and give him something to worry about for a change." She absently cast her gaze around the cabin. "I need to do something. I can't be his bargaining chip any longer."

He set her foot down. "Did suicide ever really cross your mind?"

She looked him in the eye and took his hand, and for a long while did not speak. She lowered her gaze to their clasped hands. "My life isn't worth more than all those others."

Jack sat on the bunk and put his arm around her. "It isn't worth less."

"I don't want him to use me as leverage against you." A tear streamed down her cheek. "You have to get the phage to Abner."

Jack lifted her chin and wiped the tear. "Running away won't work, and suicide is not an option. Understand? I'm going to beat Rafferty at his own game. I won't let this come down to a choice between you or the population of Washington, D.C."

She laid her head on his chest. "I love you."

"I love you too, so leave the tragic suicide thing to Shakespeare. We're going to get through this. We've got the tools, talent, and momentum on our side."

She smiled. "It's good to hear that bravado again."

"There's good reason," he said. "We just found the wreckage."

Lauren sat up and stared at him. "You did?"

He nodded.

"Why didn't you tell me?" She slapped his chest.

"My mind was preoccupied." He rubbed where she had smacked him. "It's good to see you still have your strength." He put a hand on her forehead. "And still no fever."

She took his hand and kissed it. "I still feel fine. Remember, we're just four days into the incubation period. And now that you've found the case—"

"We found the wreckage," Jack said calmly. "The case should be there in the debris, but until I have it in the recovery bay I won't relax. And Rafferty still needs to come through with his microbiologist. I'll be damned sure to hold his feet to the fire too…"

Lauren noted his voice trailing off. "What?"

A notion popped into Jack's head that he'd never considered before. Perhaps it was just a whimsical thought but it did make sense in the overall scheme of things.

"Jack, what are you thinking?"

He wasn't ready to share his thought yet, not before he had some corroborating information. He kissed Lauren on the forehead and stood. "If you're okay, I need to get back to work."

"Yes, I'm fine. Now go get that case. A hundred thousand friends and I are waiting for you to deliver."

"I will, but first I need to visit the bridge," he said. "I have to talk to Braddock before he brings the whole world crashing down on us."

- TWENTY FOUR –

"A hundred thousand dead in six months?" The number seemed to stagger Braddock, and he held onto the handrail around the port wing as if to keep from falling over.

Jack stood beside him with eyes fixed on the overcast sky ahead of the ship. "That's the government's estimate if the plague is released into a major metropolitan area."

"And this phage material in the wreckage is the only way to stop the spread?" Braddock said.

"That's what I'm told."

Braddock released the handrail and found his footing. "Why the hell wasn't I informed about this? And why the cover story about the vaccine?"

"It's all classified information." Jack said. "I found out about it the day before we shipped out, so don't think you're the only one that was kept in the dark. The critical nature of the phage requires it be kept secret. It's also the reason we have a coast guard escort with us. As far as this crew goes, they don't need to know if we're searching for a vaccine or a phage. Their job is the same. Retrieve the bio case."

Braddock thought it over a moment. "What is Shaw's role in all this?"

"Rapid response," Jack said. "He's to take the bacteriophage to a microbiologist as soon as we get it aboard and reverse engineer a living strain."

Braddock furrowed his brow. "Sounds like he's on our side. Why does Mai think he's dangerous? For that matter, why did Rezner draw down on him when he came aboard?"

Jack leaned forward and took a deep breath before spewing the next bit of story. "Mai is right. Shaw is Rafferty, the man from the *Aeneas* incident. But he's flipped. On this operation he's helping the effort."

"Rafferty?" Braddock's expression flashed to anger. "Men died aboard the *Aeneas* and he was the ringleader. I'm going to find him and snap his neck right now!"

"Hold up, Malcolm. Espionage and national security make strange bedfellows. This time around, Rafferty is on our team. He's the only reason I know about this phage in the first place. His resources will develop a living strain for us in a fraction of the time a government lab can do it." Jack let that statement of hope linger out there long enough to sink in. He added, "If Rafferty wasn't here, that hundred thousand casualty figure would be a guarantee."

"So we turn our back on what he did yesterday because he can help us today?" Braddock stomped around the wing and kicked the bridge bulkhead. "Bullshit, Sheridan. This is complete bullshit!"

"Yes, it's bullshit, but it's the hand we were dealt. The bottom line is Rafferty's involvement will save lives."

"A good bottom line doesn't make it right," Braddock said.

"I never said it was right. It's necessary."

"You were aboard the *Aeneas*," Braddock pressed. "You saw firsthand what Rafferty did. How can you go along with this?"

Jack just stared at him. "You have no idea how difficult this is for me, but it has to be done."

Braddock gestured with a fist. "My gut tells me to make this bastard pay for what he did."

"You need to promise me you won't."

"Why?"

"Because Lauren's infected with the plague," Jack said. "I can't tell you how, but she is and she needs Rafferty to develop the phage."

"Christ, Jack."

"Listen, Rafferty's presence here is extremely classified. Nobody, and I mean nobody, can find out he's aboard and involved in the recovery. Lloyd doesn't even know. This has to stay between us."

Braddock thought long and hard. "Complicated and dangerous, just how I knew it would be with you. Damn, Sheridan, are you cursed or what?"

"I'm starting to think so."

Braddock leaned on the handrail and shook his head.

"I've got you until the end of the voyage, right?" Jack said.

Braddock glanced sideways at him. "You just tell me when your wife is fixed up."

The hatchway to the bridge opened and Cooney stepped out. "Jack, the op center just called for you. They've completed mapping the wreckage."

Jack put a hand on Braddock's shoulder. "Thanks, Malcolm. We need to hang together on this." He went into the bridge and to the cage ladder aft. He checked the time on his cell phone, which didn't have service this far from shore. It was nearly eleven-thirty. He started down the cage ladder and moved as quickly as he could, skipping the last three rungs and sliding to a stop on deck in the op center.

Heads turned as he stepped from the cage. "Get me up to speed," he said.

Connor responded from the Looking Glass display. "We just finished mapping the debris field. The results are on the grid." He jabbed a thumb over his shoulder to the control console where Markus was seated. "The servos are installed and we're bringing the ROV online. Rezner is in the bay final prepping the deployment rig. We are good to go on your word."

Jack approached the Looking Glass display and assessed the grid. Dozens of triangle icons were scattered across an oblong section of lakebed almost a mile long and at depths ranging from three hundred to four hundred fifty feet. A number of icons were clustered near the southern edge of the field just west of center. "That group of contacts interests me," Jack said. "A bunch of objects the size of large travel cases all in one spot."

"Like maybe the contents of the plane's cargo hold came to rest there?" Connor said.

"You got it." Jack lifted his gaze from the display. "Mai, how many contacts are in that cluster?"

"Twenty-three," she answered.

"Evaluate the data from those hits. Compare each of them to the assumed size of the bio case and pick your top three candidates for a match."

"Yes, sir," she said monotone.

Sir? She really must be fuming about the Rafferty thing. Jack turned to Parson. "Reduce grid magnification. Let me see the location of *Achilles* in relation to the cluster of objects."

Parson acknowledged and the image on the Looking Glass screen seemed to drop away, showing a more expansive view of the search area. A ship icon appeared about three quarters of a mile northeast of the cluster. Jack went to the intercom on the starboard bulkhead. "Bridge-Ops. Come about to a heading of two-four-zero. Speed, four knots."

Braddock acknowledged and the ship began its gentle maneuver toward the cluster.

"Markus," Jack said.

"Yo," Markus replied.

"Is that ROV prepped to drop?"

"It most certainly is ready. All we have to be concerned about is my friend Joshua getting the umbilical reel spooled up in time."

Jack watched the ship icon move toward the cluster of sonar contacts. In ten minutes the *Achilles* had crossed the distance. Jack returned to the intercom. "Bridge-Ops. All stop. Standby for positioning instructions."

Jack walked to the sonar station, tapping Connor's arm in passing to get his attention. "Mai," he said quietly. "I'm sorry it went down with Rafferty like it did. In my defense, however, I did try to get you to leave the ship."

Mai frowned. "You should have told me why. I would have taken that check."

"I'm glad you didn't," Jack said.

"Me too," Connor added.

Mai eyed them both and then looked back at her monitor.

Jack cleared his throat. "I need to know that you and I are okay."

Mai looked him in the eye. "Give me your word this won't turn into the *Aeneas* all over again."

"I guarantee you Rafferty will not harm anyone on board this ship. Will that work?"

She turned back to her station controls. "I guess it will have to do."

"We won't let him try anything," Connor intoned.

Mai studied the data on her monitor.

Jack exchanged a glance with Connor. "Mai," he said, "how much longer before you've evaluated all twenty-three contacts?"

"I need another half hour." She noted Jack's disappointment. "You want this done right, don't you?"

"Absolutely. Take whatever time you need." Jack glanced into the recovery bay. Rezner was standing next to the deployment rig for the ROV's umbilical cable. He was jogging the reel forward and backward, presumably to check for unobstructed motion. Jack pressed an intercom button on the console. "Rez, are you ready?"

His voice echoed in the recovery bay, and Rezner turned around and signaled thumbs up.

Jack nodded to Connor. "Make sure all thruster pods are responsive. It's game time."

"Right." Connor took his seat at his station.

Mai continued parsing data.

Jack paced the deck. At all-stop the ship sat motionless. The absence of forward momentum felt strange to him, like the *Achilles* had somehow been becalmed in the doldrums. It made him jittery. It made him feel he was losing ground.

"Hey, Mr. Sheridan," Markus said. "You're wearing a rut into the deck."

Jack gave him a look but did not reply.

"We'll get it," Markus said with assurance.

Jack nodded slightly and went back to watching that pot, waiting for it to boil.

"Done," Mai finally announced.

Jack checked the time. Thirty minutes on the mark. "Show me."

Mai typed in a command string on her keyboard and then walked over to the Looking Glass display. "I've identified three objects that most closely match the dimensions of the bio case. They're color-coded green on the grid. They are designated as sonar contacts eleven, seventeen, and twenty-one, but I've labeled them as Larry, Moe, and Curly to simplify discussion." She glanced at Jack. "It just seemed an appropriate choice of names to me."

Markus spun around in his chair. "Oh, a wise guy."

Mai put her gaze back on the display. "I rest my case."

Jack allowed himself a brief smile. "Which one is our best bet?"

"Larry," Mai said with a measure of confidence. "Based on its dimensional data and the clarity of the image, I believe there is a 70 percent probability that it is the bio case."

"And after that?"

"Moe comes in second at 67 percent probability, and Curly rates a 65."

"Nothing in the nineties?" Connor asked.

"No. The silt, the depth, and the surrounding terrain added some clutter to the return signal. I'm surprised the numbers are this high."

"Parson," Jack said. "Feed the coordinates for sonar contact Larry to ECDIS." He went to the starboard intercom. "Bridge-Ops. Numbers coming your way. Position *Achilles* at those coordinates and shut down the screws."

"Pod status is green," Connor reported.

"Markus," Jack said. "You're up to bat."

"And I'm swinging for the fence."

Jack studied the Looking Glass grid. Of the three key sonar contacts, Larry was the deepest at three hundred eighty feet. The terrain surrounding Larry was studded with rocks and other debris, but nothing appeared obtrusive enough to impede the ROV from maneuvering close for the pick up.

After a few minutes Jack felt the *Achilles* come to another complete stop, but this time the doldrums did not follow. This time the stabilizer pods along the keel swiveled about to their holding position and the thruster engines fired. Jack felt their rumble in the deck, and he checked the ship's position on the grid.

"Right on the numbers," Jack said.

"And we're locked in tight," Connor added.

Jack went to the recovery bay intercom and keyed the switch. "Rez, we're ready to splash the ROV. Open the bay door."

Rezner checked the rigging that suspended the remote-operated vehicle over the deck one last time, and then hit a button on a nearby control station. The bay door beneath the ROV scrolled open and revealed the lake water in the recovery channel through the hull of the ship.

"I don't know about you guys, but I'm getting excited," Markus said as he checked over his controls. He tied into the bay intercom. "Rez, feed out about five meters of umbilical and then stand back. We splash in T minus sixty."

Rezner jogged the deployment reel, and a length of umbilical cable scrolled into the water. He called through a nearby intercom panel, "Five yards of cable deployed as requested."

"I requested meters," Markus said under his breath. He enabled the ROV's propulsion and video systems with a few keystrokes, and then displayed the countdown to release on his monitor. Fifteen seconds remained. "Rez, switch the reel to auto mode."

Jack prayed a silent prayer for Larry to be the bio case. He held his breath.

The countdown dwindled to zero. "Time to get wet." Markus flipped a toggle switch on his console and a magnetic latch on the deployment rig opened. The ROV dropped into the recovery channel with a moderate splash. "Depth is zero point five meters and all systems report green. Firing vertical thrusters."

The ROV sank below the surface of the water and the recovery channel became still. The deployment reel began feeding out umbilical cable at a slow, steady rate.

"Depth is three meters," Markus reported. "Descent is straight and true. Activating video."

Jack looked over his shoulder. "Parson, tie into the video feed and display it on Looking Glass."

An enclosed video camera in the framework of the ROV powered up and a pair of flood lights on the underside of the vehicle flashed on. Video of the lake environment began feeding back through the umbilical cable and appeared in a display window on the Looking Glass table. A hazy blue vista of fluid appeared. Without a frame of reference, it couldn't be determined if the camera was shooting down, up, or sideways. The lights caught a group of salmon and they scattered from the descending machine.

"That's good eatin' right there," Markus said. "Joshua and I don't see eye-to-eye on a lot of things, but he makes a great smoked salmon." He checked the depth read out. "Thirty meters."

"Stay focused," Jack said.

The water on screen grew darker as the ROV descended. The harsh white from the flood lights soon became the dominant source of illumination. Jack watched the number increase on Markus' depth gauge. He looked into the recovery bay to make sure the deployment reel was feeding cable without issue. Everything seemed to be operating fine.

Something changed in the murky water on the video feed. A pale color appeared in the fuzzy distance, like the ROV lights were hitting something solid far off in the depths. The gauge read one hundred ten meters.

"Here we go," Connor said. "I see the bottom."

Jack leaned forward on the Looking Glass table. "Markus, throttle back the thrusters and slow the descent. Let's not stir up a silt cloud."

"Right." Markus dialed back the controls as instructed.

The lakebed beneath the ROV clarified and a sandy terrain strewn with debris came into focus. Cases of varying shapes and sizes were scattered about, some half-buried, some covered in zebra mussels, several stacked one upon another, some broken open and some locked shut. Torn pieces of fuselage, structural framework, and coils of wire harnesses mixed in with the cargo hold debris. A handful of empty passenger seats stood in the sand like eerie tombstones amongst the remains of Flight 2501.

Markus stared at the video image on his monitor. "Uh, there is a lot more crap down here than I thought there'd be. I expected Larry to stand out like a sore thumb."

Mai shook her head. "That's not how it works. I tagged objects that matched the bio case specs and filtered out the rest. I didn't miss that other junk, I ignored it."

"That's great," Markus said studying the video again.

Jack did the same at the Looking Glass table. The exterior surfaces of all the cases were obscured by silt, mussels, or general deterioration. No distinct markings or features were discernable. "Mai," Jack said.

"Can you electronically paint one of these pieces of luggage so Markus knows which one to pick up?"

"Not quite," she answered. "The GPS tag can get us within a meter of the target object. That's the best I can do."

"So do it, sweetheart, you're killing my mojo here," Markus said.

Mai frowned at him. "Numbskull." She studied her sonar image of the Larry contact and identified other landmark pieces of debris around it, and then went to Markus' video monitor. "Here," she said pointing to one case among a trio of others. "Give that one a try."

"That sounded confident." Markus positioned his thumbs over a pair of small joystick controllers in the center of his station. "I'm going in."

Connor gave Mai a look. "How certain are you?"

She waggled her hand in a so-so gesture. He got concerned and she smiled. "I'm kidding. Of course that's it."

Markus took full manual control of the ROV. The left joystick guided the vehicle's position, and the right controlled a pair of grappler arms. He slowly brought the ROV in close to the case Mai had indicated on the screen. It stood on end with another case lying against it. Markus circled the ROV around to find an open spot on both sides of the case to grab onto. He used the padded claw on the left arm to hook the case's handle and touched the right arm to the other side of the case near the hinge. A small wisp of silt stirred when the grappler arm made contact. "Mai, I hope you're right about this, because once I power the thrusters to bring this thing up this whole area drops to zero visibility. The silt will be stirred up and we'll be snow blind for a couple of hours. We'll have to wait for it to settle to try again."

"I'm sure. Just bring it up," she said.

"You got it." Markus throttled up the ROV's thruster motors. The props churned the water and kicked up the fine sediment on the lakebed. The video image quickly became obscured by a thick cloud of ashen silt. "She's coming up," Markus announced. "Depth is decreasing." He checked a read-out on his monitor. "The weight of the case looks about right."

The ROV climbed toward the *Achilles*. It rose out of the milky cloud and the video feed cleared to show the case still secure in the grappler arms. Jack clutched the edge of the Looking Glass table and watched the ascent. "Come on, baby, be the one."

Topside Cargo Deck: *Achilles*

Donovan Rafferty took a drag off his cigarette and scrutinized the fishing boat far astern. It reminded him of the vessel he had seen the day before. Yes, one boat looked much like another, especially at this distance, but this vessel's trolling pattern seemed to place it in proximity to the *Achilles* during her eastern turns just like the one yesterday. Rafferty knew sport anglers often returned to sections of the lake where they had learned the fish were striking, but the *Achilles'* search pattern had moved her progressively south at least four miles from her starting point, and this fishing boat remained trolling at her stern. The overtly benign incident stirred Rafferty's instincts.

"I wonder if Abner has another set of eyes on this vessel," he said casually to Ferguson.

Straining to see the boat in question, Ferguson shrugged. "What's it matter? We're already aboard. Sheridan is going to give you the phage. Admiral Wilson isn't going to stop that."

Rafferty turned and pointed with his cigarette toward the cutter *Thunder Bay* off the port beam. "Abner has his close-range guards in place. Why would he put a long-range surveillance vessel on the water too?"

"Maybe it's just a fishing boat," Ferguson offered.

"Perhaps," Rafferty said pondering the issue. "There is another possibility."

Ferguson stared at him as if trying to figure out what he meant.

Rafferty didn't bother to elaborate. Instead he puffed on his cigarette and said, "You raise a good point, Mr. Ferguson. Abner Wilson will not stop us from acquiring the phage, but he is not the one I'm most concerned about."

"Who then," Ferguson said, "someone in the FBI or Homeland Security?"

"No, I'm concerned about Sheridan."

Ferguson laughed. "Why? You've got him in your pocket. He wants to save his wife. He's not going to screw with your deal."

Rafferty exhaled a breath of smoke. "Do I really need to remind you again? Do not underestimate Jack Sheridan. If he discovers a hole in the wall he'll slither through it. If he can scrape together the raw elements of gunpowder, he'll build a bomb and blow you to pieces. We've seen his resourcefulness before. We're seeing it now. In two days he's done what the U.S. military and scores of private researchers couldn't do in almost seventy years. He found the wreckage of Flight 2501."

"Okay," Ferguson conceded, "he's good. But you've got him flat-footed on a land mine. When he pulls that phage out of the lake, he's going to hand it over and we're going to stash it in our duffle bags and walk off this ship right under Abner Wilson's nose." Ferguson looked around at the lake. "By the way, where are they with the recovery?"

"I'm afraid Jack's been a bit slack with his reporting duties," Rafferty said through a displeased frown. "From the ship's movements I'd say they've finished mapping the wreckage and have centered us over a site of particular interest. They may be pulling the bio case to the surface as we speak."

"Don't you want to be in that op center to make sure Sheridan doesn't try anything funny?"

"Right now he's got his hands full managing the dynamics in that room. I will apply pressure when required. But that doesn't mean we won't be involved in the effort."

"How do you mean?"

"You will be my eyes," Rafferty said. "I want you to observe the crew's actions from the recovery bay. Watch but don't interfere. And keep your personal vendettas in check."

Ferguson grumbled. "Can I have my nine back?"

Rafferty shook his head. "A deal is a deal. You know that."

"Those jerk-weeds have vendettas of their own," Ferguson said. "A little life insurance would be nice in case they decide to act on them."

"They won't act unless you do," Rafferty said, "except maybe for Sweetwood. He might pose a problem, but he should be stationed up in the op center." Rafferty thought a moment. "Stay in the recovery bay. That's where the action will unfold anyway."

Ferguson turned to leave. "If they move first, I won't hold back."

"Mr. Ferguson," Rafferty said with smoke streaming from his nostrils. "If you do something to jeopardize the phage recovery, I won't hold back either. Do you understand?"

Ferguson nodded and continued toward the forecastle.

Rafferty turned back to the water. He scanned the horizon until he found that fishing boat again. Yes, there was another possibility as to who might be watching the *Achilles,* and despite how unlikely that possibility seemed it had to be considered. If true it would mean that Rafferty's bacteriophage operation had been discovered by the wrong person. It would mean a solid contingency plan had to be put in place in a damn hurry. And it would mean that Alec Cohn had become nearly as resourceful as Jack Sheridan.

- TWENTY FIVE –

The Bayliner pitched in a swell but Alec Cohn maintained his footing. He scrutinized the Neptune's Reach vessel a mile away and caressed his chin through his beard. The ship had been motionless for over an hour.

"They've hit on something," he said to Nix.

Nix sat with one hand on the wheel and kept the boat trolling on a steady course. "Yeah, but is it the airplane wreck or a shipwreck?"

"It's not a shipwreck," Cohn said. "They wouldn't be wasting any time on an old schooner."

Nix stayed silent a short while. "It didn't take them very long to find it."

"No, it didn't." Cohn spat over the side of the boat. "They might actually have a chance to stamp down the plague outbreak. It's a good thing I'm here to stop them."

Nix steered the boat into a long turn to continue their trolling pattern. "Are we going to stay out here a couple more hours to be sure they've actually found the plane?"

"No. I've seen enough. This Sheridan knows what he's doing. I say we move now."

Nix agreed. "I'll take us in."

"Do it," Cohn said. "We need to get in range of a cell tower. I don't want to use the short wave for this call. Too many amateurs monitor the channels."

"We're on the fringe now. It shouldn't take long." Nix nudged the throttle forward. "Aren't you concerned about the NSA monitoring cell calls?"

"This phone is an off-the-shelf model with prepaid minutes under an assumed name that does not appear on a watch list. Nobody at the NSA has any reason to pay attention to it."

Nix adjusted the Bayliner's heading toward the shoreline.

Cohn sat in a cockpit chair. "Are you sure about him?"

Nix stared back. "The colonel?"

"Yes. Are you absolutely sure he is aboard that ship?"

"Yeah, I'm sure. He and one of his guys showed up the afternoon she got underway."

Cohn shook his head. "That man was a mistake from the beginning."

Nix looked straight ahead. "I hate to be the one to say this, Alec, but maybe you should have killed him when you had the chance."

"I did," Cohn said. "He's just kicking up his heels on his way to the grave."

Nix put on a sarcastic smile. "What did that poet say? Do not go gently into that good night?"

"He's not."

Nix checked their position on the GPS unit on the boat's console. "Try your cell now. We should be under the coverage area."

Cohn opened his cell and dialed a number. Speers answered on the first ring. "Prompt," Cohn said. "Are you on edge about something?"

"No, just waiting on your call."

"How are the accommodations in Good Hart?" Cohn asked.

"We're holed up in Peterson's pole barn in the backwoods of northwest Michigan. The place smells like manure, the floor is dirt, and a hundred bats are living in the rafters above our heads. Besides that this place is Club Med."

"Peterson didn't lie about having an electrical utility feed, did he?"

"No," Speers conceded. "The freezers are powered, and the bugs are still frozen."

Cohn breathed a slight sigh of relief. "Good, we'll need the generators fully fueled for the next leg of the journey."

"Which is...?" Speers said to draw out an answer.

"We're flying out," Cohn said. "I'll tell you the target airfield when it's necessary for you to know. For the time being I want you and Gates to secure transportation for the equipment and the men. We can't rely on Peterson's 4x4 to shuttle everything out in pieces. When we move out we need to move as one unit, quickly and efficiently."

"How long do I have to arrange that?"

"Not very long. The other shoe is dropping right now. We're going to take care of that side job for the North Koreans today. I want eight men geared up with a full tactical package in South Haven in four hours. Rally point is the corner of Broadway and Church Street. We'll be back in Good Hart by midnight, and we'll move out from there at dawn. Clear?"

"Very," Speers replied. "Any men in particular you want sent down?"

"Give me Anders' and Erikson's squads. Gates and his men will stay with you and the bugs."

"Okay. Is there anything else?"

"No, just get the transportation set up. We'll need to move fast in the morning." Cohn ended the call and took one more look at the research vessel. After a long while, he swiveled his chair toward Nix and gave him a wry smile. "It's a nice day for a sunset cruise, don't you think?"

- TWENTY SIX –

Operations Center: *Achilles*

Larry disappointed everyone. When pulled into the recovery bay, he turned out to be a durable Skyway train case packed with surprisingly well-preserved clothing and a ruptured can of Burma Shave. Jack had Larry's contents laid out on the deck and thoroughly sifted through just to make sure nothing was missed. They went after Moe next and cherry-picked him from a collection of four similar-sized pieces of luggage. He ended up being a deteriorated Samsonite. Mai second guessed herself on Moe and scanned the area again. Another potential bio case hit resulted. Jack ordered the ROV down on the same coordinates a second time. Markus had to wait for the silt cloud stirred during Moe's recovery to settle before hooking the grappler arms around the next candidate piece of luggage.

Waiting and backtracking frustrated Jack, and when the second Moe failed to be the bio case either it compounded the emotion. He decided to abandon the site and instructed Braddock to move the *Achilles* above Curly's position. Connor locked the ship in place with the stabilizers, and Jack sent the ROV down a fourth time.

Looking Glass displayed the video feed of the now familiar blue-gray fluidic image. As the ROV approached the bed of the basin, twisted metal and remnants of luggage came into focus. Jack checked the time on his cell. They'd been pulling pieces of debris off the lakebed for five hours. Being on edge that long had begun to fatigue him.

The ROV's camera zeroed in on a cluster of five rectangular objects arrayed in a crude crescent shape beneath a thick covering of zebra mussels. Two of them seemed too small to be the bio case. The size and shape of the three on the northern tip of the crescent looked more promising. "Markus," Jack said. "Hover there until Mai pinpoints Curly."

"Roger that."

Mai studied her sonar images a moment and then walked over and touched the video screen at Markus' station, singling out the center rectangle in the crescent. "That's him," she said.

"Are you sure?" Markus said.

She gave him a cross look. "Trust me."

"I trusted you last time."

"Just do it."

"Yes, ma'am." Markus nudged the joystick controls to guide the ROV toward Curly. He spun the vehicle around to grapple the unobstructed sides of the object. A layer of silt stirred from the bottom as the thruster props rotated to stabilize the ROV.

Connor walked up next to his father. "What do you think about Curly?"

"I like Curly. He's everybody's favorite stooge."

"Seriously."

Jack opened his mouth to answer but got distracted by a message flashing across the flat screen mounted to the starboard bulkhead: *Incoming transmission.* He walked over and pulled the coax cable out of the jack.

"That was probably Lloyd," Connor said. "You're two hours overdue for your report."

"He's going to have to wait." Jack returned to Looking Glass. "Just like Abner."

In the video feed the grappler arms extended around Curly, and the claws at the end of the arms opened. They gently bumped up against the submerged piece of airline cargo and compressed a number of white-and-black-striped mussel shells. Jack thought he could make out a series of rib contours through the covering of mussels on Curly's top side, reminding him of stainless steel cases he had seen.

"Think I've got it," Markus said. He worked the controls, and the claws closed like fingers around an egg. "Nyuck, nyuck. Coming up." He dialed up the thrusters.

A swirling milky cloud engulfed the camera lens and the ROV began its ascent. Jack turned from Looking Glass and pulled open the hatchway door into the recovery bay. "Don't lose it on the way up," he said to Markus. "I'm going to give Rez a hand with the extraction." He descended the steps into the recovery bay and headed for the open recovery channel in the deck.

Rezener stood next to the deployment rig, watching the umbilical cable reel onto the spool as the ROV climbed toward the ship. Ferguson observed the activity from the opposite corner of the recovery channel, arms crossed and just about sneering as Jack approached.

Jack gave him a cursory glance. "We're bringing up another piece. Stay out of the way."

Ferguson did not respond.

Jack walked up to Rezner. "How are we looking?"

"The rig's looking good. I'm looking at that dipshit over there and want to knock his teeth in." Rezner gave Jack a once over. "You're looking like six miles of Michigan road. What's going on up there?"

"Nothing new. I'm walking a tightrope with the crew, avoiding Lloyd and Abner, and hoping Rafferty doesn't pay another visit."

Rezner studied the rippling water in the recovery channel and the umbilical cable rising out and winding back onto the rig. "This could be the bio case. What's your plan once we have it aboard?"

"Make sure the phage is inside."

"And then what?"

Jack cast his gaze to the far corner of the bay. "Honor my deal with Rafferty."

Rezner stifled a curse under his breath. "That's your plan? What about the plague? What about Rafferty's end game?"

Jack set his jaw. "I've been known to improvise."

An electronic tone sounded from a control panel on the deployment rig. Rezner checked a read out on the panel and silenced the tone. "The ROV is almost here. Ten more seconds." He glanced at Ferguson. "Any last-minute instructions, Jack?"

Jack shook his head. "Just bring it aboard. SOP."

Rezner nodded. "You got it."

The water stirred and a dark shape rose from the depths. The ROV broke the surface and bobbed in the channel, held buoyant by the thruster props spinning on the four corners of the vehicle's framework. Jack seized a hook at the end of a steel cable dangling from the boom of the extraction crane. He pulled the cable down and latched the hook through an eyelet on the top of the ROV. "Line on," Jack announced.

Rezner hit a button on the local intercom to the op center. "Markus, we're hooked up. Kill the thrusters."

"Soitenly," Markus replied with stooge-esque inflection.

The hum of the thrusters ramped down to nothing. The ROV sank until the cable caught and snapped tight. Rezner operated the extraction crane controls and lifted the vehicle out of the channel. Streams of water drained from the framework and from the encrusted case being held in the grappler arms. When the ROV and case had cleared the recovery channel, Rezner pivoted the boom clockwise with an axial drive motor.

Jack inspected the case. It looked similar to the last one they had recovered from the debris field. Of course, rectangular objects covered in zebra mussels have a tendency to look the same. Rezner slowly lowered the ROV with the crane until the case touched the deck. He signaled to Markus through the op center windows to release the grappler arms.

The claws snapped open and the arms retracted back to their stowed position on the ROV. Rezner pivoted the boom out of the way. Jack crouched in front of the case and studied it with chin in hand. It seemed fairly intact. No massive dents or obvious punctures. Rezner joined him and handed Jack a scraping tool. They went to work removing zebra mussels from the surface. Jack's thought had been correct; it was a stainless steel case. A good sign.

Jack focused intently on cleaning the mussels, so much so that he did not hear the footsteps and conversations descending the stairs from the op center, or the hatchway door swinging open across the bay. When he and Rezner had cleared the seam, hinges, and clasps, Jack set down his tool. He tried to pop the tarnished clasps but they were seized up.

"You'll probably need this."

Jack looked over his shoulder. Connor was there holding a hammer and chisel. Markus stood to his left. Lauren was behind them with her arms crossed. She made eye contact with Jack and he gave her a little smile. He took the tools from Connor and set the tip of the chisel against one of the clasps. He drew back the hammer.

"Be careful with our case."

Jack glanced across the channel and found that Rafferty had arrived and now stood beside Ferguson. Rezner came to his feet. "This is a restricted area."

"Restricted to whom?" Rafferty said.

"To you, you thick-skulled prick."

Rafferty looked to Jack. "Was Mr. Rezner's presence on this vessel really necessary?"

"Absolutely," Jack said. "It's you we could have done without."

Rafferty smiled. "Be that as it may, we are all here together now. Let's make do, shall we?"

"What choice do we have?" Jack gestured for Rezner to join him. "Hold the case steady while I shear these clasps."

Rezner reluctantly crouched opposite Jack and took hold of the corners of the cold stainless steel case. Jack set the chisel in place again and struck hard with the hammer. A clang of steel. The metal clasp tore free from the case and bounced on the deck. Lauren jumped with the sharp sound. Jack repeated on the second clasp and it clattered to the deck next to the first. He tried to lift the top lid but the seams of the case felt fused. He wedged the tip of the chisel into the seam between where the clasps had been and pried. The case creaked. Jack slid the chisel deeper and pried again. The lid popped open, tearing the deteriorated sealing strip in half.

Everyone came forward and looked over Jack's shoulder. Rafferty stepped around the channel to improve his view. Jack and Rezner forced the lid full open, pushing past the resistance of the encrusted hinge.

A plate of dark glass lay at the surface of the case. Wire clasps along each edge locked the plate down over a glass cavity. It appeared to be a case within a case. Engraved letters spanned the width of the top plate and spelled out a warning: *Biological Material – Do Not Open.*

Jack absorbed the meaning of the message. "This thing isn't packed with 'coon skin caps."

"That's a good bet," Rezner said.

Lauren leaned forward to get a better look. "Is it the right one?"

"It certainly is." Rafferty pointed to the inner glass case. "That's a liquid nitrogen cavity. This case was clearly used to transport a living organism. Jack, open that lid and check for the phage samples."

Jack popped open the wire clasps on each edge of the top plate.

"Liquid nitro? Geez, is it still cold?" Markus said.

Connor shook his head. "No, it would have evaporated within a day of the crash."

Jack lifted the glass plate. The inner seal seemed better preserved than the outer. It didn't tear when he pulled off the lid like the outer seal had done. Amazingly, the interior of the glass case remained dry. He set the plate on deck. Inside the case a series of six cylindrical pockets were arranged in rows of three so that the glass cavity surrounded each. Rafferty's supposition appeared to be on the money. If the cavity had been filled with liquid nitrogen, anything inside those pockets would have been effectively cooled.

And seated inside each pocket was a glass ampoule.

Jack removed one of the ampoules. It looked to be about three inches long with a three-quarter-inch diameter. The narrow neck at the top of the ampoule where the glass had been melted to hermetically seal the contents seemed undamaged. A clear bronze liquid swished around inside. Jack rolled the sealed vial in his hand and found a label. He felt a tremor in his hand when he read it: *Bacteriophage 731.*

"Is it a hit?" Markus said.

Jack cracked a smile. "It's a home run."

"How many samples?" Rafferty said.

Jack inspected all the ampoules. "Five intact." He lifted the upper half of a shattered ampoule from the sixth pocket. "One of them didn't survive the crash."

"Five of six seems like a good ratio," Lauren said. "Is it enough to develop a living strain?" She looked to Rafferty.

He nodded. "It's plenty."

"Connor," Jack said. "Go get our transport case. I want to transfer these into something more stable right away."

"Right." Connor took off across the bay.

Jack stared at the samples of the 731 bacteriophage. The unknowns suddenly troubled him. What the hell was Rafferty going to do with it? Jack had turned a blind eye to the moral questions raised by his deal with Rafferty, but opening the bio case forced him to consider those questions now. Abner's words sounded in his head: *A hundred thousand American deaths.* A foreboding sense of things to come closed in around his conscience like an ominous fog. Anxiety mounted, and Jack realized he wasn't ready to hand over the phage just yet.

He abruptly stood. "Donovan, you need to leave the recovery bay."

Rafferty regarded him with a puzzled tilt to his head. "Why?"

"I want to button this up clean. Prepare to head back."

Rafferty's eyes narrowed. "What are you planning to do?"

"Nothing. It's just that we never discussed the fine details of our agreement, and I think it's time we hammer them out."

"Then let's do that here and now."

Jack shook his head. "You've dictated the terms from the start. Not this time. Topside in fifteen minutes. You leave the bay now."

Rafferty's expression hardened. "You know what's at stake here. Don't be foolish."

Ferguson uncrossed his arms and stepped slowly around the recovery channel opposite his boss. Rezner pivoted to block his path. "You stay right where you are."

Markus stood shoulder to shoulder with Rezner. "I'd listen to him if I were you, dipshit."

Lauren approached Jack and put a hand on his arm. "What's the matter?"

"Nothing is the matter," Jack said, "as long as Donovan complies with my request."

Rafferty stood silent, smoldering in place. He seemed to be contemplating his position.

Deep down Jack relished the situation. For once he had the boogeyman outnumbered and outgunned. He had the bargaining power. And Rafferty knew it.

"I don't know what game you're playing," Rafferty said glancing at Lauren. "But we both know what will happen if you cross me. Are you willing to take that risk?"

"What's the matter, Donovan, don't like taking orders?" Jack thought he saw smoke coming from Rafferty's nostrils, but the man didn't have a lit cigarette in his hand.

"Don't think I won't pull the plug on this whole affair right now," Rafferty said with deadly deliberation. "I take a man's word very seriously. We have an agreement. You will honor it. If you're thinking of changing the terms, you'd better think again."

Jack gave no ground. "I'm not changing our agreement. I'm just making sure you don't try to change it either."

Rafferty scrutinized him a long while and then, unexpectedly, smiled. "I like you, Jack. You make things interesting."

"You know me. I hate to be boring."

"Yes, I do know you." Rafferty pulled a cigarette pack from inside his jacket. "Topside in fifteen minutes." He flicked open his lighter. "Ferguson stays here. Take it or leave it."

Jack checked with Rezner, who gave him a nod. "Done," Jack said.

Rafferty glanced into the bio case and then lit his cigarette. He walked around the recovery channel and past Ferguson. "Keep your eyes on those ampoules."

Ferguson held out his hand. "My nine?"

Rafferty ignored the request and left his minion unarmed as he continued across the deck.

Connor arrived from the opposite direction toting a new biological transport case. He took in the scene and read something wasn't right. "What's going on?"

"Nothing," Markus said. "Why do you ask?"

Connor glanced from face to face. "No, seriously."

Jack motioned him over. "Bring me that case. Let's transfer the samples."

Connor knelt beside the recovered bio case and set the new one on deck. "What did I miss?"

Jack crouched next to him. "I'm trying to keep Rafferty honest. Maybe figure out his end game," he said quietly.

"Is it working?"

Jack lifted an ampoule and gazed at the solution inside. "I'll let you know in fifteen minutes."

- TWENTY SEVEN –

Donovan Rafferty climbed out of the recovery bay, passed through the crew quarters, and stepped onto the cargo deck with more than a little agitation in his step. Jack Sheridan had decided to show some backbone. Obstinate bastard. He must have some rebellious plan in the works, but what could it possibly be? He had no alternatives. The parameters were set. If he hoped to save his wife's life, he had to surrender the phage. Rafferty began to think he was missing something. He tossed his spent cigarette over the side and lit another.

The sun burned low in the sky above the western horizon. Rafferty studied its orange light illuminating the underside of a passing cloud, and considered the possibility that his focus had begun to slip. He dismissed the thought rather quickly. He knew he was just as sharp today as he had been yesterday, or the day before. But despite his self-assurance, he reached into his jacket pocket and grabbed the little white pill bottle.

Rafferty cursed and popped off the lid of the bottle. He poured three tablets into his palm, removed the cigarette from his mouth, and downed the pills. Taking them dry was difficult and one of them stuck in his throat. He swallowed hard to get it down and concentrated on the sunset as the damn thing disintegrated. A set of sails rode the wind off in the distance.

Rafferty closed his eyes and imagined pulling the trigger on the Sig. Vengeance is mine. It will happen. Regardless of what Sheridan has in mind, it will happen. And then something occurred to him. Perhaps Sheridan had pieced it together.

Rafferty opened his eyes and took a drag off his cigarette. Yes, that made sense. Of course at this stage of the game it made little difference what Sheridan did and didn't know. The phage was on board and things needed to move along quickly. Even Jack would agree with that.

Rafferty lifted his satellite phone from his pocket and dialed Naughton's number.

"Yes, Colonel," Naughton answered.

"We just recovered the bacteriophage," Rafferty said. "I should have it to the house by morning. Has Simon been displaying a productive attitude?"

"Yes, your last conversation with him seemed to do the trick. He's been playing with his lab toys ever since you left."

"Good. Put him on."

"Will do."

Rafferty waited. He heard Naughton's footsteps. Thrash music on high volume swelled from the background and pounded through the line. It lasted only a moment, and then Naugthon apparently switched it off. Someone complained as the phone was handed over.

"Dude," the punk microbiologist said.

"I understand you've been busy this week," Rafferty said. "That's encouraging. How is your work progressing?"

"I'm on top of it. Making things happen. I should be ready for the samples by Tuesday like we discussed last week."

"We're having some success out here, and I should have the phage in your hands by tomorrow morning."

Simon laughed. "You rock, Donovan. I'll splice into them Tuesday and we'll be rolling."

"No," Rafferty said. "You'll have the phage tomorrow, Sunday, and you'll begin working with it tomorrow. Is that clear?"

Simon groaned. "Oh man, I can't be so random. When I work with microorganisms it's like an art, and you can't rush art."

Rafferty squeezed the phone. "You will work on my timetable and you will produce results."

"I'll do what I can, but there are some things in the microverse you can't speed up."

"You promised me success. You will deliver. You have no other option."

"What do you mean no other option?"

"You either succeed at producing a living strain of the phage and walk away with a healthy bank account, or you don't walk away at all."

"What?" Simon said with a flare of panic. "That's not what we talked about. You never said *my* life depended on this virus reboot."

"That's not accurate. You've promised success from the beginning. Perhaps it was that youthful, cocksure attitude of yours, but you never considered what might happen if you fail. For the record, our agreement does not allow for failure. Call it fine print if you like, but it is an option in our contract that I'm exploiting."

"Donovan, this isn't fair. I can't work under this kind of pressure."

"On the contrary, you must work under this kind of pressure. It's time to grow up." Rafferty let him ponder that a few seconds before ending the call with, "See you tomorrow."

Rafferty shook his head and wondered if he'd chosen the wrong microbiologist for the task. He focused on the sunset to calm himself and found that ship again. This time he recognized the sail configuration as that of the *Friends Good Will.* She was making her run on the sunset cruise, approaching from the northwest. Something in her image tightened his stomach with an unsettling twinge. He thought about the bacteriophage, and the 731 Plague, and…

"You're infected with it."

Rafferty recognized Jack Sheridan's voice but did not bother to face him. Instead he smiled faintly and took a draw off his cigarette. "What are you talking about, Jack?"

"I'm talking about the pills you took from that little bottle," Jack said. "They're the same ones you gave Lauren. I'm talking about that fever you've been fighting since you stepped aboard this ship. I'm talking about your intense interest in recovering the phage."

Rafferty did not reply.

"Speechless. That's a first."

Rafferty finally turned. "Do you think you have it all figured out?"

"I have enough figured out. You're trying to save your own hide."

"You don't know the half if it."

"At least I know you're serious about developing a living strain of the phage. Do you really intend on treating Lauren with it?"

The question irritated Rafferty. "That is our agreement, is it not?"

"Forgive me," Jack said with thick sarcasm, "but believing the things you say is still difficult for me."

"You should be getting over that by now. You've seen plenty of evidence that I've been telling you the truth."

Jack regarded him a long while. "How did you get infected?"

"That's not your concern."

"I'm curious. Did you get carless playing around with the plague?"

"Don't press for answers you're not entitled to receive."

"I just want to know how you screwed up so bad that you had to come to me for help."

"Keep that pride in check," Rafferty said sharply. "Leveraging you was an efficient means to an end." He paused when Rezner appeared over Jack's shoulder. "Mr. Rezner, aren't you supposed to be keeping an eye on my man in the recovery bay?"

Jack glanced back at Rezner.

"Connor and Markus are covering," Rezner said to Jack. "I figured you could use someone to watch your back."

Jack gave him a nod and returned his attention to Rafferty. "All right, Donovan, you won't tell me how. I guess that's irrelevant at this point. So tell me this. After you've fixed yourself up, what's next on your agenda?"

"I don't believe you need to know that either."

"A hundred thousand American lives could be at stake. The possibility of being complicit in something like that gets a man thinking. It makes him reconsider decisions made under duress. I'm sure you understand why I *need* to know your intentions."

Rafferty considered Jack a long while, pondering just how far he could go with his manipulation before all cooperation would end. Testing Jack's limits this deep into the operation would not be prudent, not when the end was so close within reach.

"Donovan," Jack insisted, "what happens once the plague is cleared from your blood?"

Rafferty took a long draw off his cigarette before answering. "I'm going to kill someone who desperately deserves it."

Jack balked. "Is that supposed to motivate me in some way?"

Rafferty parsed his reaction. "I'm not talking about you." He added, "Not this time."

Jack's eyebrow cocked. "Seriously?"

"This may come as a surprise, but everything is not always about you."

"Then who are you talking about?"

"The man who infected me with the plague."

Jack seemed incredulous. "You mean to tell me this whole thing is a revenge kick for you?"

"That's oversimplifying it."

"What ever happened to, *Revenge is mine, sayeth the Lord*?"

"I told you once. The Lord and my agendas agree in this matter."

"Are you trying to tell us you're God's hit man?" Rezner said.

Rafferty frowned. "Crude parlance, Mr. Rezener. I prefer the term subcontractor."

"I understand *your* reason," Jack said, "but why does God want this guy dead?"

"Believe me, if you knew what I know about him, you'd want him dead…too."

A crosswind carried a stream of smoke from Rafferty's cigarette across the deck. Alarm bells went off in his head. Wind direction. Telltales. Tall ships. He spun around and zeroed in on the *Friends Good Will*. She shouldn't be here. Her normal route took her just ten miles from shore, where the *Achilles* had executed her eastern turns. Today the *Achilles* held position fourteen miles out, yet there was *Friends Good Will.*

She had covered a lot of distance in a short amount of time. Coast guard cutters *Thunder Bay* and *Commodore Perry* noticed and stirred from guard duty to ward her away for the third day straight. They moved lazily toward intercept in a casual maneuver that implied they did not consider the ship a real threat. Rafferty disagreed.

"What's the matter?" Jack said

Rafferty raised a hand for silence and arranged the pieces falling into place around him. If Cohn had been the one on board that fishing boat watching the *Achilles,* it meant he knew the government was trying to recover the bacteriophage. That knowledge would certainly alter his plans, even if it meant pulling back from the outskirts of Chicago. The phage was the only thing that could stymie the 731 plot. He would have to make sure it never made it to shore.

Cohn had the resources to do it too. His crew of mercenary seamen had trained to ferry the plague across the Great Lakes in a tall ship. It made perfect sense to utilize a similar vessel as a Trojan horse to get close to the *Achilles* and terminate the threat.

That's exactly how Rafferty would have done it.

A very serious problem had just arrived.

He spun around. "Tell Braddock to radio those cutters," he said to Jack. "Do it now."

Jack paused at the sudden shift in Rafferty's demeanor. "Why?"

"He needs to tell them that sloop is an imminent threat."

Jack and Rezner exchanged a glance.

"How is she a threat?" Jack said. "We've seen her every day we've been out here."

"That's what makes her a perfect choice."

"What the hell are you talking about?" Rezner said.

"He needs to get in close," Rafferty said. "That sloop is how he's going to do it."

Jack became agitated. "Who needs to get in close?"

"No time to explain."

"Bullshit," Rezner spat. "If that sloop is a threat, it's because you set it up."

"If I set this up would I be warning you about it now?"

Jack thought hard on the argument.

"Damn it, Jack, Braddock won't listen to me. Warn those cutters. They're our only defense."

Rezner stepped forward. "Don't trust him, Jack. This is some kind of trap."

"It is a trap," Rafferty said, "but it isn't mine."

Jack bit his lip and glanced at the approaching *Friends Good Will.* The cutters were halfway to intercept. He brought his eyes back to Rafferty. "Damn you if this is one of your tricks." He turned to the forecastle. Captain Braddock was standing on the starboard wing outside the bridge, watching the sloop and the coast guard boats perform their daily ritual. Jack shouted, "Malcolm, contact the cutters. Tell them the sloop is unfriendly."

Braddock leaned over the handrail to hear him better. "What?"

"The cutters," Jack yelled, pointing at the boats. "Tell them the sloop is dangerous."

Braddock seemed to understand but hesitated. He looked at the patrol boats again and then went into the bridge.

"You're so full of shit your eyes are brown," Rezner said to Rafferty.

"Let's hope I am," Rafferty replied.

After a short while Braddock reappeared on the wing. He shouted down. "Can't raise them. All channels are full of static."

Rafferty lifted his satellite phone. Moments ago he had full service, but now the display indicated he had none. "He's jamming communications. I'm right about this."

Rafferty rushed to the starboard gunwale. Jack and Rezner followed suit. They watched as the cutters veered away from each other to circle the sloop in opposite directions. *Friends Good Will* adjusted course a few degrees west with a shift of her sails, and her port side opened up to the *Commodore Perry.* Men were visible scurrying around on the sloop's deck. The cutter stayed her course, and the crackle from her loudspeaker carried across the waves in a muted garble. It sounded like the coast guard commander was instructing the tall ship to give the *Achilles* a wide berth. Rafferty was certain the sloop would not comply.

Two jets of smoke suddenly flared from the deck of *Friends Good Will.* Fore and aft a plume of fire flashed, and a pair rockets launched directly at the *Commodore Perry.* Smoke trails blazed a straight line to target through amber sunlight. The rockets slammed into the cutter. One detonated squarely in the main cabin, shattering windows and twisting metal amid a brilliant flash and black smoke. The second penetrated the fuel tank amidships and the hull came apart under a volcanic eruption of fire.

For the very first time, Rafferty considered the possibility that Cohn might get him first.

Jack stood transfixed on the destruction. "Jesus Chr—"

Rezner drew his Smith & Wesson and aimed at Rafferty's head. "Stop this now."

Rafferty flushed with anger. "I didn't start it. How do you expect me to stop it?"

Jack turned on him. "If it's not you behind this attack, then who the hell is it?"

Rafferty glared at *Friends Good Will.* "Alec Cohn."

- TWENTY EIGHT –

Friends Good Will

Alec Cohn held on to a main mast shroud line and watched the flaming hulk of the *Commodore Perry* sinking below the surface off the port quarter. A column of black smoke rose from the wreckage into the sky. Scratch one federal vessel. It was a very good start.

The men who had fired the rockets discarded their spent M72 launch tubes on deck and hurried to open a case containing unfired weapons.

Cohn stepped away from the shrouds. "Anders, Byrne, good shooting." He turned to starboard and scanned the water. The second cutter had throttled up and was making a run. Her crew had apparently determined something had gone terribly wrong with their warding maneuver. Her props bit into the water just ninety meters out, but with each passing second she increased that distance. The effective kill range of a LAW rocket is two hundred meters. Cohn had to get her quickly.

He picked out a man stationed along the starboard gunwale. "Erickson, that second cutter is broad on our beam. Hit her before she slips out of range."

Erickson acknowledged and snapped open the launch tube of the M72 in his hands. He flicked up its front sight and lifted the weapon to his shoulder. The ship pitched over a swell as he tried to steady his aim. "I'm losing my angle on her."

Cohn shouted across the deck. "Adjust heading to two-seven-zero. Sheet in."

Friends Good Will turned slightly windward, her bow smashing through a wave crest and her main sail settling on a close reach. Erickson's angle improved and he smiled. He aimed through the sight, compensated for distance, steadied himself against the rocking deck, and depressed the trigger on the outer tube. The rocket motor ignited and propelled the 66 mm warhead from the launcher in a rush of smoke and flame. He had aimed it true and the rocket intercepted *Thunder Bay* a hundred twenty yards out. The armor piercing warhead detonated aft of the cabin, blasting a gapping hole in the cutter's hull and slamming her into a hard starboard list. Crewmen on the bow jumped into the water to escape the flames. No one escaped from the aft section of the boat.

"Propaganda of the deed," Cohn said to himself. He turned from the wreck of the second cutter. "Excellent, Erickson. Now we go after the big fish." He moved forward to the bow and studied the *Achilles* off to port. The salvage vessel had not moved from her position. She was still at a dead stop. Perfect. Cohn felt a victorious rush pass through him. "Looks like you didn't anticipate this action, Colonel," he said to no one in particular. "Not quite your best day."

He spun around and shouted aft. "Helmsman, make heading two-two-zero. Boatswain, increase our sail and set a broad reach. Squeeze all the speed you can from this wind."

Cohn had to get within striking range of the *Achilles* quickly. He had four LAW rockets left in his arsenal, and he needed to use them to maximum effect. If he didn't, preventing that ship from returning to port would get a lot more difficult.

"Anders," he called along the gunwale. "When we get in range, put a rocket inside the bridge of that vessel. We can't let them get under-way. They'll outrun us."

Anders acknowledged.

Cohn scanned the open water to the east for Nix's Bayliner. Taking the cutters out was supposed to be his signal to move into the area. No sign of him yet.

Cohn noticed movement near his feet. The grating over the hatch to below deck shifted. He drew his Glock and knelt beside the hatch. When the grating jumped again, he grabbed hold of it and heaved it away. The startled face staring up through the hatchway froze when Cohn aimed the pistol at him. "Mr. Novak," Cohn said. "You've managed to slip the tie wraps around your wrists."

Novak was a gray-headed man pushing sixty, and he seemed to be on the verge of a cardiac problem. "What's happening?"

Cohn ignored him and shouted aft. "Foley, Novak is loose. Get below and make sure the others are secure."

Novak grimaced up through the hatchway. "Why are you doing this to us?"

Cohn looked impassively at him. "You're down there because my men are more than capable of handling this ship on their own; however, I do appreciate you taking us past the breakwater. It gave us time to organize ourselves."

"What were those explosions?"

Cohn leaned close to the hatch. "Mr. Novak, I don't have time to discuss my plans with you, but try to understand that the only reason you are alive right now is that you did not ask to be a part of this. On the other hand, if you choose to interfere with me or my men in any way, I will consider that a request to get involved."

Novak stared back as if not quite understanding the implied threat.

"Let me clarify," Cohn said. "I will kill you and your crew at the first whisper of rebellion."

Novak's mouth dropped open. Foley appeared behind him and seized his arms to take him back to the hold.

Cohn stood and holstered his pistol. Novak really was partially to blame for his predicament. He should have been suspicious of a group of men paying double price to buy up all of the tickets for a sunset cruise just an hour before heading out. The TSA red flags things like that at airport terminals. Perhaps Novak will learn that lesson, if he survives the day.

Cohn put his attention back on the *Achilles*. She was very close to being in range of the LAWs. That meant Cohn was very close to ridding himself of the thorn in his side named Donovan Rafferty. Yes, killing the colonel was only a fringe benefit in comparison to the bonus the North Koreans had promised to pay, but Cohn looked forward more to a world without Rafferty than he did to the bullion from Kim Jong Um's bank.

Recovery Bay: *Achilles*

"Connor, get up here quick."

Mai's voice spilled through the PA speaker into the bay. She was nervous about something. Connor heard it in her tone. He wanted to go.

Markus stood near the bio case on one side of the recovery channel and Ferguson stood stone-faced on the other. Connor nodded to his friend. "You okay watching this guy on your own?"

Markus gave Ferguson a dismissive look. "Are you *trying* to insult me, Sheridan? Just get up there and see what's going on with your girlfriend. Me and Fergy will get along fine."

"Piss off, Sweetwood," Ferguson said.

"I'll keep an eye down here," Connor said as he made his way toward the stairs to the op center. "By the way, she's not my girlfriend."

Markus laughed. "You're only fooling yourself."

Connor climbed the steps quickly and entered the op center. He found Mai standing beside the Looking Glass table, hovering over the large graphic display of the search area. "What's the matter?" he asked.

Mai shook her head. "I don't know. One of the cutters just disappeared from the display."

Connor studied the table. The icon representing the *Achilles* floated at the center of the computer-generated Lake Michigan. The *Thunder Bay* appeared a short distance off her starboard side, moving north at a good clip. An unidentified vessel with a southwest heading seemed to be passing very close to the cutter. "The *Commodore Perry* is gone," Connor said.

Mai tapped her finger on the tabletop. "I was looking at her right here and she vanished."

Connor checked with Parson. "Did you see it too?"

"I didn't see it disappear," Parson said, "but I heard some kind of boom."

"I heard it too," Mai said, "but I thought you and Markus had done something in the bay."

Connor caressed his chin. "Maybe it's a glitch with the display program."

Mai kept her eyes glued to the tabletop. "A program glitch wouldn't affect just one element on the display. I think something really happened out there."

A muted boom suddenly pulsed through the bulkhead from outside. Everyone heard it. The *Thunder Bay* icon flickered. Pixels jumped in a random pattern, and then dissolved into nothing . The leader line and the text denoting the ship's identification and heading blinked off.

"Did you see that?" Mai said.

"What the hell is going on?"

Crewman Hart leaned into the cage ladder and cocked his head to listen to voices from above. "Something's happening. They sound excited on the bridge."

Connor went to the intercom panel to call up but Cooney's voice came out of the speaker before he could key the switch. "All hands, all hands prepare to get underway. Emergency response team, report to the launch."

Connor hit the switch. "Bridge-Ops. What's happening?"

"Don't know," Cooney replied. "The cutters. They just blew apart like they hit a mine or something. Kohler thinks he saw a missile, but that's crazy."

Mai looked up from the display. "Like hitting a mine in Lake Michigan isn't crazy."

"I'm coming up," Connor said to Cooney. He turned and put a hand on Mai's arm. "Stay here. Tell Markus something happened to the cutters. Shut down the op center with Parson and Hart but don't come to the bridge, not until I know what's going on."

"It's Rafferty, isn't it?" Mai said.

"I don't know what it is." Connor stepped into the cage ladder and grabbed a rung. "Stay here until I get back."

Topside Cargo Deck: *Achilles*

Jack watched a second plume of black smoke climb into the air. Both cutters had been taken out, and the instrument of their destruction was riding the wind like a demon, silently pressing through the water toward the *Achilles.* A klaxon sounded across the salvage vessel's deck, and crewmen hurried in every direction making for their stations and rapid response duties.

Rezner still had his pistol trained on Rafferty. "Just let me drop him, Jack. We'll knock down one problem at a time."

Rafferty scowled. "If the next problem you tackle is that sloop, you're going to need all the help you can get."

Jack looked Rafferty in the eye and saw something there he'd never seen before: genuine uncertainty. "Rez," Jack said. "Put the gun down. He's not pulling the strings on this one."

Rezner hesitated. "Are you willing to bet all our lives on that hunch?"

"I'm trusting my gut."

"You'd better listen to him," Rafferty said. "The man you want is on that sloop, and he's coming this way fast."

Rezner lowered the Smith & Wesson and glanced at *Friends Good Will.*

"Did you bring something aboard with more power behind it than that .40 cal?" Jack asked.

"I was expecting trouble," Rezner said gesturing to Rafferty. "Of course I have more firepower."

"Now is the time to get it."

"Damn straight." Rezner rushed off toward the forecastle.

Jack faced Rafferty. "You know the man on that ship. Are you the target here? Does he know you're aboard the *Achilles*?"

"I doubt it. The only logical reason he's out there is the bacteriophage."

"The phage?"

"Yes, he's here to make sure you don't recover it."

"Why?"

Rafferty seemed annoyed. "The Memorial Day plot Abner told you about is Cohn's. If the U.S. government has the phage, his grand scheme will be neutered."

Jack chewed on that a second or two. "Do you know him well enough to anticipate his tactics?"

"You've seen it yourself," Rafferty said. "He'll strike with overwhelming force to send this vessel and the phage to the bottom of the lake. Collateral damage doesn't concern him."

"So negotiation of any kind is out of the question."

"You'd have better luck negotiating with me if I were aboard that sloop."

Jack considered his options. He had only one that was viable. "We need to maneuver. We can't stay here a sitting duck."

Friends Good Will was close now, perhaps a hundred meters out. If a direct assault was coming, it would come in the next few seconds. Jack called to the captain standing outside of the bridge on the starboard wing. "Malcolm, get those diesels started. We have to make a run."

Braddock shouted down. "Already charging the ignition compressor. I'm way ahead of you."

Rafferty drew his Sig Sauer and chambered a round. The click of the action whipped Jack's head around. Rafferty smiled. "Don't lose that edge, Jack. It will keep you alive."

Jack didn't respond to the comment. Instead he said, "How do you know so much about Cohn and his plan?"

Rafferty expression turned cold. "That's a story for another time."

"Can't wait to hear it." Jack pivoted about. "I'm going to the bridge. Do I need to give you marching orders?"

"I know what to do," Rafferty said. "I'm not about to let Cohn take the phage from me."

"From us," Jack corrected. "Let's not forget that." He started for the foredeck.

"Cohn is very thorough," Rafferty said to his back. "Expect a boarding attempt."

Jack turned. "That's why I didn't let Rezner shoot you."

Jack continued on. He only covered half the distance when Rafferty shouted, "Incoming!"

A rocket streaked overhead with an eerie wail peeling off its tailfins. Jack dropped flat on deck and covered his head. The rocket struck solid at the base of the ship's bridge and exploded. Half a dozen window panes instantly shattered. Bulkhead plating folded like aluminum foil. Ribbons of expanded metal tore free from the starboard walkway and took flight in a dozen chaotic directions.

Jack stayed down until the thunder of the explosion faded and the rain of falling debris subsided. He lifted his head to check the damage. When he saw the devastated starboard wing, a sense of dread overcame him. Malcolm Braddock had been standing there a second before the explosion.

Jack got to his feet and rushed up the steps to the twisted and scarred wing. Fire from the blast burned in a gaping maw of a hole in the bulkhead at the point of impact. Braddock was lying motionless near the deformed hatchway door into the bridge. Broken glass and charred steel debris covered him. Jack knelt beside him and cleared away pieces of smoking metal. He checked for injury. The left side of Braddock's face and his left arm were badly burned, and blood soaked through his charred Neptune's Reach shirt. It seemed pieces of the walkway structure had torn through his body like shrapnel from a grenade.

"Malcolm," Jack said, gently rolling him onto his back. "Malcolm, can you hear me?"

Braddock's eyes fluttered open to a glassy stare. "I told you…Sheridan…you're dangerous."

Jack dredged up as positive a tone as he could muster. "You're not too bad off. You're going to be okay."

Braddock's breaths came short and shallow. "You…lie…too."

"We'll get you back to shore," Jack said. "Get you patched up. McElroy will take us in."

Braddock grabbed Jack's arm with a bloodied hand. "You take us…It's your mess…fix it."

Jack nodded. "Okay, I'll get you back. Just hang on."

"Plague," the captain rasped through the pain of his tattered body. "Stop…it."

"I'll do everything I can. You know I will."

Braddock's brow creased in defiance. "Go…That ship...is coming."

Jack glanced over his shoulder. *Friends Good Will* was angling her bow to make a pass alongside the *Achilles*. If they fired another rocket and put a hole in the hull at the waterline it would be all over.

"Save…the crew." Braddock's grip on Jack's arm loosened and his breathing faded.

"Malcolm." Jack checked for a pulse at his carotid artery but found none. "Malcom!" Jack looked into the captain's frozen eyes for a sign of life. There was nothing there. Jack's shoulders drooped. He recalled the heated discussion he had with Braddock at the beginning of the voyage. *Captains have a short life expectancy around you.*

"You were right about me, Malcolm. I'm sorry."

A part of Jack wanted to stay at Braddock's side to mourn his passing, but survival instincts pulled him to his feet. He had to keep this ship afloat. The lives of his wife and son, of Markus and Rezner, of the whole crew, they were all in jeopardy now.

Flames from the explosion had died down but Jack still felt the heat. He tried to push through the damaged hatchway door into the bridge. It gave only a hand's breadth before grinding to a stop. A folded hinge and a piece of debris on the other side had jammed it. He lifted his leg and kicked hard. The hatchway door screeched and jerked open another foot before stopping again, but this time Jack had enough room to wiggle through and he did.

A mix of smoke and white dust hung in the air like a thick fog. The overhead fire system had discharged its dry chemical flame retardant. Cooney and Connor were shooting jets of CO_2 from fire extinguishers into flames that were eating away at the helm console. They had cuts on their faces and on the underside of their forearms as if they had tried to shield themselves from flying glass. A long gash over Connor's right eye bled down his cheek.

"Connor," Jack called through the cloud. "Are you okay?"

Connor's fire extinguisher sputtered out. "I think so."

Jack quickly assessed the condition of the bridge. The damage had been contained to the starboard side. A good segment of the command console had been destroyed and the glass windows above it had been blown out. Bulkhead plating and electrical conduit that ran through the area at knee height was torn, twisted, and burned. A three-foot hole smoldered at the epicenter of the blast. The steel and equipment panels down there had taken the brunt of the explosion. Jack calculated that if the rocket had hit any higher up on the bulkhead, everyone inside the bridge would have surely been killed.

"What happened?" Connor asked, coughing on the foul air.

Cooney dropped his extinguisher on the deck and knelt beside crewman Kohler, who was lying at the base of the ECDIS display. "They hit us right when you stepped out of the cage ladder," Cooney said.

Connor wiped a flow of blood from his face. "Who hit us? Rafferty's men?"

"Not Rafferty," Jack said. "It's someone else, someone who doesn't want us to recover the phage."

Cooney listened for his shipmate's heartbeat. "Kohler's alive. Something knocked him pretty good on the head but he's just unconscious." He stood and faced Jack. "I saw them fire that rocket, but I didn't have time to shout a warning or anything." A breeze blew in through the smashed window panes and the air began to clear. Cooney spun around, searching the bridge and the port and starboard wings outside. "Where's Captain Braddock?"

Jack met his gaze. "The rocket hit too close—he didn't make it."

"Oh my God." Cooney looked again at the damage. "This can't be happening."

Connor scanned through the aft window panes to the water off their stern quarter. *Friends Good Will* had turned parallel with the *Achilles* and was setting up to make a run less than fifty meters off her starboard beam. "They're coming around to finish us off."

Jack clamped down the panic he felt rising inside and studied the battered helm control console. "What's left?" he said to Cooney.

"Uh…" Cooney tried to pull himself together and examined the console. "Propulsion looks okay. Rudder controls are gone. Ignition system…oh shit."

Jack came forward. "Did we get the engines started before the blast?"

"No, we were charging the ignition compressor to roll the pistons when we got hit."

"Can we still start them?"

"Not from here anymore. The bridge circuits for the compressor controls are destroyed. The whole system is shut down. We have to throw the bypass switch in the engine room and finish charging the ignition compressor from down there."

Jack went to an intercom panel on the bulkhead and keyed the switch. "Engine Room-Bridge, throw the compressor bypass—" A blast of static drowned out his words. He turned from the panel. "This intercom station is out."

"I'll call the engine room from the op center." Connor raced into the cage ladder.

"You okay to run down there?" Jack asked.

"I'm fine." He took his feet off the rung and controlled his descent with his hands along the uprights.

"Cooney," Jack said. "Once we get propulsion what can we do?"

"Straight lines," Cooney spat. "Maybe a circle. Whatever direction this ship takes off in, we won't be in the driver's seat. The rudder controls are shot."

"Moving is better than sitting. I'll take whatever I can get." Jack checked on *Friends Good Will.* She was beginning her run at the *Achilles'* stern. "Is the topside PA system still on line?"

Cooney checked an unscathed section of control panel. "It looks okay."

"Use it. Warn anyone on deck to get below. That sloop is coming locked and loaded."

"Aye." Cooney clicked on the external PA and called out Jack's warning.

Friends Good Will glided methodically into a close parallel course. Jack figured he had mere seconds to get the engines started and make a run for it before the sloop opened fire again. He knew it would take a lot longer than that to get the message to the engine room and manually roll the diesels to life. The only chance to save the ship now was to hold off that sloop from delivering a fatal blow with one of those rockets.

Jack suddenly realized everybody's life depended on the actions of Joshua Rezner.

And Donovan Rafferty.

- TWENTY NINE –

Topside Cargo Deck: *Achilles*

Rafferty crouched beneath the starboard gunwale at the stern quarter with the Sig Sauer tight in his hands. The sloop was edging forward toward amidships. He heard the creaks of her wood and rigging, and the splash of her hull cutting through the water. They had not fired another rocket yet, most likely because they had a small number of the shoulder-fired weapons in their arsenal. They were waiting until they had lined up the perfect shot at point-blank range. And why not? They were not under pressure. The *Achilles* was unarmed, she sat at a dead stop, and her crew of civilians would offer no substantial resistance. An easy mark.

Rafferty intended to use that tactical assessment to his advantage. The element of surprise would give him one free shot at them, and he had to make it count. His first priority was to take away their ability to sink the *Achilles*. From what he had seen, their rockets were a simple anti-armor infantry weapon. They did not appear to have infrared guidance or laser targeting systems of any kind. If Rafferty had to guess he would say they were M72 LAWs, an outdated weapon that was relatively cheap and fairly easy to obtain on the underground arms market. They were a crude solution to a critical need, a weapon right in line with the tactical philosophy of Alec Cohn. Hitting the mark with an M72 depended solely on the skill of the man firing the weapon, and that was the weak link Rafferty intended to exploit.

Rafferty panned the cargo deck. Rezner had not returned. Even if he had Rafferty wasn't sure if he would help or hinder the effort to fend off the sloop. Given Rezner's disposition, it was just as likely he would turn whatever weapon he had on Rafferty as he would turn it on Cohn's men. That kind of assistance Rafferty could do without.

A voice shouted commands aboard *Friends Good Will*. It was Cohn. Rafferty felt a sudden urge to rearrange his list of priorities, but what good would it do to kill the king of fools only to go down with the ship. He had to stay on task. Cohn was telling his men to hold steady, to fire on his mark when he determined the soft white underbelly of the *Achilles* was hoisted up on that silver platter. "Aim closer to the water line," Cohn ordered.

Rafferty sprang from his position. The sloop's main sail was directly across from him, about forty meters out. The *Achilles* cargo deck awarded him the high ground by perching him two meters above the main deck of *Friends Good Will.* Four men in light body armor were deployed along the sloop's port gunwale; three with automatic weapons and one with an M72 launcher aimed right at the salvage vessel's waterline. Cohn was standing aft. Rafferty blocked him out of his mind and drew down on the man with the rocket launcher. He resolved his aim in less than two seconds and squeezed the trigger, right about the same time Cohn shouted for his men to open fire with their automatic weapons.

Two bullets thundered from the Sig. The first missed the mark. The second struck the man with the launcher in the neck, sending him reeling about and reaching for his throat. He dropped the M72 at his feet. Rafferty ducked beneath the gunwale as machine gun fire assaulted his position. The ship's steel did an adequate job of shielding him against the bullets. Rafferty stayed low and scurried forward as the pops and pings of gunfire marred the *Achilles'* hull. He stopped twenty paces from his last station. It was as good a place as any to take another shot. Although the cover of the steel below the gunwale gave Rafferty comfort he couldn't stay down long. Another of Cohn's men had surely picked up the launcher by now. Unfortunately, the men with the automatic weapons knew he was there this time, and were certainly waiting for him to pop up like a duck in a shooting gallery. This second shot would be far more dangerous than the first.

Rafferty took a breath and readied himself. He considered that the sloop was moving parallel to the salvage vessel at about four knots. He considered that the man now holding the M72 might seek better cover before firing. He counted down in his head: Three, two, one.

Rafferty stood and angled the Sig Sauer as he had the last time. The sloop had traveled farther than he thought it would have, and the man lifting the M72 launcher to his shoulder was crouched lower than the previous one. Rafferty fired three shots before the submachine guns locked in on his new location and opened up. Bullets sizzled around his head and pelted the gunwale as he dropped. His target had flinched and the launcher was pulled back, but Rafferty wasn't sure if he had actually hit the man.

"Damn it, Jack, move this ship," he said to himself.

Rafferty scurried another twenty paces forward, which put him nearly amidships, the obvious sweet spot to tear a gaping hole in the hull. He figured the odds of dodging a bullet had swung heavily against him since his first surprise attack. This time Cohn would assign fields of fire to each of his men so they would catch their mark no matter where he popped up. Rafferty closed his eyes. He decided on two seconds of exposure to fire as many rounds as he could before getting back to cover. He hoped one of those bullets managed to find Cohn.

Rafferty opened his eyes and sprang to his feet. The reports from the submachine guns sounded almost immediately. He honed his focus on the launch tube among a tangle of men, weapons, and rigging and started firing. A bullet tore through the shoulder seam of Rafferty's jacket. Another grazed his earlobe. The Sig Sauer's action snapped open empty and he hit the deck.

And then Rezner came rushing out of nowhere, shouting like a crazed marine. He carried what looked like a heavy black carbine with a fat ammunition drum affixed underneath. He aimed over the side of the gunwale and lay on the trigger. An unholy series of booming reports belched from the weapon. Spent shotgun shells ejected from the side breach one after another. A maelstrom of twelve-gauge buckshot rained down on the deck of the sloop like grape shot from cannon. Cohn's men scurried for cover as hull planks splintered, shroud lines snapped, and Kevlar vests popped.

The man with the M72 depressed the trigger on the launch tube as one of his comrades who was scrambling toward a lower deck hatchway barreled into him. The launch tube angled skyward and the rocket motor ignited. The warhead sizzled upward on a seventy-degree trajectory and passed over the starboard side of the *Achilles* just an arm's length from Rezner.

Rafferty ejected the spent magazine from the Sig and smiled as he drew a fresh one from his belt. Rezner turned out to be useful after all. Who would have guessed that he had brought along an AA12 assault shotgun? Rafferty slapped a new magazine into the Sig, chambered a round, and rose to a firing stance. The sloop had finally begun to veer away thanks to Rezner's onslaught.

The AA12 ejected the last shell from the ammunition drum. The thunder subsided and Cohn rose to his feet on the quarter deck of *Friends Good Will.* He spotted Rafferty and zeroed in on him. The distance between them was increasing but Cohn drew his sidearm and opened fire. Rafferty did likewise. They stood there trading shots at one another until their magazines were empty, neither scoring a hit.

Bridge: *Achilles*

Jack watched as *Friends Good Will* moved off. She had to tack into the wind to make her break and was crawling away slow. Jack felt a glimmer of hope. Rezner and Rafferty had done it. They had prevented a hole from being blown into the *Achilles'* hull. But victory would be short lived. That Cohn character had made a mistake by coming in so close to line up a point-blank shot. He would correct that error by moving out of range of the small arms that drove him back and simply fire those rockets from a greater distance.

Despite veering off, the sloop was still very close to the salvage vessel. Jack cursed. If only he had propulsion. The *Achilles* was a three hundred-foot long steel sledgehammer displacing twenty-five hundred metric tons of water. In comparison, *Friends Good Will* was a hundred-foot piece of driftwood. If the bow of the *Achilles* struck that sloop at the proper angle, she'd split into kindling.

And then it occurred to him. "We can maneuver," he said aloud.

Cooney checked the propulsion indicators. "Diesels aren't running yet. We're still stuck."

"No, not with the main screws." Jack went to the ECDIS display. The large screen showed the surface radar contact of the sloop in relation to the *Achilles.* He picked up a grease pen and drew an arc from the extreme bow of the *Achilles* to visualize its path if the ship were to spin clockwise on its center axis. It seemed the bow would intersect the aft quarter of *Friends Good Will*, but the movement had to be initiated immediately before the sloop got clear of the radius.

Cooney watched Jack growing excited but didn't get it. "Still no engines. We'll probably get them running in under a minute, though."

"That's too long to wait," Jack snapped.

"Then how—"

"Stabilizing thrusters," Jack interrupted. "We can't gain headway but we can turn this ship on a dime with the thruster pods in the keel."

Cooney's face lit up. "Hey, that might work."

Jack rushed past the damaged intercom panel and stuck his head in the cage ladder. "Connor," he shouted down through the decks to the op center. "Put this ship into a clockwise spin with those thrusters now!"

Operations Center: *Achilles*

Connor felt he had not taken a breath since sliding down the ladder into the op center. Mai saw the blood streaking down his face and gasped. "My God, Connor, what happened?"

Hart and Parson stared at his cuts and frenzied actions. "That explosion rattled panels down here," Parson said. "Those cutters' sinking, it was no accident, was it?"

Connor made a bee line to the intercom panel on the starboard bulkhead without speaking. He slapped the panel to key the switch. "Engine Room–Ops. Throw the bypass switch and charge the ignition compressor. We need those engines started!"

A voice answered from the engine room. "Uh, the post retrofit start-up procedures say the bridge crew handles diesel ignition. We're not supposed to—"

"Do it," Connor shouted. "Bridge controls are damaged. If this ship doesn't get moving we're screwed."

A short pause played out. "Roger that."

Mai became panicked. "Rafferty?"

Connor turned to her. "No. Believe it or not, there's another psycho with heavy weapons gunning for us."

Hart came forward. "I worked with the retrofit crew. I know all the new equipment and routings better than anyone aboard. If we need the engines now I should be down there."

"Go," Connor said.

Hart took off.

Mai pulled a water bottle from the little backpack behind her station. She took off the pink hoodie she was wearing and poured some water over the sleeve. "Sit down at your station," she said to Connor.

He reluctantly sat and Mai wiped the blood from his face and cleaned around the cut on his head. "How did this happen?"

"Some shell or rocket or something hit the bridge and flying glass sprayed the whole room. Cooney is just as bad off."

"Was Braddock or your dad up there when it hit?"

Connor swallowed the lump in his throat. "Dad wasn't. Braddock is dead."

Mai didn't say anything, but Connor could feel that her hands were shaking. "This is deep," she said. "You probably need a dozen stitches to close it up."

"No doctors aboard," Connor said. "I'll have to settle for tape and gauze."

She pressed the sleeve against the wound and he winced. "Keep pressure on it. I'll get the med kit from the corridor." She wiped blood from her hands onto her white tank top and hurried out of the op center.

Connor leaned forward and rested his head in his hand to keep pressure on the cut.

Parson looked on. "What happens if we don't get underway very soon?"

Connor glanced crosswise at him. "Odds are this ship will be sunk."

"By who? I mean, who the hell would attack us over a cholera vaccine?"

"There's more to it than that," Connor said. "Anything the government gets involved with has secrets attached. This recovery mission is no exception."

"It would have been nice to know up front," Parson said.

Connor didn't reply.

Mai returned carrying a package of thick gauze pads, a bottle of hydrogen peroxide, and a roll of tape. Connor stared at the crimson stain on her tank top as she opened the bottle of peroxide. "Here it comes." She saturated a piece of gauze and set it on top of the cut. The solution foamed in the laceration and Connor gritted his teeth against the burn. "Jack should have told us Rafferty was on board," she said.

The sting subsided and Connor took a breath. "No, I should have told you. I'm sorry." He added, "But for the record, this attack right now is not Rafferty's doing."

Mai pulled the bloodied gauze away and grabbed a clean one. "Guns and killing go hand-in-hand with Rafferty."

"I can't argue with that." Connor looked into her eyes. "But what we're doing out here is important. My dad and I aren't on a treasure hunt this time. We're trying to save lives."

Mai silently tore a strip of tape from the roll.

Connor glanced at Parson. "Call the engine room for an update."

"It hasn't been very long since you talked to them," Parson said.

"We don't have a lot of time. Just humor me."

Mai continued dressing Connor's wound. He noticed her hands had stopped shaking and he gave her a smile. "You know what? You even make a blood-stained tank top look good."

She finished taping the gauze and sat next to him in her station chair. "Are we going to escape this time?"

Connor sat there trying to determine the best answer to her question. From what he'd seen on the bridge the danger seemed substantial. Was it wise to tell her that?

"They're rolling the pistons," Parson announced.

Mai still waited for her answer.

Connor opened his mouth to speak, but Jack's voice reverberated down through the cage ladder. "Connor, put this ship into a clockwise spin with those thrusters now!"

Connor sat up straight. "A spin?" He scanned the stabilizer controls on his station. Why a spin? He suddenly recalled he'd last seen the sloop setting up for a pass along the ship's starboard side. A clockwise movement made sense. He understood. "Mai, tell him I'm on it. You need to shout up the ladder because the bridge intercom panel is out."

Mai jumped from her chair and ran to the cage ladder to confirm the order.

Connor checked the status of the thrusters. They were idling in their holding positions. Good. Props turning. He touched a series of buttons on the interface screen to command the bow thruster pods to rotate full to port and the after pods to rotate full to starboard.

All along the hull the servo-driven pods oriented as instructed and locked into place.

"Spooling up thrusters," Connor said.

Mai relayed the report to the bridge through the cage ladder.

Connor punched the thruster engines to full power. The *Achilles* heaved at the insistence of props winding up to their maximum RPMs. The bow began to swing around on her clockwise arc. The sudden movement threw Connor off balance, and he kicked out his leg to right himself in the chair.

Bridge: *Achilles*

Jack staggered as the ship came about. He grabbed on to the ECDIS table and looked out through the shattered bridge windows. *Friends Good Will* was still struggling to gain distance from the *Achilles*. The salvage vessel's bow swung toward her like a scythe. Down on deck, Rezner and Rafferty moved to the point and fired on the sloop as the space between them narrowed. Muzzle flashes sparked in the waning light of day on *Friends Good Will's* quarter deck.

Jack estimated where the bow would intercept the sloop's path. "We're going to miss the mark," he said to Cooney.

Two green indicators lit up on the propulsion station. "Main engines show green," Cooney said. "The diesels are running."

Jack slapped the ECDIS display. "All ahead full, all ahead full!"

Cooney engaged the main drive shafts and ramped up the propellers to maximum. The *Achilles* lurched to starboard as the screws came to life. The ship barreled forward toward the sloop but fishtailed into a corkscrew turn. Jack immediately realized his mistake. The thruster pods and the drive propellers had not been coordinated, and the *Achilles* was careening uncontrolled. He pivoted to call down through the cage ladder but lost his footing and fell flat on his stomach near the hatchway in the deck. Close enough. He shouted down to Mai. "Abort the spin. Balance the thrusters, port and starboard."

Jack climbed to his feet using the cage ladder for support. The stern of *Friends Good Will* appeared in the water through the forward-facing bridge windows. She was close. Real close. The *Achilles'* bow swept from west to east, plowing through the sloop's wake with reckless abandon and passing so close to the wooden ship that Jack thought for sure it had scraped the paint off her transom. But it didn't hit. It didn't smash the sloop like he had hoped.

"Damn it!" Jack shouted.

And then he realized the *Achilles* was still careening from the influence of the thruster pods. The momentum of the spin had subsided, but inertia kept the ship rotating like she was caught in a whirlpool, and the salvage vessel's stern quarter now threatened to pulverize the fleeing sloop.

"We got one more shot at this," Jack said clinging to the cage ladder.

Friends Good Will

Alec Cohn commanded his crew from the quarter deck. One of his men had been killed, three others had been wounded, and the bow of that salvage vessel had just passed so close he could have counted the rivets on her hull plates. The sitting duck had turned into a hawk, and its talons were bearing down on him. He needed to get clear of its path in a damned hurry.

"Hard to starboard! Slack away the mainsheet."

The helmsman shifted the rudder. *Friends Good Will* responded to the change in heading and rode down the backside of a swell. The boatswain shouted for the crew to swing out the main sail boom. A gust of wind filled the increasing area of canvas and the sloop picked up speed. Cohn looked to port and shouted a curse.

The *Achilles'* stern was on top of them. Her steel transom towered over the sloop's aft gunwale, and her main props churned the lake white. Sheets of water doused Cohn and his men as the salvage vessel made contact, pulverizing the gunwale and rupturing deck planks in the after section of the quarter deck. The impact threw Cohn and the helmsman off their feet.

The *Achilles* kept sliding past. Cohn pulled himself up and checked the damage to the quarter deck. Fortunately it had been a glancing blow. A full-on collision would have taken the stern clean off. About a meter of after deck was demolished, and a crack in the hull seemed to jag its way down to the waterline. There could be more structural damage below. They may even be taking on water, but it didn't matter in the short run. He could still maneuver. The sails and rigging were still intact.

"Back to stations," Cohn shouted. He got his bearings and cast his gaze over the starboard bow. A white Bayliner bounced over the waves on an inbound course. Finally, Nix had arrived. Just in time, too. Cohn would need that boat soon. Over his shoulder the salvage vessel was stabilizing her course. Her wild spin had slowed, and she seemed to be trying to make way in a more controlled manner. Cohn wasn't about to let her get away. He searched and found Anders reorganizing the armed men amidships. "Anders," he shouted. "Grab a LAW and get back here."

Anders nodded and picked up one of two remaining LAW launchers out of the ammunition case. He rushed back to the damaged quarter deck and Cohn pointed to the *Achilles*. "Hit her abaft at the waterline. Damage her screws. Get her hobbling instead of running."

Anders snapped open the launch tube. "Got it."

Cohn almost called for Erickson but stopped himself. Erickson had taken the colonel's bullet in the throat and was killed. Cohn shouted for the next qualified man instead. "Byrne, grab that last M72 and take a position port side. Fire into the belly of that vessel on my command."

Cohn noted the salvage vessel's location. She was tracking southeast about eighty meters astern. Cohn frowned. The colonel had managed to stave off death once again, but it would be the last time. Cohn spotted the boatswain standing near the main mast shrouds. "Ready about."

"Ready about," the boatswain repeated to the deck hands.

"Anders," Cohn shouted. "Fire."

Anders verified his aim and pressed the trigger. The rocket ignited and rushed from the launch tube amid a cloud of smoke. It flew straight and true to target, striking *Achilles* just above the casement containing the starboard drive shaft and blowing a devastating hole in the machinery.

Cohn hollered, "Hard alee!"

The helmsman shoved the rudder leeward. *Friends Good Will* turned into the wind. Crewmen cast off the starboard jibsheet, and the sails luffed loosely as the bow crossed through the dead no-sail zone. The sloop came about and wind filled the opposite side of the sails. The main mast boom swung from starboard to port, nearly taking Byrne's head off as it passed over the deck. Crewmen trimmed and cleated the port jibsheet and the helmsman abated the turn. *Friends Good Will* had come full about and now paralleled the salvage vessel's heading a hundred twenty meters abeam.

Cohn called from the quarter deck. "Byrne. Stand ready."

Bridge: *Achilles*

Jack had nearly shouted for joy when the *Achilles* struck *Friends Good Will*, but he quickly realized the collision had not done enough damage to end the duel. He came off his emotional high, and the deck beneath his feet settled to an even plane as the inertia from the spin died away. The sloop was in the rearview mirror now, and the *Achilles* was plowing forward in an unsteady southeast heading. Jack had to decide what to do next; make another attempt at ramming the sloop or make a run for shore.

Attempting to ram the sloop would mean turning around and charging across hundreds of meters of water guided only by the thruster pods, leaving the *Achilles* open for more close-range attacks. That tactic did not appear favorable. On the other hand running had its advantages. They were already distancing themselves from the sloop, and at best speed Jack was certain they could outrun the sail vessel. The most effective tactic would be to turn into the wind and draw *Friends Good Will* into pursuit. She'd have to alternate her tack constantly to make any headway, and that would force her into a plodding zigzag course. That was the ticket.

"Cooney, get me the wind direction off of Kohler's station."

Cooney left his charred section of the command console and checked the display screens on the navigation side. "Uh, atmospherics…here it is. Wind from the northwest at twenty knots."

"Then we need to steer northwest—approximate heading, three-one-five." Jack turned to call down through the cage ladder but found Lauren's auburn hair blocking his view as she climbed up. Jack frowned. The bridge was not a safe place to be. "What are you doing here?"

She reached the top and he helped her out. "Some crewmen said that the cutters had been sunk. I went to the op center and Connor told me somebody is trying to stop us from recovering the phage. None of this makes sense." She saw the damage to the bridge over Jack's shoulder and looked to him for an answer.

"Connor shouldn't have let you come up here." Jack said.

"I wasn't going to let him stop me," she insisted.

Jack shook his head. "No time to get into it." He called down to Mai. "We need a course adjustment. Tell Connor to configure the thrusters to turn us to heading three-one-five."

Mai signaled thumbs up and went to relay the message to Connor.

"Is Rafferty still on board, or has he abandon ship?" Lauren said.

Jack returned to the ECDIS table. "He's still with us. Believe it or not he's actually helping. The guy on that sloop wants him dead. We're the closest thing to an ally he has right now."

"Likewise, I suppose."

Jack did not reply.

"Our heading is changing," Cooney said. "We're coming about to three-one-five."

Jack had reduced their speed to half to regain control of the ship, but now that they'd attained that goal he could kick it up again. "Cooney, bring us to full speed. Watch that coordination between the thrusters and the main drive."

"Connor told me about Malcolm," Lauren said.

Jack closed his eyes and pictured Braddock lying on that twisted metal. He quickly pushed the image from his mind. Emotion would only cloud his thinking right now. He had to focus on the situation at hand. He opened his eyes on the ECDIS display.

Something immediately caught his attention. A faint blip of light flickered in the grid space between the *Friends Good Will* radar contact and the *Achilles*. An instant later a second blip appeared very close to the *Achilles*. Surface radar had picked up pieces of an object that was moving very fast.

Jack knew what is had to be. He spun around to the aft windows in time to see an explosion rising from the stern. The *Achilles* shuddered and her momentum seemed to fall off sharply. "Cooney, report."

A red light flashed on the propulsion station. "Starboard screw has stopped turning," Cooney said. "Revolution count on the port screw is reading irregular, like the shaft is damaged."

Mai called up through the cage ladder. "Jack, the engine room just reported water coming in through the main drive compartment. They don't know how bad the rupture is, but they have to seal it off to avoid losing the whole engine room."

Jack fixed his eyes on the stern. Seeing black smoke pour from the hole in the drive compartment made Jack's face turn red, and the veins in his neck bulged. "Damn it!"

"Tell me what happened. In English," Lauren said.

"They hit us again," Jack explained. "The main drive shafts are damaged. Our advantage over that sloop is gone. Outrunning her is going to be real difficult now."

Cooney scanned his screens. "We've still got propulsion. Quarter speed is better than nothing."

"And we've still got the wind in our favor." Jack checked the ECDIS display. *Friends Good Will* was coming about to a new heading. She swung slowly through a turn and settled on a course parallel to the *Achilles.* Jack thought a moment on her movements. "If they put a hole in our side they won't have to chase us for long."

"Do we have any good options?" Lauren said.

"I'm working on it." Jack read the sloop to be a hundred fifty meters off their starboard. It would be a suicide run to turn and try to intercept her now, but if there was a chance of taking her down it would be worth the risk. Leaving her out there to prowl the water was a bad idea. If the *Achilles* went down and her life rafts launched toward shore with survivors, they might get used for target practice.

Jack called through the cage ladder. "Mai, heading change to zero-four-five."

He noticed Lauren watching him and they exchanged a pensive glance.

The *Achilles'* bow began to pull north, coaxed along by the thruster pods mounted in the hull of the ship. Jack tracked the position of *Friends Good Will* through the shattered bridge windows. Her sails were colored crimson by the setting sunlight. She had moved only ten degrees relative to the *Achilles* course adjustment when Jack spotted what now had become a horribly familiar sight. A puff of smoke and a flash of light flared from the sloop's deck. Another rocket had been fired, and its trajectory seemed dead on to hit *Achilles* amidships.

"Everybody down!"

Jack pulled Lauren to the deck, shielded her with his body, and waited for impact.

- THIRTY –

Recovery Bay: *Achilles*

Markus stayed close to the bio case containing the bacteriophage ampoules, and he never let Ferguson out of his sight. Serious events were going down outside the ship. He was determined to keep things locked down on the inside. Connor and Mai had reported that the cutters had been attacked and sunk, the bridge had been hit, the captain was dead, and the *Achilles* was running for her life. Amazing how quickly things had changed. Just forty minutes ago they were celebrating the recovery of the phage. Now they were hoping to just survive the voyage. His bio case guard duty had become rather intense.

When the *Achilles* had taken everyone on that Tilt-A-Whirl ride, the recovery bay got shook up pretty good. Markus had to cling to the deployment rig just to stay on his feet. During that moment of chaos Ferguson had thought about making his move. He had thought about seizing the new bio case. Markus saw it in his eyes and sensed it in his body language. A lot of things were buzzing around in that prick's head, and Markus was certain none of it benefited him.

The recovery channel still separated them.

Markus stayed within arm's reach of the new bio case, which was sitting on the deck. He didn't like the silence in the bay, so he dug a nickel from his pocket and flipped it into the water of the channel. "Heads I win. Tails you lose. Isn't that how you guys play it?"

"The object is winning," Ferguson said. "How else do you expect us to play it?"

Markus gestured to Ferguson's leg that Jack had shot. "Hey, man, why don't you take a seat over there by the maintenance crib? That bum knee must be killing you."

Ferguson didn't respond. He sent a glare across the channel instead.

"Your boss is stirring up some shit out there. Was this the plan from the beginning?"

Ferguson laughed. "If the colonel had decided to take out this ship and crew, you wouldn't be alive to ask me that question."

"Yeah, that worked out well for him the last time he tried it, didn't it?"

Ferguson thought a moment and then grinned. "How's that girlfriend of yours doing? What's her name, Alyson, is it?"

Markus felt his heart rate speed up. "How do you know about her?"

"Sheridan made an impression on the colonel. When that happens the colonel gets real interested in you. He finds out about your family and friends, and all the little details that make life so interesting."

Markus' muscles tensed. "I don't think you want to take this conversation any further."

Ferguson smiled. "If it's bothering you I do want to take it further."

Markus gave him a threatening smile. "Some guys would warn you to stay away from the girl right about now." Markus shook his head. "Let me tell you straight out. Before we're off this ship you and I are going to tangle, and when I'm finished you won't be able to lift a finger to harm her or anyone else."

"Should I consider that fair warning?"

"I don't care how you consider it. Just know that it's coming." Markus felt a slight shift in the deck under his feet, like *Achilles* was changing course. He glanced up through the windows to the op center and then back to the bio case.

It seemed Ferguson had felt it too. "Sheridan must be running us aground somewhere."

Markus squared off with him across the channel. "Hey, dipshit, you want to go right now?"

Before Ferguson could answer the starboard bulkhead across the bay burst inward with an earsplitting boom. Steel hull plates peeled back, and the flash of a high-yield explosive charge sent rivets and shrapnel flying in all directions. Markus instinctively crouched behind one of the deployment rig's support legs as water began rushing in through the hole in the side of the ship.

He tried to wrap his head around what had just happened, how it happened, but decided those questions didn't matter right then. Hundreds of gallons of water were spilling into the recovery bay and it didn't look like it was going to stop. He had to get out of there, and he had to take the bio case with him.

Markus wheeled about to retrieve the case. Ferguson was right behind him, swinging a crowbar at his head. Markus ducked and stumbled sideways. The crowbar crashed into the steel support leg. "Fore!" Ferguson yelled.

Markus found his footing as Ferguson wound up and swung again with the crowbar. Markus seized his arm in mid-swing and twisted, pulling him forward. Ferguson winced and groaned and tried to break free. Markus dug his thumb into the crook of Ferguson's arm and forced him to drop the crowbar, and then kicked straight into his ribs with tip of his right foot. Ferguson snarled in pain but managed to strike out with his off hand. Markus caught the blow square in his jaw and his teeth rattled. He lost his grip on Ferguson's arm and stepped away to clear his head.

Ferguson gasped and circled like a wolf. "Where'd you learn those moves, Marko?"

The stars in Markus' vision faded. "I didn't spend all my money on beer and women."

Water continued pouring in through the hull rupture. Its roar echoed in the bay. A large pool had already formed on deck and it spread out from the starboard bulkhead. Markus eyed the bio case. Three paces away. He estimated it was only two paces from Ferguson.

"I see what you're thinking," Ferguson said. "You're right. I'm taking the phage."

"My ass."

Ferguson lunged for the case. Markus charged and tackled him like a linebacker. They careened into the channel and the case bounced away from the fray, skidding to a stop near the deployment crane controls. The cold water shocked Markus and he kicked his legs to stay afloat. He tried to keep his arms around Ferguson but the squirrely prick was wiggling free. This was a losing proposition. If he kept trying to hold on, they would both sink below the surface. Markus reared back and head butted Ferguson, which quelled the struggle, and then pushed away. He climbed out of the channel with a dull pain throbbing in his forehead. Water drained from his clothes and pooled at his feet, but the water covering his shoes did not all come from the channel. The deluge spilling in through the hull breach had reached the center of the bay.

Markus rushed to the bio case and lifted it from the deck. Ferguson intercepted him and kicked him in the ribs with a boot heel. The impact knocked Markus on his side, and a sharp pain radiated through his rib cage.

Ferguson laughed. "We're tangling, Marko, just like you said." He kicked at his ribs again, but Markus rolled flat and dodged.

Markus had a split second of opportunity. He swung his leg around and swept Ferguson off the one foot he was balancing on.

Ferguson fell hard on his tail bone and howled. Markus scrambled to his feet, clawing his way up the side of the deployment rig. His hand smashed a button on the manual control box and the crane motor kicked on. The ROV started coming down from the end of the boom. It crashed onto the deck between the two combatants. The crane motor kept feeding out cable. Markus circled around the ROV, sloshing through the lake water at his ankles. Ferguson got back to his feet but slipped on something under his heel. Markus rushed him. Ferguson wheeled about with an off-balance right hook. Markus blocked and followed with a quick left jab that stung Ferguson below the eye. Something clicked and hummed overhead.

The big deployment reel containing the umbilical cable started turning. The heavy cable began scrolling down over the top of the ROV and the surrounding deck. Moving machinery distracted Markus, and Ferguson struck with a solid right. Markus staggered back and became enraged. Ferguson tried to press, but Markus blocked his next two strikes.

Markus went on offense. Left jab. Ferguson recoiled. Left jab. Ferguson fell back a step. Markus advanced, stepping through a loop of umbilical cable. Left jab. Ferguson tried to block but failed. He threw a wild punch. Markus ducked under. Left jab. Another step forward. Ferguson's eyes became glassy. The overhead reel kept dumping cable onto the deck. Markus set up his coup. A big right. His knuckles smashed Ferguson's jaw and a spray of blood from his mouth preceded a hard fall to the flooding deck.

Markus stood over him. "Stay away from my girl, you son-of-a-bitch."

And then the unwinding umbilical cable spilled over into the channel, splashing into the water and falling toward the bottom of the lake. It rapidly took with it the loose coils of slack that had curled up on the deck. Markus felt the bundled cable swirling around his feet like a copper python. He tried to step away. The sharp edge of a cable clamp hooked onto his pant leg and pulled him toward the channel. He struggled for balance. A second clamp hooked on. Markus fell over the top of three big loops and rode them right into the water. He frantically clawed at the side wall of the channel as the cable knotted tight around his ankle. He found the lip of the side wall with his fingernails just as he was going under. He pulled himself up, managing to get out of the water clear to his waist before the falling umbilical cable ate up its supply of slack coils and jerked hard on his leg. The weight of all that copper pulled him back into the cold channel. Markus barely kept his fingertips curled around the lip of the side wall to stop his descent.

He tried to pull up again but failed, and the strength began draining from his fingers. He fought back a wave of panic as the flood of lake water from the hull breach reached his ears.

Bridge: *Achilles*

Jack huddled over Lauren as the rocket struck and exploded. The bridge did not disintegrate around them. That was good news. But where had the rocket hit? He lifted himself off the deck. "Are you okay?" he said to Lauren.

She sat up and looked around. "Yes."

"Cooney?" Jack said.

Cooney climbed back into his navigation chair. "I'm fine, but things just got a lot worse." He nodded through the bridge windows.

Black smoke was rising amidships.

Jack faced the windows. "They finally put a hole in us."

Lauren got to her feet. "Where?"

"Starboard side, looks like the recovery bay. That's the largest open compartment aboard this ship. If it fills with water this ship is going down."

Cooney glanced over. "What do we do now?"

"Stick to the plan," Jack snapped. "Cut that sloop in half with our bow."

Mai's voice called up through the cage ladder. "Jack, the bay is flooding!"

Jack rushed over to the ladder. "Keep this ship on a collision course," he said to Cooney. "Make course adjustments with Connor. Lauren will relay your instructions."

"Where are you going?" Lauren asked.

"To see how bad off we are." He hurried down the cage ladder and stepped into the op center. More trouble. Connor had an access panel removed from the underside of his station and had his head and arms inside the compartment trying to make some kind of connection with a blue cable. The cable ran from his hands down across the deck and into a side port on the Looking Glass table. Parson intently watched a small dialog box on the display screen.

Mai ran up to Jack. "We've got a problem with the thruster pods."

Jack glanced over her shoulder through the windows into the bay. Water gushed through the large hole in the starboard hull. The bay floor was out of view and he couldn't judge how much they had taken on yet. "We've got problems all over the place. What happened to the thrusters?"

"That explosion blew apart the starboard communication junction for the pods. Connor lost all control of the stabilizers on that side of the ship."

"So we can't maneuver anymore?" Jack said.

Mai nodded to Connor, who remained buried inside the control console. "He's trying to get around the problem."

Connor ducked out of the console. "Looking Glass has a dedicated Ethernet network to monitor the status of ship equipment. I'm going to splice into that network, readdress a node or two on the subnet, and I'll be back in business."

Jack regarded him a second. "So you're going through a back door."

"That's what I said." Connor glanced over to Looking Glass. "Parson, ping my station."

Parson keyed in a command. "I got you."

Jack went to the windows across the op center. Half the bay floor was under water. The sight shocked him. And then in the shadow of the deployment rig he spotted Markus and Ferguson slugging it out near the recovery channel. Lake water slowly engulfed the bio case on deck a few feet away from them. "Ferguson is making a play for the phage," Jack said. "I need to get down there."

Mai scanned a display screen. "Jack, the ship is listing to starboard."

Jack double-checked the indicator reporting the pitch of the ship. "We're taking on too much water. The flooding in the drive compartment and the recovery bay is pulling us under."

Mai looked to Jack. "How long?"

"Don't know. It's happening pretty fast." Jack saw the umbilical cable entangle Markus and drag him into the channel. "Oh, crap!" He broke for the hatchway door into the bay. "Mai, get on the intercom. Call for all hands to abandon ship. Get everyone topside."

Jack raced down the steps into the bay and splashed into the water at the base of the stairs. He spotted Ferguson lying on deck several feet away but ignored him. Markus was in dire straits, clinging to the channel's side wall with water rising around his head. Jack sloshed to the deployment rig and hit the E-stop on the control station. The overhead reel stopped feeding out cable. Jack reached into the channel and grabbed under Markus' arms. "Hold on, I'm going to pull you out."

Jack heaved but couldn't overcome the weight of Markus and the cable working against him.

"Hold up," Markus said through a painful grimace. "The umbilical is tangled around my ankle. When you pull up it's pulling the other way and it feels like my knee is being torn apart."

Mai's voice echoed in the bay over the PA system. "All hands abandon ship. Report topside to life raft stations. All hands abandon ship."

Jack held onto Markus' arms and scanned around for something to help untangle the cable. He found nothing within reach. The water level kept rising, and Markus had to tilt his chin full up to breathe out his nose. Jack began to panic. He couldn't dive in and untangle the cable with so much tension present. Even if he could wrestle the cable loose, Markus would probably drown before Jack could work his leg free. "Damn it!"

It suddenly occurred to him what to do. "I'm such an idiot." Jack lifted Markus to get his ears out of the water. "I've got a plan, but you're going to have to hold your breath for a bit." Jack lowered him back into the water and stood. He reset the E-stop on the manual control station and reversed the direction of the drive motor for the overhead reel with a selector switch. The umbilical cable began winding back onto the spool.

A swell of inrushing water splashed against Ferguson's face. He sat up with a start and darted his eyes around the bay in a daze, trying to figure out what was happening. He got to his feet and sloshed toward Jack. "Sheridan, what are you doing here?"

Jack drew the Kimber from his shoulder holster. "Get back, or I swear I'll shoot you dead right where you stand. You got that?"

Ferguson lifted his hands as if to convey no threat. He spotted Markus straining to keep his nose above the surface of the water, and a smile curved his bloodied face. "Life's a bitch, ain't it Marko?"

Jack kept Ferguson under the barrel and glanced up at the reel. A lot of cable had fed out and it would take a bit of time to rewind it all.

Markus's face disappeared below the surface of the water.

Ferguson laughed.

Jack reached into the water with his free hand and hooked under Markus' arm. He pulled but could not get good leverage. He needed both hands. That would require holstering the pistol and leaving himself open to attack from Ferguson. Jack had no choice. Markus' life was on the line. He shoved the Kimber back into the holster and crouched into the cold water. He took hold of Markus under each arm and pulled. In his periphery he saw Ferguson's dark form slowly approaching. Nothing he could do about it. He put his back into the lift. The load seemed lighter than it had been on his last attempt, and Jack was able to elevate Markus' face above the surface. Markus gasped for air. The dark form in Jack's periphery was very close.

"Ferguson!"

Jack recognized the angry voice right away. He glanced over his shoulder and found Rafferty making his way down the sloped deck from a port hatchway with a bandage over his right ear. Jack did not comment on it. Rafferty stepped into the water that had consumed three-quarters of the bay floor and keyed in on his subordinate. "I told you to shelve your vendettas. We've got far greater problems to deal with. Now get back to the cabin and retrieve your sidearm. Meet me in the main deck corridor in three minutes."

Ferguson made a gesture to explain but Rafferty cut him off. "Now, Mr. Ferguson!"

Ferguson scurried up the port side deck.

Jack did not bother to ask Rafferty where the sidearm he spoke of had come from. He heaved Markus onto the side of the recovery channel. The water was at their chest. Jack felt around for the cable entangling Markus' foot. "Are you all right?"

"Absolutely," Markus gasped. "I could have stayed under…another minute."

Rafferty approached the bio case, which was nearly submerged. Jack saw his trajectory and pivoted about to face him. Rafferty stopped and they stared at one another. "We need to get that case to safety," Rafferty said. "In case you haven't noticed, this bay isn't safe anymore."

"This whole ship isn't safe anymore," Jack said.

"My point exactly."

The bay suddenly went dark and the hum of the overhead drive motor went silent. A few seconds later the back-up lighting switched on. "We lost the main generator," Jack said. "That's housed in the engine room. If the generator went out—"

"It's a good bet we lost the engines too," Rafferty said.

Jack turned to Markus. "Think we can get you untangled now?"

Markus tried to shift his body and frowned. "There's still an awful lot of weight pulling on my leg."

Jack felt the water inching up toward his shoulders. He had to get that bio case clear of the bay, but he wasn't about to leave Markus. The dilemma forced him to make a desperate decision. "Take it," he said to Rafferty. "Make sure you get it to a life raft."

Rafferty grabbed the handle and lifted the case from the water. "Count on it. I have a vested interest in getting this to shore." He headed forward to a hatchway on the shrinking dry portion of deck. The ship rolled farther to starboard and nosed up a few degrees, and staggered him as he stepped through the hatchway.

Jack peeled off his wet jacket. "Okay, Markus, let's get you out of here."

"Dad." Connor's voice echoed in the half-lit bay as he rushed down the stairs from the op center with Rezner on his heels. "The engine compartment flooded and the diesels are down. We're dead in the water."

Any shred of hope Jack had of saving the *Achilles* died right then. The best outcome now would be to get everyone safely off the ship and pray that that psychopath Cohn did not gun them all down. Jack called out, "Rez, hold up! Go and make sure Lauren and Mai get into a raft."

Rezner stopped on the stairs. "You need help with Markus down here."

"Connor and I will get Markus out. You take care of Lauren and Mai."

"Your concern is heartfelt," Markus said. "But get your scruffy face out of here and take care of the women. The Sheridan boys got me."

"All right," Rezner said. "But I'm not leaving the ship until I know you're all out of here." He reversed course and ran into the op center.

Connor splashed into the knee-high water at the base of the stairs. "Here I come to save your ass again, Markus."

Forecastle Main Deck: *Achilles*

Rafferty held tight to the dogging lever and fought against gravity to ease the hatchway door open. The flooded engine room and drive compartments had submerged the *Achilles*' stern and had the deck angled nearly twenty degrees bow-up. If he let go of the door, it would fall open and slam against the outer bulkhead. He didn't want that. Some of Cohn's men had probably clambered aboard by now to make certain the phage didn't make it off the ship. He had no desire to draw their attention if they were nearby.

With the bio case sitting on deck at his feet, Rafferty drew his Sig and peered through the hatchway door opening. Half a dozen crewmen were rushing across the cargo deck shouting to each other, two of them carrying a white canister containing an inflatable life raft. It appeared to be the normal disarray one would expect to see aboard a sinking ship. Rafferty held tight to the lever and glanced back through the corridor behind him. Ferguson hadn't arrived yet. He was forty seconds past his three-minute deadline to be there.

Rafferty calculated that dashing across the cargo deck and seizing a life raft canister on his own would be a tactical mistake. Confronting Cohn's men notwithstanding, the *Achilles* crew posed a potential problem as well. They didn't trust him and just might try to prevent him from securing a means off the ship. It would be better to have Ferguson as backup.

The crackle of small arms fire spilled through the hatchway door opening. Rafferty peered through. The disarray on deck had elevated to general chaos. Two men in light body armor rushed from the port side toward the crewmen with the life raft canisters. Rafferty recognized them as Duvall and Holland, two of Cohn's men. They fired automatic weapons over the heads of the crew and shouted for them to get down on their knees. The crew protested, and one of them had his leg shot out from under him for refusing to comply.

Rafferty knew Cohn and his men. He knew they were just as likely to execute the crew as let them live, and as their goal was to keep the phage lost, the fewer survivors to reach shore the better. Rafferty was determined to be among the few to survive, but to make that happen he needed to blunt Cohn's effort here, knock his numbers down, make this boarding too costly to stay engaged. Rafferty checked behind him again. No Ferguson. That could be a sign of trouble within the ship as well. Rafferty steeled his resolve and shoved the bio case into the corner of the corridor with his boot. He firmed up his grip on the Sig and let the hatchway door swing open.

It clanged hard against the outer bulkhead and Rafferty stepped through. Intent on firing first, he aimed at the closest man's core instead of the more lethal head shot and fired twice. The .45 caliber rounds blasted Duvall in the Kevlar vest and knocked him off his feet. Holland whirled about and sprayed a burst of rounds from an MP5, but his rushed aim sent bullets slamming into the forecastle steel. Rafferty pivoted and fired again, striking Holland in the forehead and dropping him like a marionette whose strings had been cut by a machete.

Duvall rolled down the angled deck into the pooling water at the stern. *Achilles* crewmen rushed after him, seizing his dropped submachine gun and throwing him over the gunwale into the lake. Rafferty strode down to the crew, measuring his steps to compensate for the list of the ship. "Have you seen any more of those men aboard?"

The crewman with the submachine gun swung it toward him.

Rafferty frowned. "I just shot the men threatening you. Point that somewhere else."

McElroy stepped out of the group. "What the hell is going on here, Shaw?"

Rafferty searched the water surrounding the ship. Daylight was fading fast. *Friends Good Will* circled off in the distance, an ominous silhouette against a darkening sky. "The men aboard that sloop didn't want you to find the airplane wreck. When you did, they took offense."

McElroy's brow furrowed like he didn't get it. "Why?"

"Does it really matter at this point?"

"Sure as hell does matter," McElroy said through an angry sneer. "Captain Braddock is dead, and Sheridan is leading this ship to the bottom of the lake right next to that airplane wreck."

For some reason the XO's comment incensed Rafferty and he glared at McElroy. "Perhaps if you had stepped up to your duty as second in command you could have done better," Rafferty said sharply. He added, "Somehow I doubt it."

Up toward the bow another small group of crewmen were breaking open white life raft canisters. Rafferty began to wonder if there were enough of them for everyone aboard. He examined the Zodiac mounted on the forecastle next to the main deck hatchway he had just come through. Its inflatable pontoons had been savaged by what looked like shotgun blasts. Rafferty scrutinized the damage. Duvall and Holland had been armed with MP5 submachine guns, not shotguns. There had to be others aboard…

Heavy reports and answering small caliber pops suddenly emerged from the main deck hatchway. The sounds confirmed Rafferty's thought. There was a gun battle taking place inside the ship. Rafferty's mind went right to the bio case sitting in the corner of the main deck corridor. He moved cautiously toward the open hatchway, keeping the Sig Sauer aimed ahead of him. He recalled his shots fired and estimated he had half a clip left. Only one fresh clip remained in his jacket pocket.

"Colonel!"

Ferguson leapt through the hatchway with a 9 mm in his hand and the bio case under his arm. His feet came down on deck, and he nearly lost his balance. "Anders and Byrne are—"

A shotgun blast cut him off. Twelve-gauge shot struck the bio case, rupturing its stainless steel skin and tearing it from Ferguson's grasp. The case tumbled end-over-end down the deck. Ferguson spun around with the 9 mm, but a second shotgun blast struck him in his chest. The impact threw him back, and he tumbled after the case.

Rafferty fired into the hatchway without a clear target. He glanced sideways at the bio case bouncing toward the stern. Anders suddenly appeared in the hatchway and took advantage of Rafferty's distraction. He charged forward, pumping shells into the chamber of his shotgun and firing frantically at the colonel. Rafferty broke hard for cover behind the starboard side of the forecastle, each stride keeping him one step ahead of the spread of deadly shot. He managed to get clear of Anders' field of fire and pressed his back against the bulkhead. Gunfire coming from the sinking stern section drew his attention. The *Achilles* crewmen had seized both Duvall's and Holland's weapons and were firing back at Anders and Byrne.

Rafferty sensed somebody approaching from the bow section behind him. He swung the Sig around and found himself aiming at Rezner.

Rezner stopped cold with the AA12 clenched in his hands. "I knew it!"

"I thought you were one of them," Rafferty said, lowering the pistol. He saw the unease in Rezner's eyes. "Aboard this ship we're on the same side, Mr. Rezner. Come to grips with that."

Rezner grumbled in frustration and then signaled behind him. Lauren and Mai, who were following, stopped their approach and crouched down. Rezner lifted the AA12 and disengaged the safety. "How many of them are there?"

Rafferty looked to the aft section of the ship. "I can't—" A shotgun blast and a staccato series of submachine gun pops cut him off. "I can't be sure."

"Can we make it to the Zodiac?"

"The Zodiac isn't an option anymore. They destroyed the pontoons." Rafferty faced Rezner. "Those men need to be taken out before they sabotage all avenues off this ship."

"That's one thing we agree on."

"There are two of them around the aft side of the forecastle," Rafferty said slipping into command mode. "One is armed with a shotgun, the other most likely with an MP5. Crewmen are keeping them at bay with suppressing fire from the stern. We can sweep them off the cargo deck with that assault shotgun. Get in position over here."

Rezner stomped around him. "Don't give me orders." He stuck the barrel of the AA12 around the corner of the forecastle and fired five shells across the cargo deck in quick succession. Someone shouted beneath the assault of twelve-gauge thunder claps.

"Time to go on offense," Rafferty said. "We move out on three."

"My count," Rezner insisted.

"Do it."

"One…two…three!"

They dashed from behind the bulkhead and aimed up the angled port side cargo deck. Anders and Byrne were falling back around the other side of the forecastle. Rafferty and Rezner opened up on them a second too late to take them down. McElroy and the crewmen kneeling in the water at the stern ceased their fire. Everyone held position in expectation of a counter-offensive. Five seconds. Nothing. Ten seconds. Nothing. Rafferty felt a cold sensation at his feet. He looked down. Lake water swirled around his ankles. Rezner drew an alarmed breath. The gun battle had distracted them so much they had not noticed how quickly the water was consuming the *Achilles*.

Rafferty searched around and found the damaged stainless steel bio case half-submerged near Ferguson's body. A spasm of remorse and loss passed through him. For all his faults, Ferguson was loyal to the end. Rafferty would miss him. But to be completely honest, the sight of that riddled bio case weighed heavier on him than did the body of his minion. Rafferty knew that if the ampoules containing the phage were destroyed by that shotgun blast, it would not be long before he would find himself in the company of Ferguson and Braddock.

"I think they're leaving the ship now," Rafferty said to Rezner. "They're done here."

"I'll believe it when I see it." Rezner strode up the pitched deck and peered around the forecastle where Anders and Byrne had fled. He caught a fleeting glimpse as Anders disappeared over the port side gunwale down a repelling line. Rezner fired a round in vain at him. He went to the gunwale. A thirty-foot Bayliner tossed in the waves amidships, picking up the boarding party. He lifted the AA12 and aimed down on the craft, but a hail of bullets flew up at him and drove him back. The Bayliner's engines revved and the boat sped away. Rezner returned to the shrinking cargo deck and called for Lauren and Mai to help him collect life raft canisters.

Rafferty pulled the damaged bio case from the water and slid it up to a dry section of deck. He crouched in front of it and popped open the clasps with his thumbs.

Recovery Bay: *Achilles*

Jack took two quick breaths off a regulator mouthpiece to make sure air was flowing from the little pony tank, and then knelt next to

Markus in shoulder-deep water. He and Connor's first attempt at untangling the cable from Markus' ankle had failed. A substantial length of the umbilical was still dangling into the depths, and the weight of all that copper put too much tension on the knot to work it free by hand. They had to try something else fast.

Jack held the regulator in front of Markus. "Open that big mouth of yours."

"This place is filling up quick," Markus said. "If you guys can't get it this time get the hell out of here."

Jack handed him the pony tank and shoved the regulator into his mouth. "Shut up, Markus. We're getting you out of here and that's the end of it."

Connor waded over from the maintenance crib with a pair of bolt cutters and a twenty-foot nylon strap. He hung the cutters on a cross member of the deployment rig and tied the strap around his waist. He handed the other end of the strap to Jack. "Let me get about four feet under and then hold me steady."

Jack took the strap. "Got it."

Connor lifted the bolt cutters from the rig. Oily, murky, debris-filled water obscured his view of the deck, and he had to test with his foot to find the edge of the channel. When he found it he stepped in and sank below the surface.

Jack let the nylon strap slip through his hands until it felt like four feet had played out, and then he held on tight. He felt Connor's weight pull hard at the other end. Only Markus's eyes were above the waterline now. Jack made eye contact with him and gave him a nod. Connor's form was barely visible through the dark water. Air bubbles percolated up as he worked the jaws of the bolt cutters on the bundle of cables.

Jack scanned the flooded recovery bay. Every square foot was under water and the level was rising by the second. The *Achilles* listed at least thirty degrees to starboard. Any more of a slant and Jack would have trouble keeping his footing on the submerged deck. He thought about Lauren and wondered if Rezner had gotten her off the ship yet. He thought about Rafferty and the bio case too. Had he done the right thing in letting him take it out of the bay?

"Dad," Connor said bobbing in the water a few feet away. "I'm nearly through. One more breath and I'll have it."

"Make sure you do," Jack said. "We've got to get off this ship."

Connor disappeared below the surface again.

Jack checked on Markus. His head was now under water but he seemed to be sitting calm and breathing through the regulator okay.

The *Achilles* suddenly groaned and rolled. Jack's foot slipped and he released one hand from the strap to grab the deployment rig for support. He heard something clatter on the deck under the swirling water, and a dark shape moved toward the channel. It was the ROV. The pitch of the deck had reached a point that unbalanced the remote vehicle and started it rolling on its outer frame. Jack tried to kick his foot out to stop it from tumbling into the channel. If it fell in it would sink to the bottom, and because it was connected to the umbilical cable that three hundred-pound ROV would drag Markus down with it.

Jack felt the frame roll over his toes. He couldn't let go of the strap. Connor needed to stay buoyant to cut the cable. He couldn't let go of the rig. He'd lose his balance and fall in too. "Damn it!"

The ROV bounced into the channel and dropped like a rock past the ship's keel. Jack estimated it would pull the umbilical cable tight in less than four seconds. He let go of the deployment rig and allowed himself to fall, taking a deep breath before going under water. His hip hit the deck and he jammed his boot against the lip of the channel. The nylon strap in his grip loosened. He took up its slack in his right hand and hooked Markus' arm with his left. Jack counted in his head. Three…four...five.

Markus jerked away like a shark had taken hold of his leg. Jack locked his arm and pulled against the force taking him down. He arched his back and fought to keep both Markus and Connor right where they were. His arms shook as his muscles strained. Air escaped his lungs and exited his nose in a stream of bubbles. A collage of shadowy blurs filled his vision. A dark mass moved near Markus' feet. It had to be Connor cutting the cable. Hurry up, son.

A high pitched twang sounded in the water and Markus shot up onto Jack's chest. The nylon strap fell loose. Markus was free. Connor had dropped the cutters. All three paddled to the surface of the water together; Jack and Connor taking deep breaths, Markus pulling the regulator from his mouth. Jack noticed he couldn't touch the deck with his feet anymore. "Head for the op center," he shouted.

They swam for the stairs leading up and out of the recovery bay. At the base of the steps they grabbed the handrail and pulled themselves out of the water. "Make your way topside," Jack said, "toward the bow."

Connor started up the stairs with water draining from his clothes. The gauze dressing on his head was so wet and loose he just tore it off and kept going. Markus limped after him. Jack followed. At the top of the stairs he looked back. The recovery bay appeared to be a great holding tank with water curling against the bulkhead as the level rose. The deployment rig was completely submerged. The *Achilles* pitched again to starboard, and the bow angled up another several degrees. Jack held on tight to keep from falling. He rushed into the op center.

Emergency lighting was dim, but it lit the place well enough to guide him toward the cage ladder across the room. Connor and Markus had already started up. Jack climbed in and hurried up the rungs to the main deck access. The guys met him in the corridor as he stepped off, and they all ran through the forward hatchway door onto the bow.

Scant light remained in the sky. Night air chilled Jack through his drenched clothes. He searched left and right to get his bearings. In the water off to starboard *Achilles* crewmen paddled away from the ship in a trio of lift rafts.

Rezner ran down from the tip of the bow. "Jack!"

Jack took hold of his arm. "Where's Lauren?"

"She's in a raft with Cooney and Parson. She's all right."

"What about Mai?" Connor said, wiping a trickle of blood from his cheek.

"She's with them too." Rezner smacked Markus' shoulder. "Glad to see they got you out of that bay, you jackwagon."

"Thanks," Markus said, "but let's save the bonding crap until we get off the ship."

"This way." Rezner led them toward the starboard gunwale. "I've got the last life raft secured. It will be a little tight with five of us aboard."

Five? Jack looked over the side and saw a single raft several yards out. A small battery lantern in the hand of a sole occupant lit the perimeter of the raft. It was too dark to make out who it was sitting there. Jack didn't waste time contemplating the question. He patted Connor on the back. "Over the side. I'm right behind you."

Connor and Markus scrambled over the gunwale and jumped off the ship. Jack and Rezner followed suit and leapt from the listing *Achilles* before the guys had splashed in. Already cold and wet from the recovery bay, the water did not shock Jack's senses like he had imagined it would. His feet hit first and he sank. The lake enveloped him in cold blackness. He heard Rezner splashing in and the guys' kicks and strokes through muted ears. He pressed his lips together and made his way to the surface, taking a great breath when the water streamed off his face. He swam hard for the raft, and his mind took him back to the Fourth of July and his desperate swim away from Garity's sail boat. He remembered dodging bullets, and the judge's hysterical rant. Jack shook his head clear. Another time, another place. His hand hit the side of the rubber raft and he reached up. Someone grabbed his arm.

Jack lifted his chin and looked into Rafferty's eyes.

A miraculously dry cigarette burning between his lips and a wry smile on his face, Rafferty hauled him aboard the raft. Jack was too numb and exhausted to conceive the irony of his arch nemesis pulling him to safety. Connor and Markus were already aboard and were helping Rezner out of the water. Jack lay back to catch his breath, but Rafferty handed him a paddle. "We can't get caught in the backflow when the ship goes under."

Jack snatched the paddle from him. "Right." He knelt on the port side of the raft and began rowing. Rafferty did likewise on the starboard side. "Where is the bio case?" Jack asked.

Rafferty slapped something underneath a damp blanket in the nose of the raft. "Right here."

Across the water the *Achilles* floundered. She was submerged clear up to her forecastle with her bow pointed skyward at a forty-degree angle. Her hull and upper decks glowed ghastly in the moonlight as she heeled over and groaned in her death throws. The light from her portholes blinked off one deck at a time as water filled her compartments and shorted out the emergency lighting system in large segments. Jack thought he could hear the crash of bulkheads giving way deep within the vessel. The bow kept rising until it pointed straight up. Half the forecastle was inundated when the *Achilles* began her final descent. She sank straight down, leaving less and less of her bow above the water's surface as the lake consumed her from the stern on up.

Jack and Rafferty picked up the pace of their rowing, although Jack felt they were far enough away now from the sinking vessel to avoid being drawn in by the backflow. Connor, Rezner, and Markus sat transfixed by the sight of the newest, most technologically advanced salvage vessel on the Great Lakes descending into the graveyard that had claimed so many ships before it.

"Lloyd Faulkner is really going to be pissed off," Rezner said.

Markus watched the tip of the bow sink closer to the surface. "Going…going."

It disappeared from view within a swirling, percolating radius of water.

"Gone," Connor said.

Jack didn't linger on the scene for long. "What happened to that sloop?" he said to Rafferty.

"She took off west," Rafferty said. "Cohn couldn't hang around long. Our little conflict will surely attract some attention very soon. He can't be caught in an old sail boat if the coast guard arrives in force on a full-scale search and rescue mission. He has to get back to his primary mission to disperse the 731 Plague in Washington." Rafferty rowed a while in silence. "Besides, he thinks his job here is done."

Jack glanced over. "Is it?"

Rafferty stopped rowing and pulled the blanket off the bio case. The shotgun damage revealed in the lantern light shocked Jack. He dropped his oar on the floor of the raft and popped open the lid of the poked case. The twelve-gauge pellets had caused extensive damage inside. The thermal nests designed to secure and cool the ampoules had been blasted apart and twisted. The ampoules themselves looked to have been completely shattered. Jack held the lantern above the case and searched the dark recesses of the riddled interior but could not find a single intact ampoule.

Jack dropped his head and his heart nearly stopped.

Lauren was going to die from the 731 Plague.

Rafferty took a long draw off his cigarette and blew a stream of smoke into the moonlight. "This isn't the end, Jack."

Jack lifted his eyes to him and set his jaw. "What are you talking about? The phage is the only means we have to kill the plague, and now it's gone."

"It is," Rafferty said coolly, "but I know where to find more."

BOOK IV:
CLEAN SLATE

- THIRTY ONE –

Alec Cohn looked down on the Bayliner from the bow of *Friends Good Will.* He counted three people in the boat. There were two missing. Gathering darkness concealed the men's faces, and Cohn could not make out who had made it back from the boarding operation. In the overall scheme of things it did not matter who had been lost, but Cohn preferred to keep an accurate account of the resources at his disposal. The names of the survivors, however, would not be the first question he asked of his returning men.

"Nix," Cohn called over the side of the sloop. "Were they successful?"

Nix pulled the throttle lever down to idle the engines. "I'll let Anders report out."

One of the men in the stern of the boat threw up a line to the sloop's gunwale. A crewman named Iverson caught it and tied it off. The man who tossed the line said, "The job is done."

Cohn recognized Anders' voice. "I saw life rafts in the water. Are you sure they didn't manage to load the bacteriophage aboard one of them?"

Anders shook his head, which Cohn could barely see through the darkness. "One of the colonel's men tried to make off with a biohazard transport case. I think it was Ferguson. I hit the case with the twelve-gauge. It didn't survive for a trip to shore. Neither did Ferguson."

"What about the colonel?"

"He was there. He's the reason we're light two men."

"Are you sure?"

"Yeah, I put eyes on him."

Cohn felt a bristle of irritation. "Did you put a bullet in him?"

"No, I didn't get the opportunity."

Cohn remained silent for a moment. "Who did we lose?"

"Duvall and Holland."

Cohn made a fist and considered the loss. In exchange for seeing the phage return to the lakebed it was an acceptable price. "Are you absolutely certain you destroyed the bio case?"

"We've been dealing with this biohazardous crap for months," Anders replied. "I recognized the design of the case and the markings on it, and Ferguson was determined to keep it from us. It had to have had the phage inside."

"Did you check out the contents after you shot it?"

Anders paused. "I couldn't get to it. The colonel and the crew were all over us by then."

Cohn mulled it over. It seemed they had succeeded but he could not be 100 percent certain, not without visual confirmation. He considered the merits of returning to the site of the attack to finish off the survivors, but Foley walked up from amidships with a report.

"I powered down the jammer and started monitoring the coast guard channel as ordered," Foley said. "They're aware something happened out here and are dispatching a cutter and search chopper to investigate."

"Did the patrol boats we sank get an emergency signal out through our interference?"

Foley shook his head. "Not likely. It's more probable that a civilian boat passing by saw some of the action and called it in. Either way, this whole section of Lake Michigan is going to get a lot of attention real soon."

Cohn stroked the scar tissue along his jaw. He couldn't go back and deal with the survivors. Risk of detection by the coast guard was too great, and if that happened the primary mission would be put in jeopardy. He would have to settle for the assumption that Anders' assault had removed the phage from the equation. But the colonel had survived, and in that fact alone Cohn knew the issue was not completely put to rest. He would have to address it somehow.

Cohn snapped his fingers at Iverson. "Go astern and tell Lars we're abandoning the sloop. Collect all the weapons, ammunition, and gear that will fit in the Bayliner and transfer them over. Deep-six the rest of it over the side."

Iverson nodded and headed aft.

Cohn looked to Foley. "Make sure this boat's SSB and VHS radios are destroyed before we leave. I'll take care of the staylines and halyards."

"What about Novak and the crew below?" Foley asked.

"Leave them. They know nothing about us. Once they're found, the guard will waste hours questioning them about what happened. That will give us plenty of time to get clear of the area." Cohn glanced at the moon as a cloud drifted by. "We've got the night to cover our escape. We'll head west and then circle back to shore north of South Haven. We'll reconnect with Speers in Good Hart before morning."

"I just came from below," Foley said. "The collision with the salvage ship did some damage to the hull. This boat is taking on water."

Cohn drew a hunting knife from a sheath on his belt and approached a section of running rigging. "Then Novak better pray the coast guard finds him sooner rather than later."

- THIRTY TWO –

Jack counted nineteen souls packed into five life rafts. They paddled east under a near-full moon on a fourteen mile exodus to the coastline. The tiny flotilla got its heading off a compass that Cooney had managed to grab during his evacuation of the doomed salvage vessel. They were twenty minutes into their journey, and Jack had been rowing in silence the whole time. He kept an eye on Lauren in the moonlit raft ahead and wondered if he would be able to save her without the bacteriophage.

After the *Achilles* had gone under the survivors had gathered their rafts together to decide on a course of action. The race to abandon the rapidly sinking ship and the chaos caused by Cohn's boarding party had left them lacking in survival equipment. The portable shortwave did not make it into a raft, and any cell phone that did was four miles out of range of the closest cell tower signal. Jack's phone had shorted out on his swim to safety anyway. And although Connor's head wound had been effectively redressed, there were three other crewmen who had sustained more critical wounds in the attack who needed medical attention beyond what they could get from the first aid kit available to them.

On the plus side, Rezner had managed to get his hands on a flare gun, and had stowed it in the raft beside the AA12. Also, Lake Michigan offered drinkable water. And fourteen miles was a surmountable distance to reach shore.

They decided to head back on their own to get into range of the cell towers along the coast. They had calculated that help would not come to them any time soon. Cohn's electronic jamming had prevented their radio signals from being heard. Waiting to be found in need of help didn't make much sense.

Forty minutes into their voyage, Jack felt it time to get the answers to the questions plaguing his thoughts. He handed his oar back to Rezner and indicated for Rafferty to do the same.

Rafferty passed his oar over his shoulder to Markus and smiled. "You finally want to talk."

"The phage," Jack said. "If you knew of another source to get it from, why did we go after the airplane wreckage?"

"Because recovering it from the wreckage was the easier of the two options."

Jack frowned. "If finding Flight 2501 was the easy route to the phage, we're in serious trouble."

"I don't deny the difficulty of what lies ahead, but it beats the alternative of not having a second option."

Jack begrudgingly agreed. "So where do we get it from now?"

Rafferty fished a cigarette pack from his jacket pocket. "We're in close quarters," he said indicating to Connor, Markus, and Rezner behind them. "Do you mind if I smoke?"

"Would it matter if I did?"

"No, I suppose it wouldn't." Rafferty smiled and casually set a cigarette between his lips.

"Where are we going to find the phage, Donovan?"

Rafferty flicked open his silver lighter and sparked a flame to life. He let its light flicker on their faces a moment before saying, "Alec Cohn has it."

"Cohn?" Jack processed that. "The guy who just tried to kill us?"

"Yes, he has the phage. Alec Cohn may be a maniacal psychopath but he isn't suicidal. He's ferrying a deadly plague to Washington, D.C.; of course he's going to keep an antidote against it on hand." Rafferty lit the cigarette and snapped the lighter closed.

"Where did he get the phage from?"

"The same place he got the 731 Plague: North Korea."

"How do you know so much about Cohn's plan?" Jack stared at Rafferty, and it all came clear. "You were part of it. You and Cohn were working on this plot together."

"I wouldn't put it quite like that," Rafferty said bitterly.

"What happened? Did he refuse to take orders from you, or was it the other way around?"

"Let's just say our respective philosophies are diametrically opposed."

Jack let out a sarcastic little chuckle. "You two are not so different from my perspective. Executing a terror plot against America and selling mercenary services to a hostile nation are right up your alley."

Rafferty exhaled. "We couldn't be more different. Cohn wants to break the world. I want to order it."

Jack laughed. "Order it to your specifications, I'm sure."

"Would you rather a radical Islamist set up his vision?"

"Don't make me answer that."

Rafferty regarded Jack. "America is in decline," he said abruptly. "I intend to stop it."

"By killing and extortion?"

Rafferty straightened his back. "The greatest threat to America is its complacency." He took a drag off his cigarette. "I kick that complacency square in the balls. I wake people up and show them just how off-track they are. I show them shadows of a dismal future that could be if they don't turn the ship around."

"I see. You're like a militant ghost of Christmas yet to come."

"It worked for Scrooge, didn't it?"

Jack scoffed. "How is the plague attack on Washington supposed to turn the ship around?"

"In my estimate it won't. That's where Cohn and I had our falling out." Rafferty flicked a plug of ash into the lake. "The damage caused by the plague will be too substantial and the geopolitical aftershocks will be too unpredictable for the 731 operation to be of any constructive use, but Cohn doesn't care about any of that. He just wants the chaos the plague will ignite and the money he will reap from it."

"The government knows the 731 Plague comes from North Korea," Jack said. "There will be military reprisals if it's unleashed in America. Doesn't Cohn see the danger in his plan?"

"You don't understand him," Rafferty said. "The son-of-a-bitch is a textbook anarchist and a delusional egoist. He thrives on discord."

"You don't seem to share that passion."

"I abhor chaos. It's quite an impasse between us."

Jack looked at him funny. "Then how did you two hook up to begin with?"

"At first I thought our skills and resources would complement each other, but when the North Koreans contracted him to deploy the 731 Plague and I saw his eagerness to do so without hesitation, I realized our objectives could never reconcile."

"Are you actually casting yourself as the White Knight in this fairy tale?"

Rafferty ignored the comment. "I began formulating a contingency plan on my own. As I've explained before, I discovered the existence of the phage samples aboard Flight 2501 from my contacts at Military Intelligence. Initially I intended to retrieve the bacteriophage and force the government to bargain for it, but once the North Koreans made it clear they were not interested in extortion, I kept the information secret. I decided I had to move against Cohn before he carried out this foolish plan. Two weeks ago I did."

"Since you're sitting here with me now, infected with the plague, I assume your assault didn't go off as planned."

"Very astute," Rafferty said deadpan. "Cohn is intelligent and sensed I was going to come after him. He was ready when I did. I lost four of my men in a gun battle at his staging compound in the Canadian Rockies. That's when he exposed me to the plague with a dart very similar to the one I shot your wife with."

Jack tensed up. "You liked the idea so much you used it yourself."

"I needed to find that plane to recover the phage," Rafferty said. "You were the best candidate for the job. You had to be properly motivated."

Jack did not reply.

"Step back and use logic," Rafferty said. "Finding the phage is best for everyone. You have to admit you would not have helped in any other scenario."

"Abner had already gotten me involved in the search for Flight 2501 before you showed up. The government had caught wind of the North Korean terror plot on its own."

"As impressive as it was that U.S. intelligence agencies detected the North Korean plan, they still needed help uncovering the Memorial Day connection."

Jack stared with disbelief. "Are you saying you tipped them off?"

"A third string backup in case I fail to stop Cohn myself."

"I don't believe it."

"It doesn't matter what you believe. What's important now is that we take the phage from Cohn and in the process stop him from deploying the plague in Washington."

Jack shook his head. "You won't convince me you've flipped sides."

"I'm not saying I've flipped anything. My primary goal here is to take Cohn down and take him down hard. I won't allow him to undo the work I've done over the years."

"Right," Jack said dismissively. "The fact that Cohn is trying to kill you with the plague has no bearing on your actions. Getting revenge on him is just icing on the cake."

Rafferty looked ahead and took a drag off his cigarette. "I never said that either."

"I'll be honest, Donovan, I'm not feeling too sympathetic to your cause."

"I don't expect you to feel sympathetic," Rafferty said. "I expect you to do whatever it takes to save your wife's life, and if you happen to save thousands more in Washington at the same time, I suspect you'd call that a good deal."

Jack looked across the water at Lauren and wondered again how he got stuck in this mess. "How do we find Cohn?" he finally said. "You were on the inside. That gives us an edge, right?"

"Don't get too excited about my knowledge of Cohn's plan. I know his target and roughly when he'll strike. His action tonight has shit-canned any other detail I knew. Attacking the *Achilles* was never on his agenda. He did it because he believed his plan had been compromised in some way, and if he believed that, you can bet he's changed up everything by now."

Jack felt irritated. "How *was* he going to get the plague to Washington?"

"He was transporting it from Canada across the Great Lakes to Chicago in a tall ship, and from there to Washington by truck. I never knew exactly when he intended to ship out, or from what port either."

"Is *Friends Good Will* the ship he chose for transport?"

"Negative. He needed a vessel free to circumvent the lakes on his timetable. My understanding is that *Friends Good Will* berths in South Haven at a museum and doesn't stray."

Jack thought on it a bit. "Then his transport ship could be anywhere around the crown of the Lower Peninsula. That's a big area."

"You're constraining your thoughts," Rafferty said. "If Cohn suspects his plan is compromised, my guess is he will abandon his original means of transportation."

"You mean he might be moving it over the road or by air now?"

"All options are on the table."

Too many possibilities had dropped into the equation for Jack's liking. "We can't roll the dice and strike out after him on our own. Too much is at stake if we miss."

"If you're thinking of handing the ball over to Abner and letting the government handle this forget it. They'll mobilize too slowly and botch the window of opportunity we have tonight."

Jack frowned. "Define opportunity."

"Cohn is improvising on the fly. He's most vulnerable now, when he's structuring a new plan to move the plague."

"It's going to be difficult for us to take advantage of his *precarious* situation while we're shipwrecked in Lake Michigan."

"I'm sure you'll think of something."

Jack stared at him a long while in silence. "Going after Cohn on our own is not about a window of opportunity, is it? The last thing you want is for the government to seize the phage. If that happens you won't get treated, and I won't need your microbiologist to save Lauren."

Rafferty cocked his head. "Are you willing to put your wife's life in the hands of a government bureaucracy? You're more brazen than I thought."

"Abner would never stand in the way of Lauren getting treated with the phage."

"Abner is not calling the shots when it comes to 731. The men in control will confiscate the phage and the plague and call in a team of microbiologists from the CDC to study the material. They'll run tests to determine that it is what it is, and they will lock everything down until a special congressional committee is selected to determine what to do next. We're talking weeks if not months. Do you really think Lauren has that long to wait?"

Jack did not reply.

"Simon will administer the phage to Lauren within hours of getting it in his hands."

Jack shook his head. "A Spec Ops team will have a better chance of getting the phage from Cohn than we will. I'd rather cut through bureaucratic red tape than a dozen mercenaries."

Rafferty flicked his cigarette into the water. "Don't fool yourself. Cohn will destroy the phage and disperse the plague at the first whiff of a strike team descending on him. He desperately wants to set off a chain of events that will lead to an anarchist utopia. A plague with North Korean fingerprints on American soil will do the trick."

"You said he wasn't suicidal."

"If he knows he's finished, he'll do his best to take everyone down with him."

"If we go after him alone, he'll do the same thing," Jack countered.

Rafferty chuckled. "Where's your confidence, Jack? He'll never see us coming."

"That's what I'm afraid of; he'll never see us coming because we won't find him." Jack looked skyward and thought about the shattered phage ampoules in the bio case. If only one of them had survived. Then they would not be in this desperate situation. If only…

Jack sat up straight and rocked the raft. "Hold on a minute. Cohn's men damaged the bio case but they didn't bring it back to verify mission accomplished. Cohn has to *assume* he was successful. How do you suppose he'll take that?"

"It will drive him crazy," Rafferty said. "The fact that I survived will concern him too."

"Will it bother him enough to keep watching us?" Jack asked.

Rafferty thought a bit. "I see where you're going. Your idea has merit."

Jack sat forward and for an instant forgot he was talking with the dreaded boogeyman. "Cohn hasn't come back to finish us off. He's probably afraid of getting caught if he hangs around here too long." Jack tapped the side of the bio case. "Without this in his hands he really doesn't know if we have a remnant of the phage with us or not."

Rafferty nodded. "Without complete assurance that all of the ampoules have been destroyed, he'll definitely try to keep tabs on us. He'll want to know what we do once we get to shore."

"If we act as if we still have the phage we won't have to search for him. He'll come to us."

Rafferty grinned. "I knew there was a reason I didn't kill you two years ago."

"Heartwarming," Jack said.

"Divine Providence," Rafferty insisted.

"Whatever." Jack glanced at the stars again. "Now call in the guard and let's get rescued."

Rafferty stared at him but did not reply.

"You managed to keep your cigarettes dry. I'm certain your phone is dry too." Jack gestured to the clip on Rafferty's belt. "It's a satellite phone, isn't it? You're always in range of a signal."

Rafferty smiled and grabbed the phone from its clip. "Good catch."

Jack felt a hand on his shoulder. It was Rezner.

"Listen," Rezner whispered.

Jack did. Far off to the east he heard the faint sound of a thumping helicopter blade.

Rezner snatched up the flare gun from the floor of the raft and fired into the night sky. High over the water the flare ignited into a brilliant ball of light.

Jack looked at Rafferty.

"I guess someone beat me to it," Rafferty said.

"I guess so," Jack said. "Good for us."

Rafferty watched the flare descend toward Lake Michigan and smiled. "Very good."

- THIRTY THREE –

Michigan Intelligence Operations Center (MIOC)
Lansing, MI

"Judas Priest, what's happening out there?"

Abner Wilson sprang from his chair and burst out of his cubicle. Lieutenant Walker's report had gotten him very keyed up. Apparently a coast guard chopper had just spotted a handful of life rafts a dozen miles off the coast of South Haven, very close to where the *Achilles* should be trolling for that airplane wreckage. The news troubled Abner.

He strode through the operations area past the array of video screens and zeroed in on Walker's cubicle. The coast guard officer stood and met him at the opening. "It's confirmed, Admiral," Walker said. "Five life rafts. Nineteen to twenty people aboard. No word yet on who they are or where they came from. The chopper is plucking the first person out of a raft now."

"It has to be them," Abner said. "It's got to be the *Achilles* crew. Damn, what happened?"

Abner was not happy with Jack Sheridan. Yes, he was concerned about his friend, but he was furious with him as well. Ever since the *Achilles* had shipped out, Jack had not kept in constant contact with him as was expected. Earlier in the day Lloyd Faulkner had called to complain that Jack had failed to make his afternoon report and wondered if Abner had spoken with him. He hadn't. The communication blackout from Jack was bad enough, but when the coast guard lost contact with the cutters escorting the *Achilles,* Abner's instincts told him something very bad had happened.

"Can the chopper crew send us a live video feed of the rescue?" Abner asked.

Walker shook his head. "No, MIOC isn't set up to receive live feeds from the guard."

"Do we have a visual or radar confirmation that the *Achilles* is still out there?"

"No, sir, but we've got vessels en route to the area and they'll be able to get us a surface radar sweep in a few minutes."

Abner felt his blood pressure rising. "What about *Thunder Bay* and *Commodore Perry*? Any word on them?"

"Negative, Admiral. No response to our calls and we can't locate their transponder signals."

"Damn it, Gabriel, what the hell can you tell me?"

Walker waited for Abner to settle down before speaking. "I can tell you that we're converging on the site with two HH-65A Dolphin helicopters, three motor life boats (MLB), and the cutter *Buckeye*. Once they're on site we'll get our answers."

Abner grumbled at the lieutenant and stomped over to the op area. He scanned the video monitors, looking for any indication that the news media had caught the scent of the story unfolding on Lake Michigan. It seemed they had not.

Someone came up alongside him. Abner looked over and found State Intelligence Officer Paul Dutello there, looking just as fresh and unruffled at this late hour as he had in the morning.

"Do we know if those rafts are from the *Achilles*?" Dutello said.

Abner crossed his arms and frowned. "Lt. Walker and I were just discussing the matter. We apparently don't know where they came from yet."

"What would be your best guess?"

Abner nodded. "It's them."

Dutello set his hands on his hips and studied the carpet in the op area. "Do you think Rafferty is involved?"

Abner glanced over. "My kneejerk reaction says this is his handiwork. I've got nothing to back that up, but it's a logical assumption given his recent contact with Jack."

"If you're right this is bad."

Abner did not reply. He figured it was bad no matter who was involved.

"How long until we have solid information?" Dutello asked.

"The picture should clarify in about a half hour."

Somebody entering the fusion center from the main entrance across the room drew Abner's attention. Over the tops of the cubicle walls he identified Special Agent Chatfield making his way to the op area dressed in a dusty baseball jersey and jeans to match. It looked as if he had just walked off a softball diamond.

"I called Ben in," Dutello said. "Maybe he can shake loose some information from the Bureau on this incident."

Chatfield walked up to the admiral and the SIC.

"Don't tell me. Designated bench warmer," Abner said.

"No, Admiral, I bat clean-up in the Al Capone league."

"Ben," Dutello said to cut the exchange short. "Does the Bureau have any idea what's happening out there tonight?"

Chatfield dusted off his jeans. "I made some calls on the way in. We've got nothing on this. No intercepts, no chatter, no tips."

"On top of things as usual," Abner said.

"Hey, this is your operation. Not mine."

"In case you've forgotten, this is our operation," Abner countered.

Dutello stepped in. "The issue at hand is finding out what happened to the *Achilles.* You two get your damned focus on that."

Lieutenant Walker approached them. "New reports in from the site," he said. "The first person rescued is a guy named Kohler. He's the navigation officer from the *Achilles.* He's got a pretty nasty head wound, and he says he got it when the ship was attacked. The rescue team leader says Kohler is in and out of consciousness, so his take on things is sketchy."

"But Kohler is from the *Achilles,*" Abner said. "This looks grim."

"It gets worse," Walker said. "The first MLB on site found a *Thunder Bay* crewman in the water who says the tall ship *Friends Good Will* attacked them with a rocket barrage."

Chatfield's jaw dropped. "Christ, that's no amateur operation. Paul, is this the kind of thing you expected from that Rafferty character?"

"Unfortunately it is," Dutello said.

Abner made eye contact with Walker. "Is that tall ship still in the area?"

"We don't know," Walker said. "The MLBs are just reaching the site now. Their focus will be rescuing survivors. *Buckeye* will be on site in about twenty minutes. She's going to make a sweep around the perimeter to look for the ship."

Abner shifted his weight. "How is she armed?"

"She's got a fifty-caliber machine gun on her bow and a squad of guardsmen with assault rifles on deck."

"If the *Buckeye* crew locates *Friends Good Will,* you tell them to proceed with extreme caution," Abner warned. "Rafferty's proven to be one dangerous SOB. If he's the one behind this, those guardsmen are going to have their hands full."

"Point taken," Walker said. "I'll pass that advice on to *Buckeye.*"

"What about that strike team you assembled to back up Sheridan?" Chatfield said to Abner.

"They're staged at Selfridge," Abner replied. "If we find that ship, they'll be on their way in a hot minute."

Dutello shook his head. "I'm afraid the damage is done. If the *Achilles* is sunk, the bio case is probably lost as well."

"And Memorial Day is right around the corner," Chatfield added.

Abner regarded them both. "You two just keep that doom and gloom talk to yourselves. Jack Sheridan was on board that salvage ship and until I hear from him, I will not assume the effort to recover the bio case is a lost cause."

"That's touching," Chatfield said, "but what if Sheridan didn't survive the attack?"

"I'm sure he did. He knows how to take care of himself. If anyone could survive that type of assault it would be him."

Chatfield laughed sarcastically. "You don't know that. They were attacked by a rocket barrage. All bets are off regarding the casualty list."

Abner looked him square in the eye. "Special Agent Chatfield, you don't know Jack."

- THIRTY FOUR –

Somewhere Over Lake Michigan

The guardsman pulled Jack in through the side door of the helicopter and disconnected the harness from the cable that had lifted him up from the raft. Jack leaned in close to the crewman's flight helmet to thank him, and then stepped over and dropped into a bench seat on the other side of the cabin. The Dolphin had taken on all the survivors from the raft, and the pilot veered away from the remnants of the flotilla below on a course back to shore. Jack checked the damaged bio case at his feet. It took some convincing, but the rescue team had finally let him bring it aboard. He wasn't sure if they bought into its importance, but they did realize that Jack had no intention of leaving the raft without it.

The first step in the plan to bait Cohn into action had been taken.

Jack found himself seated next to Rafferty. Connor, Markus, and Rezner comprised the balance of the passengers in the chopper. Before the guardsman pulled the side door closed, Jack looked out through the opening to try and spot the rafts still carrying survivors in the water. He didn't see any of them.

Normally Jack would have insisted on being the last one off the lake, but in this case time was of the essence. He had made sure that the first helicopter picked up Lauren and the injured, but he and Rafferty had agreed that the quicker they got to shore to carry out their ruse the better chance they would have of snagging Cohn in the deception. As such they were the first ones taken by the second chopper on site. Jack took solace in knowing that three motor life boats had arrived on the scene and had commenced pulling survivors to safety as he flew to shore aboard the Dolphin.

Jack leaned toward Rafferty and spoke with as much discretion as he could and still be heard over the noise of the helicopter engines. "We need Abner's strike team."

Rafferty looked nonplused. "Did you forget our conversation in the raft?"

"I haven't stopped thinking about it. If nothing else we need serious backup."

"And where would you have us send this strike team?" Rafferty said.

"I'd suggest the site where you have your microbiologist holed up."

Rafferty glanced crosswise at him. "Do I really look that foolish?"

"After the team is in place, we make a few conspicuous phone calls and rush to that address with the case. When Cohn makes his move, the professionals take him down."

"I am a professional," Rafferty said, sounding a bit insulted.

"After what I saw on the lake today, I think a Special Forces team is in order."

"And who knows, it just might be your lucky day if I get caught in the crossfire." Rafferty felt around his jacket for a pack of cigarettes. "You'll have to try harder than that to get rid of me."

"Believe it or not, that's not what I had in mind."

"Besides," Rafferty continued. "You don't know how or if Cohn will come after us. We may capture one of Cohn's hired guns who know nothing of the main plan and there we'll be, stuck with military involvement and all the baggage that goes with it. Meanwhile, Cohn slips away to Washington and Lauren's symptoms advance."

"You're determined to have us do this on our own, aren't you?"

"We are the tip of the spear. It has to be that way in order for us to have the best chance of getting the phage from Cohn and stopping him cold."

"Bullshit. You just want to kill Cohn yourself."

"That's beside the point."

"That is the point."

Rafferty shook his head ever so slightly. "Once we have a handle on Cohn's location and a solid plan to box him in, we can discuss calling in Abner's team."

Jack regarded him. "You don't trust me any more than I trust you."

"Is this a surprise?"

"No," Jack said. "But given our situation, I figured you'd be more open to compromise."

"Compromise?" Rafferty frowned. "Just saying the word tastes sour. I'm certain you understand."

"Now I'm the one insulted."

"We'll be back on dry land soon," Rafferty said. "Do we agree on the way forward or not?"

Jack didn't like Rafferty's cavalier approach to the issue, but his argument had merit. They had to go out on a limb alone to draw Cohn in one last time. Bringing in the government too soon could have all the unintended consequences Rafferty had thrown out there. Again Jack found himself in the unpleasant position of agreeing with his enemy.

Jack looked across the cabin at Connor. "What do you think?"

Connor nodded. "We can do it."

"Markus?"

Markus sat up straight. "This Cohn guy almost drowned me. You bet I want a piece of him."

Jack smiled and shifted his gaze down the bench. "Joshua?"

"Do you really need to go around the horn?" Rafferty said to Jack with a bit of exasperation. "You lead, they follow."

"That's not how I do things."

"It's inefficient." Rafferty found a pack in a jacket pocket with one cigarette left. "Unlike me, they trust you. They trust your decisions. They will do what you say."

"I value their input," Jack said. "Maybe if you had listened to your team more you wouldn't be in the position you're in now."

Rafferty smirked. "If I had listened to my team, you would be dead."

Rezner scoffed. "If Jack took my advice back at the dock, you'd be dead too."

Rafferty extracted the cigarette and crushed the pack. "This conversation is pointless."

The guardsman who had helped Jack aboard turned from the helicopter cockpit and stepped into their space. "Are one of you gentlemen named Jack Sheridan?"

Jack kept silent. There was only one reason he would be asking.

"There is an Admiral Wilson from the Maritime Affairs Office on the radio," the guardsman continued, "and he wants to speak with Mr. Sheridan."

Jack remained silent. If he intended to go along with Rafferty's plan he could not contact Abner yet. Jack stared across the cabin at Connor. Neither of them spoke. Jack realized that he had just made up his mind on the way forward. They were striking out alone.

Rafferty sat back and lit his cigarette. "It appears Jack Sheridan is not on board."

The guardsman glanced around at their faces a moment longer before nodding. "Okay, I'll tell Admiral Wilson to check with the MLBs. We'll have you folks in Grand Haven in ten minutes." He moved toward the cockpit.

Jack felt a bit like he'd just thrown away a life line.

Rafferty smiled. "Smart decision."

"It doesn't feel smart."

The Dolphin flew on through the darkness and conversation in the cabin dried up. Connor stood and looked out through the cockpit window. Lights along the Michigan shoreline appeared far ahead of the craft. "Why are they taking us to Grand Haven?" he said to Jack.

"It's the guard's main station on the west coast."

"I'll have Naughton pick us up there once we land," Rafferty said.

Connor reclaimed his seat across from Jack. "Does Mom know the phage ampoules are destroyed?"

Jack didn't know. He checked with Rezner.

"No," Rezner said. "She didn't see the case get hit, and I didn't bother showing her."

"We need to keep it that way," Jack said. "The fewer of us who know the truth the better." He added, "Besides, I refuse to tell her our last hope is gone until it really is gone."

Rafferty let the burning cigarette dangle between his lips. "That's the trick, isn't it? How do we clearly communicate to Cohn that we still have the phage?"

"He had to have learned about our salvage operation from you," Jack said. "He's obviously got a line on you somehow. Let's use it."

"Don't be so sure about that." Rafferty pulled the cigarette from his mouth. "When we last parted Cohn was confident that I was on my way to die in a dark corner somewhere. I never revealed the existence of Flight 2501 to him, and I know he isn't monitoring my phone. Trust me on that. My guess is he learned about the salvage from you."

"Me?" The implication irritated Jack.

"He had to have planted electronic surveillance of some kind on you for him to discover the Neptune's Reach plan. You did tell Abner about our meeting in the cemetery, didn't you?"

"The only reason Cohn knows I exist is because of you. He must have had eyes on you too."

"Unlikely," Rafferty protested. "I'm very careful in my travels."

Jack pivoted toward him. "The fact that we both led him to the *Achilles* is irrelevant. We just need to figure the best way to feed him the bait." Jack lifted his cell phone. "The lake fried my cell. If Cohn was listening in on my line, there goes option number one."

Rafferty waved his cigarette in a dismissive manner. "Cohn would not rely solely on your cell phone to gather information from you. He would plant listening devices around your home and in your car too."

"Not in my house," Jack said. "Not with my security system, not to mention Ike."

"I was listening in on you," Rafferty said with droll inflection. "Long-range directional microphones work well if you place them properly."

Jack didn't want to believe that. "Are you serious?"

"Of course I'm serious. But since I was watching your property and did not pick up on anyone else doing the same thing, you may be right about your home not being bugged. It's more than likely, however, that your car is compromised. I'll tell Naughton to bring the frequency detector with him and have him scan your vehicle."

"My Jeep is parked in Muskegon at the dock. Have him scan it before he comes to Grand Haven. If Cohn is watching us he doesn't need to know we're on to his surveillance."

Rafferty dialed Naughton on his satellite phone. "Done."

Connor stared at his father a long while. "You told me, and I didn't want to believe it."

Jack cocked his head. "Believe what?"

"You said we could succeed out there on the lake and still fail. That's happening, isn't it?"

Jack shook his head. "No, I was wrong. I can see the whole field of play now. This is going to work. We're going to get the phage and stop Cohn. Lloyd would call it a win-win scenario."

"I wanted to hear that kind of talk before. Now that you're saying it I have a hard time buying in."

Jack jabbed a thumb at Rafferty. "He needs the phage just as bad as we do. It turns my stomach to say this, but I'm glad he's on our side for this one. He's motivated to take Cohn out. That will boost the odds in our favor."

"If we're going to win a lot of breaks have to go our way," Connor said, sounding not too convinced. "The way I see it Lady Luck will have to crawl in bed with us."

Jack smiled. "Ms. Luck and I have a long history together. She's fickle but she always comes back."

"I hope she's good-looking," Markus said.

Rezner leaned into the conversation. "I just hope Cohn takes the bait."

"He'll take it," Jack said. "He sank two coast guard cutters and the *Achilles* to keep the phage lost. With psychotic determination like that he certainly won't give up now."

- THIRTY FIVE –

Grand Haven, MI

Nix sipped a hot coffee and welcomed the warmth flowing from the car heater. After riding in the Bayliner's open cockpit all day and half the night, he still felt the chill of the cold lake air in his bones. That salvage vessel could not have gone down soon enough. As soon as it had heeled over, Nix set the Bayliner on a beeline back to shore and warmer temperatures. Inside of forty-five minutes he had Cohn and the men on an isolated section of beach north of South Haven. They had split up immediately after stepping onto dry land. Cohn took most of the team north to hook up with Speers in Good Hart while Nix went back on surveillance duty, this time with Iverson. After spending several days on windswept Lake Michigan Nix found the confines of the car quite comfortable, even if conversation with Iverson was somewhat lacking.

Nix had parked the car in the lot of the Snug Harbor restaurant just northeast of the Grand Haven Coast Guard Station and had been waiting there thirty minutes for something to happen. Cohn had dispatched him to that spot based on information Foley had gathered while monitoring the guard's operational channel on the shortwave. The survivors from the Neptune's Reach salvage vessel were being brought to that station, and Cohn wanted to confirm that his effort to completely destroy the bacteriophage had been successful. Nix and Iverson were to be his eyes.

Iverson reclined his seat a few notches and kicked his foot up on the dash. "Turn that heat off. I'm burning up over here."

Nix took another sip of coffee. "In a minute."

"It isn't *that* cold outside."

"You weren't out on the water all day. After a while the wind cuts through you."

Iverson glanced over. "Maybe if you'd been more involved in the action your blood would warm you up."

"I've seen enough action to last a lifetime," Nix said. "Surveillance and ferry duty suits me fine."

"Once the deed goes down in Washington you may not have a choice," Iverson warned. "The world is going to get crazy, and Cohn is going to need more guns."

Nix didn't reply. What he had to say might sound sacrilegious to Iverson. Nix had known Cohn a long time. They'd been stirring up trouble together for years, longer than most of the men on the team knew. Nix never had a problem with the things they had done in the past. Stealing and extorting from the dark characters they dealt with never bothered him. Killing them or bombing their assets never kept him up at night either. But the 731 operation took them to a whole new level, and deep down Nix wondered if Alec Cohn had bitten off more than he could, or should, chew.

"Everyone has a choice," Nix said. "The hard part is learning to live with the consequences of your decisions."

"That's deep, Nix. I think the heat in this car is getting to you."

Nix lifted the coffee cup to his lips and gazed into the night sky beyond the coast guard station. A single light appeared southwest of their position. He watched its approach long enough to determine that it was heading toward them. He scrolled down his window and listened. The distinctive sound of a helicopter grew as the light came closer. Nix grabbed the cell phone on his belt and pressed the speed dial key to call Cohn, but the unfamiliar keypad configuration caused him to hit two buttons at once and the call failed. "Damn throw-away phone." He angled his thumb differently and hit just the one key.

Cohn answered quickly. "Yes, Nix, you have something to report?"

"A helicopter is coming toward the station. I'd bet real money it's filled with survivors from the salvage vessel."

"Watch what happens closely," Cohn said. "Find out if the colonel is among them."

"What if he is?"

Cohn stayed silent a moment. "Inform me immediately. I'll give you further instructions at that time."

"Got it, Alec, I'll let you know."

Cohn ended the call and Nix put the phone back on his belt clip.

"How do you stand all this watching and waiting?" Iverson said.

Nix lifted a pair of binoculars from the car seat and peered through them, trying to get a better look at the rear of the coast guard station where response personnel had gathered to await the chopper's arrival. "Like I said, I've seen enough action to last a lifetime."

Aboard Coast Guard Helicopter #2

They were close to shore now. Jack watched through the cockpit windows from the passenger cabin, keeping his balance with a nylon handhold affixed to the overhead. He could make out the coast guard station landing zone as they descended toward it. The first helicopter was on the ground. Guardsmen and paramedics swarmed the aircraft, prepping the wounded for transport to a hospital and evaluating the condition of the other survivors on board. Down there somewhere Lauren melded with the crowd. All Jack wanted to do was get to her, talk to her, touch her; the ordeal with the plague had made their every moment together more significant to him, and for good reason. With the situation in flux as it was, he didn't know how much time they had left.

But Jack's emotional burden went beyond the threat to Lauren. Her life was one among many threatened by the plague. If Cohn succeeded in his plan a lot of other people would die as well. Throughout most of the Flight 2501 salvage Jack had managed to compartmentalize that fact and focus primarily on Lauren, but that was when the terror plot was still an ethereal rumor. It had become very real now, and Jack couldn't marginalize it any longer.

The *Achilles* was gone and the man who sank her still prowled in the darkness. Given the brazen nature of Cohn's attack, it would be no surprise at all if he showed up at the coast guard station to finish the job he started on the lake. No survivors. No phage. End of story.

The guardsman in the helicopter cabin turned away to converse with the pilot, and Jack discretely drew the Kimber from its holster. He kept the pistol concealed under the blanket he had draped over his shoulders and chambered a round. The noise from the chopper's twin engines masked the click of the weapon. Jack engaged the safety and returned the weapon to its holster.

"Are you expecting trouble down there?" Rafferty said nodding toward his covert action.

"Aren't you?" Jack replied.

"I have to say I've considered it. I guess great minds think alike."

"I'd appreciate it if you didn't say garbage like that."

"I have two rounds in the Sig and a fresh magazine in my pocket." Rafferty made a cursory search of the cabin floor. "What happened to Mr. Rezner's assault shotgun?"

"They wouldn't let him bring it aboard the chopper. He'll have to show his permit for it before they'll return it." Jack shrugged his shoulders. "That's why I'm keeping this blanket over me. I've got a CCW for my .45, but I figure the fewer questions the better."

"It's a shame," Rafferty said. "That AA12 would be good to have on our hunt for Cohn."

"Don't worry. Joshua will have it before he leaves the station."

The helicopter dropped through a patch of turbulence and Jack's stomach fell.

"We'll be on the ground in less than five minutes," Rafferty said. "Naughton will arrive thirty minutes after that."

"Good. That will give me time to find Lauren and check in with the crew."

"That also might give Abner just enough time to drive here from Lansing to find you."

Jack glanced sideways at Rafferty. "Then you better hope Naughton gets here early."

The pilot lined up his approach and slowed his air speed. The helicopter descended over the landing zone. Paramedics and guardsmen waited on the periphery. Jack turned and addressed the others in the cabin. "Once we're on the ground, stay together and stay close. Our ride arrives in thirty minutes. Then the fun begins."

The landing gear touched the concrete pad and the helicopter bumped to a stop. Jack lifted the bio case from the floor. The guardsman in the cabin turned around. "Gentlemen, stay put until we secure the craft."

Rafferty leaned toward Jack. "Keep your eyes open for unfriendly faces in the crowd."

"Funny," Jack said. "I was about to tell you the same thing."

Rafferty checked through the window in the side door of the helicopter. "It's unlikely Cohn will make a move against us here."

"It was unlikely he'd attack the *Achilles* too. I think it's safe to say conventional thinking is out the window."

"Indeed."

The guardsman threw open the side door and a gust of fresh air filled the cabin. In unison Jack and Rafferty rested their hands over their concealed weapons. The guardsman hopped out of the helicopter and gestured for Jack to follow. Jack scanned the group of responders and officers waiting outside and then stepped down from the aircraft. He ducked under the rotor wash and held the blanket tight over his shoulders. A pair of paramedics ran up to him. One of them said, "Welcome to Grand Haven, sir, do you need any medical attention?"

"No," Jack said, "but my son is cut up pretty good. He's coming off the chopper behind me."

The paramedics circled around him and Jack continued forward. He searched for Lauren in the crowded landing zone. The first rescue helicopter sat just ahead with rotors slowly winding down. An ambulance sped away from the scene with wounded crewmen aboard. Another ambulance was parked outside the landing circle with lights flashing and a group of people gathered around. Jack recognized faces; Cooney, Parson, Hart. He headed toward them, all the while scanning for someone who looked out of place, someone not fitting the demeanor of a survivor or a responder. Jack sensed Rafferty to his left doing the same thing.

Jack spotted Lauren's hair amongst the crowd. Her auburn locks were like a beacon to him. She stood with Mai behind the ambulance. She seemed to be searching too, trying to get a look at who had come off the second helicopter. When she saw Jack their eyes locked and she smiled wide. Jack picked up his pace and wrapped her in an iron embrace. He kept the bio case tight in his hand.

"You scared me," she said. "I didn't think you were going to make it off the ship."

"But I did make it. And I brought Connor and Markus with me."

She felt behind his back for the bio case. "It feels like there are holes in that thing."

"There are." Jack released her and looked around. Rafferty had positioned himself a few paces away and kept his eyes probing every movement in the crowd. Connor and Markus were heading toward the ambulance at the insistence of the paramedics. Rezner was nowhere in sight. Jack turned back to Lauren. "How was your flight to Grand Haven?"

"What happened to the case, Jack?"

Jack's lip twitched. "Cohn's boarding party happened."

Concern set into her eyes. "Is the phage okay?"

"Uh…"

"Jackson." Mai grabbed his forearm. "Where's Connor?"

Jack turned and nodded. "Paramedics are patching him up by that ambulance."

Mai rushed over there. She threw her arms around Connor's neck and he lifted her off the ground. They kissed, and then a paramedic told Connor to take a seat so he could work.

Jack scrutinized the perimeter of the landing zone.

Lauren read his expression. "What's wrong?"

"Hopefully nothing."

"You're expecting something to happen. I know that look."

"Hey, after what we just went through, allow me a little paranoia."

"Are you afraid Cohn is going come after us again to get the phage?"

If only it was that simple. Jack gave her a little nod. "That's pretty much it."

"Let's contact Abner," she said. "Have him send in his men to protect us."

"That's not our best option at this time." Jack avoided looking her in the eye.

"Why?"

"It's a little complicated."

"What do you mean?" She regarded him. "Look at me, Jack. Tell me what's going on."

He met her gaze but could not speak.

Her eyes went to the damaged bio case. She seemed to be piecing it together.

Jack felt his heart breaking. He put his arm around her. "It's going to be all right." The words sounded hollow as he spoke them.

"The phage in that case was our only hope." She stared at the pock marks in the stainless steel. "What about all those people in Washington? How are we going to stop this now?"

Rafferty walked over and spoke in a low, determined voice. "The plague is in my blood too. Rest assured we will have the bacteriophage in our hands before sun up tomorrow."

Lauren looked to Jack. "How?"

"Cohn carries the phage with him." Jack hoped he was not lying to her. "We're going to draw him to us and take it from him. Give me ten minutes and I'll fill you in on our plan."

She looked angry. "Why didn't you tell me about this?"

"I didn't know the ampoules had been damaged until I got into the raft."

"If the ampoules are broken, why are you carrying that case around?"

"It's part of our plan."

"What part of your plan does a bullet-riddled bio case play?"

Jack gave her a reassuring smile. "Chum for the shark."

Snug Harbor Parking Lot

Nix had left the car and had scrambled to the end of the concrete pier at the rear of the parking lot to get a better look at things. He held the binoculars to his eyes and watched the rescue activities at the coast guard station. Two helicopters were on the ground now, and he was certain that the colonel and Sheridan had gotten off the second. Sheridan carried a case, and it looked like he wasn't letting it go for anyone. They had coalesced into a group and had been talking for a while now.

"What are they doing?" Iverson asked, crouched beside him on the pier.

"Still talking." Nix adjusted the focus on the binoculars. "They're anticipating something because they're keeping watch all around. It's really odd though."

"How so?"

Nix lowered the binoculars. "The last time I saw those two men together they were shooting at one another."

Iverson shrugged. "Maybe they have a love/hate relationship."

"Maybe." Nix grabbed his cell phone and carefully hit the speed dial key to call Cohn.

Cohn answered. "Report."

"The colonel is here. And so is Sheridan…"

"And?"

"They've got a case that Sheridan is carrying around. Their body language is very defensive."

Cohn remained silent a moment. "That could be a problem."

"Could be," Nix said.

"I'm halfway to Good Hart. I don't have time to tie up this loose end myself."

Nix glanced at Iverson. "How do you want us to proceed?"

"Stay on them. Don't let them hook up with the colonel's men in Bangor or anywhere else. Find a suitable location along the road and take them out."

"Understood," Nix said. "Just hope they don't pull out of that station in an armored car. You played your hand on the lake. They know they're marked now."

"If the situation becomes too difficult for you to handle, contact me immediately. That phage has to be eliminated."

Nix wasn't in the habit of asking for help. "I think I can handle it, but I'll let you know otherwise."

Cohn disconnected.

Nix scanned the coast guard station through the binoculars. "So you like action, eh, Iverson? It looks like you're going to see a little more before the night is over."

"Good. No more watching and waiting."

"Not for long," Nix said. "One of the colonel's men just arrived. They're moving out."

- THIRTY SIX –

Fortunately the Buick Enclave was designed to carry seven people, just enough to take everyone away from the Coast Guard station that needed to go. A little after 1:00 a.m. Naughton pulled out of the parking lot with Rafferty riding shotgun. None too pleased that he couldn't take the wheel, Jack sat in a second row captain's chair next to Lauren. The third row bench seat had Connor, Markus, and Rezner crammed together. Talk about all the eggs in one basket. But Jack knew this initial leg of the trip had to be this way. Until they got to Muskegon to disperse into other vehicles they were one big, fat target for Cohn.

"Take Jackson Avenue to hook up with 31 North," Jack said to Naughton.

Naughton did not acknowledge that he had heard.

Jack glanced at Lauren bemused. "Communication is a two-way street, Naughton."

Rafferty looked back. "He knows the way."

"Does he know there are already two cars that could be tailing us?" Rezner said from the cramped rear seat.

"Of course," Rafferty said annoyed. "Once we're clear of town, we'll know for sure if we've picked up a shadow or not."

"Just make sure your man stays well ahead of whoever is back there," Jack said. "We'll need about a minute out of sight to set the game in motion."

"I appreciate the advice, but we've done this before."

"I'm sure you have."

Naughton drove through sparse traffic on Jackson Avenue and connected with 31 North toward Muskegon. He proceeded out of town, leaving the street lights and glowing signs of late night bars and restaurants behind. Not long after crossing over the Grand River, Grand Haven faded into the darkness, but the headlights of both cars that Rezner had identified still followed, staggered behind the Enclave about a half mile back.

Jack swiveled about to face Connor. "What did you tell Mai we were doing?"

"I told her we were concluding our business with Rafferty."

"She didn't ask for more details?"

"I don't think she wanted to know the details."

Jack regarded him. "According to Petty Officer Barrows back at the station, Neptune's Reach is putting up the crew in a nice hotel tonight and arranging transportation there. If things go well you can swing by and pick her up in the morning."

Connor gave him a little smile. "Don't you mean *after* things go well?"

"That's my boy."

Jack dug into his damp jean pocket. He had gone through so much that day that he really wasn't certain if he still had the key ring for the Jeep on him. He breathed a little sigh of relief when he felt the metal and pulled the keys out. "Markus, make sure you have your car keys."

"Please, Mr. Sheridan. I don't go anywhere without the keys to the big, bad 'stang." He jockeyed for elbow room in the cramped seat and squeezed his hand into his right pocket. He grumbled and checked the left pocket. This time he produced the key fob. "Got 'em."

Rafferty turned and faced Jack. "I was right. When Mr. Naughton scanned your Jeep he detected an audio transmitting device."

"Good. That will be our direct line to Cohn's ear. All we have to do now is confirm that we have a tail."

Naughton crossed into the passing lane and sped around a flatbed trailer hauling steel coils. He quickly cut back into the right lane just ahead of the truck. After a few moments one of the two cars behind them duplicated the maneuver with a little more urgency than seemed normal, as if perhaps the driver might be trying to keep the Enclave in line of sight.

Rezner watched the car settle in behind them again. "It's confirmed. We have a tail."

Jack, Rafferty, and Rezner all drew their pistols.

"Whoa, guys," Lauren said. "Check those safeties."

Jack watched the headlights through the tinted rear window.

"If you were in their shoes, what would you do?" Rafferty asked him.

"How do you mean?"

"Assume Cohn and his men are in that car. They're back there for a reason. They suspect we have the phage. They're not just going to follow us across the state. Logically their intent is to stop us, kill us most likely. How would you accomplish that goal?"

Jack thought on it a moment, considered the problem. "I'd wait to make my move until the conditions were right. I'd want the target vehicle isolated and away from a populated area, and I'd use darkness to mask my approach and make it more difficult for them to defend against me."

Lauren looked on. Jack could see she was troubled with the discussion.

"I concur," Rafferty said. "Unfortunately you've just described our tactical situation." He addressed his minion behind the wheel. "Speed up, Mr. Naughton. Make sure our tail is for real."

Naughton put his foot down on the accelerator. The speedometer needle ticked up toward eighty-five. The trailing vehicle hesitated a moment and then its speed increased too. Rezner pivoted about and aimed his Smith & Wesson at the car through the rear window.

"Hold your fire, Mr. Rezner," Rafferty ordered.

"Eat me, Donovan."

"Joshua, he's right," Jack said. "We don't want to start a firefight. Remember, we need to take them alive. We have to draw them in to capture, not kill."

Jack swiveled around and looked out through the windshield. An interchange was dead ahead. "That's our exit to Business 31. Maybe we can lose them on the cloverleaf."

"My thoughts exactly," Rafferty said.

Naughton kept picking up speed. He steered into the right lane to catch the exit ramp, braking just enough the keep the Enclave from sliding as he started into the loop. Centrifugal force shoved everyone to the left of the cab, and the tires squealed on the pavement. The trailing car made a move to the outside as if trying to overtake and assault the broad side of the vehicle.

"Muzzle flash," Rezner reported. "From their passenger side. Everybody down."

Jack heard the muted reports of an automatic weapon firing but did not detect a hit on the Enclave. "Tell me you've got bullet resistant glass in this thing." he said to Rafferty.

"Glass, yes. Tires, no."

Up ahead a gray Nissan negotiated the off ramp. Naughton straddled the Enclave over the white line between the soft shoulder and the ramp and moved to pass the car. The Nissan's driver cursed at them through his window. The Enclave pulled even with the car, and Rafferty scrolled down his window, letting in a cacophony of wind noise and revving engines. He aimed his Sig at the Nissan's front end.

"What the hell are you doing?" Jack shouted.

"Buying time." Rafferty fired two rounds into the front tire of the Nissan. The driver's expression changed from anger to panic in a split second. He struggled with the steering wheel to maintain control and jammed on his brakes. Naughton sped around him. The Nissan screeched into a three-sixty spin.

The car that had been following the Enclave slowed and broke hard to the left to avoid a collision. It almost worked. The rear quarter panel of the Nissan smacked the trailing car's front bumper and deflected it onto the soft shoulder, where it smacked hard into the guard rail.

Naughton steered the Enclave out of the curve and merged onto Business 31. Behind them their tail slowed to a crawl as the car scraped against the guard rail at the crest of the off ramp and the Nissan skidded to a stop down the inner embankment.

"That did it." Rafferty closed his window. "There's your minute, Jack."

"You could have killed that guy in the Nissan."

"He would have died for a good cause. We're on a rather important mission."

Jack fumed in silence. He didn't like Rafferty's tactics at all, but their common need for the phage had chained them together like the Defiant Ones. He decided he had to draw the line somewhere. "If you pull something like that with an innocent bystander again, you and I are going to have a major problem. You got me?"

Rafferty ejected the empty clip from the Sig. "Your complaint is duly noted."

Naughton sped down the road. Rezner and the guys kept the car that had been following them under watch as the distance between them increased. "They're on the move again," Rezner said. "Coming off the guard rail with one head light burning."

"Ease up some," Rafferty said to Naughton. "Keep the carrot in sight."

"This is insane," Lauren said.

Jack grabbed her hand. "It gets crazier. It's our turn next to be the rabbit."

She looked him in the eye and he could see her uncertainty.

He gave her a smile. "You go with Connor. Joshua and I will take the Jeep."

"No," she protested. "I'm staying with you." She added, "That Mustang has a tiny rear seat."

Naughton kept driving at a fast clip. Up ahead the darkness of Lake Muskegon appeared beyond the lights of Muskegon's marine industrial shoreline. The road curved north and Jack knew they were very close to Mart Dock. The car with one headlight had stayed with them and had managed to gain some ground. Jack lifted the damaged bio case from the floor. "Everybody get ready."

The marine terminal that the *Achilles* had shipped out from came up fast on the left. Naughton spun the steering wheel and the Enclave screeched onto Fifth Street. He veered off the road, rumbled across a dirt lot, and bounced over a set of railroad tracks. Mart Dock lay just ahead. Naughton headed toward the cars parked along the far edge of the concrete lot and slid to a stop behind Jack's Jeep and Markus's Mustang.

"Move out!" Jack threw open his door and sprang from the Enclave. Lauren jumped out the other side. They ran for the Jeep. Jack unlocked its doors with the key fob and the taillights flashed. The bio case banged against the Enclave's grill as he rounded the front of the vehicle.

Rezner and the guys piled out after them. Connor and Markus made for the Mustang. Doors flew open and engines roared to life. Rezner had barely gotten in through the Jeep's rear passenger door when Jack slammed the shifter into drive and hit the gas. The rear wheels spun and kicked bits of gravel into the side of the Enclave. Naughton peeled out of the lot toward the service drive while Markus fish-tailed the Mustang into a screeching parallel path.

The car with one headlight turned off Fifth Street and halted in the middle of the dirt lot that Naughton had raced through. It seemed the driver was realizing that he no longer had just one car to contend with but suddenly faced three. His moment of indecision allowed the stampede of steel to rush past him. The car abruptly wheeled about to give pursuit.

Jack turned hard onto Shoreline Drive heading south. He glanced left through his window to confirm Markus and Rafferty were heading north. "Lauren, get out your cell and call Abner."

She pulled the phone from her jean pocket and dialed the number from her contacts list that would go straight to Admiral Wilson's home voicemail, just as Jack had instructed her. She handed him the phone.

He took it and waited for the tone on the admiral's machine. "Abner, this is Jack. Listen close. We have the phage but a guy named Cohn is chasing after us right now. He's the one who attacked the *Achilles*. He wants to destroy the phage. The Memorial Day plot is his. The guys and I are playing a shell game with him. We scattered from him in three cars but I have the phage with me in the Jeep. I'll contact you when I get to Bangor. Get your team ready."

Jack disconnected and, keeping in mind the Jeep was bugged, gave Lauren a nod.

"We did it," Rezner said with the same obvious thought. "We slicked him good."

They drove in silence for almost a minute when Lauren looked back and saw a car in the distance behind them. It had only one headlight.

"Jack," she said. "I think they're on to us."

- THIRTY SEVEN –

Nix sat gripping the steering wheel as three sets of headlights barreled toward him. The SUV containing the colonel, Sheridan, and the bio case had gone into the marine terminal alone, but three vehicles were coming out. Nix beat a fist against the dashboard and cursed. First the fiasco at the off ramp and now this; how could he be so sloppy? He should have known what they were up to when they headed north into Muskegon out of the coast guard station instead of south toward the house in Bangor. Now he had a one-in-three chance to intercept the phage and eliminate the threat it posed to Cohn's plan.

Iverson fidgeted in the passenger seat and lifted an MP5 submachine gun. "Which one?"

"Don't know."

The Enclave, a Mustang, and a Jeep blew by in a cloud of dust.

"Damn it!" Nix slapped the gearshift into drive and hit the gas. He spun the car around and set a pursuit course down Fifth Street. The taillights of the fleeing vehicles flashed on as they reached the Shoreline Drive intersection at the end of the road.

"They're breaking up," Iverson said.

Nix shook his head. "Of course they're breaking up, Einstein."

The Jeep went right. The Enclave and the Mustang went left. Nix thought fast. Two cars together made sense if one of them contained the phage. The second could act as a blocker. Then again it could be a ploy to draw attention away from the single vehicle. Which one?

Nix suddenly had an epiphany. "Grab my surveillance bag from the back. Quick!"

Iverson turned and reached into the back seat. The car pounded through a pot hole and he bumped his head on the ceiling. He came back with a brown canvas bag. "Now what?"

Nix stepped on the brakes and screeched to a stop at Shoreline Drive. He swiped the bag from Iverson's lap and unzipped it in a blur. He ripped out a black electronic device and switched a power button on the side of the case. The unit clicked on and belched a burst of static. Nix stared at the green LED bars of a decibel level indicator on the face of the unit. "Come on, Sheridan, tell me something."

He and Iverson listened as road noise from inside the Jeep made the green bars on the indicator vibrate at the bottom of the scale. They jumped to midrange when Jack Sheridan's voice emerged. "Lauren, get out your cell and call Abner."

"All right, we're in business," Nix said.

They listened to Jack's call to Abner and heard the message they needed to hear.

"The phage is in the Jeep," Iverson blurted out.

"Nothing gets past you, does it?" Nix turned onto southbound Shoreline Drive and ratcheted up the speed. The taillights of the Jeep were far ahead, but at least he knew he was chasing the correct vehicle. The road curved away from the lakefront and led into a more residential area. Nix kept his eyes fixed on the Jeep and his ear tuned to the listening device.

"Jack," a woman's voice said through the speaker. "I think they're on to us."

"You got that right, honey," Iverson said.

"I'll try to lose them on a side street," Sheridan said in reply to his wife.

Far ahead the Jeep made a quick turn onto a crossroad. Nix picked up speed and found that Sheridan had turned off onto Hackley Avenue. Nix slid through the intersection and reacquired the Jeep's taillights. Less than a mile down Sheridan turned again, this time onto a small, dark side street. The Jeep's headlights disappeared behind a stand of trees. Nix smiled. "I'm still with you."

He almost reached the side road when the green bars on the decibel monitor jumped to max. "Jack, look out!" the woman shouted.

A loud crash sounded. Sheridan cursed and the Jeep's engine revved again and again. "We're stuck. We've got to make a run on foot."

Nix slowed the car and turned onto Glen Avenue as Sheridan had done. "Get ready, Iverson."

A street sign informed them they were entering McGraft Park. Tall, old trees bounded the road on both sides. There weren't any houses within sight anymore, and a ravine on the right fell away from the roadside to a creek. The road seemed to run straight for a while, and the car's single headlight beam reflected off the back of the Jeep just ahead. Skid marks on the road implied Sheridan had swerved to miss something, perhaps a deer, and had slid partially down the embankment into a cluster of trees. The doors were open and it didn't appear that anyone was still inside.

"Search the Jeep for the case," Nix said. "They may have left it hoping we'll leave them alone if we have the phage."

Iverson checked his weapon. "Are we going to leave them alone?"

Nix put his gaze on the road ahead. "The phage is our only objective here."

* * *

Jack ran from the Jeep through the woods, Lauren holding his right hand and her cell phone gripped in his left. He had speed-dialed Rafferty as soon as his boots hit the ground, and he listened intently for an answer. Rezner ran beside them ten yards to the left with the bio case under his arm. It was dark amongst the trees, and all they had to navigate by were beams of moonlight shining through the openings in the branches.

The cell line clicked and Rafferty answered. "What's happening?"

Jack pulled Lauren behind the thick trunk of an ancient oak and glanced back at the Jeep thirty yards away. "The plan is working beautifully. Get your ass over here."

"Where is here?" Rafferty said.

"McGraft Park, just past the fork on Glen Avenue. GPS it."

"On the way." Rafferty disconnected.

Jack pocketed the phone and drew the Kimber.

Rezner took up a position behind a nearby tree.

"You still have the case?" Jack asked him.

"Sure do. You still have your wife?"

"Yes, he does," Lauren answered. She regarded their surroundings. "Jack, didn't you bring me to a place just like this in the cemetery?"

Jack clicked off the safety and aimed toward the Jeep. "You know, honey, I think you're right. We'll have to expand our horizons."

"Please do."

The car with one headlight crept up behind the Jeep. It rolled to a stop and the doors swung open. Jack couldn't make out distinct shapes in the darkness and glare of the headlight. He steadied his aim at the car behind the Jeep. "Take out the light on my mark," he whispered to Rezner.

"Roger that."

Two dark forms moved against the blackness and rushed to the Jeep. One stood and looked out into the woods from behind the driver's door while the other searched inside the Jeep with the aid of the dome light.

"Rez," Jack whispered. "Lights out."

They both fired one round and the headlight shattered. The thunderous report of the pistols echoed in the woods, and the man behind the driver's door fired a spray of bullets wildly into the trees. The muzzle flash lit his face with a macabre yellow flicker. The dome light in the Jeep went dark, and Jack could hardly see the vehicles on the road any longer.

A voice called out. "All we want is the case, Sheridan. Hand it over, and you and your wife can go."

Jack didn't reply. The two men on the road fell silent too. After a moment Jack sensed they were moving. A dry piece of deadwood cracked on the forest floor. Jack pulled back so a beam of moonlight touched his face, and he silently signaled to Rezner. *Two rounds down range. Twenty yards. Back to cover.* Rezner signaled okay.

They aimed around their oak concealment and fired twice toward the road, trying to hit ten yards shy of the Jeep. They quickly crouched behind the tree trunks again. The submachine gun answered almost immediately, but this time it was joined by a semi-auto pistol. The incoming bullets landed closer to their position than the first haphazard volley. Jack and Rezner's own muzzle flashes were giving them away.

The two men held up at the edge of the soft shoulder, perhaps unsure of how to approach. Jack didn't care much for this game of keep away. The longer it went on the greater the risk. He turned to signal Rezner to fall back when he heard the growl of a Shelby Cobra Mustang racing up Glen Avenue. Headlight beams pierced the darkness, lighting the Jeep like daylight and catching the two men in their glare like rabbits on the road. Side by side the Mustang and the Enclave slid to a stop just short of the car behind the Jeep. Doors clicked open, and an onslaught of gunfire shattered the night. Bullets struck all around the men, kicking up clouds of dust and bits of gravel.

The gunfire subsided and Jack stepped away from the tree trunk. Naughton and Rafferty had moved into the light and were ordering the men to raise their hands. Jack glanced over at Rezner. "Joshua, let's go." They rushed to the road with Lauren a step behind them. When Jack got close he saw the men had dropped their weapons and had their hands clasped behind their heads. Rafferty approached them with his pistol in hand and Naughton standing guard behind. Jack stepped up to the road. "Are one of these guys Cohn?"

"No," Rafferty answered, "but I know them." He regarded the shorter of the two. "Nix," he said with a sense of recognition. "I thought you'd be smart enough to abandon Cohn when he took on this plague foolishness."

"Cohn and I have a history," Nix replied. "I'm sure you understand."

Rafferty turned from him and walked up to the taller man. "Iverson, isn't it?"

Iverson didn't reply.

"You were at the complex in the Canadian Rockies."

Iverson smirked. "I sure was. Had your ass handed to you that day, didn't you?"

Rafferty swung the butt of the Sig like a hammer and struck Iverson in the face with enough impact to drop him. Iverson moved on a surge of anger to stand but Rafferty aimed the Sig between his eyes and stopped him cold. "You handed me my ass. Let me return the favor."

Jack moved into the road. "Donovan! Stay on task. We need to find Cohn."

"That we do." Rafferty kicked Iverson in the shoulder and sent him tumbling on his tail. He returned to Nix. "Tell me where to find Alec."

Nix shook his head. "I can't."

Rafferty shoved the barrel of the Sig under his chin. "You can and you will."

Nix took a nervous breath but said nothing.

Rafferty stood nose to nose with him. "Think this through, Nix. I have nothing to lose by killing you. I'm already dead, remember?" He let that thought hang out there a bit and then said, "Do you really want to be part of what he has planned?"

"I picked this path a long time ago," Nix said. "I knew where it might lead."

"What a waste of loyalty." Rafferty lowered the Sig from Nix's chin but held him in place with a commanding stare. "He wouldn't do the same for you. His only loyalty is to himself."

"Cohn is loyal to his cause. He believes in what he's doing."

Rafferty's eyes narrowed. "Yes, he's a true believer. He's a pious zealot in the church of anarchy, and anarchists are remarkably self-serving people."

"Don't fool yourself, Colonel, deep down we're all anarchists."

"Then act like one," Rafferty snapped. "Be selfish. Live to see the sunrise and tell me where to find Cohn."

Nix stood silent but his eyes searched the ground.

"Don't say a damned thing," Iverson warned.

Rafferty spun and kicked a boot heel square into his chin. Iverson fell onto his back clutching the point of impact and spitting a venomous curse at the colonel.

"Joshua," Jack said quietly. "Shut that guy up before he ends up dead."

Rezner strode across the road and gestured for Markus and Connor to come. The three of them took Iverson off the ground and brought him to the back of the Enclave to be bound and gagged. Naughton stood vigil over their every move. Rafferty didn't bother to interfere.

It occurred to Jack that Nix wasn't going to talk any time soon and time was getting short. Cohn was getting farther away with each passing second. They needed to try a different approach. Jack considered the problem from a dozen angles and hit on a memory from a few days before. He regarded Nix. "How do you keep in contact with Cohn?"

Nix seemed unsure of the question. "By phone."

Jack held out his hand. "Give it to me."

"Why? Are you going to call him and ask where he's hiding?"

Rafferty aimed the Sig at Nix's right kneecap. "Give it to him. No more chances."

Nix lowered his hand and pulled a cell phone from his pocket. Jack took it from him and walked to the Mustang. "Connor, get over here."

Connor returned from the rear of the Enclave. "What do you need?"

"That IT magic you did in my Jeep the other day," Jack said, "when you tracked the location of Markus's boat with your laptop. We can do the same thing with a cell phone, can't we?"

"It depends," Connor said. "The first thing we need is the cell phone number."

Jack flipped open Nix's phone and scrolled through the call history. One number kept appearing in the incoming and outgoing call list. "My guess it that's Cohn's number there."

Rafferty walked up to them. "No stomach for interrogation, Jack?"

"We need to try something more reliable. He'll tell us whatever he thinks we need to hear if you thrash him hard enough. We don't have time to chase shadows."

Connor took the phone from Jack and searched through its menu selections. "It's a prepaid cell."

"Cohn probably uses them to communicate with his men anonymously," Jack said.

Connor studied the phone a little longer. "The GPS chip is disabled."

Jack shook his head. "If this guy's phone is off the grid, I'll bet Cohn's is as well. There goes my great idea."

Connor handed the cell back to him. "We can still do it."

Jack didn't follow. "Without the chip?"

Connor nodded. "You can track a phone using cell tower triangulation."

Rafferty smiled. "Very astute. If you're ever interested in contract employment let me know."

Jack frowned at the suggestion. "Connor, how do we triangulate on Cohn's cell?"

"We have to query the cell towers in the area to find which ones are communicating with Cohn's number," Connor explained, "and then calculate the distance of the phone to each tower with signal strength algorithms. With that info we triangulate on the phone's location. It will get us within a couple hundred meters of his position."

"That sounds too easy," Jack said skeptically.

"I left out the hard part," Connor said. "Location data and the signal algorithms we need are only found on the service provider's network. We have to get inside to track that phone."

Jack's hope in the plan began to fade. "Can you do it?"

Connor bit his lip. "If I can get past their firewall I think I can find everything we need, but those networks are pretty secure and I'm not an expert hacker."

"Leave that to me," Rafferty said.

Jack raised an eyebrow. "You're quite a renaissance mercenary."

Rafferty looked at him crosswise. "My contacts inside Military Intelligence are hackers, among other things."

"What if they can't break into the network?" Connor asked.

Rafferty drew a perturbed breath. "Mr. Sheridan, these people infiltrate computer systems at Iranian nuclear facilities and hack into Chinese satellites as a matter of course. I doubt Verizon's service network will prove too formidable for them. I'll get you inside."

"Then I'm going to need a computer with 4G connectivity," Connor said. "My Toshiba is on the bottom of Lake Michigan right now."

A police siren wailed off in the distance.

"The Muskegon authorities just woke up." Jack said bending his ear to the sound. He called Rezner and Markus over. "Police are on the way to investigate our gun play. We need to scatter."

Rafferty lifted his satellite phone and tapped Naughton's shoulder. "Secure Nix in the back with Iverson. We're moving out." He dialed a number and headed for the Enclave.

"Where are we going?" Rezner asked Jack.

"The only place around that's open all night and sells electronics."

Rezner cocked his head. "You better drive."

Jack rushed over and took Lauren's hand. "Let's go, dear." He called over his shoulder to Connor and Markus. "Get moving. We'll regroup in fifteen minutes at the Walmart on Sherman Boulevard."

Markus signaled thumbs up. "Got it."

Jack climbed into the Jeep and started the engine. After Lauren slammed her door closed he switched into four-wheel drive mode. He backed away from the tree that he had parked up against and climbed the embankment. Rezner met him in the middle of the road with the AA12 he had retrieved from the Enclave slung across his back. He hopped in and they were off, leaving Nix's battered car on the soft shoulder.

The three vehicles fled McGraft Park and dispersed in different directions. Jack drove calmly down Shoreline Drive as an oncoming police car with flashing lights sped past and turned onto Hackley Avenue. Jack released his breath and headed into the heart of Muskegon.

"Assume this idea works and we locate Cohn," Lauren said out of the silence in the cab. "He isn't going to just let you take the phage from him."

Jack didn't reply right away. "I know," he finally said.

"We've seen what he's capable of today. How can you confront that?"

Jack shrugged. "Bring a big hammer to persuade him."

"If you bring a hammer he'll have a wrecking ball." Lauren closed her eyes. "I don't like it."

Jack exhaled. "I don't like it either."

- THIRTY EIGHT –

Connor fired up a brand new laptop in the rear of the Jeep. The hatch was open and he sat with the computer on his lap, testing out the 4G connection amid the smell of new plastic and packaging foam. Markus had parked his Mustang behind the Jeep at an angle to the parking spaces so that his door swung open toward the group standing around Jack's vehicle. Positioned equally between the Jeep and the Mustang, the Enclave closed the triangle of cars. They were parked on the very fringe of a lot adjacent to Walmart, just out of range of roving security cameras. The configuration of the vehicles reminded Jack of a tail gate party at a football stadium, only this gathering did not impart a festive mood on the small crowd in attendance. The participants of this tail gate gathering were gearing up for a very different kind of contact sport.

The computer wasn't the only item Jack's credit card had purchased in the wee hours that morning. A fresh box of ammunition for the Kimber, and one for Rezner's Smith & Wesson, sat in the back of the Jeep. Rezner had picked up a .308 hunting rifle, which he now instructed Markus on handling, loading, and firing. Lauren watched them a moment and then looked away. Her eyes found Jack near the Jeep inserting .45 caliber rounds into a spare clip for the Kimber. She frowned and walked over and hugged him but did not say a word. He held her tight. "What do you say, sweetheart? Next week we go to the Caribbean. No hardware allowed."

"You're on," she said.

Rafferty stepped down from the Enclave's driver's seat and returned his satellite phone to its belt clip. He walked to the Jeep holding a piece of paper with handwriting on it. "It just so happens that attaining data from cell service networks without consent or court orders is not uncommon for certain elements of the intelligence community. There's actually a covert protocol and decryption system in place to hack into these networks at will, all sanctioned under Top Secret executive order."

Jack regarded him. "You don't seem too concerned with keeping this information a secret."

"It's not my secret to keep." Rafferty handed the piece of paper to Connor. "There's a URL that leads you to the back door of Verizon's network. That's the provider currently servicing Cohn's prepaid phones. There's also a pass code to let you slip under their firewall. It's a twelve-hour key. Once the time expires you'll never be able to use it again."

"This thing will be over in half that time," Jack said.

Connor read the handwritten information with apparent excitement. "This is the coolest thing I've ever done…from an IT perspective." He began keying in the URL.

"If Cohn has the battery pulled from his phone, this idea isn't going to work," Jack said.

Rafferty nodded. "Cohn sent Nix to finish us off. I have no doubt his cell phone is powered up and roaming the towers while he anxiously awaits word of my demise."

"That could turn into a problem," Jack said. "Cohn is going to get suspicious that he hasn't heard back from his men yet."

"Quite right. Let's remedy that." Rafferty returned to the Enclave and pulled the bound and gagged Nix from the rear seat. After loosening the gag he faced Nix toward the car and stuck the barrel of the Sig into the base of his spine. Rafferty handed him the cell phone. "Call Alec. Tell him Sheridan and I are dead and the phage is destroyed. Understand?"

"You'll never get to him," Nix said. "Alec is at his best when he's winging it. He's hell-bent on getting to Washington, and nothing is going to stop him."

"Do as you're told or live the rest of your life in a wheelchair."

Nix dialed Cohn's number and raised the cell phone to his ear.

"If you say anything I construe as a code word I will shoot. Stick to the script I gave you."

"Alec," Nix said. "It's done."

"Both of them?" Cohn said.

Nix paused and Rafferty pressed the Sig into his back. "Yeah, the colonel and Sheridan are dead. They had an accident outside of Grand Haven."

"What about the phage?" Cohn asked.

"The case and the ampoules inside are destroyed."

"Send a picture of the case."

Nix glanced over his shoulder. Rafferty was standing close to listen to the conversation. He gave Nix a nod. "Will do," Nix said. "I'll send it right away."

"Good work," Cohn said. "I'll contact you tomorrow."

The line went dead.

Rafferty took the phone from Nix's hand and removed the pistol from his back. He gestured for Naughton to return the prisoner to the rear of the Enclave and then went over to Jack. "Where is that bio case?"

Jack jabbed a thumb inside the Jeep.

Rafferty opened the Jeep's side door and snapped a photograph of the open case with Nix's phone. Before sending the picture he typed in a short message: *Propaganda of the deed.*

"What's that for?" Jack said.

Rafferty pocketed the phone. "Evidence that Nix did his job."

"How much time do you think it will buy?"

"Enough."

Jack looked around at the faces in the parking lot. One week ago he would never have imagined these people working together in an alliance, no matter how tenuous. One week ago he could not have conceived the possibility of standing beside Rafferty without trying to stab, strangle, or shoot him. Jack was certain Rafferty felt likewise. Through an uncanny series of events Alec Cohn had managed to do the impossible. He had forced Jack Sheridan and Donovan Rafferty to rely on each other for survival.

"Holy crap, I got it!" Connor waved everyone over to the computer.

Jack and Rafferty turned.

Connor looked at them with the glow of the computer screen on his face. "I located Cohn's cell phone."

Everyone crowded around. Connor tilted the screen back and pointed to a blue dot pulsating on a map of northern Michigan. "He's in Good Hart at the northeast tip of the Lower Peninsula."

Jack felt his breathing accelerate. This was it, his last chance to save Lauren and half the population of the nation's capital. "Are you sure?"

"Of course I'm sure. It's right freaking there."

Rafferty stared at the screen. "Let's get moving. He won't wait for us to arrive."

"Hold on," Jack said. "This whole posse isn't going."

Rafferty looked at him as if he'd just uttered something very obvious. "Of course not. I'm sending Naughton to protect my flank."

"How so?"

"My microbiologist is sequestered at a house in Bangor. There's a good chance Cohn knows about the house, if not the man inside it. He may have dispatched another hit team to take care of business there, make a clean sweep of it. I won't let him snatch victory from the jaws of defeat."

Jack thought on it a moment. "Does the microbiologist need to work on the living phage too?"

Rafferty checked the time on his phone. "Simon has been studying the 731 Plague for months. He'll know right away if Cohn's phage needs to be modified to be more effective against it. I'm sure you agree this is a good idea."

"I do," Jack admitted. He thought the situation through and then said, "Lauren is going to Bangor too."

Lauren looked at him but held her tongue.

"I don't have an issue with that," Rafferty said.

"Hold on a minute." Lauren came forward. "I get a vote on where I go, and I think you guys could use all the help you can get."

Jack faced her. "We're going to get the phage to save your life. It will be counterproductive if you get yourself shot while we're doing that. You're going to Bangor."

Lauren stood there and stewed.

"Joshua," Jack said. "You're going with her. I want you there if a hit team shows up."

"Just a damn minute," Rezner protested.

Lauren shook her head. "Jack, you can't— "

"Discussion over," Jack barked. "Rafferty and the guys and I are going to Good Hart. We will call in Abner's cavalry to support us. We will not be alone up there."

Rafferty checked the time again. "Get your people in line, Jack. Time is of the essence."

Jack glared at him. He went to Lauren and put his arms around her. They held the embrace a long while. Jack knew this might be their last moment together. Going up against Cohn was a very dangerous game. He closed his eyes and tried to block out any thought of defeat. "I love you," he said. "And I will be back."

"I love you too," she whispered with a shaky voice. "And you better be."

He kissed her and the significance of it all hit him. The next few hours would define the rest of their lives. He wanted more years to spend with her, not just this fleeting moment. He held her tight and silently vowed to wrestle those years away from Cohn and Rafferty. Somehow. He slowly pulled away. "I'm coming back with the phage."

He could tell she was fighting hard to keep from breaking down. "Keep Connor safe."

"We'll watch each other's back." Jack turned and slapped his son on the shoulder. "You're mobile with that laptop, right?"

"You know it," Connor replied.

"Then let's roll."

"All right!" Markus slid the hunting rifle into the back seat of the Mustang and stood up on the doorframe. "We'll take the point. Try not to fall behind."

Jack smiled and tossed him Lauren's cell phone. "We'll need to know every move Cohn makes. It's almost a four-hour drive to Good Hart. He may not stay there long. I programmed Rafferty's number in that phone. Use it to keep us up to date."

The guys acknowledged and jumped into the Mustang.

Jack spun around and found Rafferty staring at him.

"Get in the Jeep," Jack said.

"It's about time."

Rezner walked up with the assault shotgun and handed it to Jack. "You'll need this more than I will." He wrapped his knuckles against the ammunition drum. "It's a twenty-round magazine, after that you're down to your .45. How are you sitting with ammunition for the Kimber?"

Jack took the AA12. "Half a clip loaded, two fresh in my jacket."

"Watch your ass, Jack." Rezner leaned in and whispered. "I still don't trust Rafferty."

"That makes two of us."

Rezner slapped his bicep. "No quarter."

Jack set the shotgun in the Jeep and slammed the door shut. "Protect Lauren."

Rezner patted the Smith & Wesson in its holster. "You know I will."

Jack climbed into the Jeep and started the engine. He looked one last time at Lauren. She gave him a faint smile and wiped a tear from her cheek. Jack put the Jeep in gear. "Markus, move out."

The Mustang's engine roared and the rear wheels squealed on the pavement. Markus screamed out of the parking lot. Jack hit the accelerator and the Jeep jumped forward. In the rearview mirror he saw Naughton, Rezner, and Lauren get into the Enclave to head down to Bangor. He put his eyes back on the road.

"Mr. Rezner has the right idea," Rafferty said from the passenger seat.

Jack glanced over but didn't follow.

Rafferty smiled. "No quarter for Alec Cohn."

- THIRTY NINE –

Jack raced down the expressway, keeping the Mustang's taillights in sight. Good Hart was a long way off and he began to feel anxious, not because of the coming encounter but because there was a reasonable chance they might miss it. They were defying the odds by going on offense, but it was a risk they had to take. If Cohn slipped from their grasp now everyone would lose.

"We need to tell Abner what's going on and get his team in play."

Rafferty exhaled. "Triangulation locates a cell phone within a two hundred-meter radius. We don't know if Cohn is sitting in a house, parked in a car, or if he has left his phone in a diner to draw us away. Given the unknowns, what would you have Abner do with his men? Carpet bomb Good Hart? I certainly hope the phage survives the assault."

It infuriated Jack to hear Rafferty make sense. "We have to nail down his exact position."

"I believe that's what we're attempting to do."

Jack thumped the steering wheel with his palm. "All right. Cohn is in Good Hart but we know he isn't going to stay there. He needs to move the plague. How will he do it?"

Rafferty settled into his seat. "In my opinion he has only two options. He'll either go back on the water in another vessel to follow his original route to Chicago, or he'll fly the plague out of the state from a regional airport."

Jack nodded. "He won't try to drive it out. Once we sound the alarm about a madman hauling a deadly plague through Michigan, the roadblocks and checkpoints will stop him before he reaches Toledo."

"Returning to the water is unlikely too," Rafferty said. "The coast guard, Homeland Security, and the FBI will be swarming the lakes by morning thanks to the *Achilles* attack."

"That leaves only one viable option for him," Jack said. "He's going to fly the plague out."

"It's best not to jump to conclusions," Rafferty warned. "We'll know for sure which option he's chosen when he makes his move away from Good Hart."

"Let's not waste time either." Jack pointed to the passenger door. "There's a Michigan Atlas in that pocket. Use it to find all the airports in northern Michigan. Mark them with the highlighter in the center console here."

Rafferty flipped through the pages of the book, searching for the correct map. "Don't get comfortable giving me instructions."

"Instructions?" Jack laughed. "I was giving you orders."

"Even worse."

Jack kept the Jeep three car lengths behind the Mustang as they barreled down M46 toward the U.S. 131 junction. Rafferty clicked on the dome light and highlighted each airport symbol he found on the map, public and private. His phone vibrated and he checked caller ID. "It's Mr. Sweetwood calling from your wife's phone."

"You better let me take it." Jack held out his hand and Rafferty gave him the satellite phone. "What's happening, Markus?"

"Cohn is on the move."

Jack glanced at Rafferty. "Which direction?"

Markus checked with Connor in the background and said, "South along the coast."

"Are you absolutely sure?"

"Yeah, what kind of dimwits do you think we are?"

"The best kind. Hang tight." Jack lowered the phone and addressed Rafferty. "What's the closest airport south of Good Hart?"

Rafferty inspected the map. "Harbor Springs. It's less than twenty miles away."

"And over three hours from us." Jack's anxiety ratcheted up. If Harbor Springs Airport was Cohn's destination, the plan to take the phage from him was doomed. But Cohn could still be stopped and thousands of lives could be saved. The only catch is the phage would surely be lost. Jack clenched his teeth and slowly lifted the phone. "Markus, tell Connor to watch that tracer close. If it stops in Harbor Springs I need to know immediately."

"Got it." Markus ended the call.

Jack began dialing Abner's cell number into the phone.

"Who are you calling?" Rafferty asked with a good amount of suspicion.

"Cohn will have to offload the plague from his vehicle onto an airplane. He'll need to stay on the ground a while to do it. Abner's strike team might have enough time to get there and take him down."

Rafferty slapped the atlas into his lap. "Don't be irrational! We don't know if he's stopping in Harbor Springs. If you call in the strike team now, you will all but guarantee our failure. We will not capture the phage."

"Damn it, Donovan, don't you think I know that? Your hide isn't the only one on the line here. Lauren's life is at stake too, but if we can't get to Cohn ourselves, we have to do everything in our power to make sure he doesn't reach Washington."

"Careful, Jack, your altruism is showing."

"A Special Forces team from Selfridge has a good shot at intercepting him in Harbor Springs and burning him at the airport."

"That's an extreme long shot," Rafferty countered.

"Cohn will be dead and the plague will be neutralized. It's everything you want, except..."

Rafferty flipped to the back of the atlas. "I'm surprised you don't have a nose bleed from standing on that moral high ground of yours."

"What are you looking for in that book?"

"Statistical information for the airports." Rafferty scanned through the index and flipped another page. "That plague isn't packed in neat little boxes. A lot of it is needed to make the D.C. plot feasible, and it all must be kept frozen in cryogenic freezers. Those freezers need a portable energy source, most likely a generator. Do you see what I'm getting at?"

Jack did see it. "Cohn has a lot of equipment and a group of men to transport by air. All that stuff won't fit into a Piper Cub. He needs a decent-sized cargo plane."

"And if Harbor Springs doesn't have appropriate aircraft based on the field or the facilities to support one, Cohn will not be stopping there." Rafferty lifted the atlas to catch the dome light better. "Operational statistics: Harbor Springs Airport. Fifteen total aircraft based on the field. Twelve of them are single engine craft. Too small. Only one is listed as multi-engine, but there is no major airframe service available. The airport has just two runways, moderate length with eighty-foot obstructions two hundred feet back from the edge of asphalt. Not quite ideal for a mid-sized aircraft."

Jack felt a little encouraged. "Odds are Cohn couldn't get what he needed from Harbor Springs."

Rafferty looked up from the book. "Don't make that call yet."

Jack cleared Abner's number from the phone and dialed Markus. "Where is Cohn now?"

"He's coming up on Harbor Springs."

"Give me play-by-play, Markus."

"He's entering the town."

Jack tapped his fingers on the steering wheel and prayed for Cohn to keep moving.

"Still passing through," Markus reported.

A minute ticked away. And then another.

"I don't think he's going to stop," Markus said. After a long stretch of silence he added, "Elvis has left Harbor Springs and is continuing along the shoreline."

"Back in business," Jack said holding down his enthusiasm. "Markus, continue as planned but give me updates in five-minute increments." He disconnected and looked to Rafferty. "All right, let's figure out which airport Cohn *is* going to stop at."

- FORTY –

Michigan Intelligence Operations Center (MIOC)
Lansing, MI

Abner Wilson stood in the operations area and watched a local news station's live broadcast from the Grand Haven Coast Guard Station on one of the monitors. His neck ached and his eyes burned after catching an hour of sleep in his cubicle chair, but his vision was clear enough to take in all the detail of *Achilles* crewmembers climbing into a coach bus on the television screen. He checked the faces in the foreground and the background and grumbled.

"Can someone please explain to me how ten crew members report seeing Jack Sheridan either in a raft or at the station, but his name does not appear on the guard's roster of survivors?"

Paul Dutello shrugged. "At this stage of a rescue the operation is still organized chaos. My guess is the paperwork hasn't caught up with the event yet."

"What if he doesn't want to be on the roster?" Ben Chatfield said from a few steps away. "Maybe he's involved in the attack somehow."

The comment incensed Abner and he glared at Chatfield. "You mind repeating that?"

Chatfield cocked his head in an irritated way. "You told us Sheridan was in contact with Rafferty before they shipped out. It's starting to look like that wasn't a coincidence. They could be in on this together."

Abner stepped toward him. "You and I have had our moments of levity, Agent Chatfield, but this isn't one of them. I recommend you back off from what you've just suggested."

"Sheridan hasn't reported in to you since he left port. You told me that isn't like him. Maybe there's a reason."

Dutello shook his head. "That's not what's happening here, Ben. From what I know of Sheridan he would never flip. But I agree with you on one thing. Rafferty has his hand in this somehow."

Lieutenant Walker wheeled out of his cubicle and hurried to the operations area. "Fresh report. The *Buckeye* found *Friends Good Will* adrift. They've secured her and have her in tow."

"Who was on board?" Abner asked."

"Just the crew from the museum. They were tied up below deck."

"Who tied them up?" Dutello asked.

"We still don't know for sure, but they had to be part of a terrorist or militia group of some kind. They booked the sloop for the sunset cruise using a cover story. Said they were professional photographers working a project for an ad agency. When they hit open water…"

"Let me guess," Abner said. "Their photographic equipment turned into weapons."

"A rescued crewman named Novak witnessed more of the action than the others. He says the salvage vessel put up quite a fight, nearly smashed the sloop to pieces. The men who took her were afraid of being sunk at one point."

"Now that's Jack," Abner said emphatically.

"Sheridan wasn't the captain," Chatfield said. "And the *Achilles* eventually went down. In my mind he's still the prime suspect."

Abner nearly drew back his massive fist when his cell phone rang. His wife's number appeared on caller ID. He checked the time. It was almost four in the morning, far too early for this to be a casual call. A pang of nervousness tightened his stomach as he answered. "Candice?"

"Abner, you got a message from Jack. I think you need to hear it right away." Her voice sounded distressed.

This isn't what Abner expected to hear from her. "Honey, calm down. What do you mean I got a message from Jack? I've been waiting all day and haven't heard a thing from him."

"I never sleep well when you're not home," she said in prelude. "So I got up early, and when I walked past your study—"

Abner rolled his eyes. "Candice, dear. The message. What about the message?"

"The light on the answering machine in your study was blinking. It was from Jack."

Abner processed that for half a second. "What time did he send it?"

"The machine says it came in at 1:25 in the morning."

"Play it for me."

She did, and Abner listened intently to Jack's frantic message about a man named Cohn attacking the *Achilles*, his pursuit of Jack to Bangor, and the Memorial Day plot unfolding right under their noses. He had her play it again and jotted notes this time just to make sure he got all the information right. "Candice, you may have just saved a lot of lives. I love you, lady. Now I've got to go."

Abner disconnected and faced Dutello and Chatfield. In the back of his mind he wondered why Jack had not called his cell phone instead of the answering machine. He shelved the peculiar question and zeroed in on Chatfield. "Time to share, Ben. I just got a message from Jack. He says a guy named Cohn is the Lake Michigan assailant and that the Memorial Day plot is his. Who is this guy?"

Chatfield licked his lips and glanced from Dutello to Abner. "Did you just say Cohn?"

"I most certainly did."

Chatfield looked at the monitors in the operation area and cursed. "According to CIA briefs, Cohn is an anarchist who has pulled off mid-level terror attacks in a handful of countries. His goal is the collapse of all organized government. He's a real nut job."

"Why the hell isn't he on your prime suspects list?" Abner growled.

"And why does the Bureau know more about him than Homeland Security?" Dutello added.

"The Cohn plot is a fringe theory with no hard evidence to back it up," Chatfield explained. "All we had is an unconfirmed report that Cohn crossed paths with a North Korean operative in Dubai. This NK operative is also linked to activity concerning the newly discovered 731 facility on the Korean Peninsula. Cohn's connection to him is thinner than rice paper."

"We've got a lot more now," Abner said. "Jack mentioned taking the phage to Bangor and that he'd contact me again with more information regarding Cohn."

"I'm still not convinced Sheridan is clean," Chatfield said.

"I'm telling you he is." Abner glanced at the news broadcast on the flat-screen. The coach bus was pulling away. "I'm having my boys at Selfridge warm up the Blackhawk's engines. If Cohn is in Michigan, it's a good bet the plague is too. We've got an opportunity to end this terror threat once and for all, and I'll be damned if I don't take my shot at him this morning."

North of Alba, MI

Alec Cohn sat in the passenger seat of the late model GMC Denali and checked the side mirror for the vehicles trailing behind him. Two other SUVs of the same make followed in a little convoy, rushing over the concrete of Highway 131 on a southerly heading. Speers drove the vehicle and kept the speed near eighty, fast enough to make time but not fast enough to attract unwanted attention.

Over an hour had elapsed since Nix's last report. Although Cohn was pleased with the news of the colonel's death, he regretted not being the one to pull the trigger. He opened the photograph of the damaged bio case on his cell phone and studied it one more time. The case was severely bullet riddled and clearly the ampoules inside were all smashed. He lowered the phone to his lap and stared out the side window. Something was bothering him. The scar tissue along his jaw itched, and he scratched at his beard. "Did you follow our protocol when you secured these vehicles?" he said to Speers.

Speers nodded. "I got one rental from three different agencies using three different identities. There is no record of one person renting out a fleet of Denalis from any one place."

Cohn looked out the driver's side window. The sky was dark but it wouldn't be long before dawn broke. He had wanted to be airborne by sunrise. It seemed unlikely they would meet that timetable. It would be close though. Making arrangements for air transport on a specific type of cargo plane at the last minute had limited his airfield options and had forced him to drive farther from Good Hart than he would have liked. All things considered, however, he was confident to be out of the state in a few short hours. And then on to Washington.

Propaganda of the deed.

The anarchist motto popped into his head and struck at the root of his unease. He lifted the cell phone and looked at the picture again. He saw what had been bothering him subconsciously. It wasn't the case but the background surrounding it. It seemed to be sitting in the back seat of a car. Nix's sedan had light gray interior, but the one in the photo was black. It could be the inside of the colonel or Sheridan's vehicle, but then when would Nix have snapped the picture? Cohn did not request the image until well after Nix had assaulted them, and Nix certainly would not have been hanging around the vehicle that long after the incident. Cohn could not reconcile the problem with the photo.

He dialed Nix's number and let it ring. Nix did not answer. He dialed again. Same result.

Something had gone wrong, and it wasn't a very big leap for Cohn to conclude that the colonel had somehow turned the tables on his hit team. That damned mercenary had found another way to evade his demise. If that was the case then Nix's report could not be trusted.

Cohn stared at the phone and tried to get inside Rafferty's head. What would he do next? The man wanted revenge. He would try to discover where Cohn was and then come after him. But how would he do it? He couldn't coerce Nix into divulging the location of the airfield they were heading to because Nix did not know. So how then? The answer was staring Cohn in the face.

He tore open the back of his cell phone and pulled the SIM card.

Speers looked over. "What are you doing?"

"The colonel might have captured Nix. If he did he has Nix's cell phone along with my phone number. He could be using that information to track us."

"Without GPS?"

"They can triangulate off cell towers," Cohn said. "It's not simple to do but the colonel is resourceful. Call Anders and Byrne and have them pull their SIM cards too. We're going silent the rest of the way to the airport. Disable your phone after you've contacted them."

Speers started making the calls.

Cohn pounded his door panel. "Damn you, Donovan, how many lives do you have?"

South of Howard City, MI

Jack's knuckles turned white on the steering wheel. He and Rafferty had been hanging on Markus' position updates for almost an hour. After Harbor Springs, Cohn bypassed Charlevoix Municipal Airport and did not veer toward the airfields in Antrim or Ostego County either. He was on the verge of bypassing Gaylord Regional. Gaylord concerned Jack the most as its operational statistics made it sound like an excellent airfield to accommodate the kind of aircraft Cohn would need, but when Cohn failed to alter course toward it Jack figured the decision was based on its location at the center of a dense population area. It made sense that Cohn would want to use a fairly isolated airport with minimal daily activity to lower the odds of someone witnessing his illicit cargo transfer. For the same reason Jack and Rafferty agreed that Cherry Capital Airport in Traverse City would be bypassed as well. There was far too much activity there to conduct covert activity of any kind.

Jack continued north on 131 while the tracer signal for Cohn's phone headed south on the same highway. "Scratch Gaylord and Cherry City off the list."

Rafferty studied the map for the next candidate airport in Cohn's path. "We may have miscalculated. Cohn may not fly the plague out."

"If he doesn't we're going to play a real interesting game of chicken in about an hour."

Rafferty set a finger on the map. "He's coming up on Roscommon and Wexford County airports."

"Does either of them look promising?"

"They're both decent options," Rafferty said. "Comparable length asphalt runways, major airframe service, they both have adequate facilities to accommodate a mid-sized cargo plane."

"How many planes are based at each field?"

Rafferty turned to the statistics page. "Wexford has fifty aircraft based there, four of them multi-engine. Roscommon has only eleven single-engine craft."

"Daily activity?" Jack asked.

"Roscommon reports about fifty operations a day, but 80 percent of that is local general aviation. Wexford averages twenty-two operations a day, half of which is transient general aviation."

"Transient general," Jack said. "Does interstate air transport fall into that category?"

"I believe it does."

"Wexford seems the better bet based on aircraft and activity, but Roscommon can accommodate Cohn's plane and it is a little more rural."

"We'll get a better sense of his destination in a few minutes," Rafferty said studying the map. "If Cohn intends to meet his plane in Roscommon he will turn east onto Route 38 very soon, or perhaps Highway 72."

A cell phone rang with an unfamiliar ring tone. Jack and Rafferty looked at each other a bit perplexed, and then Rafferty seemed to realize which phone was ringing. He pulled Nix's cell out of his pocket and checked the incoming call ID. "It's Cohn. He's trying to reach Nix."

"Don't answer," Jack warned.

"Thanks for the advice."

The ringing stopped. Jack picked up Rafferty's satellite phone from the center console and dialed Markus. It rang once.

"Yo," Markus answered.

"Where is Cohn right now?"

Markus conversed with Connor in the background. "Driving through Alba," he finally said.

"Watch him close and stay on the line."

Nix's phone rang again. Rafferty looked as if he was contemplating answering it.

"If you answer Cohn will know for sure we're on to him," Jack warned.

Rafferty did not reply.

"Don't let your hubris screw up our plan. When we meet him he'll know it's you who came to get him."

Rafferty stared at Jack and the ringing stopped. "You can be very irritating, Jack, do you know that?"

"Coming from you I'll take that as a compliment."

"That's not how I meant it."

Jack nearly grinned but remembered who he was talking to and what they were doing. He lifted the satellite phone to his ear when he heard Markus' excited voice calling out. "Slow down, Markus, what's going on?"

"We lost him," Markus said. "We just lost Cohn's cell phone signal."

"Maybe he's driving through a dead zone," Jack offered. "Give it a minute or two for his phone to reacquire a tower."

Rafferty shook his head. "It's not service. Cohn has disabled his phone. He's finally figured it out. I have to say it took him longer than I thought it would."

"Markus," Jack said. "Where was he when you lost the trace?"

"He'd just passed Alba."

Jack's mind raced. They had not gotten close enough to pin Cohn down yet. Not good. "Stand by, Markus." Jack lowered the phone to his lap. "We need to make a decision. Wexford or Roscommon?"

"It could be neither of them," Rafferty said.

"It has to be one. Both airports have ideal facilities and locations for Cohn's purposes. I can't see him traveling any farther from Good Hart to reach his escape airfield."

"Based on operating statistics both make sense," Rafferty said. "If you were Cohn, which would you choose?"

Jack shook his head. "Why do you keep asking me to stand in his shoes?"

"If there is one thing I learned about you from our past encounters, it's that you have acute intuition."

Jack considered the situation and all of the facts they had just discussed. He let his instincts guide his thoughts, and his mind drew decidedly toward one destination. "Wexford."

Rafferty regarded him a moment. "Why Wexford?"

"My gut is telling me to go there."

"If we're wrong about this, Cohn makes a clean getaway."

"Would you rather pick Roscommon?"

"I have no substantial argument to pick one over the other."

"Then Wexford it is. My instincts haven't let me down yet." Jack glanced over. "They got me past you once, didn't they?"

"That they did."

Jack dialed Abner's number into the satellite phone. Rafferty opened his mouth to speak but held his tongue. Jack noticed. "I'm impressed. You really do want Cohn dead, don't you?"

"I'd prefer it by my hand, but if the last thing he sees is the barrel of a Special Forces rifle I can live with that."

Jack hit the send button. "You may get your wish. We're about an hour away from Wexford, and so is Cohn. Even if Abner gets his guys in the air in sixty seconds, we'll probably get to the airport first."

"A beautiful way to start a new day," Rafferty said.

After two rings the line clicked in Jack's ear. "Hello," Abner said.

"Abner, this is Jack. Listen close—"

"Judas Priest!" Abner shouted. "Jack, where the hell have you been?"

"No time to explain. You need to get your team in the air right now and send them to Wexford County Airport. Cohn and the 731 Plague will be there in one hour. You got that?"

"Yeah, I got that. How about a target? I need something more specific."

"Just get them in the air. I can't be more specific yet. The next time I call I'll be able to point to Cohn's vehicle myself."

"Okay, consider my guys on the way, but tell me one thing. Is Rafferty involved in this?"

Jack glanced at his passenger. "Yes."

"Don't worry, Jack, we'll get him."

"Concentrate on nailing Cohn. I'll be in touch." Jack disconnected.

- FORTY ONE –

> "See, the storm of the Lord will burst out in wrath, a driving wind swirling down on the heads of the wicked." - Jeremiah 30:23

Jack noticed the black night sky had begun to dissolve and the sun threatened to crest the horizon. Silhouetted industrial plazas materialized in the faint first light of day to the right of the Jeep and the open darkness of the airfield appeared to the left. Landing lights illuminated the edges of the primary runway even though Wexford County Airport did not officially open for business until seven o'clock. It being Sunday morning and the airport's location being two miles from downtown Cadillac there was precious little traffic on Highway 131, save for one throaty Mustang and one dust-covered Jeep Cherokee.

They had lost Cohn's trace signal nearly an hour ago and had been driving in relative silence ever since. Jack had felt confident about his decision to go to Wexford, but when he actually saw the airport through the windshield a fragment of doubt surfaced. If he had guessed wrong, Lauren would likely die and a devastating terror attack would continue on track toward the nation's capital. In that event Jack would feel duty-bound to remove Donovan Rafferty from the face of the Earth, just for recompense.

No worries.

Jack squeezed the steering wheel and cursed under his breath.

"You've been quiet," Rafferty said. "What are you thinking about?"

"You don't want to know." Jack glanced at the dim sky over the airport. It was clear and devoid of activity, no Blackhawk helicopters, no cargo planes taking off, nothing. The airport grounds and buildings beside the tarmac sat dark and quiet as well. "Looks like we made it here first."

"That is, of course, if anyone else is coming," Rafferty added.

Jack lifted the satellite phone and dialed Markus. "Markus, make a left onto Boon Avenue up ahead. The airport entrance will be on the left. Find a concealed positioned and watch that entrance. Call me if anyone rolls through it."

"You got it. Where are you going?"

"I'm taking a short cut." Jack disconnected and threw the Jeep into four-wheel drive. He swerved off the highway and down a side street named Bell Avenue, and then off the road completely and up a slight embankment. The Jeep bounced over uneven terrain, smashing through a thicket of saplings, and then crested the hill to open field. Jack switched off the headlights and picked up speed, heading for the runway bisecting the airfield. He threaded the Jeep between landing lights and barreled toward the structures across the field.

Rafferty hung on as they rumbled over a taxiway. "Do you know where you're going?"

"Not really." Jack swerved to avoid a Cessna parked at the edge of the tarmac. "The airport is deserted at this hour. I figure I'll head for the only building with a light on. It'll have to be the hangar for Cohn's plane."

"There." Rafferty said pointing through the windshield. Three buildings to the east appeared to be a group of hangars, and the center one had a large sliding door half open with light spilling out through the opening into the dawn.

Jack adjusted course toward the tall hangar. "Cohn may already be inside."

"I doubt it. Those doors would be wide open, and we'd see a lot more activity." Rafferty reached under his seat and pulled out a compact submachine gun. "Just in case."

Jack looked at the weapon. "Where did you get that?"

"Mr. Naughton packed some things for our trip."

Jack judged the hangar door opening to be wide enough to allow them inside. Barely. He steered for it. "Hang on."

He maneuvered the Jeep through the opening and rattled the big sliding door with his front quarter panel. The glancing blow crashed loud in the cab, and Jack found himself driving under the wing of a cargo plane with a big, boxy fuselage. He hit the brakes and slid to a screeching stop near the tail of the plane. He threw the gearshift into park and jumped from the Jeep, drawing the Kimber as his boots touched the concrete floor. Rafferty burst out the passenger door, and they moved quickly around the tail section toward the center of the hangar.

Bright lights burned in fixtures mounted in the overhead trusses and lit the space well. A man dressed in a leather flight jacket and jeans stood with his jaw dropped open in front of a worktable and maintenance crib across the floor. Jack drew down on him with the Kimber. "Hands behind your head. Now!"

The man stammered but complied with the order. "What do you want?"

Rafferty noticed a door on the plane near the cockpit was open and a portable metal stairway rolled up in front of it. He got Jack's attention and nodded toward the stairs.

"Are you alone?" Jack asked the man.

"Uh, yeah. I'm waiting for the guy who chartered my plane this morning." He looked nervously between Jack and Rafferty. "Is it you?"

"Not quite." Jack nodded toward the plane. "Is anyone on board?"

"No. I was just going over my preflight checklist. My charter didn't want anyone here but me when he arrived."

"I'll check it out." Rafferty cautiously made his way up the stairs to the open door.

Jack didn't see a weapon on the man, who looked genuinely terrified. "Lift your jacket and turn around." The man did. Jack still did not see a holster or outline of a weapon anywhere. "You can put your hands down."

"What's this all about?" the man said a little more steady, as if he was starting to think the men who just broke into his hangar might not shoot him dead. "If you want money I've got fifty bucks in my wallet, but the plane is empty."

Jack walked over to him. "What's your name?"

"Tom. Tom Lanuzza."

Jack lowered the .45 but did not holster it. "Tom, my name is Jack Sheridan. I'm not interested in chartering your plane, but I am interested in the man who did. What's his name?"

Tom Lanuzza seemed a bit confused. "His name is Max Stirner. Said he'd be coming in with some perishable medicine he needed to get to the East Coast in a hurry. Why do you want to know? Why do you guys have guns? Are you a cop or something?"

"Or something."

Rafferty emerged from the fuselage and started down the stairs. "The interior is clear."

Jack met him at the bottom. "The pilot said Max Stirner chartered his plane."

"It's definitely Cohn," Rafferty said bemused. "Max Stirner is a nineteenth-century anarchist, an egoist no less. It makes perfect sense Alec would use his name. Ridiculous bastard."

"Chalk one up for instincts."

Rafferty gave the gray and blue two-tone cargo plane a once over and stepped off the stairway. The aircraft's nose had a steep sloping profile, and the tail sported dual stabilizing fins. "This is a Short 330. It has an eight thousand-pound cargo capacity and twin twelve hundred horsepower turboprops to get her in the air. We used a variant of it in the military, the C23 Sherpa. She'll carry whatever Cohn has to transport."

Jack hurried around the plane and retrieved the AA12 from the Jeep. He returned to Tom Lanuzza. "How much does one of these engines cost?"

Lanuzza stammered. "Uh, replacing a Pratt & Whitney PT6A would put me back forty thousand, and that's just the cost of a rebuilt unit."

Jack grimaced. "This one's going to pinch a bit."

He swung the assault shotgun around and fired three blasts into the engine on the starboard wing of the plane. The explosive reports echoed in the hangar and Lanuzza's eyes opened wide. "What the hell are you doing?"

"Mr. Stirner isn't bringing medicine with him," Jack said with the acrid smell of gun smoke in his nose. "And this plane isn't going anywhere with the stuff he does show up with."

Rafferty reviewed the holes in the engine cover and the riddled machinery inside. "That should do it."

Jack shouldered the AA12 and faced Lanuzza. "I'll cover the cost of a replacement. Don't worry, I'm good for it."

Rafferty's phone rang and he lifted it from his belt. "It's Mr. Sweetwood." He tossed the phone to Jack.

Jack answered. "What's up, Markus?"

"Three Denalis just came down Boon Avenue and are turning into the airport's service entrance. What do you want us to do?"

Cohn had arrived. The news hit Jack in the gut like a sucker punch. He toyed with the phone and scanned the inside of the hangar, trying to formulate a plan of some kind. "You and Connor stay put. Understand?"

"Sure. What are you and Rafferty going to do?"

Jack fumbled for a response. "We'll try to negotiate with Cohn until Abner's guys get here. I'll call back when it's safe to come in." He disconnected and dialed Abner's cell number.

Rafferty peered around the corner of the hangar door. "We're not negotiating with him."

"I know." Jack put the phone to his ear. Abner picked up right away. "This is Jack," he said before the admiral could utter a word. "Is your team en route?"

"Hell yes," Abner said. "I'll get an ETA from the squad leader, but by my watch they should be there soon."

"I've got a target for them," Jack said moving to the hangar door. "Three GMC Denalis. Cohn and his men are transporting the plague to the airport in them."

"Are you on site?" Abner asked.

Jack hesitated. "Yeah, I'm on site."

"Well, don't get caught in the crossfire."

"I'll do my best. Gotta go, Abner." He added, "Wish me luck."

"Luck? What are you doing there?"

Jack disconnected and tossed the phone back to Rafferty. He pulled the AA12 off his shoulder and searched the morning sky. Nothing was flying overhead but a murder of crows. Fitting. He listened for the sound of an approaching helicopter engine, but all he heard was the song of a robin perched on the roof and the gravel crunching under the tires of the vehicles entering the airport.

"We can't let him leave here," Rafferty said. "Not by plane or by car."

"I know, I know. We have to get the phage from him before the strike team arrives."

The first Denali appeared from the entry drive, emerging from behind the easternmost maintenance shed and starting into a wide loop on the tarmac. It seemed the driver was aligning the vehicle for a straight-on approach into the hangar housing the cargo plane. The second Denali followed a length behind the first, and then the third. A lump rose into Jack's throat and he squeezed the assault shotgun. He glanced back at Lanuzza. "Find something to hide behind. Make sure it's made out of steel."

"Pull open your door," Rafferty said. "Let's make this look as inviting as we can."

Jack saw his point and slowly rolled his hanger door open, staying concealed behind it and keeping intent watch on the approaching vehicles. The dark SUVs formed up in single file as they came out of the loop and headed straight for the cargo plane.

"Although they fast, I will not listen to their cry," Rafferty said lifting full magazines for his submachine gun from his pocket. "Though they offer burnt offerings and grain offerings, I will not accept them." He transferred the magazines to the ammunition belt he had strapped around his waist and unfolded the stock of the submachine gun. "Instead, I will destroy them with sword, famine, and plague."

Jack released the door and checked the AA12 for firing. "What are you rambling about?"

"Jeremiah," Rafferty said gazing at the SUVs. "The man knew a thing or two about prophesying death and destruction."

Jack whispered a short prayer of his own and then made eye contact with Rafferty. In a million years he would never have dreamt of fighting side by side with him. "Ready?"

"Absolutely."

Go time.

Jack pivoted around the hangar door, leveled the assault shotgun at the lead vehicle, and fired a thundering barrage of shells that disintegrated the front grill. Rafferty focused his fire on the tires. At thirty yards out the first Denali swerved left and ground to a halt with smoke pouring from under the hood. The second vehicle broke right, clipping the rear of the disabled SUV and rocking it back and forth. Jack lifted the AA12 and aimed at number two. He cut loose another volley of blasts, the weapon spitting spent shells onto the hangar floor. The second Denali's passenger window and windshield cobwebbed white under the assaulting rain of shot.

Rafferty ejected a spent magazine and reloaded with practiced precision. He didn't miss a beat and shredded the rubber on the second SUV's front end. It careened forward several yards, weaving left and right before coming to a stuttered stop. The passenger door flew open and a man jumped out firing a submachine gun at the hangar. Bullets whistled and popped through corrugated steel walls. Rafferty crouched low and returned fire, sending the last two rounds from his magazine into the man's shoulder and forcing him to drop his weapon. Rafferty shouted, "Foley, you lucky bastard."

Another man burst from the rear of the Denali and followed after Foley, shooting a semi-auto pistol as fast as he could work the trigger. Jack swung the AA12 around and hit him with two blasts in the leg, shattering his knee with twelve-gauge pellets and dropping him a writhing mess on the tarmac.

And then a maelstrom hit. A squad of men had formed a firing line using the first disabled SUV for cover and had cut loose with their automatic weapons. Rafferty pressed tight against a thick steel I-beam while Jack crouched for cover behind a Craftsman tool box. Incoming ammunition laced the hangar like deadly hail, perforating wall panels and pounding structural steel. The cockpit windows in the cargo plane shattered. Lanuzza shouted above the staccato reports from a corner of the maintenance crib.

Two men on the firing line seemed to realize shooting from the hangar had stopped and moved cautiously from their cover, inching forward. A lull settled over the airfield like the passing eye of a hurricane. Jack suspected they were attempting to advance but to poke his head out to check would likely get it shot off. He stuck the barrel of the AA12 around the corner and fired a wide spread. The advancing men retreated from the shot, and a volley of 9 mm suppressing fire answered the booms of the assault shotgun. Jack pulled back behind the tool box and realized that the last shell from the AA12's ammunition drum was bouncing across the hangar floor. He set the weapon down and drew the Kimber.

* * *

A trickle of blood flowed down Cohn's cheek. A stray pellet of shot had pierced the windshield and grazed his temple. He wiped away the blood and crouched behind the dead SUV while clenching his Glock 9 mm. Booms from the assault shotgun were deafening, but they did not intimidate him. It would take much more than that to derail him from his mission. The plague had to be released. The first domino had to fall, and neither the colonel nor Jack Sheridan would stop him.

He and Speers had scrambled out the passenger door of the lead Denali after the first wave of gunfire had disabled it. The situation was worse than he had imagined. Not only had the colonel tracked his location, he had managed to get to the airfield ahead of him to lay this trap. Cohn's anger was palpable.

At the onset of the attack the third Denali in the convoy had stopped short, directly behind the smoking hulk of the first. It had found shielding from the onslaught there, but Anders and Byrne had yet to make a move to get out of it. Unacceptable. Cohn signaled for them to rally to his position and then turned to Speers. "We have to shut down that incoming fire."

His voice was nearly drowned out by the blasts from the assault shotgun and the reports from the automatic weapon now targeting the second Denali that Gates was driving. Cohn reached into the rear seat and pulled out a Kevlar vest. He slipped it on as Anders, Byrne, and a man named Lufkin emerged from their sheltered SUV and approached. The men were careful to stay out of the line of fire. "Anders," Cohn shouted when they had gotten close enough to hear. "You, Byrne, and Lufkin form up here and saturate the hangar with fire. Stop those rounds from coming at us."

Anders nodded, but Byrne spat on the ground and gave Cohn a cross look.

"You have something to say?" Cohn barked.

"You led us into this," Byrne said. "You lost half the team on this plague op. I'm through taking orders from you."

Without a blink of hesitation, Cohn lifted the 9 mm and fired two rounds into his chest. Byrne dropped there on the concrete. "A man determines his own future, Mr. Byrne." Cohn turned away from the body of his rebellious minion. "Speers, take his place."

Speers snapped to and picked up Byrne's submachine gun. The three of them laid down a wilting stream of fire on the hangar entrance. Cohn stared at the cargo area of his disabled SUV. Canisters of the 731 Plague sat frozen within a steel reinforced cryo freezer inside. The plague was the point. The outbreak was the linchpin. Cohn decided right then that his mission could not end without the plague's release, be it in Washington, D.C. or Cadillac, Michigan.

Foley stumbled to the rear of the smoking Denali with blood flowing freely from the wounds in his shoulder. Cohn assessed his condition. "Where is Gates?"

Foley grimaced with pain and shouted above the reports from the automatic weapons firing behind him. "Gates bought it behind the steering wheel. Jacobs got his leg shot off on the tarmac. Riley's still in the back of the SUV. His wounds from the fight with the salvage vessel stopped him from making a run."

Cohn cursed and looked toward the hangar. The colonel had bloodied his nose good. That would not go unpunished. He faced Foley again. "Can you drive a vehicle?"

"I think so," Foley said as the gunfire subsided.

Anders and Lufkin tried to advance on the hangar but were forced back by that damned assault shotgun. Speers opened fire to cover their retreat. When they had gotten back to cover, Cohn grabbed Lufkin's arm and pointed to the undamaged SUV. "Go with Foley. You two get in that vehicle and charge into the hangar. Kill the colonel any way you can. Shoot him or run him down I don't care which, but I want him dead."

Lufkin seemed unsure of the order.

"Don't be a damned coward. I've only counted two men with automatic weapons in there, and they have to be running out of ammunition soon."

Lufkin nodded and headed for the unscathed Denali with Foley.

"Anders," Cohn said. "Keep the colonel and Sheridan pinned down to cover Foley's advance. Speers, come with me."

"What if they try to escape out the back?" Anders asked.

"They won't," Cohn said with confidence. "The colonel wants me dead as much as I want him dead. One of us is going to get our wish today, and I intend it to be me."

* * *

"He said stay put."

Connor lectured Markus from the hood of the Mustang outside the service entrance to the airport. He bounced his heel off the front tire and watched Markus pace to the road and back.

"It may have been more of a suggestion," Markus said. "He was talking pretty fast."

Connor hopped off the hood. "He said he wanted to negotiate. He needs time to do that."

Thunderclaps suddenly arose from the airfield, and then rapid reports that the guys had come to know as automatic weapon fire. Markus dashed to the road and tried to see between the airport buildings. "Sounds like your dad just started negotiating."

Connor stood beside him. "Dad or Rafferty."

"You want to give them time to talk this out?"

"Screw that." Connor hurried back to the car. "Let's get in there."

"All right!" Markus raced alongside him and reached for the door handle but stopped. "What are we rushing into?"

"Seriously?" Connor said with incredulity. "You pick now to be cautious?"

"You're right. Screw that. We go in and do what feels right."

Connor hopped into the car. "That's the Markus I know."

Markus turned over the engine and clutched into first. He popped the gear, spit gravel from the rear mags, and flew across the road into the airport service entrance.

* * *

Jack saw a guy throw something from behind the first SUV. The fist-sized object bounced once on the hangar floor, and he knew what was coming.

"Flash-bang!" Rafferty shouted.

Jack had already blocked his ears and had looked away with eyes pressed shut. A concussive blast rocked the cavernous hangar, and a flash like a nuclear detonation overpowered the overhead lighting. Having the .45 clamped in his hand prevented Jack from forming a good seal over his right ear. The sonic assault on his eardrum shut down his hearing and replaced it with a high pitched ring. He had managed to protect his eyes, though, and he checked across the floor to see how Rafferty had fared.

Amazingly the man seemed unfazed. Rafferty stood firing his submachine gun out the open hangar door, and when it stopped vibrating in his hands he dropped it and drew the Sig Sauer in one fluid movement. Jack shook his head to try to counteract the effects of the stun grenade and looked outside at what had captured Rafferty's attention.

Jack drew an alarmed breath and raised the Kimber. The third Denali was coming at them. It had swerved around the first and now roared full ahead toward the hangar opening. Shattered headlights and a bullet-riddled hood from Rafferty's submachine gun had failed to stop it. Jack fired, pumping round after round into the windshield and frosting the tempered glass with cracks. The driver ducked below the dash. Rafferty fired his Sig too, but it didn't seem the slugs from their pistols were stopping the oncoming three tons of steel.

Markus slapped the gearshift into third and hit the gas. "Front or rear?"

"Rear," Connor shouted. "More trajectory impact, less repercussion."

"Are you sure?" Markus shifted into fourth. The speedometer topped fifty.

"Yeah, I'm sure. I aced Dynamics. You didn't. Do it."

Markus altered course and clutched into fifth. "You owe me a car, Sheridan."

Connor braced himself on the dashboard.

"Don't lock your arms," Markus warned. "Your bones will snap."

Foley and Lufkin had hunkered down below the windshield to avoid getting shot so far that they never saw the midnight blue lightning bolt coming at them. The Mustang clipped the Denali's rear quarter near the bumper at sixty-five miles per hour. Their steel frames collided and a ghastly loud crash pulsated across the airfield. The Denali's cargo doors burst open and the vehicle spun clockwise, rearing up on the driver's side wheels. A shockwave hammered through the Mustang's frame and crushed the front end, deploying the airbags on impact. The rear of the car kicked into the air and swung around.

Jack and Rafferty shielded their faces from the collision as the two vehicles heaved up in a twisted mass of steel and fell hard back onto the concrete. The Denali settled on its side with rear wheels spinning wild. The Mustang came down on all fours with the hood folded up like an accordion to the shattered windshield.

Jack stood transfixed on the scene for a brief, brutal moment. "My God, Connor, Markus."

Rafferty let none of it dissuade his focus. He stepped from the hangar with purpose, ejecting a spent magazine from the Sig and slapping in a fresh one. He led with the pistol and walked around the crashed vehicles. He assessed the situation in an instant and shouted back to Jack. "They're prepping to release the plague."

The plague. Jack pulled himself away from the wreckage. "How?"

"Speers is removing canisters from the second SUV we took out. Stop him!"

Jack circled around the front of the overturned Denali. Two men sprawled behind the shattered windshield were not moving. Jack did not know if they were alive or dead but he did not linger on their condition. He moved past the vehicle with the Kimber steady in his hands and focused on the Denali sitting idle several yards west. The cargo doors were open and the dark-haired man Rafferty had called Speers moved about behind them, reaching into the back and manipulating something inside. Plague canisters. A bio freezer unit. Jack fired three rounds at him, praying not to hit a canister. The tinted glass in the rear door blew apart. Speers ducked behind the panel. Jack sidestepped for a better angle at his target, but Speers reached under the rear door and fired a volley of rounds from a 9 mm. Jack's thigh burned and he returned fire, but the Kimber's action froze open after only one shot. Empty. He pulled back for cover behind the hood of the overturned SUV with blood soaking his pants over the wound in his leg.

Rafferty was blasting away with his Sig on the other side of the wreckage, and it sounded like more than one weapon was firing back at him. The thought of him getting killed frightened Jack. What if the microbiologist reneged on the deal to treat Lauren with the phage because his benefactor was dead? Jack had to prevent that from happening, but he had to deal with Speers first.

He reloaded the Kimber with a magazine from his pocket. Speers had continued to put something together behind the SUV's rear door. That man had to be taken down. Jack chambered a round and left his concealment, edging along the roof of the overturned vehicle. He thought he saw movement behind the Mustang's deployed airbags but could not stop to check. He needed to get to Speers. Jack limped along knowing he should be petrified, but he wasn't feeling fear. The stakes of the situation did not afford him that. He had to stop Speers. No other option existed. That simple truth steeled his nerves and steadied his hand.

He reached a vantage point that gave him a line of fire. As if sensing this, Speers spun around with his pistol. Both men fired, but Jack triggered his weapon a split second sooner and put a bullet through Speers' chest. Speers fell back into the SUV, dropping a metal-cased device and wildly firing his pistol until the ammunition ran out. He slid down to the concrete limp and motionless.

Jack held him under the barrel until certain the threat was gone, and then spun around and hobbled to the smashed Mustang. His thigh burned as he tried to open the passenger door, but the front end damage had jammed up the hinge. He heaved with all he had and forced the door past the obstruction. "Connor, are you okay?"

Connor flailed behind a half-inflated airbag. "My leg. I think it's broke."

Jack checked it out. The collision had collapsed the cockpit around Connor's legs, and a piece of frame had smashed his shin. The unnatural angle of his leg below the knee told Jack his tibia had been fractured. It did not appear to be pinned.

Jack looked to the driver's seat. "Markus?"

"I'm good," Markus said a bit dazed, trying to push the airbag out of his face. "Connor's side took most of the damage."

Another volley of gunfire sounded behind the car. "If you can walk, get Connor out of here," Jack said. "Both of you get into the hangar."

"You got it." Markus kicked open his door.

Jack squeezed Connor's arm. "Markus will get you out. I have to get the phage from Cohn." He pulled back out of the car and crouched painfully near the trunk. Twenty yards south two men took pot shots from behind the smoking Denali. They were not interested in the people near the Mustang. And then something happened to really capture their attention.

Rafferty suddenly stepped away from the undercarriage of the overturned SUV as if tired of exchanging ineffective fire from a concealed position. His faced glistened with sweat, and he aimed the Sig Sauer carefully down range. For an instant Cohn and Anders appeared not to believe what they were seeing, but Anders quickly decided an opportunity had just presented itself. He stepped from behind the Denali and raised his submachine gun. In haste or excitement he fired before lining up a clean shot. Rafferty paid no heed to the errant bullets and advanced on their position, shifting his aim toward Anders and firing a single round. Anders' head snapped back and he fell to his knees, falling face down on the concrete.

Cohn opened up with the Glock.

Rafferty kept moving forward, shifting his aim left. A 9 mm round struck him in the chest before he could fire again. He staggered and squeezed the trigger with the Sig's barrel aimed high. The bullet flew well over Cohn's head. Another round hit Rafferty high on his right shoulder. The impact ejected the Sig from his hand and he dropped to one knee.

No!

Jack sprang from behind the Mustang with a searing pain like a hot knife radiating from the bullet wound in his leg. He aimed quickly and fired twice. Both slugs blasted Cohn's upper body. Dual .45 caliber impacts knocked him off his feet. Jack limped out to Rafferty and grabbed his arm. "What the hell was that?"

Rafferty breathed heavy and frowned. "Is Cohn dead?"

"I don't think so. He's wearing a vest." Jack struggled to pull Rafferty behind the overturned SUV.

"Damn it, Jack, you should have taken the head shot." Rafferty grit his teeth against his pain and staggered as best he could. He fell onto his back near the rear axel. "Always take the head shot if you have it. And you had it."

"What were you trying to do?"

"End this." Rafferty rasped. "I drew him out. You were supposed to take him down."

"Maybe you should let me in on your plan next time." Jack glanced over his shoulder and saw Markus helping Connor totter into the hangar. At least they were clear.

Rafferty tried to prop himself up on an elbow but failed. "He's going to release the plague."

"Stay still," Jack said sternly. "You have to survive this. You have to tell Simon to treat Lauren with the phage." The ringing in Jack's ear from the stun grenade was not subsiding. All the gunfire wasn't helping the situation. He covered his ear as if to block the sound from getting in, but it did nothing to alleviate the ring.

"Where does Cohn keep the phage?"

Rafferty coughed and drew a labored breath. "He knows we have him. He's going to do it. The plague is weaponized. Fine particulate. The wind will carry it into Cadillac. It'll spread from there. If you care about all those people, you have to kill him."

"I understand. Now tell me where Cohn carries the phage. Is it in one of the SUVs?"

Rafferty tried to work his right hand but couldn't seem to articulate his fingers. "I can't finish him off, Jack, you have to do it."

"Where is the goddamned phage, Donovan?"

Rafferty grabbed Jack's forearm with his uninjured hand and locked eyes with him. "Kill Cohn and you get the phage…Kill Cohn and I wipe the slate clean between us."

Jack stared at the man who had haunted his dreams and terrorized his thoughts for two whole years, and he contemplated the end of his long nightmare. He gave Rafferty a nod. "Just make sure you stay alive long enough to see it."

Rafferty grinned. "Give him my regards, Jack, right between the eyes."

Jack stood with the Kimber locked in his hand and peered around the overturned SUV. He did not see Cohn near the smoking Denali. The cargo doors were open but nobody was there. Jack felt a surge of panic.

The memory of Speers dropping a metal case among offloaded plague canisters flashed into his thoughts. Speers had begun setting up the equipment to disperse the bacterium. Cohn wouldn't begin from scratch with the equipment in the smoking SUV, he would pick up where Speers left off in the other one. Maybe all he had to do was press a button on that metal case.

Jack circled around the overturned Denali with his head ringing and his bloodied leg burning. He steadied himself on the totaled Mustang and hobbled with a frantic limp toward the SUV where he had shot Speers. Cohn was there, standing behind the vehicle surrounded by six stainless steel canisters arrayed on the concrete. A small black device had been placed atop each canister, and a tiny red LED blinked on each. Cohn turned, revealing that he had the metal case in his hands.

The ringing in Jack's head seemed to get louder, but the sound of his heartbeat matched its intensity. His leg went numb and his vision narrowed into a tunnel as his entire focus turned on Cohn. If that psychopath released the plague, it would set in motion a hundred thousand agonizing deaths. Jack lifted the Kimber and set the gun sight square on Cohn's head.

Wind blew in Jack's face and voices shouted beneath the ringing in his ear. He felt the pulse in his head like a mechanical thump. Or was he hearing it? It didn't matter. He caressed the warm trigger with his finger and solidified his aim on the anarchist's forehead.

Cohn glanced up from the metal case with a twisted smile on his face. "Propaganda of—"

Jack fired.

Alec Cohn, six steel canisters, and the rear of the Denali were suddenly erased by a brilliant flash. A ball of fire consumed them all, and a wave of intense heat hit Jack so hard it knocked him to the ground. Stunned and disoriented, he struggled to right himself as pieces of smoking debris rained down around him. The heat of flash burn stung his cheeks, and the odor of singed hair filled his nostrils. Jack focused his eyes on the firestorm before him and watched as its heat reduced Alec Cohn to carbon on the tarmac.

Abner's team had apparently arrived.

And in a terrible moment, Jack realized that the phage had just been incinerated.

- FORTY TWO –

Jack looked skyward. A Blackhawk helicopter hovered in the near distance, suspended like a wasp with one missile missing from its arsenal. It began descending to the ground and Jack turned away. With the heat of the burning wreckage behind him, Jack staggered back to the overturned SUV and dropped on his good knee beside Rafferty.

"Cohn is dead," Jack said flatly.

"I heard." Rafferty coughed and felt around his jacket. Blood from his wounds smeared his hands and he frowned. "You don't happen to have a cigarette do you?"

Jack raged inside. "Cohn is dead and the phage is gone. That means Lauren is gone too." He shoved the barrel of his .45 into Rafferty's temple. "I guess I don't need you anymore."

Rafferty froze and his eyes betrayed genuine fear, but only for an instant, just long enough to pick up on Jack's hesitation. "Cohn's bullet missed my heart. Are you sure you want to finish the job?"

"More than you can possibly imagine." Jack's hand began to shake.

"Before you dispense your self-serving brand of justice…" Rafferty fished with his left hand for something in his pocket. He pulled it out and lifted it up.

It was an ampoule from the bio case.

Jack snatched it from his hand. "You son-of-a-bitch, you had it the whole time! We didn't need to go after Cohn."

"I needed to go after Cohn," Rafferty said coolly. "And your help proved invaluable."

Jack sneered. "Always manipulating. Always deceiving. Nothing about you is true."

Rafferty laughed and coughed at the same time. "The only truth that matters now is you still need me to give Simon his marching orders."

Jack pulled the gun from his temple and stared angrily at him.

"Mr. Sheridan." Markus came running up from the hangar. "We tried to warn you about the helicopter, but you didn't hear us. Didn't you see it?"

Jack looked up at him. "No, I didn't see anything but Cohn and those canisters."

"Well, they're gone now, all of them. That had to have been a Hellfire with an incendiary warhead. It should have vaporized the plague."

Jack struggled to get up. He needed a little help from Markus. "How do you know that?"

"I don't," Markus said. "That's what Connor thinks. He's geeky smart about stuff like that."

The Blackhawk had touched down and a squad of soldiers in bio hazard suits swarmed the tarmac, seizing survivors from Cohn's team and securing the area. Sirens pulsed from Boon Avenue, and a pair of hazmat trucks screamed into the airport entrance. A local fire engine and an ambulance followed close behind. Jack figured they had been waiting for Abner's strike team to pounce on the airfield before coming in. Not a bad call, he just wished he had known.

"Weapons down and hands behind your head." One of the soldiers barked the order from inside his sealed suit as he neared Jack with an AR-18 assault rifle at the ready.

Jack set the Kimber on the concrete and complied with the soldier's order.

Markus did likewise. "Easy boys."

The soldier glanced at the screen of what looked like a smart phone of some kind in his hand. He studied Jack's face. "Are you Jack Sheridan?"

Jack lifted an eyebrow. "That's me."

"Sir, I have orders to secure your safety and put you in immediate contact with Admiral Wilson." The soldier handed Jack the phone.

Jack took it and looked at a picture of himself on the screen. "I shaved the mustache," he said absently. "Guess that's why you didn't recognize me right away."

The soldier did not crack a smile behind his face mask.

"Right." Jack lifted the phone to his ear. "Abner?"

"Jack! Thank God you're all right. You had me worried, mister."

"I made it through. Thanks for the assistance."

"Is Rafferty at the airport? Did he survive?"

"I can't answer that for sure."

"Don't sweat it. My guys will sort it all out. As long as you're safe and the plague is contained, that's all that matters. Now play nice with the hazmat boys. They're going to want to quarantine you for a while, just in case."

Jack shook his head. "Abner, you have to do me one more favor. I can't explain why just yet, but I have to leave the airport right now. They have to let me go."

"Why? It's over, Jack. Relax, and let's make sure you're not sick. You can't mess around with a plague."

Jack thought about his exposure to Rafferty. He did have an elevated risk of infection, but where he intended to go promised the best remedy for that possibility. "I'm fine. Trust me. I have to do this. I need this, Abner."

Abner let a long stretch of silence play out. "I wouldn't do this for any other person on the planet. You realize that, don't you?"

"I know." Jack handed the phone back to the soldier, whose name he finally read off the suit. "The admiral wants a word with you, Lieutenant Pooley."

Pooley plugged the phone into a jack on his bio suit so he could talk with Abner. "Yes, sir." He listened intently for a few seconds. "No, sir, I cannot allow that."

Jack saw Pooley's eyes grow increasingly concerned through the face mask of the suit. Abner must have been coming down pretty hard.

Lieutenant Pooley nodded. "Understood, sir." He looked at Jack. "Mr. Sheridan, you are authorized to depart this area. Admiral Wilson has informed me that you are clear of infection. I do not understand how he knows this, but he emphatically assures me that you are clean."

Jack couldn't stop the smile from curving his lips, and the burned skin on his cheeks stung. "If anybody knows I'm clean, it's the admiral."

A pair of medical techs dressed in biohazard suits hurried over from the ambulance and set a stretcher on the ground next to Rafferty. They began checking over his condition to determine if he was safe to move.

"Be careful, guys," Jack warned. "There's a good chance he's infected."

Pooley shouldered his rifle. "Mr. Sheridan, one more question."

Jack faced him.

"I also have orders to find and apprehend Donovan Rafferty. The admiral didn't have a photo of him for me but told me you could point him out. Where is he?"

Jack looked around at the wrecked cars and burning debris. "I don't know, Lieutenant."

"Was he at the airfield this morning?"

"Yes, but a lot happened here. I lost track of him in the chaos. I'm sure he'll turn up." Jack nodded to the flaming Denali. "You may have char broiled him."

Pooley gestured to Rafferty as the med techs loaded him onto the stretcher. "Who is that?"

Jack looked at Rafferty and considered his answer. "Joshua Rezner," he finally said.

Rafferty grinned ever so slightly and then asked the paramedics for a cigarette.

The med techs put a quick dressing on Jack's leg wound, and he hobbled back to the hangar. He embraced Connor at the door. "That was a stupid move, son, you're lucky you only broke your leg. You could have been killed."

Connor balanced on one leg and frowned from the pain of his broken tibia. "You're not very good at saying thank you."

Jack limped to the Jeep and pulled open the driver's door. "I'm going to Bangor with a special delivery for a guy named Simon. I'll give your mother your love."

"What about us?" Markus said.

Jack slowly climbed into the Jeep and slammed the door closed. "I'm afraid you two are stuck in quarantine for a little while. I'm clean so I get to roll." He started the engine and maneuvered out of the hangar. As he rolled past Connor he opened his window. "Thank you."

Connor hung on to the hangar door for support and smiled. "You're welcome."

Jack put his foot down on the accelerator and steered around the emergency vehicles. Lieutenant Pooley instructed the other soldiers to let the Jeep go. Jack turned onto Boon Avenue and drove into the sunrise. He hopped onto 131 South at the intersection and mapped out his course to Bangor.

- FORTY THREE -

> "I'll try to carry off a little darkness on my back,
> 'til things are brighter, I'm the man in black."
> - *The Man In Black*, Johnny Cash

Jack made it to the house in Bangor by mid-morning. He handed the ampoule containing the bacteriophage residue to the young microbiologist, seconds after Naughton had opened the front door for him. Simon went to work with the phage immediately, just as Rafferty had told him to do. Simon had already drawn a blood sample from Lauren to help tailor a phage strain that would best treat her infection. He took a vial from Jack's veins too, just to be sure that after all the time in close proximity to Rafferty he had not contracted the plague.

Lauren had gone to tears when she saw her husband limp into the house. He looked beaten and broiled but he was alive and he had brought back the phage, just like he had promised. Rezner embraced Jack too, glad his friend had won the day. They settled in the tiny, decrepit living room of the house to begin the period of waiting. They watched breaking news coverage of a foiled terror plot in Cadillac, Michigan, on an old television that Simon had finally talked Wexler into picking up in town.

On day two Jack got debriefed via conference call by Abner and Dutello, although Jack kept some aspects of Rafferty's involvement secret. He was, after all, still waiting on the phage.

On the morning of the third day Naughton and Wexler left the house before sunrise. Jack watched them leave from the window of the Spartan bedroom upstairs. He crawled out of the tiny bed, half-amazed he did not wake Lauren with all his groans and clumsy movements, and made his way downstairs. He found Simon still working in his little lab room. It looked like he had pulled an all-nighter. Jack approached the table that was loaded down with bio equipment he just didn't understand. He noticed a little handwritten cardboard sign sitting next to Simon's computer keyboard. It read, *Old bacteria don't die, they just phage away. - Mark Mueller.*

"Cute," Jack said.

Simon jumped in his chair. "Jeez, dude, don't do that!"

"Who's Mark Mueller?"

"A primo microbiologist." Simon gave Jack a once over. "Why are you awake so early?"

"Naughton and Wexler left the house. Do you know where they went?"

Simon turned back to his computer screen. "No. Those guys don't tell me anything."

Jack had only known Simon for a couple of days, but something didn't seem right with him. "You're a little edgy this morning. What's the matter?"

"Nothing, except this is the day I promised to deliver the 731 phage."

"Did something go wrong, because yesterday you said everything was on track?"

"Dude, chill, I'm still on track. As a matter of fact, why don't you take the little woman out to breakfast for like, a celebration. Come back around noon and I'll be ready."

Jack looked at him funny. "Shouldn't we stay away from the public? Contagion?"

Simon shrugged. "Stick to the drive-thru."

After two days sequestered at the squalid house, the idea sounded good to Jack. Simon had no car to pack up and leave, and besides, Rafferty was still sealed up at the hospital. Naughton would never let the microbiologist disappear without administering the phage.

Jack woke Lauren, and they threw themselves together for a drive into South Haven. It was a warm morning and they got a carry-out breakfast from a diner near the marina. They ate on South Beach overlooking Lake Michigan and talked about booking that trip to the Caribbean. Jack mailed a large check to Tom Lanuzza to replace the starboard engine on his cargo plane. They called Connor for an update on his broken leg, and learned that he and Markus had to undergo a few more days of quarantine before they would be released. Mai had been checking in on them too. It seemed something serious had started there between her and Connor.

Jack and Lauren returned to the house at eleven thirty and walked into the makeshift bio lab.

Simon was busy cleaning up the lab table; gauze wrapping, medical tape, a used syringe. A portion of his equipment had been packed for transport, like he was closing down shop. He appeared a bit flustered at their arrival before noon. "Hey, how was breakfast?"

Jack didn't reply and let silence settle in the old house. The ringing from the stun grenade had faded from his ear a day ago, and he listened for noises upstairs. It was very quiet. Something didn't feel right. "Didn't Naughton and Wexler come back?"

Simon nodded. "They did. They left again." He pulled a chair away from the table and angled it toward Lauren. "I've got some news. You should sit down."

Lauren slowly sat and concern set into her eyes.

Simon noticed. "Oh, I mean good news actually."

Jack leaned against the wall. "What's the matter, Simon? You look nervous." Jack glanced at the syringe Simon had thrown into a little garbage pail. "What was that for?"

Simon swallowed. "Uh, Rafferty. That was for Rafferty. He was just here."

Jack stood up straight. "He was just here? How? He's lying in a hospital bed with a chest full of bullet holes, locked up in quarantine indefinitely."

"Naughton and Wexler got him out somehow. I just gave him his first phage treatment."

Jack pointed at the equipment cases on the table. "He's treated and now you're leaving? What about Lauren?"

"Dude, relax. That's just the thing I want to talk about. I've been screening her blood for three days, and the bug hasn't shown its ugly face."

Jack cocked his head. "It's a slow replicating bacterium. Maybe three days isn't enough time for it to show up on the test?"

"That might be true for your blood test, but from what I understand she was exposed over a week ago. That's plenty of time for me to pick it up."

Lauren processed the news and a smile broke across her face. "I don't have the plague?"

"No. Don't have it. Never did." Simon lifted his hand for a high five.

Lauren jumped up and slapped it. "Yeah, dude."

Jack stood dumfounded. "He played me. Rafferty played me the whole time. That dart never contained the plague. We went through this whole thing for nothing."

Lauren hugged him. "This wasn't for nothing. You stopped Cohn. It was worth it."

Simon gestured to Jack. "The verdict is still out on you, dude. Your blood screen came up negative too, but like you said it's only been three days." He lifted a sealed vial and a packaged syringe from the table. "I'll keep watching your blood culture. If the bacterium is there I'll find it. In the meantime if you get a fever, shoot up with this. It's the living phage. Keep it in the fridge. Should last about ten days."

Jack looked at the vial. "So this is it? You're out of here?"

"Hey, I survived my contract agreement with Donovan Rafferty. You bet I'm out of here."

Lauren gave him a hug. "Thank you, Simon."

Jack shook his hand. "I know what it's like to be put in irons with Rafferty. Just be glad your misery was short lived."

Simon's cell phone rang and he looked at caller ID. "Last thing," he said handing the phone to Jack. "He knew you'd be here with me now."

Jack put the phone to his ear. He knew who it had to be. "Hello, Donovan. Feeling better?"

"Much," Rafferty said. "Cohn is dead, and I've stopped bleeding. And Simon's phage has started eating away the plague bacteria in my blood. What more could I ask?"

Jack held Lauren's hand. "It'd be less than honest of me to say I'm glad you're on the mend."

"I like your honesty, Jack." Rafferty laughed. "I trust Lauren is feeling better."

"And you wonder why I never believe anything you say. I hope you enjoyed your game."

"Immensely. But it was for a good cause, don't you agree?"

Jack simmered on that thought for a moment. "Do you remember what you said at the airport about a clean slate?"

Rafferty did not reply right away. "That whole affair in Wexford is a bit hazy, but I do recall something to that effect."

"Did you mean it, or was that a lie too?"

"I take a man's word very seriously, and my word is no exception. Consider our business concluded. And I hope you appreciate my parting gift."

"What gift, Lauren's health? That should never have been a gift for you to give or take."

"I'm talking about the gift in your hand right now. You wanted to give Abner the phage. Now you have a living strain to do with as you please. Just hope that you don't need it after you give it to him."

Jack shook his head. "You're an enigma, Donovan. The things you do don't make sense."

"Someday you'll understand. I'm not the evil you think I am."

"It's funny how an evil man doesn't think of himself as evil. He always seems to think he's just misunderstood. Can you shed some light on that for me?"

Rafferty chuckled. "Good and evil will never be the same for you, will it?"

"Don't bet on it."

"I serve a purpose," Rafferty said. "You see, a man wearing a white suit is not the man you need to clean up a mess. Sometimes it takes a dark stranger to get the job done right and like it or not, Jack, that's who I am. Until I see the changes I'm after, I'll be out here. Until the days are brighter, I'm the man in black."

The line clicked off and Jack stared at the phone.

Lauren squeezed his hand. "So what did he say?"

"He said our business is concluded." Jack looked into her eyes. "It's over." He wrapped his arms around her and they stood there in a tight embrace. "For the first time in two years, I'm going to get a good night's sleep."

"You might want to cross your fingers," Simon said. "Donovan likes to put a lot of fine print into his agreements. If he promised to leave you alone, I'm sure he's got an escape clause."

Jack handed the phone back to him. "I know, but I think this thing with Cohn set the scales right…at least for now."

For more information on *Allied In Irons*, the state of Michigan, and other works by J. Ryan Fenzel, visit the author's website at www.jryanfenzel.com.

ACKNOWLEDGEMENTS

I first wish to thank all the readers of *Descending From Duty* and *Inherit All Things* for their overwhelmingly positive feedback. Knowing there were people out there eagerly awaiting another book added fuel to the fire to write *Allied In Irons.* I truly appreciate the support and encouragement.

Writing and editing a novel is a time-consuming business proposition, and I thank my family for putting up with me during the whole ordeal. As always, I'm indebted to my wonderful wife Melynda for her insightful critique of the manuscript's early drafts. Most of her impressions have made it to the page, and this book is far better because of it. I'm blessed to have her in my life.

My daughters are fantastic young ladies, and I thank them for keeping me grounded as I wrote a tale of terrorists, mercenaries, and global catastrophe. They are a constant reminder of what is important in life. Jack Sheridan's extraordinary exploits would often be put on hold to attend a band concert or basketball game. That's the stuff of life, and it's something I try to carry over into the fictional worlds I create.

Special thanks to long-time friend Tim Lee for his invaluable research assistance. Tim is the deputy director of the Michigan Intelligence Operations Center (MIOC) in Lansing, and the tour he guided me on through this nifty law enforcement facility made the scenes at the fusion center in *Allied In Irons* possible.

Once again I owe a debt of gratitude to my "inner circle" for their candid perspectives on my writing. Brian Shureb has been reading my stories since junior high, and I've come to rely on his eye for action as well as his surprisingly astute instincts regarding sentimental matters. Thanks to Jon Lillemoen for keeping watch over the cold, hard facts. And thanks to Tony Nielsen for being the one true constant in the universe, listening to my story concepts, and saying "depends" a lot when I ask legal questions.

As per usual, Julie L. Hamilton did a bang-up job on the cover art. That's three in a row now, and when four comes around we'll be working together again.

Finally, thanks to Jeanmarie Martin for editing the manuscript. Our first pairing on *Inherit All Things* worked so well I had to have her talents for *Allied In Irons.* She does a remarkable job with the material I give her, and if any errors in grammar or punctuation have managed to survive to press, please be assured that the fault lies with me.

Don't miss these other titles by J Ryan Fenzel, available online through Amazon, and at chain and independent bookstores.

INHERIT ALL THINGS (Ironcroft 2009)

The best place to hide something
is in the past...

Read the story that launched Jack Sheridan into action. This west Michigan treasure hunt with a historical puzzle at its core has received widespread acclaim from reviewers and readers alike, and has been given the following honors.

- 2009 Michigan Notable Book nominee
- Selected #14 on *Traverse Magazine's* 2010 list of 30 Great Summer Reads

"A fine read crossing large chunks of time and geography...Reading an adventure on Lake Michigan is not a bad way to spend a few cold, winter nights."

- Steve Begnoche, *Ludington Daily News*

DESCENDING FROM DUTY (Ironcroft 2006)

She's out there stalking the Great Lakes...

Read the submarine thriller that has captured the imagination of the Great Lakes region. Fleet boat submarine *U.S.S. Silversides* is unleashed from her moorings in Muskegon onto the unsuspecting Great Lakes by mercenaries executing a deadly quest for revenge.

"[*Descending from Duty*] is a crisply-paced military thriller which steams full speed ahead around Lake Michigan."

– Dave LeMieux, *Muskegon Chronicle*

"Fenzel has managed to weave a seafaring yarn, political intrigue, and a detective story into one enjoyable read."

- C. Williams Coane, Rear Admiral USN (Ret), Exec. Director of Naval Reserve Association

Ironcroft Publishing
www.ironcroft.com